Silver City Roils

By
Diane Stuart-Wright

airleaf.com

© Copyright 2007, Diane Stuart Wright

All Rights Reserved.

No part of this book may be reproduced, stored in a retrieval system, or transmitted by any means, electronic, mechanical, photocopying, recording, or otherwise, without written permission from the author.

ISBN: 978-1-60002-268-5

Publisher's Note:

This book is a work of fiction based on historical events.

Preface

Step back into a simpler time when America was a sleeping giant. Close your eyes, take a deep breath, and wander back into the past.

The westward expansion held many perils for the unseasoned traveler but the adventurous spirit of early Americans led them into the land of dreams.

The New Mexico Territory was a haven for prospectors, health-seekers, and nomadic Indians. The windswept desert, with its brilliant sun during the day and star filled nights, provided sustenance to all and filled them with hope of a bright future.

When dawn silently streaked across the eastern sky, it appeared jaded. In contrast, the pure gold and vivid colors of the blazing western sunsets called to courageous hearts.

The gold is still here in the western skies but its brilliance is fading. The pulse of life quickens. The rutted stagecoach routes wearily surrender to the blistering sands.

Dedication

This book is dedicated to my loving and supportive family; my husband, David; daughter and research assistant, Paula, daughter, Amy, and grandson Clell. I want to express my appreciation to my parents for their unwavering beliefs in my abilities. To my sisters, sisters-in-law, brothers-in-law, nieces and nephews, thanks for being there for me.

*In memory of Smoky (1962-2002),
Appaloosa extraordinaire and my friend for 32 years.*

Acknowledgments

For Inspiration and Encouragement: M. June Cary, (my mother), Keith E. Stuart (my father), Barbara Phillips Stuart (my stepmother), Angelita Y. Lara, Lois Wood McWilliams.

For Cover art, Charles Messenger (www.messengerartgalleries.com)

For Editing Assistance, Advice, and Encouragement: David M. Wright (my husband), Lena M. Wright (my mother-in-law), Claire Cosper, Sondra Martucci, Elisabeta Szekely, Dana Pellegrino, Robert Swisher, Mary and Ted Lynn, Lucile and Rider South.

For Helpful Interviews: Robert Hall, Adolph Zapata, Belle Eaton, Don Miller, Ena Osborne, Violet Ball, Terry Hupp, Betty Menard, William Lee, Alvin Franks, and Ruth Bound.

Assistance with Research: Paula K. Wright, Peter Crum, Ruby Steltzer, Maggie Andersen, Dale Pruit.

A Special Thank You to Silver City Museum, Silver City Library, Miller Library, WNMU Museum, and Pinos Altos Museum.

Chapter 1. New Mexico Territory, Late 1800s

A rutted passage wound through a maze of silvery thorns across a desert valley. Distant mountains shimmered behind a powdery haze. Something was approaching; timid rabbits scampered toward their burrows and a covey of quail exploded into the sky.

Robert Jensen, a St. Louis banker and Union supporter, settled back into the lumpy, coarsely padded seat of a westbound Concord stagecoach. The efforts of his lifelong friend, R.D. Farnsworth, had finally come to a satisfactory conclusion. Robert stared out at the bright, cloudless sky and laughed.

Thinking back, the world had changed drastically. It had been over a year ago when his friend, R.D. Farnsworth suggested that the Jensen family move to the small mining town of Silver City in the New Mexico Territory. Farnsworth, his face flushed with excitement, told his friend about the small general store he was building in Silver City. As construction of the store neared completion, Farnsworth encountered some financial difficulties and was forced to return to St. Louis in search of backers. Competition for trade contracts with local mining interests and surrounding towns was proving to be a lot fiercer than he expected.

Robert promised to loan his friend some money, scoffing at his offer of a full partnership. As a senior alderman, Robert Jensen was aspiring to run for mayor of St. Louis. As his influence grew, it became likely he would be a successful candidate.

Emma Jensen, Robert's daughter, was a piano virtuoso by the age of seven. By sixteen, she was attending the Academy of Music in New York and enthralled by city life and culture. Emma was being taught by some of the most renowned musical masters in the world.

When Emma left St. Louis to pursue her studies, she was given a beautiful parting gift. Her proud father placed a silver locket with her name engraved on it around her neck as she prepared to board the train bound for New York City. The locket held tiny portraits. On one side a picture of Robert and his wife, Florence, Emma's mother; and on the other side a picture of Emma. Robert explained that it kept the whole family together. The locket became Emma's special talisman.

The Academy's course of studies was grueling and a slight winter cough developed into tuberculosis in less than 3 months. Her illness forced Emma to abandon her musical pursuits and return to her parents in St. Louis, soon after Robert's conversation with Farnsworth. Failing health and depression took their toll on Emma. Medical experts watched as her condition worsened, partly due to an unusually wet spring.

Robert reconsidered his friend's offer because the New Mexico Territory was touted as an ideal recuperative climate for people with respiratory ailments.

Even so, Robert was reluctant to move his family. Without knowing what to expect, he went to Silver City alone, deciding to travel as far as possible by train.

During the long train trip, Robert developed an extreme antipathy toward Indians. One morning, the train hurtled past a burning wagon. A brave, in the act of scalping a screaming woman, held his bloody trophy up for the train passengers to see and waved his gory knife in the air. Robert choked on the bile in his throat and ran to the door to be sick. At night, the sight returned to his mind and caused fearful nightmares. He worried he was making the wrong decision, but with Emma's health at stake, he knew they had little choice.

Shaking and rattling, the stagecoach lurched to a stop, startling Robert out of his reverie. A cloud of dust choked the passengers inside the coach, Robert, his wife Florence and their daughter, Emma. Emma was dozing, her head resting against her mother's shoulder. She moaned slightly and began to cough with as much force as her weakened condition would allow.

Frank Parnell stood outside the Deming stage depot. He pulled a tattered bandana from his pocket, carelessly dragged it across his forehead then quickly clapped it over his nose and mouth as the stagecoach swathed him in its dust cloud. The last few days had been grueling and he was anxious for a chance to rest. The exhausted driver, Chet, a friend of Frank's, stood and leaned back with all his weight to stop the horses. Frank tossed his bedroll and worn saddle up and greeted his old friend, before climbing into the coach.

"Mornin' Chet. Any trouble this trip?" he asked.

"Naw, nothin' so far. Heard tell of a hold-up last week along this route, though," Chet responded, slapped his dusty gloves together and reached down to shake Frank's hand.

Frank ignored his fellow passengers, shifted himself into a comfortable position in the seat next to Robert and pulled his hat down over his eyes. By the time the stage began its journey to Silver City, Frank was sound asleep. Frank was dreaming of roses when he suddenly jerked awake, feeling that someone staring at him. He dozed again. *Roses were everywhere, fields and fields of them, blinding colors, red, yellow, and pink. He could even smell them.* The dusty traveler opened his eyes and pulled back his hat.

A tall, slender young woman sat in the seat across from him. She smiled shyly, revealing pretty dimples. Her eyes were cornflower blue and her hair the color of harvested wheat. She resembled a china figurine Frank had once seen in a store window. Her smile seemed to be just for him and he sat transfixed by its radiance. Then she frowned and began to cough. Frank's gaze was drawn to a beautiful silver locket around her neck. Shifting in his seat, he was enveloped by the heady scent of roses. Sighing contentedly, Frank pulled his hat down over his eyes.

A spray of pebbles lashed the side of the coach, Emma gasped and choked but her eyes never left the stranger's face. She was so tired, she envied the man's ability to sleep. He had the look of someone official but wore no uniform. His clothes were of good quality material but very wrinkled and travel-stained. His features were regular but not extraordinary, his clean-shaven chin, decisive. High cheekbones and an angular face, he was of medium height and build but appeared regal with a military bearing. She made up a story about him.

The young man awoke and Robert was bored. "Good afternoon, sir. Robert Jensen from St. Louis. Where are you headed?" Robert extended his hand.

"Fort Bayard," Frank grasped the outstretched hand firmly.

"Have you been to Silver City?" Robert asked, unable to determine Frank's occupation.

"Yes, sir. I've been in the area for a few years. I am with the Bureau of Indian Affairs," Frank said politely, although he was beginning to resent the man's curiosity.

"Ah, very interesting," Robert said, tenting his fingers. "So you are making the territory safe for families like mine."

Frank drawled. "The Indians are protecting their land."

Robert sputtered and his face reddened. Uncharacteristically speechless, he coughed violently into his fist. Florence reached over and patted her husband's hand. The impertinence of that young man was shameful. Florence remembered the horrible nightmares after last summer's trip out west. Thrashing and screaming, Robert bolted upright in bed, his face flushed and perspiring, he wouldn't sleep for the rest of the night. Several weeks later, he related the horrible scalping incident.

Emma was surprised by the anger on her father's face. Shyly, she smiled at the young man and he smiled back; his teeth white against his tanned face. The stagecoach slowed and Frank opened the door and disappeared. Emma craned her neck to see where he had gone and was pushed back against the seat by her mother.

"No more of that young lady. That man is a disgrace! Imagine taking sides with those savages," Florence said forcefully.

Frank swung himself up beside the stage driver. The atmosphere in the coach was suffocating and he needed some air. When the stagecoach jerked to a stop, Frank instinctively reached for his rifle. "Why are we stopping?" Frank asked Chet.

"Look over yonder, behind them trees," Chet said quietly.

"What is it?" Frank asked and jumped from the seat.

"I saw something moving over there and didn't want to get too close 'til I knowed what it was."

"You'd better warn the passengers to stay inside," Frank whispered.

Chet nodded and jumped, putting the stage between him and what might be trouble. Chet was relieved Frank offered to see what was going on up ahead because his old bones were too stiff to move quickly. He did his best to reassure the Jensen family and climbed into the coach with them. His rifle trained in the direction of the cottonwoods, Chet tried to spot Frank. Even his eyesight was getting bad.

Frank crouched in tall grass. Near the Mimbres River, the air was cool. He longed for some water but could see three men up to no good. A scruffy lot, one was tall and lanky, one of medium build, and the youngest was short and stout. The short man cut a hole in a new barbed wire fence and snapped the tall man's boot.

"What in tarnation are you trying to do, Lem?" Then he let loose with a string of curse words.

Lem, the short man, grinned and slapped his partner on the back. "Aw, that didn't hurt ya. I saw some calves over in them trees."

Frank crept through the waist length grass. Outnumbered and outgunned, Frank waited for his chance to surprise them. The tall man barked some orders. "Lem, you keep a lookout for that foreman. He'll try to sneak up on us. Jesse, grab that calf over there, I'll get its mother's attention."

Jesse grabbed the calf around the neck as the tall man waved his arms around in front of the cow. She looked at him curiously. The cow turned around in alarm and charged when the calf bawled. Jesse yelped and ran for the opening in the fence. Frank heard rifle shots. Six men rode up brandishing ropes as Lem, Jesse, and their leader scattered. Quietly, Frank retreated back to the waiting stagecoach.

"Rustlers were trying to catch a calf and the rancher caught 'em," Frank explained to Chet who climbed out of the cabin of the stagecoach. The older man cringed, the penalty for cattle rustling was hanging and few were tried for their crimes.

Robert, upset by the delay and heat, yelled loudly. "You call yourself a stage driver. My daughter is ill forced to sit here for so long in this heat."

"Keep your shirt on," Chet mumbled. He stuck his head in the window and said,

"Sorry, sir. I've been in this business a long time and you can't be too careful."

Robert's face was flushed and beaded with perspiration. Florence patted his hand and offered him a handkerchief moistened with water from the large canteen provided for the passengers. Robert jerked it out of her hand and dabbed his forehead angrily. "Emma is exhausted and so are you," Robert said irritably.

"We will be fine, dear. Try to relax, those men have the situation well in hand," his wife replied gently.

Robert closed his eyes defiantly. The vein on his right temple pulsed wildly. His temper was notorious and Florence hoped, for his sake, they would reach Silver City soon. The stagecoach gathered speed and Florence settled back against the uncomfortable seat. Towns in this primitive land were few and far between and Florence longed for the comforts of home. A hot bath and clean clothes would be a luxury after this long trip.

Chapter 2

The Dragoon Mountains in southeastern Arizona territory were a perfect location for Apache raids. Small marauding parties attacked isolated ranches and faded into the rocks.

One summer evening thunderheads piled against the rocks. Three men had delivered a message to General Crook at his temporary quarters near Camp Huachuca and were returning to Captain Beyer, at Ft. Bayard, with his reply. Captain Beyer sent three volunteers to insure the message got through. Beyer couldn't send it by telegraph, the Apaches had cut the wire again!

Frank Parnell sensed crackling electricity in the air. Massive granite pillars growing straight out of the ground provided some shelter for their horses. At this height most of the valley could be seen from their camp. The other two men were looking for jackrabbits for supper.

Frank knew he was being watched. He set the pot down on the rocks near the small campfire and pretended to reach for a canvas coffee bag. Grabbing his pistol, Frank twisted around and dropped to his knees. Finger on the trigger, he was ready to shoot.

An elderly man approached, his hands in the air. In an old Army issue uniform, he wore his graying hair in long braids.

"Stay where you are," Frank growled menacingly.

"I mean you no harm," the old man said hesitantly. "I'm looking for the camp of the Indian Police. I saw some smoke and had been told that they were in the area."

Frank knew the man was lying about the smoke, the fire was built with very dry wood.

"What do you want?" Frank's finger twitched on the trigger.

"Some people need help. Please come with me," the man pleaded.

Frank knew Victorio, an Apache leader, was in the area. *Could this be a trap?*

"Are you going to help them?" Urgency quickened the old man's step.

"Who are you?"

"Name's Jal. I was an army scout. Listen, do you hear that?"

Frank heard a low keening sound. He hesitated for a moment then motioned for the man to proceed, keeping his pistol trained on the stranger's back. The keening grew louder. Frank squinted in the fading light. He could see a shadowy figure crouched beneath an overhanging boulder. An old Chiricahua woman held her hands clasped above her head, wailing loudly, and rocking back and forth. A dying child was sprawled on the ground in front of her. There was blood everywhere and a bone protruded from his thigh.

Silver City Roils

"What happened?" Frank asked. He removed his belt and applied a tourniquet above the wound.

"He fell," the man was standing behind Frank and pointing upward. A broken spire of rock stood in relief against the dusky sky. The boy had been shot. Dark blood bubbled from a wound beneath his rib cage. *Who would have done this and why? The boy wasn't old enough to be a warrior.*

"Help me get him back to camp." Getting no response, he turned. The man was gone. Grunting loudly, Frank picked up the unconscious boy and made his way back to camp.

The old woman followed Frank but stopped at the edge of their camp. Frank's companions were sitting near the campfire and the smell of sizzling meat permeated the thick humid air. The men gathered their sparse first-aid supplies and cleaned the gaping wound in the boy's leg. But the boy shuddered suddenly and stopped breathing.

A loud clap of thunder and a huge, blinding shaft of lightening split the night sky. A granite pillar reverberated from a lightening strike and a shower of sparks and rocks rained down on the men. Pebble sized hail pelted down on their heads as they ran toward their tied horses. A torrential downpour broke over their heads and the boulders provided little shelter. Mountain storms were common this time of year and would soon pass through.

In less than an hour, the storm was over. Rivulets of muddy water cascaded down the rocks, forming large pools in the sandy earth. The air exploded with the pungent smells of wet sage and creosote.

At least it'll be easier to dig a grave, Frank thought.

The wind whipped tendrils of mist into their faces as the saddened group went to bury the child. The old woman and child's body were gone. The rain-scoured ground showed no traces of them. Jim Dougan and Fred Bascomb, Frank's companions were very quiet. He sensed they were spooked. Drenched and miserable, the three huddled under some rocks until dawn.

About a mile from camp, they found hoof prints of roughly 30 unshod ponies, headed in the direction of the Chiricahua Mountains. The Indians must have come through after the rain the night before.

It was an arduous journey to Fort Bowie and they found the soldiers involved in a flurry of activity when they arrived. The soldiers had heard about the raiding party and had to catch it before it disappeared into Mexico. "We saw tracks headed toward the mountains," Jim reported to the captain.

Jim and Fred accompanied the soldiers to point out the pony tracks. Frank cut two fresh horses from the Army's remuda and ate a meal in the canteen. Anxious to get started, he saddled a horse and put a pack on the other. Going deeper into Apache country, Frank crossed the flat, barren valley able to see for miles in any direction. The low Peloncillo Mountains lay to the north and it would be safer to skirt along their edge. He picked up moccasin tracks, toes turned inward Indian fashion, headed in the direction of the Dragoons. The tracks the men found earlier showed the Indians were on horseback. Where had they obtained mounts? The air was deathly still and it was hard to breathe. Frank was out of water and must stop at the Pritchard ranch.

Something was wrong!

The house looked deserted but Frank approached cautiously. The hair on the back of his neck stood up despite the intense heat. His uneasiness turned to dread, Elizabeth Pritchard, the family's six- year old daughter, stood in front of the house. Clutched tightly in her arms a tiny, blood-soaked bundle. The look on her face appalled him. She looked at him but through him.

Frank gently took the bundle from her.

Last week, Frank, Jim, and Fred stopped at this ranch on their way to Arizona Territory. Charlie Pritchard's wife, Mary, graciously prepared a meal for the travelers. Elizabeth sat nearby, as her mother washed the dishes, and tended her three-month old sister Sally. The baby reached up and grabbed a handful of Elizabeth's curly brown hair, Elizabeth gently opened her sister's fingers and removed her tangled hair from Sally's clutches and kissed the baby's fingers gently.

"Would you like to hear a story about an old horse I used to have?" Jim asked.

Elizabeth nodded shyly.

"Old Smoky was a blue roan Appaloosa. That means he was kind of gray with a white rump and black spots," Jim began.

Elizabeth giggled as Jim related Smoky's many escapades. Smoky used to crawl under corral fences on his knees.

Mary laughed. "You're a wonderful storyteller, Mr. Bascomb. We never have company since the ranch is so far from anywhere. My sister, Claire lives in Stine but hardly ever visits us."

Elizabeth bounced up and down wanting more stories.

"I've got a whole passel of 'em young lady. I'll bet you've never heard the story about the little princess that lived in a big castle."

"No, I haven't," Elizabeth smiled dreamily. Leaning her chin on her hands, she gazed adoringly at the tough old soldier.

Elizabeth was no longer an innocent child. Oblivious to her surroundings, Elizabeth stared dull eyed toward the distant mountains. Frank shook his head. As he suspected, the bundle was what was left of Sally. Behind the house, the bodies of Charlie and Mary were stretched out on the ground, their arms reaching toward each other. Frank buried them and the baby as Elizabeth watched silently.

Only a sliver of a moon lit their way to Steins that night. Elizabeth appeared to recognize him and the sound of his voice soothed her. She pressed against him and whimpered.

Steins was a railroad town in New Mexico Territory and lay at the bottom of Doubtful Canyon. Dismounting slowly, Frank struggled to make his legs hold his weight. Dried mud caked the wooden steps of Miss Jennie Owens's boarding house. The pretty young woman who answered the door recognized Elizabeth. Her face paled, she screamed and fell to the floor. Two cowboys carried Claire, Elizabeth's aunt, into the parlor and laid her on a lounge chair. An elderly woman ran to fetch some smelling salts. Claire's eyes flew open when she inhaled the potent fumes.

"Elizabeth?" Claire whispered. The room grew quiet as Frank carried the little girl to her aunt and placed her in a chair beside the lounge. Claire reached for Elizabeth's hand. "What happened to my sister and her family?" Claire asked, tears glinting in her eyes.

"Their ranch was attacked by Indians," Frank looked down at his hands. "I found Elizabeth and Sally first. Charlie and Mary were around back."

Claire studied Frank's face. "I buried them behind the barn. I'll tell the sheriff what happened," Frank's voice shook with emotion.

Sheriff McGrew locked his office door and turned to find Frank standing behind him. "What can I do for you, young man?" he asked.

"I just came from the Pritchard place about 10 miles northwest of here. Apaches raided it sometime yesterday. I found their six year old daughter, Elizabeth Pritchard alive and the rest I buried," Frank told him, sadly.

"I'll send a couple of men out there tomorrow to see what they find. What became of the girl?"

"I brought her to her aunt. She lives in the boarding house up the road," Frank replied. So tired he could barely stand, Frank leaned against the hitching post.

"How long since you've eaten?" McGrew asked kindly.

"Around 5:30 this morning," Frank grinned weakly.

"I'll buy you a thick steak smothered with onions." The sheriff led Frank to a saloon called Doubtful Dan's. The hot food revived Frank temporarily but when he returned to Jennie Owens's boarding house, he gratefully accepted her offer of a free bed for the night.

The following morning, Frank caught a train to a station just north of Lordsburg. Timing was critical but he feared he might succumb to exhaustion before he reached his destination. He unloaded his horses and started out across the flat land that rose to meet the Burro Mountains.

The Bureau of Indian Affairs offered opportunities to men like Frank. As a child, he dreamed of being a soldier and when he was old enough, he applied to West Point Military Academy. Then he went to spend a week on a military post in Texas and decided that the regimentation of military life was not for him.

When he was attached to the Indian Police, Frank found that he disliked many of the policies the United States government employed to subdue the Indians. Treaties were as worthless as the paper they were written on and often those treaties were broken before the ink was dry. Being of ordinary build and coloring suited his line of work allowing him to maintain anonymity and blend in with a crowd. Many of Frank's duties exposed him to the government's attitudes toward the Apaches. In 1877, Geronimo met with John Clum at Ojo Caliente. Accused of killing, stealing, and violating a treaty, Geronimo and his followers were outnumbered and overpowered. Instead of being treated with the respect due a prisoner of war, Geronimo was shackled like an animal. Frank recalled how relieved he was not to have to witness any further mistreatment of the group. The following day he was assigned to accompany General Beauford to investigate reports of Indian raiding going on in Arizona Territory,

Frank was involved in many mediation efforts between U.S. military forces and Indian leaders. But his opportunities were limited and were likely to remain so unless he committed himself to the Bureau for the next twenty years. Sensing the growing animosity during peace talks and palpable mistrust between the military and Indian leaders, Frank experienced a rare sense of awe. Primitively dressed men carried themselves with the pride and dignity of uniformed generals. Their solemn faces were etched with the weathered wisdom of their ancestors.

The hot sun pounding on his head, Frank considered his future. What he really wanted was his own piece of land and maybe a family. He closed his eyes and pictured a cozy house surrounded by grazing land, a few head of cattle, a good well, maybe a few fruit trees.

It took three days to reach Ft. Bayard. He delivered General Crook's message, dirty and unshaven, and reported the Ft. Bowie search for Victorio's band. When he told Captain Beyer of the tragedy at the Pritchard Ranch, the Captain sighed, "We have to stop these raids."

Chapter 3

Emma tossed and turned on the narrow bed, her face was flushed and her nightgown was soaked with sweat. Her mother, Florence sat beside her and every few minutes, Florence dipped a towel into a washbowl of cool water and wiped her daughter's feverish face. Emma cried out suddenly and sat up, her eyes were wild and frightened.

"Please, help me, help me!" she screamed, clawing at the throat of her nightgown.

"Emma, mama is here," Florence struggled to keep the young woman from leaping out of bed. Despite her illness, Emma was remarkably strong.

"Janie, come quickly!" Florence said loudly. Janie ran to her assistance and tried to soothe Emma. It took several minutes for Emma to calm down. When she realized that she was in their new home in Silver City, and that her mother and Janie were there, she sighed loudly and settled back against the pillows.

"It was just horrible, Mama. I was walking through a bunch of trees and I could hear birds singing. Then I was lying on my back in a deep hole. I heard voices and when I looked up I could see faces looking down at me," Emma shivered.

"Oh, my dear, what a terrible dream," Florence patted her hand.

During the three weeks since their arrival in Silver City, Emma was so ill, she was unable to eat and could barely sip water. Dr. Woodville, a local practitioner, was amazed she could survive in such a state. Sensing that Florence was exhausted, Dr. Woodville persuaded Robert Jensen to hire Janie Grandy, a young nurse to help with Emma's care. Florence barely stirred from Emma's bedside but Janie could tend to Emma's needs under her supervision and allow her to rest.

Determined to keep busy, Robert spent his time between his new business and their house. He learned his friend and business partner R.D. Farnsworth had things well in hand at the store. So Robert studied the books and familiarized himself with the stock. In the evening, long after sunset, he returned home to the tedious process of putting the house in order. Most of the family's household goods remained in St. Louis. Many items that had been sent to them in Silver City, arrived damaged. Robert sighed as he rubbed his sleeve over a deep gash in the finish of his desk. He and Florence had always had a close relationship while living in St. Louis. Now, thousands of miles from family and friends, their daughter's illness had driven a wedge between them.

Robert looked around the room full of packing crates of dishes, trunks of clothes, and sawdust in the cracks of the floors. He wondered again if he had done the right thing, this was no place for his family. Walking to the back of the house across newly varnished floors, he gently pushed open the door leading to Emma's room.

His beautiful girl was so healthy and alive when she left for the Academy of Music. Full of hopes and dreams, she was immensely proud of her piano. Leaving it in St. Louis had been the hardest thing Robert had ever done in his life. Emma smiled tremulously when he explained why they couldn't take her piano with them. "It might be possible to have it delivered later but not immediately," he told her. Emma blinked back tears and nodded bravely.

Robert winced when he saw Emma's frail body lying in the large bed. He closed the door and went down the narrow hallway to his room. It was Florence's room too, but it felt like his alone because she was so rarely in it. Loosening his cravat, he sat on the edge of the bed and covered his face with his hands. He was not religious and had forgotten how to pray; but he needed to talk to Someone. "Dear Father, I am not sure what to say. I'm begging you to let Emma live. I will give up everything I have just to see her well again. Please help her. Amen."

In Emma's room, Florence sang a lullaby. She remembered a time when she held tiny Emma in her arms and rocked her to sleep. With her last ounce of strength, she changed her daughter's nightgown and resettled her in the bed. Emma's eyelids drooped and she drifted to sleep. Florence sat beside Emma until she was certain her daughter was asleep. Taking a deep breath, Florence forced herself up out of the chair she slept in for so many nights. *Robert must be told about Emma's condition!.*

She found her husband, lying on his bed staring at the ceiling. "I'm so frightened! The doctor was here about an hour ago. He said she's much worse. He thinks the trip was too much for her and wants us to keep her in bed and as quiet as possible," Florence choked and started to cry, "I know he thinks she is going to die,"

"Don't cry, Flo. For God's sake, please don't do this. Did he tell you she might die?" Robert persisted as he put his arms around his wife.

"No, but he looks worried. She is so frail that she can barely cough. Janie and I spend hours trying to coax some fluids into her. What can I do? Tell me what can I do?" her voice dissolved into sobs.

"We brought her here so she can get better. There is nothing else we can do except pray it will happen. Just try to be cheerful while she's awake," Robert kissed her head and offered her a clean handkerchief. "All the doctors in St. Louis and Dr. Woodville agreed Emma needs fresh air and sunshine. R.D. warned me about the dust here. That's why I had this house built away from the main streets. Soon we'll be able to take Emma out on the porch and let the sun restore her strength."

Their house on Black Street was built with Emma in mind and was as well equipped and designed as any in town. Robert's fingertips stroked the tears on his wife's cheek. "What can I do to help you, Flo?" he asked gently.

Florence shook her head sadly. She shrugged off her husband's arms and walked back to Emma's room. Her shoulders sagged in defeat. *It was impossible to turn to Robert for help. Why is Robert all thumbs and elbows in the sick room? He spills slop jars and curses. When her father is upset, Emma is upset and she needs to be calm and she thinks she is dying. What will I do if she dies? Can I go on without her?*

Florence stayed in the hall until she could compose herself and then gently pushed open the door to Emma's room. Florence dragged a heavy chair to the window and looked outside. The sky turned pale then pink. *The streetlamps in St. Louis would be lit now. Carriages drawn by fine horses are taking people to their evening entertainment. Perhaps they were visiting friends or dining out in their favorite restaurant. It seemed so far away. Tomorrow, I will write a letter to mother and tell her we have arrived*, Florence decided. *Mother will understand, I can tell her how I feel.* Leticia Renard tried not to judge and could be relied upon to offer loving suggestions and not harsh advice.

Draping her shawl around her shoulders, Florence sat down heavily in the big chair, resigning herself to another long night. Briefly, she closed her eyes. Emma saw her mother sitting next to the window when Janie came to bring Emma some fresh water. Janie motioned for Emma to keep still and held a cup to her cracked lips. When Emma finished with the water, Janie pulled a hairbrush from her apron pocket, "Let me brush your hair and plait it into two braids. It will make you more comfortable." She tied the ends of the braids with some bright green ribbons, adjusted the pillows, and tucked the thin coverlet around her patient's fragile shoulders. "Doesn't that feel a lot better?" Janie asked. Emma nodded and closed her eyes.

Robert awoke the following morning and sleepily reached for his wife. She wasn't there. She always stayed with Emma. He poured water into the cracked basin and splashed some on his face. *What a relief it would be to leave the house*, he thought guiltily. He adjusted his cravat in the mirror and carefully combed his thinning hair. *Why can't I help Flo take care of Emma? She won't tell me what needs to be done. She acts like she expects me to know and when I don't, she just shakes her head. I know I'm not much good in the sick room but its just that I have no experience. I just don't know how to help.*

From an upstairs window, Florence watched her husband walk down the road. She sat down to write at her escritoire and ran her hands lovingly over the polished wood. The last time she used it was in St. Louis. It was one of the few pieces of furniture she was able to bring. A few small nicks marred its surface but they didn't matter. Her hands trembled as she opened the inkwell and began her letter.

Dearest Mother and Father,

I hope this letter finds you well. We've arrived in our new home. Some floors still need to be varnished, the roof has been shingled, and the porch covered. The house is large by Silver City standards. A porch goes around the entire house. We want Emma to enjoy the fresh air when she is better.

I'm sorry to worry you but I know you'll understand. Emma is so thin and pale. The trip was hard on all of us but especially on her. I'm so tired I fall asleep fully clothed most nights. I hired a young woman with nurse's training to help me. She is competent but very opinionated. I need to hire a cook soon as my culinary talents, as you know, are very limited. Anyway, I'm too tired to cook most of the time.

Florence straightened her shoulders, she must not indulge in self pity. The tone of her letter changed and became more formal. For a moment, she was tempted to tear it up and start over. But she decided to finish it.

We're told wild Indians are everywhere. When smoke rises from a mountain in the distance, it's their primitive way of communicating with one another. A fierce renegade called Victorio enjoys killing soldiers and stealing horses in the vicinity.

Silver City can hardly be called a town and there are no cities nearby only several small settlements of mostly miners and a few families. There is a fort about 8 miles away and all of the soldiers, except the officers, are Negroes.

I am unable to leave Emma so I can't attend church. Robert tells me the mercantile is impressive. His partner, R.D. Farnsworth is sending freight wagons to various camps and settlements. Robert thinks it will bring customers from out of town, into their store.

Pray for us, Mama. I feel so alone and frightened.

Your loving daughter,
Florence

Emma's condition slowly improved and by the middle of November, she'd regained some of the weight she had lost and was able to walk around the house.

"I'm not supposed to tell you but I overheard your mother and father discussing a Christmas party. Mr. Farnsworth is inviting most of the people in town and it'll be grand," Janie confided as she assisted Emma with her bath.

"Janie, do you think I could go?"

"Well, I don't know what Dr. Woodville will say, but he might let you."

That was all Emma needed. She was determined to be well for the party. Dr. Woodville was astounded at her recovery but when Dr. Woodville asked to speak to Florence and Robert one evening, Florence was frightened. Emma seemed better but how could they be sure?

"As you know," Dr. Woodville began, "I've had some reservations about your daughter's condition. She appears to be getting stronger but it may be only a temporary improvement. She needs something to keep her mind occupied, such as that Christmas party. I can't say now if she can go, only that it may be possible." Dr. Woodville shook Robert's hand and nodded to Florence as he took his leave.

On a cold, clear December night, Robert, Florence, and Emma took their small trap to R.D.'s house and were greeted at the door by their host. "Emma!" R.D. exclaimed, "How well you look! Please come in and meet the other guests." He clapped Robert on the back and took their coats.

R.D.'s house was large and beautifully decorated with fragrant pine boughs framing the windows. Musicians stood in one corner of the main room and the furniture was pushed back against the walls to make room for dancing. A roaring fire in the hearth snapped and crackled causing two elderly gentlemen to jump to avoid being singed by errant sparks. At the other end of the room, a huge table groaned with food. Smoked hams, turkeys, cakes, pies, spiced hot cider, yeasty rolls, fresh butter, all wonderful delicacies provided by the host. R.D.'s wife, Beatrice, had arranged everything to perfection. Dancers of all ages filled the room.

Emma could barely breathe, as the room grew hot and stuffy. Her parents stood near an important looking gentleman. The man was waving his arms in the air and Emma heard her father's booming laugh. She exclaimed to no one in particular, "I just have to get some fresh air."

Frank Parnell leaned against the wall of the livery stable. Across the street from R.D.'s house, he watched the dancers until he saw the door open and someone slip outside. The full moon bathed her face in its soft light so he could see her features plainly. Recognizing the girl from the stagecoach, Frank couldn't take his eyes off of her. Joe, the livery stable owner, nudged him with his elbow.

"She's that new store owner's daughter. Heard tell she's been mighty sick," Joe cut off a plug of tobacco and shoved it in his mouth.

Frank nodded. Whistling a tune, he walked across the street. Emma was looking up at the moon. She smiled that smile he felt was especially for him when she recognized him.

"Hello," she said.

"Pleased to see you again, miss," Frank said as he tipped his hat politely.

"You rode on the stage with us from Deming. I wasn't sure you would remember me. You slept nearly the whole way."

"I was tired. Your folks made it clear I wasn't good enough to talk to you," Frank said. "And they didn't care much for my opinions."

"I must apologize for them. They are very protective. I've been sick, you see, and they're worried about me," Emma said quietly.

"You don't need to apologize. If you were my daughter, I wouldn't let you talk to strange men either," Frank admitted.

Emma blushed. Instinctively, she touched the locket around her neck. This man made her feel so strange inside, kind of warm and fluttery. She took a deep breath and tried to compose herself. The warmth in her cheeks must be evident to the young man standing so close to her.

Frank removed his bandana and brushed off a bench situated just outside the Farnsworth garden. When Emma was seated, he sat down on the edge of the bench.

"If you introduce yourself, we won't be strangers," Emma was surprised at herself. She was never forward. The next twenty minutes passed quickly as they talked about Silver City and their stagecoach ride from Deming. Emma couldn't remember ever enjoying a conversation as much.

Caught up in the excitement of the party, Florence was captivated with John Fleming's charm and storytelling ability. For awhile she forgot about her troubles and listened to Fleming's conversation with Robert. When she looked around the room, she realized Emma had disappeared. Alarmed, she excused herself and started looking for her missing daughter. As she approached the dining room door, she saw Emma sitting outside on a bench. She wasn't alone. Dismayed, Florence called to Emma as she hurried toward her. The man, Emma was sitting with got up, hurried across the street, and disappeared into the livery stable. Emma was flustered when her mother reached her and Florence's heart pounded in her ears.

"What are you doing outside?" Florence asked anxiously, pulling off her own shawl to put it around Emma's shoulders.

"I came out for some air. A man was passing and stopped to talk. It was all perfectly innocent, Mother," Emma shivered.

"A young lady never speaks to a man without a proper introduction," Florence admonished, "Let's get inside before you catch your death." Instantly, she regretted her words. "I knew this party wasn't a good idea."

"I'm sorry but I've been indoors so long," Emma opened the front door of the heavily heated house.

"Why did the man run when I came out?" Florence demanded.

"I think you startled him. He was very polite, Mother," Emma said.

Florence tried to disguise her feelings as she smiled and took her daughter's arm. A young woman with Emma's breeding could have her pick of men in St.

Louis. She shuddered to think of delicate Emma in the arms of an uncouth ruffian.

Back inside R.D.'s house, the party continued with lively fiddlers and dancing. Although Emma was asked repeatedly for a dance, Florence stood beside her daughter to be sure she declined. When Robert asked Emma to dance, she smiled at him gratefully. When her father took her in his arms and they waltzed, Emma closed her eyes tightly and pretended she was dancing with Frank Parnell.

After a couple of beers with Joe, the livery stable owner, Frank returned to his small hotel room. As he stared at the ceiling he pictured Emma's pretty face and knew he had to see her again.

Chapter 4

Frank's job kept him away from Ft. Bayard for weeks at a time. He had some decisions to make because he couldn't get Emma Jensen out of his head. There had to be some way to see Emma and continue doing his job. Her house was easy to find but it was difficult to get a message to her. He spotted Janie walking toward town.

"Pardon me, Miss. I wondered if I might speak to you?" Frank asked politely walking along beside her.

Janie looked him up and down. Deciding he didn't look too dangerous, she agreed. "What can I do for you?"

"I'm trying to get a message to Miss Jensen. Would you take it to her?"

Janie stopped. "Why don't you take it to her?" She smiled and nodded. "Never mind, I know why." She took the folded paper and put it in her pocket. "I'd be happy to."

Emma was lying down when Janie returned to the Jensen house. Mischievously, Janie giggled and poked Emma's arm. When Emma opened her eyes, Janie dramatically produced the note from her pocket. Snatching it from Janie's grasp, Emma's eyes filled with tears. Frank wanted to ask permission to court her.

While preparing a basket for a church family, Emma decided it was time to discuss her feelings for Frank with her mother. She didn't know what to say but felt she should let her mother know that she was interested in someone. Emma stood beside her mother in the large kitchen as Florence arranged the baked goods, Janie had prepared, in a basket. Emma laid her head against her mother's shoulder. Florence paused and kissed her daughter's forehead.

"Are you all right dear," she asked.

"Yes mother. But I want to discuss something with you," Emma said. She paused, not knowing how to continue.

Florence continued to fill the basket. "I told Mrs. Henry we would deliver this basket today. She has been ill for nearly two weeks and all of the church ladies are taking turns providing meals for them. I'm sure she'll appreciate some homemade baked goods. Janie has a way with baking. I'm sure I'll never be any good at it," Florence laughed.

"Mother, would you and father, allow young men to court me?" Emma interrupted.

Florence stopped, feeling the heat rising in her cheeks.

"The doctor said you should take it easy and rest, Emma dear," Florence struggled to hold her temper. "You're very young and don't understand the dangers you could be exposed to in a place like this. Your father would never allow someone in this town to court his daughter. When the time comes, perhaps we can move to a more suitable place. Now help me finish this basket."

"But mother, I..." Emma began.

"I'll hear no more about it," Florence said with an angry snap of her jaw. "I must be off."

A large cottonwood in the corner of Jensens's garden served as a message center. Frank crept to the tree after dark and left a note. Janie checked the large knothole high in the trunk every day and relayed any messages promptly to Emma.

Late one February afternoon, Janie watched Emma slip out the back door and into Frank's waiting arms. Janie kept busy with her work, determined to do everything she could to help Frank and Emma continue to meet. Janie brought Emma some warm tea to drink when Emma returned. "Tell me more about your mysterious young man. He is so handsome and seems to love you very much."

Emma longed to confide in someone and was thrilled Janie was interested. "He is so wonderful, Janie," she gushed. "He makes me laugh. Sometimes we both start to say the same thing. I miss him so much when he is away. We always have so much to talk about."

"Emma, why don't you invite him to meet your parents? I know they're strict but I'm sure they'd like to meet this man," Janie said.

Emma gasped. She blushed and examined the locket around her neck. "He has met my parents and didn't make a very good impression. My mother made it clear that I am not allowed to have a courtship of any kind. We'll have to meet secretly. I'm thankful that we live near the edge of town because it is easier for me to sneak out," Emma yanked a brush through her hair.

Janie approached her employer the next day when Florence was reading a letter from her mother. "I'd like to speak to you about Emma, ma'am," Janie said.

"What is it?" Florence asked impatiently.

"I think Emma is tired of staying home all of the time. Maybe she could begin to attend some of the local dances," Janie said. "She needs to be around people her own age."

Florence jumped up from the chair. Her letter fell, unheeded, to the floor. "Emma has been very ill! The young men in this town are rough and unruly. I'll not allow her to become involved with someone who might hurt her or cause her to suffer a relapse," Florence said forcefully.

"I didn't mean to intrude on private matters, ma'am. I just thought..." Janie was curtly interrupted.

Indignation made Florence's words cut through the air like a knife. "My husband and I pay you to guard Emma's health. Don't presume that we want or need your advice about anything else. We know what's best for our daughter. Guard your tongue, young woman, or you'll be looking for another position!"

Janie was headstrong and refused to leave the matter alone. While speaking to Dr. Woodville, she decided to discuss Emma's lack of recreation with him. She was careful not to mention Emma's young man. Emma was afraid to tell her his name.

"I am concerned about Emma having to stay inside so much of the time. I was wondering if you might suggest to her parents that she be allowed to picnic on warm days?" Janie asked timidly.

Dr. Woodville didn't like to have nurses offer him advice. "Mind your own business, Nurse. It isn't your responsibility to tell me how to treat my patients."

Janie had the satisfaction of knowing she planted the idea in his head. She watched him pause and look out his office window.

Soon Emma was allowed to go on picnics occasionally. Florence accompanied her and Janie several times but felt she was wasting too much time. The two young women were allowed to venture out each Tuesday and Friday afternoons, weather permitting, with a picnic basket to their favorite picnic spot at the top of a hill. From their vantage point, they spent afternoons watching the town's activities. Frank joined them whenever he could. Sitting on an old blanket, Janie could hear snatches of their conversation and Emma's laughter. Tears welled up in her eyes. *It would be so nice to have someone love me that much. Emma wants a normal courtship and to be allowed to grow up*, she thought.

One April day when the fruit trees were in bloom, Frank kissed Emma for the first time. His courage nearly deserted him when he looked into her trusting, innocent eyes. He knew he loved her when he saw love reflected in her beautiful, blue eyes; his shyness vanished and he took her in his arms.

"I love you, Frank," Emma whispered.

"Not nearly as much as I love you," he told her.

Emma's legs felt shaky and weak and shivers ran down her spine when Frank kissed her. Frank struggled to catch his breath and maintain control. *She is so thin, I might hurt her if I hold her too tightly*, he thought.

Emma looked into his eyes when he ended the kiss, abruptly. Reading his thoughts, she laughed. "Don't worry, you won't hurt me. It was wonderful, like soaring through the air!"

Janie worried when Emma was gone so long. She packed up the picnic basket and the couple appeared just as she finished. Janie smiled happily. Emma's cheeks were pink and they were both smiling.

In late November, Frank and Emma decided to elope. Several times, Emma tried to speak to her parents about her relationship with Frank. They wouldn't approve of any man in Silver City as a prospective son-in-law. Janie made plans of her own; it was time for her to live somewhere more civilized.

Frank resigned from the Bureau of Indian Affairs when he and Emma decided to get married. With his saved wages, he purchased a small piece of land from a homesteader, near Columbus. The homesteader, John Collins, had a few head of cattle and grew alfalfa. The two men met in Deming while Frank was there on business. Emma wouldn't have to leave the climate that was doing her so much good but would be far away enough from her parents to give them a chance to accept the marriage before they discovered the couple's whereabouts. Frank was worried about banditos and Indian raids, their land was about 10 miles from Mexico. Could they protect themselves?

"We've seen some Indians from time to time but most leave us alone. As for Mexican bandits, we haven't had no trouble," John assured him.

Emma cried as she packed her valise. It was frightening, embarking on a new life, leaving her childhood, and loving parents behind. A rough life faced her, unlike anything she'd ever known. She held her locket in her hand and tears streamed down her face. "Am I doing the right thing?" Emma asked Janie.

"Oh, Em, it's so romantic. You love him and he loves you. I'm sure you'll be very happy," Janie reassured her. Janie took Emma's valise and stashed it behind the large potted plant in the foyer.

Emma's tears mixed with the first snowfall of the year. She stepped out of the Jensen home, carrying all her important belongings in the valise, and whispered goodbye to her parents. Frank took her arm and led her across the street to a small wagon with a mule harnessed to it. Emma smiled bravely and he smiled back.

They were married in a simple service performed by an itinerant preacher. During the entire ceremony, Emma clutched her locket. The picture of her Mama and Papa was inside. She closed her eyes and tried to imagine them standing beside her.

Snow flurries and cold wind threw a veil of white on the new bride's hair as she and her husband headed toward their new home. Their first night was spent near the Mimbres River. The wind died down and snow fell silently. The bare branches of the cottonwoods along the river stood starkly against the night sky. The couple ate and Frank set up the tent.

For the first time in their relationship, they couldn't speak. Shyly, Frank reached for Emma's hand. When he led her into the tent and drew her into his arms, no words were necessary.

Chapter 5

Robert and Florence awoke on December 4th to find Emma and a few of her belongings gone. A note was propped up on Emma's dresser against the mirror. Florence's hands were shaking as she hastily pulled off the ribbon tied around the note.

Dearest Mother and Father,
I love you both so much. It's hard for me to write this letter. I can't tell you how I feel. I've met a man and want to be with him. We'll be married by the time you read this. He is wonderful, kind and gentle, as well as strong.
Please forgive me. I know you wouldn't approve of him. He has nothing and we'll be poor; but he'll never let me go hungry. You came here so I could get well. Now that I am better, I need to make a life for myself. Please try to understand, I want to have children and grow old with my husband.
I love you.
Emma

Huge tears fell on the paper Florence held tightly. She was numb with grief. Her beloved daughter was lost to her. *Where was she? Was she safe?* Florence handed the tear stained note to Robert. He groaned loudly when he read it and sat down heavily on the edge of his daughter's neat bed.

"My God! How could she do this?" he murmured. What had they done to drive her away? She was their whole world and she was gone without saying goodbye or even telling them where she was going.

"She thinks she's a grown woman now. We gave up everything so she could get well and then she runs off with the first man she meets!" Florence said angrily. The pain of her loss was overwhelming. "Our little girl is gone for good and we don't know where she is or if we shall ever see her again. Why couldn't she tell me about him? I'd have listened," Florence cried.

A chill ran down her spine when she recalled Emma asking if she could be courted. Then Janie suggested Emma spend more time with people her own age. Maybe, she should have allowed it. She had made decisions with Emma's best interests in mind, hadn't she? Anger took over where uncertainty left off. *Emma's elopement was certainly not her fault!*

She stomped out of the room and in a shrill, shaky voice, Florence summoned Janie. "Janie, where are you?" Tears flew from her face as she ran down the hall.

"Here I am ma'am," Janie said. She was horrified by her mistress' appearance. Florence's face was blotchy and swollen. A large vein pulsed in her forehead. Janie mentally braced herself for the confrontation.

"What do you know about Emma and that man?" Florence demanded.

Janie shrank back against the wall. This was much worse than she expected. Robert came up behind Florence and placed a restraining hand on her shoulder.

"Calm yourself, my dear. Janie, you must tell us about this man," Robert said.

Janie confessed she knew about Emma and Frank. There wasn't much else to tell, she didn't know where they had gone, Emma refused to tell her.

"Get out! You might as well leave Silver City because I'll be sure you never work here again!" Florence shoved Janie toward the door. Wrenching it open she pushed her outside.

Janie stood on the porch with her mouth open, still in shock. As she walked down the steps and through the front gate, some of her clothes came flying by her head. She looked around in embarrassment to see if anyone was watching. Fortunately, it was still early and few people were out yet. Janie hurriedly scooped up her belongings and put them into her valise also laying in the street. Slowly, she walked toward town, her clothes poking through the sides of her valise.

On the morning of December 8th, reluctantly bidding her friends goodbye, Janie boarded a stage going to San Francisco. Her sister Margaret, a recent widow, lived in a house on Nob Hill. Margaret's two small children needed looking after while Margaret tried to settle her late husband's affairs. A letter from Margaret had arrived two weeks earlier, begging Janie to come. Fate intervened and Margaret wired Janie money for the trip. Florence refused to pay Janie's wages for her last week of service.

Robert was a wreck. He went to work early and locked himself in his office, not eating for days at a time. His sense of guilt was overwhelming. He failed to protect his daughter, the most precious person in his life. *What had he done wrong?*

R.D. tried to comfort his grief stricken friend as he tried to find out everything he could about Emma's husband. The young man had covered his tracks. R.D. learned he was attached to the Bureau of Indian Affairs and assigned to Ft. Bayard. R.D. arranged a meeting with Colonel Peter Swain, the new commander of Ft. Bayard.

Colonel Swain answered his knock impatiently. "I'm sorry Mr. Farnsworth, I have more important things to do than keep track of ex-Indian agents. Parnell was gone by the time I arrived. I understand he was a good man but that's about all I can tell you."

A courier knocked at the door interrupting their meeting. Swain read his message hastily and Swain pushed past R.D. "Urgent business demands my attention, I must ask you to follow up on this at a later date," Swain was gone before R.D. could protest.

R.D. Farnsworth was furious. He decided to waste no more time with the military. He offered a large reward for any news of Frank Parnell or the couple's whereabouts. The men R.D. questioned could give him little information. Frank anticipated Emma's family would look for her and was careful not to divulge their plans. R.D. sent a wire to the Bureau of Indian Affairs in Washington, D.C. The paperwork on Frank Parnell had been misplaced, was their reply.

Florence plunged into the Ladies' Sewing Circle activities and wrote letters to Emma. Not knowing where to send them, she kept them in a trunk in Emma's old room. She felt foolish but found it helped stay connected to her daughter. Florence wrote about her own early childhood in St. Louis and her time as a debutante. Vividly, she recalled the men who courted her and described them in detail, reliving her youth. Later, Florence decided to keep a journal and poured out her heart, aching for something to fill the void.

As months went by, Robert and Florence realized Emma wasn't coming back. They found comfort in each other, spending evenings sitting on the porch not speaking just enjoying each other's company.

Spring came and imported fruit trees blossomed, along with the native juniper and scrub oak. The parched earth sucked up every scant drop of moisture. Desert wildlife, deer, coyotes, and elk appeared more frequently in and near town. Wild pigs, called javelinas, snuffled around in gardens, rooting for food.

Houses sprang up all over town. Many didn't have the means to buy a house and property, so row houses were built. The founding fathers of Silver City realized cheaply fabricated houses were a fire hazard. An ordinance was passed to outlaw "frame houses" within the city limits because strong winds could wipe out a whole block in a matter of hours.

Chapter 6

Li Soo carefully touched her stinging cheek wondering if her father's hand left its imprint on her skin. She was forbidden to speak to Chan Cho, her friend and playmate since childhood.

The morning started out badly with a dirty pile of miners' clothes reeking in the hot, steamy laundry room. It wasn't cool outside but at least she could breathe. When she stepped outside, she saw Chan beckoning to her and she went to speak to him.

"I haven't seen you for awhile," Chan said, slurring slightly and swaying on his feet.

"I have been working," Li Soo answered shyly. He had been in the opium den again.

Chan was a very handsome man and Li Soo daydreamed about having him as her husband. Lan Soo, Li Soo's father, observed the two and rushed from the laundry. He grabbed his daughter's arm and dragged her inside, screaming in Chinese.

"You have been warned, my daughter, not to associate with the pigs that spend their lives as slaves of the poppy," he yelled, trembling with anger and frustration. Chan Cho was no good! He must keep that evil young man away from his daughter.

"But, my father, I was only speaking to Chan Cho. I have known him since we were small children," Li Soo said quietly.

Before Li Soo knew what was happening, her father slapped her across the face. The slap wasn't very hard but it hurt her pride. Li Soo went back to work as her mother, Mai, shook her head. Her daughter wouldn't listen to reason. "I have told you, my daughter, this is one thing your father will not tolerate," Mai scolded.

"It cannot be that I can never speak to Chan again," Li Soo replied sadly. Large tears filled her eyes and threatened to spill down her cheeks. Why didn't her father understand how she felt?

"Let us have some tea and talk more of this," Mai suggested, taking her daughter's slender arm and gently guiding her to the back of the laundry. The small room behind the larger one, held a wooden table, a stove, four mismatched chairs, a lamp, and tea making equipment.

Mai was a compassionate woman and knew Li Soo loved Chan. It hurt her heart when her daughter was sad. But she agreed with her husband, Li Soo must never become involved with someone who used opium. The two sat side by side silently, while they waited for the water to boil and the tea to steep. Fifteen minutes later, Mai was pouring fragrant jasmine tea for herself and her young daughter.

Li Soo was their only daughter. Five years ago, Mai's son and husband left Mai and Li Soo in China to come to America to start a laundry business. No one was sure how they ended up in Silver City but the men decided to start their business in the small mining town. When they had saved enough money, they sent for Li Soo and Mai. Now Li Soo was of marriageable age but without prospects.

Mai spoke softly to Li Soo, not wishing to be overheard. "You are my beloved daughter and I want your happiness. In this business with your father, you are wrong. By defying your father you are breaking a sacred law. You are in love with Chan; but you must try to forget him. He is no good for you," Mai said.

"We played together as children. As I grew older, my father told me we could no longer play together. He said that it was improper. Now, my father tells me I can no longer speak to the man I love," Li Soo sobbed. She reached for her mother's work roughened hand. Mai took Li Soo's hand and gently stroked it.

"When you are older, you will understand some things that you do not now," Mai said. "Drink your tea and sit down outside beneath the trees, for a time. I will finish your chores. Will you try to compose yourself before you meet your father for this evening's meal?" Mai asked gently.

"I will do as you ask, my mother," Li Soo answered.

Li Soo sat under some trees that lined Main Street. Closing her eyes, she listened to water swishing in the tubs and sounds from the street. When she opened her eyes, little, white, puffy clouds floated overhead. She imagined she was one of the clouds scudding across the sky. Li Soo craved freedom, she didn't want to spend her life washing dirty clothing.

When she went back inside the laundry again, Li Soo had trouble breathing for a few minutes. The dryness of the air outside contrasted sharply with the heavy humidity inside. The acrid smell of lye soap caused her nose to burn and eyes to water. She stirred the water in a large vat with a wooden paddle and continued to stir until the water turned a murky gray. Then the soapy clothes were run through a mangle, rinsed in another vat of water, and run through the mangle again. Her crisp white uniform was limp and wrinkled. Sticking to her body, it hampered her movements.

Li Soo preferred to wait on customers but was allowed to only when business was slow. During the summer, laundry needed to be done more frequently and business was seldom slow.

Mai watched Li Soo change the water in a tub. She waited until Li Soo completed her task before asking her to wait on customers.

"Thank you, my mother," Li Soo said gratefully.

As Li Soo approached the counter, she saw a carriage stop outside. A well-dressed woman entered the laundry and Li Soo greeted her politely.

"I've come in search of a house servant. I realize this is a laundry but I have been told the people working in this establishment are very well educated. My name is Florence Jensen and I live on Black Street," Florence said, handing Li Soo her calling card. "My husband is Robert Jensen of Miner's Mercantile. Perhaps you've heard of him? I'd like to employ an intelligent, well-spoken person."

Li Soo's eyes widened. This was an important lady. "What is the job of a house servant?" Li Soo asked, accepting the card.

Florence explained that the servant would be expected to oversee the cleaning of the house and laundry for two adults. In return, she would receive room and board and the generous salary of $1.00 per week.

"What of the cooking?" Li Soo asked.

"The house servant would be responsible for finding a suitable cook for the family as soon as she is settled," Florence said.

"I would like to request that you return tomorrow so that I may discuss your offer with my family."

Florence smiled and said, "Of course, that would be perfect. I'll return in the morning."

Li Soo bowed her head. Other customers, mostly miners, came and went until the laundry closed for the day. The miners stared at her rudely but Li Soo ignored their behavior. It was hard to hide her beauty under the shapeless clothes. A delicately bridged nose, bright almond shaped eyes and long black hair, worn in a queue, were her best features. Hard work roughened and reddened her slender, young hands so her mother insisted she apply almond oil to her hands twice a day. Her figure was well shaped but hidden beneath the long white cotton shirt and baggy pants that were her daily uniform.

The family gathered around the supper table. There was no speaking at the table until the food was served. Carefully, Li Soo composed herself and practiced in her head what she would say. "I have been offered employment as a house servant. I would like to accept this position, with my father's permission," Li Soo said quietly.

Her family sat in stunned silence. Finally, Lan Soo spoke. "I will need to be told more of this before I make a decision," Lan Soo said.

The dinner continued. When Mai rose slowly to clear the table, their new daughter-in-law, Concha, stood also. She was a sweet girl but Mai and Lan Soo believed their culture should be kept pure.

When Li Soo was preparing to retire for the night, her father sent for her. She told him what she knew about the position and explained that Mrs. Jensen was the wife of Robert Jensen of Miner's Mercantile. Lan Soo sat quietly as his daughter talked.

"My daughter, do you wish to accept this position you have been offered?" he asked solemnly.

"I would like to accept this position and be allowed to send part of my wages to my family to repay them for the problems I have caused," Li Soo replied, bowing her head with respect.

"What problems?" Lan Soo asked, his hands were folded in his lap.

"There will be no one to perform my duties at the laundry," Li Soo replied, "I have not been an obedient daughter. For this, I am sincerely sorry."

"You are a fine daughter and I am honored to be your father. You may accept this position with my blessing," Lan Soo said quietly. He turned away from his daughter's gaze so she couldn't see the tears of pride in his eyes.

"With your permission, I would like to prepare for tomorrow," Li Soo said.

"You may prepare," Lan Soo said.

Li Soo bowed slightly and walked out of the room, scarcely able to contain her excitement. Florence was grateful to relinquish the running of the household into Li Soo's capable hands. She learned quickly and took the initiative to do things without being told. Janie cared for Emma and acted as housekeeper. She brought in young women to do the actual cleaning but oversaw their work. After she was fired, Florence was at a loss. She was incapable of caring for her own house and unable to find things. Florence sought help from R.D.'s wife, Beatrice, but was told she needed to find her own servants. Beatrice was still upset that Janie had been fired.

When the household was running smoothly, Li Soo asked permission to hire a local woman, Enriquetta Tovar, to do the cooking. Quetta, as she liked to be called, was a fabulous cook and introduced the family to Mexican American food. Robert, with a tendency to be stout, gained 15 pounds. Li Soo took his clothing to the tailor for alterations. Florence asked Quetta not to prepare so much food.

"But Señora, I have cooked for a large family all of my life. It is *muy difícil* to cook for only four," Quetta said. It was true, the fewest number Quetta ever cooked for was fifteen. Determined to comply with Florence's wishes, Quetta continued to have massive quantities of leftovers. At night, when the household was asleep, Robert crept downstairs and found leftovers he could eat without listening to his wife's nagging. He even oiled the door hinges.

Chapter 7

John Collins converted a small shed, used to store his feed, into a house for Frank and Emma. It wasn't much but it kept out most of the wind that continued to howl for the rest of December and most of January. Emma set about making the little shack livable. She made curtains from pieces of an old dress for the only window. She scrubbed the plank floor with a scrub brush and soapy water every day until it was possible to walk on the floors barefoot and not get splinters.

Frank was out checking on a newborn foal early one morning when Emma feared she was dying. She arose early and made breakfast on their small cast iron stove. The smell of frying eggs made her stomach churn. She slammed a plate down in front of Frank when he returned from the barn. Without a word, she ran for the outhouse and was ghastly pale when she returned.

"What's the matter? Are you all right?" Frank asked fearing a relapse of consumption.

"I'm just fine. Just a little touch of dyspepsia," Emma groaned.

"I'll stay close today, in case you need something," Frank said, after he finished his breakfast. He went to work on a fence for the garden Emma wanted to plant in the spring. Weather and everyday demands of cattle ranching had prevented him from getting it done. He was determined to have their garden plot and fence ready by time to plant.

Frank asked Emma if he should go get Betsy.

"Don't bother Betsy, she has too much to do with her little ones. I'll be just fine," Emma assured him.

As the day wore on, she made innumerable trips to the outhouse and each time it got harder to walk back to the house. Finally, she put a small cooking pot outside the door so she wouldn't have to go clear to the outhouse to be sick.

Frank checked on her several times and decided to go get Betsy. Betsy came over in her wagon with her two small children in tow.

"My goodness, Emma, you look terrible!" Betsy said without thinking and promptly clapped her hand over her mouth. "I'm sorry. What have you had to eat today, dear?"

"Nothing will stay down," Emma groaned. "I tried to eat a little bread and a few sips of water. I can't think what could be wrong, I was fine yesterday."

Betsy smiled knowingly. She put her arm around Emma's thin shoulders and whispered something to her. Frank was bewildered because Emma was smiling. He noticed she was holding the locket around her neck.

"Do you think so? Oh, how wonderful!" Emma said as tears streamed down her cheeks.

"I'll leave you two alone. Farley, don't hit your brother! Let's go home now." Betsy separated her two small sons, herded them out the door, and closed it behind her.

Frank sat down beside his wife and held out his arms. "What did she say, Em?" he wanted to know.

Emma smiled mysteriously. "She thinks I may be on the nest," she said.

"On the nest? What? Ohhh…," Frank jumped up and ran outside.

Emma struggled to her feet and followed him. He was standing in front of the house looking out across the fields. "What's wrong, dear? Aren't you happy" she asked putting her arms around his waist.

Frank took her hands firmly and turned to face her. "You aren't strong enough to have a child. I don't think I could bear to lose you," he looked grief stricken as he pulled her toward him and wrapped his arms around her frail body.

"I'll be just fine. Betsy is here to help me and I'll go into town and see a doctor, if you like."

Frank nodded. "I'll take you tomorrow. You must do everything the doctor tells you."

Early the next morning, Frank hitched up the mule to their little wagon and they headed for town. The wind whipped up the dirt so Emma tied a bandanna across her face. The jolting of the wagon caused every muscle in her body to ache. With nothing left in her stomach it continued to rebel.

In Deming, Frank lost no time finding a doctor. Doc Cain insisted Emma stay in his office for a few days on a cot. He administered several disgusting smelling concoctions during her stay. By the second day, she was able to get a little sleep and could eat and drink small amounts.

Frank heard that Doc Cain had a tarnished reputation in Deming because he was frequently in the local saloons. When Emma was able to travel, she and Frank returned to the homestead. Doc Cain confirmed Emma was expecting a child and the baby would be born sometime in mid-October.

The months flew by. Emma's morning sickness subsided and she developed a healthy glow. Frank was elated to see Emma so well and happy. It was truly a miracle.

Chapter 8

Night after night, Emma stared at the ceiling. Familiar piano etudes swam in her head and her fingers throbbed. The familiar strains of Chopin's Prelude No. 4 in E minor lulled her to sleep.

At the Academy of Music, the works of a young Russian composer, Peter Ilich Tchaikovsky, enraptured her. His music stirred her imagination conjuring up faraway lands full of mystery and magic. One of her instructors had studied at the Moscow Conservatory. He brought many of Tchaikovsky's compositions with him to share with his students. Emma attended the first American performance of George Bizet's opera Carmen. The production was performed in Italian at the Academy. Later, Emma arranged many of the beautiful melodies into piano compositions. It was so long ago.

As Frank worked around the homestead, Emma hummed loudly to herself, occupying her hands with menial tasks to keep her fingers from feeling the familiar throb. Frank found her lost in thought, holding her silver locket, tears streaming down her face. He questioned her gently. Emma smiled through her tears and admitted she missed playing the piano. Her dear husband could never understand music was as much a part of her existence as breathing.

Deming was a bustling little town with dusty streets filled with wagons and itinerants. One late spring evening Frank was in town for supplies. After he finished helping the clerk load the wagon, he headed to the saloon for a drink. Near the saloon, a mule harnessed to an old cart chomped noisily, his nose buried in a deep feedbag. As Frank walked by, he paused; something caught his eye. The cart contained a spinet. Frank stood for a moment looking at it and smiled. Inside the saloon, he ordered a whiskey. The old bar piano was being tuned. An old man surrounded by tools was tinkering with something inside the case. Frank sat down at a nearby table and waited. When the old man finished and was gathering up his tools, Frank cleared his throat loudly.

"Excuse me, sir," he said.

The old man looked toward him. His rheumy eyes blinked several times. "Did you say something? Well, speak up!" he said.

Frank rubbed his jaw with his fingers. He wasn't sure how to ask the old man. "Is that your rig outside in the street?"

"What ya want to know fer?" the man asked.

"No reason, except I saw a piano in the back and wanted to know if you would sell it to me," Frank replied.

"Tain't a pianny. It's what some folks call a spinet. Can you play the pianny, son?" the man chuckled.

"No sir. It's for my wife," Frank grinned.

"It don't stay in tune very long with all the jarring it gets. I play it while I'm on the road. What would ya give me fer it?" the man asked, his eyes beginning to gleam. He liked the idea of a shrewd deal.

"How much are you asking?"

"I guess I could take forty dollars fer it," now an evil twinkle danced in his eyes.

"Forty dollars, that's a joke, right?" Frank exclaimed.

"Reckon you must want a pianny awful bad to want that 'un," the old piano tuner smiled, revealing his gold teeth.

"I could give you fifteen for it, maybe," Frank said as he did some quick calculations in his head. He still needed to buy more supplies before heading home the next day.

"Why did ya say ya wanted it?" the man asked.

"My wife went to school in New York to study piano before she got sick and moved here," Frank said. "She's so unhappy sometimes, I thought maybe it would cheer her up."

Now it was the old man's turn to rub his chin. This young feller's wife would be about the age of his daughter. Frank found his soft spot.

"Well, I guess I could take twenty fer it," he said grudgingly.

"Can't spare more than seventeen. Honest mister, I would be much obliged," Frank said.

"I'll sell it to ya fer eighteen dollars and not a penny less," the old man said shrewdly, knowing he was still getting the better end of the deal.

"Done!" Frank said laughing. He wasn't sure if he had enough money to buy the feed but it would be worth it to see the look on Emma's face. He borrowed the supply money from John and needed to pay him back. After finishing his drink, Frank paid the man. The older man smiled, counted his money, and ordered himself a drink from the bartender. Frank went outside and climbed into the cart. He plunked on the chipped keys of the spinet. Even to his untrained ear, the sounds the spinet produced were discordant. Frank went back inside the saloon and spoke to the old piano tuner. After fifteen minutes of haggling, the man reluctantly agreed to tune the spinet for an additional three dollars.

Scarcely able to contain his excitement, Frank left for the homestead before the sun came up the following morning. He spent most of the evening securing his precious cargo in his wagon with ropes and baling wire and even obtained the rest of the supplies he needed. The battered finish was protected with gunnysacks and old horse-smelly rags from the livery stable. Frank felt guilty because he had spent so much money on the spinet.

The journey home was arduous. Frank drove slowly over the smoothest areas he could find and stopped every few miles to check the ropes and to be sure the spinet hadn't moved. It was very late when he arrived home. Emma was waiting at the door with a lantern.

"What kept you? I have been so worried," she asked as Frank jumped down and came toward her.

"Sorry, Em. I was delayed," Frank grinned.

Emma looked at her dusty, disheveled husband. *Why on earth was he grinning like that?* "What happened? I kept imagining all kinds of things," she said sternly.

"Nothing happened, I had trouble finding some things," he said, twisting his mouth sideways to hide his silly grin. His face hurt with the effort it took to hide his excitement. On the way home, Frank decided to wait to give Emma her present until the next day. Shined up with beeswax, it would be more presentable.

Emma knew Frank was up to something. She kissed him on the cheek and he patted her rounded belly. "I'm sorry if I worried you. How is our little one?" he asked.

"After working in the garden all day, my back was sore, so I lay down for awhile this evening and I felt a fluttery feeling. Maybe it's because I haven't eaten yet. I think he moved," she smiled triumphantly. "Oh, I kept dinner warm for you."

Frank put his hand on her abdomen. He didn't feel anything but was excited anyway. "Thanks, I'm starved," Frank admitted. He took some bags of flour and sugar from the wagon and followed Emma into the little house. The wagon was full of supplies, she could hardly wait to see what Frank brought home.

"I'm pretty tired. I'll get up early and unload the wagon, Em."

That night, she drifted to sleep holding her silver locket. At dawn, Emma lit the stove. The rich smell of frying bacon greeted him when Frank came inside. After breakfast, he reached across the table and stroked Emma's hand with his fingertips and then squeezed it gently. "Come outside with me, it's a beautiful day," he said quietly.

"I need to clean up the dishes first. I'll be out later to work in the garden," Emma stood slowly, smoothing the folds of her dress.

"The dishes can wait. Come with me, I brought you something." Frank held Emma's arm and guided her toward the door. "Close your eyes," he said.

"I knew you were up to something. You can't keep secrets from me," Emma giggled. She closed her eyes and allowed her husband to lead her outside. She shuffled her feet so that she wouldn't trip over a loose rock.

Frank laughed, "I won't let you fall, silly. Come on." When they reached the wagon, Frank told her to open her eyes. After polishing the spinet, he was pleased with the results.

"Frank, oh, Frank, oh, Frank!" Emma collapsed into his arms sobbing. She clutched her locket.

"Emmy, are you all right? Tell me, what's wrong? Say something!" Frank was alarmed by her reaction.

Her eyes filled with tears when she looked up at him. "I don't know what to say. Where did you find it?"

"I bought it from a piano tuner in Deming. He wanted a lot of money for it but I haggled with him. It doesn't sound too good but he tried to adjust it some. You're so sad sometimes. I know this isn't the life you're used to and soon you'll have a baby to mind. I wanted to somehow make it a little better here for you."

"You're a wonderful man," Emma kissed and hugged him tightly.

John Collins witnessed the touching scene. He was working on the fence and waited until they were finished before he approached. He helped Frank unload and carry the spinet into the house. It took up a lot of room despite its small size. John wasn't sure what happened between the young couple but knew it was significant. He and his wife were settled and comfortable with each other. Had they ever been as much in love as these two?

Emma stroked the old spinet lovingly. She pulled a chair over to it and started to play. It was out of tune and tinny sounding but Emma didn't care. The man she loved, really loved her and gave her something back she thought was lost forever.

Every day, Emma played her spinet for at least an hour. Frank stood beside her with his hand on her shoulder, amazed at the beautiful sounds coming from the little instrument and the look of rapture on his wife's face when she played.

Chapter 9

In the middle of a cold autumn night, Emma was awakened by a strange sound. Gathering her nightdress around her, she approached the door cautiously and looked outside. The mule was restless, running around the corral, snorting and stomping. Frank was fast asleep and snoring gently. Reluctant to disturb him, she lit the lantern and went to see what was disturbing the mule. She lifted the lantern as high as she could so that most of the corral was illuminated. She didn't see anything but heard a muffled growl when she approached the barn. The sound was indistinct and she crouched down to get a better look. A movement caught her attention and the lantern light revealed a grimy dog. Cowering, it slunk closer to the building. Even in the dim light, it was obvious the little creature was matted and starving.

"I won't hurt you," she said softly. To her amazement, the dog quit growling and timidly wagged its scruffy tail.

Emma went to get her shawl and a piece of meat left over from their supper. She feared the dog was gone but it had hidden itself under the woodpile. She could just see the tip of its nose.

An icy gust of wind penetrated her thin shawl. Kneeling down on one knee, Emma gently coaxed the little dog from under the woodpile. The tiny creature crept forward, its tail between its legs, to accept the offered meal. The large chunk of meat was gone in two gulps.

Emma laughed then was disappointed when it retreated quickly to the woodpile as soon as it finished the meat. A frigid gust like needles against her face made her retreat toward the shack, a shooting pain in her abdomen felt like a knife, then another pain drove her to her knees.

"Oh no, it's the baby," she thought. She struggled to stand but her strength deserted her. Numbed fingers sought the locket around her neck. "Frank, help me!" she screamed. The wind moaned in response. "FRANK, FRANK, help me!" she screamed. She lay on the ground with her knees drawn up to her swollen belly. The pains grew sharper and more prolonged. Her voice weakened with each episode.

The little dog crept from it hiding place and sniffed the ground near Emma's feet. So severe was her agony, she didn't feel the cold nose against her chapped bare leg. The dog left her and ran to the cabin door. It scratched at the door and howled.

Frank heard the howling and reached for Emma. She was gone! He grabbed his rifle and when he opened the door, the dog ran. Emma lay on the ground, the lantern on its side emitted a faint glow. His rifle fell to the ground as he ran to kneel beside his stricken wife. "Em, is it the baby?" he asked, cradling her in his arms.

"Frank?" she moaned.

"Em, is it the baby?" he asked again. She nodded.

"Let me get you into the house. Hold on to me and I'll try to carry you," Frank said. He struggled to lift his wife. Her water broke as they entered the shack, her pains came closer and closer. Frank laid her on the bed; she screamed then gritted her teeth and pushed. There wasn't enough time to get Betsy to help with the birth. Frank tried to think what to do. Emma told him to light the stove and get some water and clean rags. Usually cool and collected in the midst of a crisis, Frank was seized by panic. He followed Emma's instructions but made two trips to the well for water. Frank dropped the first bucket on the way in the door, leaving a huge puddle on the floor.

Emma yelled for the leather strap she made with Betsy's help. Frank handed it to her and she bit down on it as the pains ripped through her and she pushed with all of her strength. He managed to light the stove and stuff some clean rags under Emma's hips. His hands were shaking so badly he was afraid he would drop the baby.

Within minutes, he saw the top of the baby's head and soon he held his newborn daughter in his arms and wiped her with a clean rag. He placed her on her mother's chest. When the baby started to nurse, Emma fell asleep. Frank cleaned up the room and collapsed in a chair near the stove.

A light mantle of snow covered the ground on the first day of Prudence's life. Her father stoked the stove with all of the firewood in the wood box and still the little room was cold. Frank covered Prudence and her mother with two more blankets and went outside to the barn.

The little dog crept from its hiding place to see if the man had any more food. Frank saw it and went back into the house to look for scraps. Wagging its tail, it accepted the food from Frank's outstretched hand.

Black clouds threatened more snow as they moved in to cover the blue patches of sky. Frank decided to stay near Emma and not tell Betsy about the baby's arrival. He went to the barn for some little pieces of lumber, hammer, and nails. Frank went around the shack tapping boards and nails into the flimsy walls to keep out the wind.

Emma was sitting up nursing Prudence when he came in. He coaxed the dog inside and secured the door. His daughter made loud smacking noises, Frank bent to kiss her tiny head. Then he stroked the soft blond fuzz with his rough fingers.

"She's beautiful," he said.

"Yes, and she's strong too," Emma said. "Our little Prudence will be quite a girl, I think." She smiled up at her husband with tears glistening on her cheeks. Emma missed her mother desperately. Florence would forgive her when she saw Prudence. She opened her locket and looked at her parents' faces.

Frank assured her, in the spring, their little family would make a trip to Silver City to see Florence and Robert. "Rest now dear. You need to regain your strength," Frank said gently kissing her on the forehead.

Each day, fierce winds raged against the shack's flimsy walls. Frank made sure Emma had her meals. Clumsily, he tended the baby but within a week, he could change Prudence's soiled napkins as well as Emma.

Betsy was six months pregnant and exhausted from trying to keep track of her growing brood. When Frank rode over to tell her about Prudence, she hurried to prepare some food and pack up some clothes for the baby. She really had to struggle to get into the wagon. Frank found John in the barn and he was congratulated heartily. John and Betsy argued about Betsy going over for a visit.

"I have to go see my new goddaughter!" Betsy insisted. Enthusiastically, Betsy rushed into the Parnell's tiny shack and threw her arms around Emma who was sitting on the side of the bed, braiding her hair. Prudence was asleep, lying on the bed beside her. "My, my he is quite the young man. John made sure I was near a doctor for my first two. Most likely, he'll have to deliver this one himself."

Emma struggled to regain strength as Prudence thrived. When Prudence was nearly two months old when their world turned upside down.

Chapter 10

The late fall weather turned warmer and the wind died down. Frank lit the stove, and put on some coffee. He and the little mongrel dog, called Homer, went to the barn to gather some scrap lumber, nails, and hammer to repair a hole in the barn roof. Frank sipped his coffee and thought about how to proceed. The roof was flimsy and the hole was directly in the center so he'd have to be careful. Setting his cup on a corral fence post, he tossed up a sack of nails and a few small pieces of wood, climbed up on the fence, and eased up on the roof. On his belly, he crawled toward the hole. Frank hadn't been able to do anything other than minor repairs to the barn and cabin. After selling their cattle, Frank and John invested in a contraption called a windmill. It was expensive but was proving invaluable. If John was right, they could expect a rough winter. Frank wanted to be sure of a dry place to store his feed. Several hundred pounds of corn and cottonseed for winter fodder needed to be stored. Most was in John's larger barn but Frank needed some as well.

A loud cracking sound and Frank flailed to grab anything to keep from falling. Instinctively, he seized a plank with large nail protruding from it. The plank was loose and the nail caught in the flesh below his elbow and dug a furrow into his arm from his elbow to his wrist, as he crashed to the barn floor below. His head hit an old anvil and he lay there stunned and bleeding when Emma found him a few minutes later.

Nursing Prudence, she heard Homer at the door. She wrapped Prudence in a blanket and placed her in the middle of the bed. "I'm coming, give me a minute," Emma said as she crossed the room.

Once inside, Homer barked sharply several times, causing Prudence to cry. Emma went back to the bed and picked her up to soothe her. Homer continued to bark as Prudence screamed and refused to nurse. Emma yelled for Frank. Not getting any reply, she pushed Homer outside with her foot and shut the door. After a long, sleepless night, Emma was not going to tolerate that noise. Homer continued to bark and scratch at the door. Impatiently, Emma bundled up the baby, and followed the excited dog to the barn. *Couldn't Frank hear all the commotion? Why didn't he come to help her?*

He was lying on the floor of the barn, hemorrhaging from his right arm. Clotted blood soaked the straw. Emma screamed and Prudence wailed, Homer barked. The noise did not arouse Frank. Panic stricken, Emma ran to the cabin and put the baby in her cradle. Prudence gasped for air and threatened to choke. Emma tried to soothe her but nothing helped so she laid Prudence on the bed on her side with a pillow behind her back. Emma left the door open, grabbed some clean rags from a box and ran to the barn.

Unable to staunch the flow of blood welling up like a fountain from Frank's injured arm, she gulped air through her mouth trying to hold down last night's supper. Emma tied a large strip of cloth, tourniquet fashion above Frank's right elbow and the bleeding began to subside. Later she wondered how she knew what to do. When the bleeding slowed to a trickle, Emma ran to the house to check on Prudence. Despite the cold, Emma's nightdress was drenched in perspiration and dried blood made the soft material to chafe her skin like burlap.

Homer was in the cradle with the baby and wrapped around her head. Prudence lay on her back, her eyes wide open with her tiny fingers tangled in the dog's coat. She cooed and kicked her feet, excitedly. Emma left Homer where he was. When she untangled the baby's fingers from Homer's fur, Emma considered what to do next. First, she thought about leaving Frank in the barn and keeping him covered with blankets while she went for help. But when she went back to the barn with the blankets, she saw that the rest of the roof was about to collapse.

Desperately, she tried to think what to do. The wagon was just outside she could manage to drag Frank by his feet only a couple of inches. Her swollen breasts were leaking milk and Prudence was wailing. Frank's breathing was shallow. Emma grabbed the mule's harness from the wall. Frank must have let the mule, Sassy, out to graze the night before and hadn't put him back in the corral yet. She saw Sassy out in the field about 100 yards from the house and called to him. He shook his head and continued to graze.

Emma ran to her garden. "Sassy, look, I have carrots," Emma yelled, waving the carrots she had just pulled. Sassy paused and studied the situation. Deciding the carrots looked tempting, he broke into a trot toward the garden. Emma silently thanked God. When Sassy accepted the carrots, Emma harnessed him and led him to the barn. Still unconscious, the rags on Frank's arm were saturated. She tightened the tourniquet and applied dry rags over the soaked ones. Lifting Frank's head, Emma positioned herself so she could reach under Frank's arms. Underneath his shoulders and arms, Emma secured the harness reins. Fairly patient during this whole procedure, Sassy the mule started stomping impatiently. Emma positioned a canvas so when Sassy pulled, Frank would slide on to it.

She found some rope, and gently coaxed Sassy to pull. Once Frank was on the canvas, Emma tugged hard on the reins and the mule stopped. Prudence wasn't crying so she ran to the house to see if she was all right. Exhausted, Prudence hiccoughed in her sleep. Emma assured herself Prudence would be fine for a few more minutes and went back to the barn. She used the rope to tie the bottom of the canvas around Frank's boots. Taking his knife from its sheath, Emma cut the remainder of the rope and used it to tie the canvas above Frank's head. With the harness reins tied around the canvas at the level of his shoulders and his knees, Emma clucked to Sassy while supporting the canvas on the side. Slowly, Sassy dragged Frank toward the wagon outside. She maneuvered the mule so Frank's head was even with the back end of the wagon bed. When she untied the reins for the third time, Emma led Sassy to the front of the wagon and secured the reins to the singletree. Emma tied a long rope, she found in the wagon bed, around Frank's waist and the other end to Sassy's harness. Untying the reins from the singletree, she supported Frank's head and clucked to Sassy who moved forward as commanded.

"I think it is working," she said. "Come on Sassy, keep going."

Finally, Emma and Sassy managed to get Frank into the wagon. There was no time to waste. As quickly as she could, she hitched Sassy's harness to the wagon. She went to the pump and got a bucket of water and sponged off as much of the blood from the front of her gown as she could. Prudence needed to be fed and the gown was stuck to her skin. She ripped off the bloody gown and went to the house, returning shortly in an old dress with Prudence securely feeding at her breast.

"Thank God, John and Betsy are so close. John will know what to do," she said to Prudence. It took longer than usual to reach the Collins' home. The house was unnaturally still. No one was home! Mustering every ounce of strength, Emma went into the house and laid her sleeping baby on Farley's cot. Nearly twenty miles to town, she knew Frank couldn't make the journey.

What if he dies? I love him so much. Maybe it's a bad dream? She pinched herself hard and blew her nose on an old handkerchief she found in her pocket. Frank's fingers on his right hand were blue but the bleeding had stopped. With the wagon near the cabin door, Emma dragged Frank out of the back of the wagon to just inside before she collapsed on the floor beside him. Emma heard Prudence crying. She tried to stand up but could only crawl to her daughter. Putting the baby to her breast, she fell asleep on the floor. Sunlight streamed through the window. *How long had she been asleep?* Prudence lay beside her, her tiny rosebud mouth moving in a sucking motion. Emma buttoned the bodice of her dress and gently lifted the baby to the cot.

Frank thrashed around on the floor. Emma touched his forehead and pulled back her fingers quickly. He was burning up with fever, she loosened his shirt and peeked under the blanket at his hand. The fingers were black and a rotten odor exuded from the dirty rag bandages.

Diane Stuart Wright

"Please God, give me strength, and tell me what to do," she prayed. Slowly, she loosened the rag tourniquet, there wasn't any bleeding so Emma removed the tourniquet completely. The rags had to be soaked loose with warm water, and after carefully removing them, Emma went outside to be sick. The wound was fiery red with thick yellow pus oozing from it. Muscle and tendons lay exposed and Emma gritted her teeth as she washed the area with soap and water. Loading the stove with wood, she started a fire. Frank moved very little until she had finished binding his arm. She emptied the bloody water outside, rinsed the bowl with boiling water, and filled it with cool water from the pump. Frank moaned loudly when Emma removed his clothes and boots and sponged him with cool water. She was nearly through when Prudence woke up. Quickly, she finished her task and covered Frank with a light blanket.

Prudence was washed, fed, and dressed in some baby clothes Emma found in a chest in the corner of John and Betsy's room. Satisfied that Prudence was asleep, Emma looked for a change of clothes for herself. Betsy was a much larger woman but she found something she could wear behind a blanket slung over a rope, the family's closet. She went outside again for a bucket of water and remembered Sassy. He was stilled harnessed and had pulled the wagon over to stand in the shade of the barn. She took off the heavy harness, climbed into the loft, pitched down some hay, and went in search of oats.

When Emma finished bathing, she searched for something to eat. A stale piece of bread, some jerked beef and water made her supper. Feeling some of her strength returning, Emma set about tidying up. A loud commotion outside, dogs were barking and a child yelling, meant the Collins family was home.

Overjoyed, Emma rushed into the yard, stopping short when she saw John's face.

"I lost her Emma. I lost my Betsy. The baby came early and the doctor couldn't stop the bleeding," John sobbed.

Toby Collins and the dogs raced around. Farley, the eldest, realized something bad had happened. He stood beside his father, reached up and took his large hand in his small one. Tears sprang to Emma's eyes. *Why does anyone come to this cruel land?* She went to John, put her arms around him, and led him gently into the house.

Now what was she going to do? John was so lost in grief he barely noticed his surroundings. He must go to Deming to get the doctor for Frank.

"Listen, John. Frank had an accident, his right arm is badly infected. You have to bring Doc Cain to tend to him. Please, he could die!" Emma pleaded.

John sat at the kitchen table staring at the print tablecloth Betsy said made the room look cheery. Shaking his head back and forth, he murmured something over and over. Emma felt like grabbing him by the collar of his coat and shaking him. Then she saw the hungry faces of Betsy's two little boys. There was very little food in the house and the rest of the bread and jerked beef was quickly consumed. Dried beans took too long to cook but she put them to soak in water. Emma found some flour, baking powder, salt, and bacon grease and made some biscuits. The boys needed no coaxing to eat.

"John," Emma said, taking his face between her hands. "Please forgive me but you must bring Doc Cain. I'm sorry to have to ask, but you must! Frank may be dying and he needs a doctor." Her pleadings continued for the better part of three hours.

Finally, John was able to hear what she was saying "I'll go in the morning, Em. I can't tonight," was all he would say. He went to his bed and laid down fully clothed.

Emma got the boys ready for bed. When they were settled, she fed Prudence and bathed Frank's face and chest again. He was still feverish and breathing shallowly. She spread a blanket on the floor for herself and Prudence after stoking the woodstove and setting a pot of beans on the stove to cook over night. Emma lay beside Frank and prayed for God to help him.

John was difficult to awaken the following morning. Emma shook him several times. When he opened his eyes, he blinked and looked around as though unfamiliar with his surroundings. "I was hoping it was a bad dream. What will I do without her? What will the children do? Yesterday, she was making a list of supplies we needed in town. She laughed and told me if I didn't get to the store soon we'd have to eat the corn we bought for the cattle.

I said if she didn't eat so much, the supplies would last longer. That struck her funny and she laughed again. The boys both wanted to go to town but I thought Farley should stay with his ma. He was promised a penny's worth of licorice and he agreed to stay. Toby and I were just going past the barn when Farley yelled for me to stop.

I came back to the house. Betsy was bleeding awful bad. I picked her up and carried her to the wagon, Farley climbed in beside Toby and we headed for town. The baby was born dead in the wagon soon after we started out," his voice cracked and he wiped his streaming eyes with dirt-caked fingers. "I sent the boys out with the dogs to look for jackrabbits so as not to scare them. There was so much blood. Betsy tried to hang on but she died just as Doc Cain and I carried her into his office." He struggled to compose himself and sipped some coffee.

"I'll get Doc Cain," John finished his coffee with a gulp. He helped Emma lift Frank onto Farley's cot. It was too short for Frank's legs but it kept him from being exposed to a draft when the door was opened. Realizing how ill Frank was, John grabbed his hat and coat from their pegs near the door.

"Papa, where are you going?" Farley asked. "When will Mama come home?"

"Papa will be back in a few hours. He went for the doctor," Emma assured him.

"I don't like that old doctor. He took my mama and didn't give her back. Will Papa make him give her back?" Farley asked, putting his hand in Emma's.

"Your Papa will explain everything when he comes home. Let's get your breakfast."

Emma served beans and made more biscuits for the boys. She tried to eat but had no appetite. The boys went to do their chores while Emma fed Prudence and changed the bandage on Frank's arm. Too late, she wished she had reminded John to bring food from town.

Doc Cain and John arrived in the late evening. It was obvious Doc had been drinking. He pulled a flask from his pocket, uncorked it and took a long draw on the bottle. Feverish and hallucinating, Frank called out for Emma. Doc Cain slowly removed Frank's bandages and dropped them carelessly on the floor.

"It sure stinks. That arm needs to come off," he said matter-of-factly.

Luckily, John was standing next to Emma when she fainted. He barely caught her before she hit the floor. "You son of a bitch! You haven't got the decency of a rattlesnake!" John shouted. Remembering his boys were asleep, John struggled to keep from killing the man on the spot.

Doc Cain pulled out his flask and gulped. He slapped the cork back in with the palm of his hand. With a deep sigh, he wiped his mouth with the back of his hand. "I just call 'em like I see 'em. Sorry if I upset your sensibilities," he snorted. "Now, let's get down to business. I'll need to use that table for the operation. You, over there, yes, you young man," Farley rubbed his sleepy eyes. "Fetch my bag from the wagon and be quick about it." Doc swept his arm across the table sending plates and cups flying. John grabbed the hurricane lamp or it would have been pushed off as well.

"Get me some hot water, clean towels or rags, an old bucket to catch the blood and some whiskey. I can't do this alone, so you or the lady will have to assist me. Do you have a strong stomach?" Doc asked.

"I'll try to help," John said weakly. Having seen Frank's arm, he was swaying on his feet. Doc peered at John's face now a sickly green shade.

"Help me put him on the table," Doc ordered. "Now fetch the stuff I need."

John staggered to the well and brought water to heat. He found very few rags, Emma had used most of them already. He searched for a bucket in the barn and brought it along with all the whiskey in the house. Emma stood beside the table and looked at Frank. He looked ghastly. She coaxed small sips of water between his lips. Blood loss, lack of nutrition and fluids made him seem small.

Doc Cain pulled a rusty saw from his bag and set it in a pan of hot water. Bits of rust floated to the surface and Emma shivered when she saw its jagged teeth. Amputations were difficult procedures. Cain was experienced and performed it quickly and efficiently. Emma held Frank's head and poured whiskey into his mouth, John tried to hold him still while the doctor worked. Cain tossed the severed limb into the bucket at his feet. Emma slumped into a nearby chair as the doctor expertly stitched up the wound.

"That should do it. There was gangrene up to the elbow but luckily not beyond. He should live, I think, as long as the infection doesn't spread further," Doc Cain stated. When he was finished suturing, he poured a small amount of whiskey over the wound, Frank bellowed in pain. John struggled to hold him down while Doc finished off the bottle.

"You can put a bandage on that stump now, missus. I'd like some more of that whiskey," Doc said as he wiped his hands on a rag. He pulled a cigar from his pocket, chewed off the end and spit it into the bucket. "Nothing like a good cigar after a hard day's work."

"I haven't got anymore," John mumbled.

"Haven't got anymore what?" Doc grunted, tipping his own flask up to reveal it was empty.

"Whiskey, I haven't got anymore whiskey," John said.

Doc stood up and shook his fist at John. "What do you mean you don't have anymore whiskey. How did you expect me to perform this operation? You homesteaders are a pack of idiots."

Indignantly, Doc scooped his bloodied instruments into his bag, stomped out and slammed the door. He mounted his horse, shifted unsteadily in the saddle, and headed in the general direction of Deming. Emma and John walked outside and watched him ride off. It was dark but there was a full moon. Doc Cain was a talented physician but they both sensed that drinking would prove to be his downfall.

Chapter 11

Emma awoke the next morning and little Farley Collins's nose was nearly touching hers. Startled, she drew back. "What's wrong, Farley?" she asked.

"Toby said he wants Mama," Farley replied.

Emma rubbed her eyes and yawned. Toby never talked, he yelled and made noises but Emma never heard him utter a single intelligible word. Emma looked around the room, John was out to doing chores. Frank was sleeping peacefully with Prudence beside him, chewing on her fist.

"Your Papa will talk to you about your Mama when he comes back," she said.

That seemed to satisfy the boy and he went to sit by his brother who was sitting quietly in a corner of the room chewing on a wooden block. Emma leaned over to kiss Prudence and was seized by paroxysmal coughing. She sat up to turn her head away from the baby and clapped her hand over her mouth instinctively. She choked as a salty, metallic taste flooded her mouth. "Oh, no!" she whispered searching the room for a cloth. Her hand was bloody but she forced herself to remain calm not wanting to frighten the children.

Frank felt a severe pain in his right hand. He flexed his fingers and the pain grew worse. Sleepily, he lifted his hand to look at it. "Em, what happened to my arm? Em, where is my arm? Oh, dear God!" he tried to sit up but fell back against the pillow.

Emma ran to her husband and lifted his head, sitting down beside him, she cradled his head in her lap. Knowing Frank was a proud man, she shooed the boys outside. She could see them through the window, playing with Homer and their dogs.

"What will we do? I can't run a ranch with only one arm," Frank choked on the lump rising in his throat.

"Don't worry, dear. God will provide. I've spent a lot of time praying and I'm sure He will help us get through this," she said.

With his limited strength was spent, Frank drifted into a troubled sleep.

Not only did John refuse to talk to his boys about their mother's death, he barely spoke to her and even less to his sons. Capable of carrying out his ranch chores, when he was in the house, he lay on the bed and stared at the ceiling. Emma kept the boys occupied so they wouldn't bother him. His grief was excruciating to witness.

"You have to buy some food, John. There is absolutely nothing left. Your boys are hungry and Prudence isn't getting any nourishment from my milk," Emma admonished. "Here is a list Betsy made. Please go buy what's on it."

John turned to look at her. His face crumpled suddenly and he broke down completely. Covering his face with his hands, he murmured over and over, "Betsy, Betsy."

"I'll go to our house and get what I can," Emma said. She dressed the children and loaded them into the wagon. Sassy was grazing nearby and Emma went to harness him. Able to find enough food to last out the week, Farley helped Emma load it into the wagon. Back at the Collins's house, she fixed a large nourishing supper for everyone.

Emma's cough and night sweats grew worse each night. She kept a pail of water outside the back door so she could sponge herself off before nursing Prudence. When their food supply was nearly gone, John made an announcement.

"The boys and I are going to Texas," John said staring at his hands in his lap.

Emma was seated near him at the table making a list of supplies.

"Are you sure you want to do that?" Frank asked from the shadowy corner of the room.

"No, I'm not. What can I do with two younguns and no wife? With Emma here, I can work around the ranch but when you leave I won't be able to manage alone."

Frank struggled to raise himself up on his left arm so he could see his friend's face. The coal oil lamp cast shadows into the hollow faces of the two people sitting at the table. Grief and despair permeated the room.

"My brother, Wes, has a place in Texas near San Antonio. He built a large hacienda and has quite a few people working for him on his ranch. I reckon I can go to him for a while. I can't stay here no longer. I keep expecting to see her walk through the door," John hid his face in his hands.

Emma patted him on the shoulder and rose to get more coffee from the stove. It was going to be a long night. With John and Emma's help, Frank came to sit at the table. There they sat until dawn discussing their plans in hushed voices.

Three days later, the morning was crisp and cold. Emma fixed biscuits for breakfast and when everyone was fed and dressed, John helped Emma get Frank to the wagon. Frank tried to walk around the house but was still a little unsteady and weak. Homer ran ahead of the wagon, apparently happy to be going home. Nearing their home, Emma pulled hard on the reins, causing Frank to jerk awake. He raised himself up and saw smoke coming from their chimney. Frank struggled out of the back of the wagon into the wagon seat. He took the reins from Emma and turned Sassy away from the house toward a shallow arroyo just south of the cabin.

Prudence began to whimper, she was asleep but when the rocking motion of the wagon ceased, she realized she was hungry.

"What are you going to do?" Emma asked, her voice tinged with concern. She unbuttoned her bodice and started to feed Prudence.

Frank put his fingers to his lips. "Stay here and be as quiet as you can," he whispered. He leaned over and kissed Emma and the top of Prudence's head. Frank put a loop of rope over Homer's head and secured him to the wagon to keep the little dog from following him. He located a stout piece of wood to use as a balancing aid or weapon, if necessary and scanned the area around the house for signs of people, as he struggled toward the cabin.

Reaching the window, he saw that the curtains were drawn but through a little gap between them could see a dark haired man sitting in Frank's chair, his feet propped up on the table. In his hands, he held a wicked looking bowie knife. The man held the knife lovingly; he stroked the blade and held it to the light, polishing it with a cloth. Frank looked around the room and saw that the knife appeared to be the man's only weapon. Frank's own rifle was leaning against the wall near the door, exactly where he left it nearly two weeks earlier.

Deciding that it would be smarter to come back when the man was asleep, Frank returned to the wagon. Emma and Prudence were huddled in the back. Emma had unhitched Sassy and staked him out to graze nearby. Homer was in the wagon now and he barked happily when he saw Frank. Emma silenced Homer with the sharp tone in her voice. She put Prudence down, got out of the wagon and ran to Frank, whose face was white and pinched with pain.

"Who is in our home?" Emma wanted to know. She was holding her locket, Frank noticed, a sure sign that she was very upset.

"One man with a very big knife," Frank said as Emma helped him sit on the wagon bed. He collapsed against the pile of burlap bags that John thoughtfully put in for his friend's comfort.

"What are we going to do?" Emma asked as she checked the bandage on Frank's stump, relieved to see there was no blood on it.

"I'm going to wait until he is asleep and try to get my rifle," Frank said.

Emma shivered. "Isn't that awfully dangerous? What if he wakes up before you can get it?"

"I'll just have to take my chances. What else can I do?"

"You are so brave," Emma said proudly taking his hand.

Frank grinned weakly. "I'll rest here awhile and then go back and wait."

Chapter 12

The dark haired man at the table was very content. He was inside a house for the first time in several months. His life in Mexico was behind him and soon he'd be living in style, with the elegance he deserved. The solitary lifestyle was beginning to wear thin, though. He missed his creature comforts and the companionship of his amigos.

A born leader of men, Nicholas Oso, was handsome and cunning. His only weakness was the ladies and what a weakness it was. He was generous with the *señoritas*, when it suited him, but sometimes his generosity would give way to cruel, sadistic pleasures.

His first sweetheart was a young girl in the small *pueblo* of his birth, in southern Chihuahua. She was as delicate as a flower, a young beauty at the age of eight years old.

At twelve, Nicholas knew she would be his the first time he saw her. He took his time teaching her the pleasures of the flesh and in twisting the young girl's mind to believe that his sadistic propensities were normal.

Nicholas enjoyed watching through windows. In this way, he learned about passion at an early age. Unfortunately, the examples he witnessed were not based on love. Dominance over the weak and helpless gave him such a rush of power that he got a buzzing in his head and a feeling of invincibility. He searched for ways to force others into submission. As a small child, Nicholas enjoyed torturing insects and later graduated to cats and dogs. Eight-year-old Luz was entranced by the attention afforded her by an older boy. She followed him everywhere. Fascinated by his cruelty, she even assisted him in his acts of torture.

Luz was nearly 10, when Nicholas stopped to talk to his friend Francisco at the village square. He noticed Luz looking at Francisco the same way she used to look at him. Nicholas said nothing at the time but plotted to rid himself of the little tramp.

Nicholas promised Luz a present. He told her it was in a cave in the mountains near the village. She was ecstatic, she wanted a pretty red dress and was sure Nicholas had gotten one for her. Her once gentle lover, raped and beat her and left her in the cave. Three weeks later, a hunter found her mangled remains. Nicholas was long gone. The fourteen-year-old murderer decided to become a *bandito*. His mercurial temper was restrained as he sought lovers like Luz on whom he could lavish his attention. If he caught any of his girls looking at another man, he would tie her up and carefully carve an "L" on her right breast with the tip of his bowie knife that he kept very sharp. Cutting only deep enough to leave a lifelong scar he reveled in the girl's screams.

Nicholas Oso was a successful *bandito*, honing his craft like he honed his beautiful knife. Stealing horses while ranchers were asleep was particularly enjoyable. Two days ago, he happened upon this *ranchito*. Nicholas was puzzled when he discovered the blood in the barn and the drag marks.

There were no horses to steal but there was some food and coffee. A few chickens in the coop beside the barn were jumping, flying around and pecking each other. They appeared to be hungry, so he fed them. He took delight in wringing the neck of a plump hen. He pulled his knife from its sheath and cut off its head. Deftly, he plucked off the feathers, chopped it in half and removed the internal organs. Using a large pot he found in the cabin, he cooked the chicken in water and ate the whole thing. Sated, he lay down on the bed and buried his face in a pillow that smelled like the roses his mother used to grow in the tiny garden behind their house. Growing restless, he knew it was time to move on but hesitated because the cabin kept him out of the cold winds, the chickens provided meat and eggs.

The day that Emma and Frank returned home, the winds died down and the sky was clear. Frank returned to the cabin to wait for the dark haired man to go to sleep, and was relieved to see the man was gone but realized he had taken all of their supplies. Frank was greatly disturbed by the condition of the house and how it would affect Emma.

Frank went to get his family quickly because winter nights in the desert come with a sudden drop in temperature. When the family was secure inside, Frank dragged a big clothes chest over against the door. The man left some wood by the stove and as soon as Frank thought it was safe, he built a fire. He was so clumsy and everything took at least 3 or 4 tries. Having only one arm even affected his balance. Silently, he thanked the drunken doctor for his skill because although phantom pains continued to plague him, the wound seemed to be healing without infection.

Emma held Prudence tightly and kept looking at the door. When Prudence was ready to eat, Frank noticed that Emma's fingers trembled.

"I'm sure he won't be back," Frank said. "He got what he came for."

"How can you be sure? He might come back and murder us all in our sleep," Emma sobbed.

Frank had never seen his wife so frightened. "I promise I will protect you and Prudence. Try to get some rest now. You're exhausted," Frank said as he picked up his rifle and propped the barrel on the back of a chair and pointed it toward the door.

"Frank, you are just now getting back some of your strength, you shouldn't try to sit up all night," Emma said quietly. Her pupils were dilated with fear and she resolved to stay awake with him.

Frank wanted to stroke her hair and reassure her but he had to hold the rifle stock. He practiced taking aim at the door and shuddered to think what would happen if it became necessary to protect his family. Emma finally slept but stirred restlessly and coughed.

The night dragged on. Frank tried hard to concentrate on something so he could stay awake. The old rifle, he held, was a gift from his father. *Frank's father, James was a Confederate soldier in the War Between the States. James had joined a Mississippi Regiment, determined to fight for his native state. If anyone asked James Parnell what he thought about slavery, he would run his fingers through his thinning sandy hair and cock his head to one side. In low menacing tones, he would mutter his philosophy that could have come from Mr. Lincoln, himself.*

"It ain't right for any man to own another. But no Yank is going to take my farm. My people have lived in these here parts for as long as anybody can remember and I'm not gonna be the one to leave."

After the war, James did leave his farm. The war changed him. Frank recalled watching his father staring out over the bleak Texas plains with tears glinting on his cheeks, watching the sunrise in the east. The wagon train was headed west, James stopped to look back in the direction of the only home he ever knew. His roots sank deep in the Mississippi clay and his identity and values were in the earth of his farm. Until his regiment marched off to meet the Yankees, James was never farther away than Jackson.

Anxious for new adventures, Frank was puzzled by his father's sadness. To distract his pa, he asked him to help him learn to shoot. James patted Frank's head and smiled, "Reckon that's a good idea, young Frank. We can start tomorrow," he said.

Every evening, James sank deeper into his depression and Frank tried to find ways to make his pa laugh. Even Frank's elder sister, the irrepressible Felicity grew solemn. Charlotte, the children's mother, appeared distracted and shooed Frank off to play with some children his age, when he expressed concern over his father's behavior.

Frank practiced his marksmanship when his father avoided him in the evening. Charlotte, a fiery redhead, curbed her tongue when she addressed her morose spouse. Naturally optimistic, it was difficult to understand the intensity of James' pain.

Charlotte's childhood was spent in the squalor of a sharecropper's hut. When James first saw her, her hair flew wildly around her head as she chased a chicken across a muddy yard. On his way to Jackson to buy a new plow, James stopped to gape at the amazing creature with hair the color of fresh carrots. Charlotte was distracted from her task of tackling the evening supper when she heard her dog bark. She slipped in the muck, fell flat, and with her face covered with mud, she saw a young man watching her. Embarrassed, she tried to jump to her feet. The young man dismounted and tried to assist her. The mud was sticky and one of his boots plunged into it and stuck. He fell face down as he reached out to grab Charlotte's arm. She went down again. They sat up and looked at each other. Their appearance was so comical that they laughed hysterically.

After that, James looked for excuses to visit the city, and it soon became apparent to Charlotte that James was in love with her and she didn't hesitate for a moment when he asked her to marry him.

Life was wonderful for the young couple and after the first year of their marriage, Felicity was born. Three years later, James held his newborn son in his arms. Their happiness was cut short by the onset of tension over the issues of slavery. When war broke out, James was compelled to protect his family and farm. The small ragtag company trudged off leaving not only dust in their wake but wives and small children. Felicity was nearly four and Frank was a babe in arms.

During their journey west, a disillusioned James related the story of the worst night of his life to his enthralled offspring. Efforts to win the war for the Confederacy were in vain. Many Rebel soldiers held on to hope but there were a lot who gave up and deserted. When the wagon train was nearly half way across Texas, Frank persuaded James to talk about the War between the States.

"Two of my best friends, George Unger and Nolan Black, fought beside me through so many battles, we could anticipate what each would say before it was said. One night, our infantry division marched toward Knoxville and our commander, General Humphreys, announced that we would attack Fort Sanders. I remember it was a frosty night in November. George thumped me on the back suddenly, Nolan was standing just behind him. Playfully, I took a swing at George and he ducked.

George was grinning when he told me that he and Nolan were going to leave before the attack on the fort. He said, "We just can't take it no more. Are you coming with us?"

Well, I didn't know what to do. You see, I felt like I was all fought out but I wasn't going to be a deserter neither. So I shook my head. Nolan and George just shrugged and walked away from me. About an hour later, we made our advance on that fort. It commenced to raining and snowing. It was a bloody battle and some of the men lost sight of our positions and the noise, smoke, and mud was so thick we couldn't see what we were doing. I felt like lying down on the icy ground and giving up." James choked suddenly and stopped his narration. Frank ran to fetch his father a drink of water but James shook his head and pulled a whiskey flask from his coat pocket and took a long pull.

Frank's father never mentioned his war experiences again. Maybe they were too painful because James seemed to retreat more and more into his whiskey bottle as the wagon train neared their new home. It was frightening to the children to see their drunken father staggering *around, nearly falling into their campfire one night. Charlotte admonished him loudly and James waved her off and went out into the darkness to sleep it off.*

The wagon master, Mr. Mills, had a long talk with James one evening after supper. Mills held his arm as he and James went to be sure that the horses were bedded down for the night. James managed to stay sober for a couple days but then started to sneak off. Charlotte held her tongue and kept the children away from their father when he became enraged.

"Where did you put my bottle?" he slurred.

"You don't need to be drinking, it is time to go to bed," Charlotte said, gently.

"I axed you, whare dih you put my bah...tle woman?"

"I poured it out over in the rocks," she said.

"Wha...ah? Ish mine, you can't do that!" he ran at her, tripped and fell headlong over a rock.

Charlotte watched as two men escorted her husband to the wagon master.

Frank's head felt like it was filled with gunpowder. He stood up and stretched and walked around the small room as quietly as he could. He had to stay awake at least until morning. Maybe things would look better tomorrow.

Chapter 13

Emma felt violated. A strange man invaded her house, looked through her belongings and even slept in her bed. The day after the departure of the mysterious man, Emma pulled all of the bedding from the bed and dragged it outside. She wanted to burn all of the linen but instead she built a big fire and filled her laundry pot. She scrubbed the sheets and quilts until her hands were raw and bleeding and then she boiled them. Next, she dragged all of the furniture outside and proceeded to scrub the floors and walls of the cabin with a brush. It was well after dark when she finished, having started before dawn. Stopping only long enough to feed Prudence, she was totally exhausted. Frank returned from checking on the cattle and found Prudence lying in the middle of the bed crying and Emma sound asleep beside her. Frank washed himself quickly and tended to the baby.

Just before dawn, Emma was seized by severe chest pain and started coughing and wretching violently. Her handkerchief was covered with blood.

Frank watched helplessly. Emma's cheeks were sunken and her skin was sallow. Her once beautiful hair looked dull and brittle and hung limply down on her frail shoulders. Every morning, Emma got up at dawn and cleaned furiously. Each night, she fell into bed totally exhausted. It became necessary for Frank to help her change her nightgown nearly every night when it became saturated with perspiration and blood. Prudence fussed more and was restless. Emma's milk dried up and she was forced to feed the baby with cow's milk diluted with water.

Frank noticed darkness in Emma's eyes as their sparkle was replaced by a haunted dullness. Struggling with a growing sense of despair, Frank tried to find ways to compensate for his missing arm. Simple tasks around the ranch were very difficult and he longed to talk about it with Emma.

Doc Cain came from Deming to examine her. Frank didn't really care for the man but he was a doctor and might be able to help her. Cain made regular visits to the ranch but was usually so drunk, Frank wondered how he found his way.

"There isn't much I can do, I'm afraid," Doc Cain announced, one evening in February. "The consumption is eating up her insides. I can give her laudanum for the pain. Don't know how long she has left, probably no more than a few months. Doc Cain shook his head sadly, climbed into his wagon and headed back to town.

Frank stood outside the house and watched the doctor's wagon grow smaller and smaller in the fading twilight. It began to rain lightly. Mist on his face mixed with tears. Men don't cry, he thought.

The next year passed with little change in Emma's condition, she had her good and bad days; but she kept moving because sitting and lying down made her feel weaker.

Chapter 14

Slowly Frank walked up Main Street in Deming. The mule was at the blacksmith to be shod and he needed to pick up supplies. Emma's cough was worse during the past week and Doc Cain promised to mix up a batch of medicine that would help her sleep at night.

The sun was setting and it looked as though Frank wouldn't make it home. The smell of roasting meat drifted toward him and his stomach rumbled loudly. Following his nose, he soon located the source. He pulled up the collar on his jacket and tucked his chin, the wind was cold and he wished he could be at home in front of the woodstove with Emma and Prudence.

A newly constructed lodging house was inviting with its freshly painted exterior and delicious cooking smells. Two middle-aged sisters were the proprietors and there was a line around the block waiting for supper. Frank watched the line start moving and decided to wait his turn to eat.

"It's getting kinda cold, ain't it young man?" a grizzled old man asked Frank.

Frank grinned and nodded. About to reply, he was interrupted by a loud shout from some passersby and shots rang out. Frank pushed the old man back against a rock wall and shielded him with his body. Doc Cain staggered out into the street toward the line of waiting people, brandishing his pistol. He fired off two more shots before Frank tackled him. Most of the crowd ran for cover. Frank wrested the gun from Doc's hand and shoved it into the back of his pants. Doc smiled at him in recognition.

"What's all the fuss about? Can't a feller have some fun 'round here without everybody getting all shook up?" he asked.

"Let's get you back to your office," Frank said. He half dragged, half carried Doc to his office. By the time he got him settled, he was too tired to eat. Frank made camp on the edge of town and waited until morning to collect his mule and the medicine he needed for Emma.

Hazy sunlight woke Frank early and he gathered his belongings and headed for the blacksmith shop. He paid the smithy and led his mule, Sassy, to the wagon and hitched him up.

Before long, he was headed toward the mercantile to get the rest of his supplies that were to come in on last night's train. A bell rang as he entered the store. Several people were gathered at the end of the long room and they seemed to all talking at once. Daniel Weatherby, the owner of the mercantile, knew Frank as Latimer Jones. He said something to a man standing near him and came to speak to Frank. "Heard what happened last night. That was a mighty brave thing you did last night, Mr. Jones," Weatherby said, patting Frank on the shoulder. "Is there something I can get for you?"

Frank smiled, "I came for the rest of my supplies. I stayed to get some things you didn't have in stock. I gave you my list and you said they were coming last night."

"Sorry, I had forgotten. I guess you haven't heard the news," Weatherby said. He reached under the counter and started searching for Frank's list.

"What news is that? Did something happen? Everyone sure seems upset," Frank noticed one woman had fainted and another was holding smelling salts under her nose.

"Judge McComas and his wife from Silver City were slaughtered by Indians. Their son, little Charley, was captured and taken near Thompson Canyon, they were on their way to Lordsburg. No telling where them Apaches will strike next. If I were you, I would get right home to my family," Weatherby said as he gathered up Frank's supplies and put them on the counter, along with his list.

Frank hurriedly gathered and loaded his supplies and went to Doc Cain's to get Emma's medicine. It took nearly an hour to coax Doc out of bed and another to sober him up enough to concoct the medicine. Frank wanted to shake the inebriated fool but he managed to stay calm. Bile rose in his throat, feeling that he was leaving his family vulnerable while he dealt with a drunken sot.

He urged Sassy to a trot when he finally set out for the homestead. Seeing clouds of dust on the horizon, he panicked and slapped Sassy hard on the flanks with the reins. He jerked and the wagon lurched sideways. Frank was barely able to stay on the seat. Supplies rattled and bounced. Feeling that an Indian attack was imminent, Frank drove Sassy at a gallop for several miles.

Two years earlier, an old prospector was killed by Apaches, just east of the homestead in the Floridas. John warned Frank to be on the lookout for rustlers, Indians, Mexicans, and whites.

"Don't leave your kinfolk alone, ever!" John said.

Frank had no choice now. Emma couldn't make the ride in the wagon to town anymore. Most days she could barely get out of bed. He left a loaded shotgun close to her and told her just to aim it in the direction of any varmint, man or beast and pull the trigger and she would hit it.

The little house was quiet, as he guided Sassy into the yard. Jumping from the wagon, he lost his balance and fell headlong. Struggling to his feet, he brushed the dust off his clothes, and ran into the house. Prudence was asleep in her bed and Emma leaned weakly against the table holding a fragile teacup in her hand.

"I thought tea sounded good. I didn't realize how weak I was," she sighed as Frank set her cup on the table and assisted her into bed. He adjusted the pillows and handed her the cup.

"I'm so glad to be home. I'll just see to Sassy and come have a cup of tea with you," Frank whispered as he leaned to kiss her on the forehead.

Deciding it was best to wait until Prudence was settled for the night, Frank told Emma that the McComas family had been killed. He didn't mention young Charley McComas, knowing that it was information best kept from her. She lay staring at the ceiling when he told her. Her sunken eyes filled with tears. Emma's hand reached for his and she squeezed his fingers gently.

"Thank you for telling me Frank. I liked Mrs. McComas. She was a very nice lady and a good mother. What will become of the children, I wonder?" she asked.

"I'm sure they have family back East who will see to them, I'm sure. Now you try to get some rest. Do you want me to make some tea?" Frank asked gently.

"That would be nice dear," Emma said, dabbing her eyes with the corner of her tattered lace handkerchief.

Frank prepared the tea and set Emma's cup on the table beside the bed. Emma's eyelids drooped and she drank only a few sips. Frank took the cup from her hand and placed it on the table. He sat beside her and kissed her forehead. Sighing, he blew out the lamp.

Chapter 15

Beatrice Farnsworth was a vain woman. She had to look her absolute best for her meeting with Mrs. Elizabeth Warren. Beatrice smoothed the folds of her dress with her gloved hands and adjusted her new bonnet. The brass knocker, that read "O.S. Warren" was new and highly polished, she noticed with pleasure. She lifted it and rapped smartly.

A young maid answered the door. Beatrice sniffed disdainfully and said, "I am Mrs. Farnsworth, vice president of the Ladies' Sewing Circle."

The young woman was very polite and ignored Beatrice's haughty manner as she led her through the foyer into the parlor and asked her to wait. An avaricious gleam lit her eyes as Beatrice surveyed the room. Some magnificent oil paintings adorned the walls. The wallpaper was a pale cream color with faint pink rosebuds. The flowers were unobtrusive enough to serve as a tasteful backdrop for the imposing landscapes. *Obviously, the Warrens have good taste*, she thought.

Elizabeth Warren greeted her guest and took her into the sunny dining room. She motioned for Beatrice to sit and she sat down nearby. Joan Warren, Elizabeth's daughter was seated at a piano, practicing her scales. Her face was flushed and she was perspiring heavily, her blond curls drooped. The women fanned themselves as Joan continued. The scales were replayed for the next 15 minutes. When Elizabeth allowed Joan to stop playing, Beatrice was ready to scream.

"That was very good, my dear. Remember not to let your wrists sag. Run along and play. Mind that you stay out of the street. Traffic is very bad this time of the day," Elizabeth warned her daughter.

"Yes, mama," Joan said obediently as she shook Beatrice's hand. The look on the child's face was one of total relief. She skipped out of the room, smiling happily.

"I'm sorry you had to wait. I remembered our appointment after Joannie started practicing. It is so hard to keep that girl indoors. I insist that she practice for at least 30 minutes every day," Elizabeth said. "I'll have Dorrie serve tea."

Elizabeth picked up a tiny silver bell. Dorrie appeared instantly with a tea tray. Beatrice envied this tiny woman and her orderly life. The iced teacakes were perfect; but Beatrice refrained from eating more than two.

"I understand children must have self-discipline and that practice is a good way to learn it," Beatrice said. She was an expert in the art of raising children, although she had none of her own.

"Mrs. Miller wanted to meet with you herself but was unavoidably detained. She is, as you know, the president of the Ladies' Sewing Circle. Mrs. Miller, Mrs. Jensen, and myself would like to offer to have you become a member of our elite group," Beatrice paused, waiting for Mrs. Warren's response.

"I consider it an honor to be asked. I'll have to speak to my husband before accepting, of course," Elizabeth rose to her feet and extended her hand.

Beatrice had been dismissed. Since she had other calls to make, she was not offended, and bade Mrs. Warren good day. She planned to discuss Sewing Circle projects with Mrs. Warren and see if she could discover what had happened at the parade last weekend.

A parade down Main Street brought most of the town out during the heat of the day.

Unseasonably warm for April, the overheated crowd was raucous and several fights broke out. Elizabeth and O.S. Warren's children were with some other children standing in the shade of a large cottonwood tree. The adults were standing somewhat apart from the children. O.S. bent his head so that his wife could hear what he was saying. While speaking to her, he noticed John Fleming walking down the crowded street. Warren excused himself from his wife and went to catch Fleming before he got further away. Fleming was walking quickly and Warren had to run to catch him.

Warren tapped Fleming on the arm. Fleming turned and looked at Warren intently, nodding his head occasionally. When Fleming turned abruptly and started walking on, Warren grabbed his arm. Fleming shrugged his hand away and kept walking. When O.S. Warren rejoined his wife, his face was flushed and a large vein pulsed in his forehead. He took Elizabeth's arm roughly and led her to the children.

Seeing their father's angry face, the children followed obediently. They didn't protest even though it meant missing the rest of the parade. Fleming was an influential man and had made O.S. Warren look like a fool in public. Elizabeth made sure that her husband was undisturbed by the children for the rest of the day.

The night after her visit from Beatrice Farnsworth, Elizabeth asked her husband about the Sewing Circle. "It consists of a group of ladies in the community interested in raising money for charitable purposes. It meets twice a week, I believe," she told him.

"I suppose it is a good idea. Be sure to bring up the subject of insurance now and then," he said.

When Elizabeth laughed, her husband gave her a disgusted look. She saw that he wasn't joking. "Of course dear, if there is ever a lull in the conversation," she said sarcastically.

Chapter 16

The town of Deming was overrun with transients. Most of the buildings in town were strung along Main Street. Teamsters with their cumbersome wagons loaded with ore, plowed up the packed earth in the street. Many residents believed the town was sinking into the bowels of the earth and they were suspended in limbo between heaven and hell. The weather was hot until two weeks earlier and now winter had returned with a vengeance. Some heard tell it had even snowed in Pinos Altos.

A retired railroad conductor sat at the table with the owners of the boarding house. He smoothed his four strands of reddish hair over his freckled pate and smiled disarmingly at the younger of the two unmarried sisters. His gold tooth winked at her and she giggled girlishly.

"Madam, I believe that is the best breakfast I have ever eaten," he said rubbing his moist palms over his ample stomach.

The room was stuffy and a huge fire roared in the grate. The women were worried someone in their lodgings might take pneumonia and that would mean tending to them. Neither one had the stomach to take care of a sick person.

"I'm pleased that you enjoyed it Mr. Dick," the spinster simpered.

The door burst open suddenly and Doc Cain staggered in. "Madam, did you make me my breakfast?" Cain demanded as he jerked out a chair and sat down at the table.

Mr. Dick stood up. He couldn't abide such behavior in the presence of ladies. Unceremoniously, he grabbed Doc Cain by the collar and held on as Doc struggled to free himself. "You need to be taught manners," Mr. Dick exclaimed as he opened the door and shoved Cain out. He slammed the door and went back to the table.

Doc Cain was not a man to be trifled with. Later that day, he returned to the boarding house and shot Mr. Dick in the stomach while he was napping in the parlor. He was taken into custody protesting his innocence. Mr. Dick died from his wounds. Doc's drinking had finally gotten the best of him.

The 4th of July was a day of celebration because the railroad between Silver City and Deming was completed. Elizabeth Warren was elected as secretary of the Grant County Women's Sewing Circle earlier that week. Beatrice and Florence were happy for her but felt that one of them would have been more suitable for the position.

The Sewing Circle meeting was held at the home of Dr. Henry Woodville. The topic of discussion was, as usual, the appalling lack of hospital facilities in the community. Every day, reports of amputations due to gangrene reached the committee members, fortunately no smallpox had come to town, but it was just a matter of time.

Elizabeth sat beside Beatrice and Florence. She was squinting slightly and concentrating on the piece of fine linen on her lap. Her fingers were deft and she handled the needle like a professional seamstress. Unable to contain herself for another moment, she stabbed the needle into the cloth with finality and rose to her feet. "Instead of all this talk, why don't we do something about it?" Elizabeth's face was flushed and she was obviously angry. The room grew very quiet. A few discreet coughs and murmurs began a few seconds later. The ladies considered Elizabeth's vehemence alarming.

"What can we do, dear? We are ladies after all. None of us have any money of our own except the pin money that our husbands allow us," Beatrice smiled.

"The town should donate the land or perhaps a building and each of us could collect donations. In a short time, we could have a fine hospital," Elizabeth replied. It was apparent to everyone that she was having difficulty controlling her temper.

"My dear…" Beatrice began.

"Just a moment. Hear me out. More families are moving to Silver City. We need a hospital. If we all work together, I am sure we can accomplish it," Elizabeth said, her eyes sparkling with excitement behind her spectacles.

"Hospitals need doctors. We have only a few doctors and they are so busy, they wouldn't be able to staff it adequately," Mrs. Woodville said.

"I'm sure that our doctors would welcome a place where they could bring their patients to receive proper attention under hygienic conditions. Some of the miners live in leaky tents and die before they can receive proper medical attention. Think of the possibilities," Elizabeth said. "Doctors could treat more patients if the patients came to them."

"Well, I for one, would not make a good nurse. All of that blood and other bodily fluids, the very idea makes me want to swoon," Sally Carew said, putting the back of her hand against her forehead.

"If you don't want to be a nurse, maybe you could do laundry," Elizabeth said affectionately, patting Sally's arm.

"Thank you, but no. I think I'll stay home with my babies and leave hospital life to you older ladies," Sally giggled. Sally brought up her age difference whenever possible. She was only about three years younger than Elizabeth but she loved to tease her friend whom she admired greatly.

"Maybe your daughters will become nurses," Elizabeth laughed. Everyone joined in their laughter and there was a collective sigh of relief as the tension in the room abated. Elizabeth decided it would be better to drop the subject and see what she could do on her own before discussing it with the Sewing Circle. So the next morning, Elizabeth made arrangements to speak to Mrs. John Miller, director of the Sewing Circle. Mrs. Miller had not attended the meeting because unexpected guests had arrived from Tucson. Mrs. Miller's guests were just passing through town and Elizabeth wanted to speak to Mrs. Miller before she heard what transpired during the meeting from one of the other ladies.

John Miller was the Commissary Purchasing Agent at Ft. Bayard and owned a mill near the edge of town. He was well known as a generous man and his wife's standing in the Sewing Circle was a source of pride. Miller was very supportive of her and was happy that she was such an integral part of the community.

Mrs. Miller met Elizabeth at the door of her modest residence. It was apparent that she was attempting to return her house to order after the departure of her guests. "It is so good to see you. Come into the kitchen, I just made some coffee and I need to sit down," she laughed, tucking some stray hair into place with her fingers.

Elizabeth liked Mrs. Miller's easy manner and felt comfortable saying what was on her mind. Mrs. Miller listened carefully and did not say a word as Elizabeth explained the reason for her visit. When she was finished, Mrs. Miller stood and walked to a cupboard. She took out a plate of cookies and offered them to Elizabeth.

"I think the idea is wonderful. I've been thinking about it myself for quite awhile. The first thing we must locate a building we can use. Let me discuss it with my husband. I will call on you later in the week and let you know if he'll help us," Mrs. Miller said.

Elizabeth didn't want to take up anymore of her friend's time so she placed the delicate china cup on the table, carefully picked up her reticule, and started for the door.

"I didn't mean that you had to rush off, my dear," Mrs. Miller said kindly.

"I know that you are very busy and I need to run a few errands. I'll look forward to hearing from you," Elizabeth said. Barely able to contain her joy, Elizabeth rushed up the street toward town. At last, Silver City would have a proper hospital.

Her husband's office was her next stop. Told by his secretary that he was in a meeting, Elizabeth waited patiently. She asked the secretary for pen and paper and started writing down ideas as they occurred to her.

Nearly an hour later, the door to O.S. Warren's office burst open and a young, untidy man emerged clutching a thick sheaf of papers to his chest. He tripped and the sheaf of papers exploded into the air like blinding blizzard. Apologizing in a mumbling tone, he bent to retrieve them, his limp, greasy hair, flopping against his flushed forehead. Elizabeth felt sorry for him and started to help him pick up the papers when she heard her husband clear his throat. He was standing in the doorway of his office, frowning darkly.

"Jarvis, pick up those papers and get them sorted right away. Mr. Fleming is waiting for them in his office," Mr. Warren said, unable to keep disgust from creeping into his voice.

Elizabeth was concerned. Her husband hadn't been himself lately and was becoming increasingly short-tempered. Even with his children, whom he adored, he was decidedly cross. She'd tried to discuss it with him and was told to mind her own business. Her heart leapt into her throat. It wasn't a good time to discuss hospital plans with him. He wasn't in good humor.

"Hello, dear. I stopped to see if I need to have dinner brought to you today. I can see you are busy, so I'll be on my way," she said.

"Nonsense, I'm never too busy to speak to you. I have a dinner meeting tonight, thank you for asking," Warren said politely. "Now if there is nothing else, I should return to my books."

Elizabeth smiled wistfully and shook her head. She said goodbye to Warren's secretary and proceeded to the mercantile to do her shopping.

Chapter 17

As the hot summer crept by, Emma slowly regained strength. Using less and less laudanum for the pain, she found that she was more clear-headed and felt more like herself. Even a small draught of the pain killer caused her to sleep for hours.

Prudence was learning to talk. She came with a picture book, left behind by Betsy's children, and set it on her mother's lap. Emma smiled and lifted the tiny girl into her lap and squeezed her. "My beautiful girl, your Mama loves you so much," Emma murmured.

Prudence turned her head and smiled at her mother. Emma gasped. She hadn't realized how much her daughter resembled her. "Mama is going to play the piano. Would you like to help?"

Prudence nodded happily and clapped her hands. She liked to watch her mama's face when she played. Emma sat quietly for a moment and took a deep breath. Her slight frame shook with the effort. It was so hard to breathe. Sometimes she had to remind herself to breathe, it would be so easy not to make the effort. Prudence sensed something was wrong and was looking at her with concern on her tiny features. Emma struggled to smile at her. Her daughter was much too young to be left without her mother. *Concentrate,* Emma chided herself. *The music will help you feel better, but you must concentrate.*

She played with her daughter sitting on her lap. The beautiful melody helped, she stroked the keys, her muscles relaxed and her emotions took over. Tears streamed down her face as she felt the music coming from deep inside her, transferring itself to the sagging keyboard and filling the air with vibration.

"No cry, Mama," Prudence said when her mother finished playing.

"I'm so sorry, my darling," Emma said, laughing suddenly.

Prudence jumped down from her lap and stood in front of her with her arms folded. A grumpy frown on her baby features, made Emma laugh until she was gasping for air. Prudence stamped her foot indignantly. Emma picked her up and set her on her lap. She choked to prevent breaking into laughter again. Taking her daughter's tiny fingers, Emma plunked out a tune on the worn keys. Prudence squealed with delight. Homer, lying quietly nearby, jumped up and barked. Prudence bounced up and down so hard that Emma nearly dropped her.

"Was that fun?" Emma asked.

Prudence squealed again. Frank came hurrying into the house.

"What happened?" he yelled.

"Pru is playing the piano. Listen Papa!" Emma said as she helped her daughter plunk out a tune.

"My, my, she is a big girl," Frank laughed.

Prudence jumped down from her mama's lap and toddled over to her father with her arms extended. Frank knelt down and wrapped his arm around her. Emma sighed and smiled contentedly.

Prudence loved music and would abandon her beloved rag doll, made by her mama, when she was allowed to play the piano. Climbing eagerly into her mama's lap, she would clamor for her turn to play and knew not to touch the keys when her mama was playing. Sometimes, Frank would join in, when he knew the words to a song. He would even make them up and lend his slightly off-key baritone to the merriment. His wife and daughter would burst into gales of laughter.

Emma stayed home when Frank went to town for supplies. The cabin was a long ride from Deming in a wagon and the trips were too much for her. Frank planted an apple tree next to the house. Emma watched as Frank tried to dig the hole. Homer observed Frank's progress for a few minutes, his head turning from side to side. Suddenly, Homer began digging and dirt flew in all directions. Prudence was standing nearby and some of the dirt pelted her in the face. She grabbed the little dog's tail and tugged on it. Homer stopped digging and jumped on the little girl, knocking her down. On all fours, Prudence crawled over to the hole and began digging frantically alongside Homer. Emma and Frank laughed so hard that they had to hold each other up.

"What made you decide to plant an apple tree?" Emma asked Frank at supper that night.

Frank winked and smiled. "I am not getting enough apple pie. I decided if I grow my own apples, I could have apple pie whenever I want it."

By September, Emma was bedridden. Frank promised to take her to Silver City to see her parents but she was too weak. The homestead was neglected except for the barest minimum of chores. Early one morning, Frank awoke with his arms around Emma. Her breathing was shallow and her face was so pale that the skin appeared translucent. Prudence crawled into their bed a few minutes later and went back to sleep. Frank dressed quietly and went out to check on the stock.

When he returned less than an hour later, Emma was no longer breathing. Frank laid his head on her chest and sobbed. Prudence woke up and tried to console him. "Tell Papa not cry, Mama," Prudence demanded. Unable to get a response from Emma, she started patting her mama's arm.

"It's going to be all right, baby. Mama can't hear you anymore," Frank sobbed as he picked up Prudence and set her on the floor. Prudence started to cry and tried to climb back up on the bed. "Find Homer and give him this bone," Frank said, handing his daughter a small bone left over from soup. He kissed his wife's face and gently removed the locket she loved so much.

Obediently, Prudence went to look for Homer. Frank washed Emma and dressed her in her favorite dress. He buried her in their picnic spot about a mile from the cabin. Prudence watched not knowing what was happening. It took Frank several hours to dig the shallow grave and he covered it with large rocks. Emma was only 20 years old. Her last request was that Prudence be given her locket when she was old enough to take care of it.

After a week, Frank sat down and wrote a letter to his sister Felicity in Santa Fe. He had nowhere else to turn, he needed help and Felicity was the only person he could depend on.

Dear Sis, it read, *My wife has died and I am unable to carry on alone. Could you please come for a time to help? Your loving brother, Frank.*

He received Felicity's reply two weeks later.

Dear Frank,
Of course I will come if you need me. Love, Felicity.

Chapter 18

Dear Mother and Father,

I hope this letter finds you both well and happy. I still have had no word from Emma. I pray every day that my next letter will tell you that she has been found healthy and has come home to us. I dreamed last week that she came to see me. She told me she was sorry and I woke up crying.

Conditions in Silver City, during the summer months are very different from those in St. Louis. There is no humidity but a dry heat until July. Then large cottony clouds begin to pile up, one on top of another during the afternoon. By evening, the clouds have turned dark gray and grip the mountains like moist, wrinkled hands. Lightning flashes and is almost immediately followed by the loud rumble of thunder arising from the earth like a long dead giant. The sky splits open and rain pounds the ground. Within minutes, rivulets form and soon the streets become seas of mud.

Main Street seems to be the worst. For years, large pits were dug at the northern and southern ends of the street. The earth in those particular areas are rich in clay. Clay is used, for making adobe brick. Adobe bricks are an inexpensive building material made by mixing clay, straw, and water. The mixture is poured into forms and allowed to dry in the hot desert sun. When the bricks dry, they are used to make buildings that are cool in summer and warm in the winter.

The large adobe pits have robbed the earth of vegetation in those areas. The roots of trees and plants serve to hold the earth in place. When the rains come, the earth tears loose and cascades into town. All of the water seems to converge into Main Street making it impassable to wagon or horse during the rainy season. Business owners along Main Street place gunnysacks filled with sand along their walls and when it begins to rain, shops close and sandbags are placed in front of the doors as well. Last week, the rains were particularly heavy. Several wagons got stuck in the mire and frustrated drivers whipped their horses and cursed, to no avail. It took 7 men to dislodge each of the stranded rigs and all were so covered with mud that onlookers laughed and laughed. The situation is serious because privies are overflowing and business owners on Main Street are unable to restock their supplies.

I will close my letter for now. Give my love to all. With much love and continued prayers for my dearest parents,

Your daughter,
Florence

Florence carefully blotted the letter and put it in an envelope, sealing it with sealing wax. She smiled as she thought about her mother's excitement when she got letters. There was a knock on the door, Florence smoothed her hair and went to open it. A young man stood on the porch with a telegram in his hand. He tipped his hat and silently handed her the wire. She went to her reticule and retrieved some coins and pressed them into the young man's hand. Taking a deep breath, she closed the door and went to sit down. Carefully opening the message, her hands began to tremble uncontrollably. It read:

Dear Mr. and Mrs. Jensen,
  Regret to inform you that your daughter Emma has succumbed to TB. She wanted me to tell you that she loved you both very much.

Frank

Frank was careful. He sent a telegram to Felicity in Santa Fe asking her to send a telegram from there before she left for Deming. He hoped it would keep his in-laws from finding him and taking Prudence. Frank was sure that with the Jensens's money and power, they would have little trouble taking his daughter away from him.

Felicity was to train a replacement for Judge McCoy before she left. She found a very nice young lady, Jade Finderley, to assume her housekeeping duties. "Please respect my brother's privacy and don't speak a word about my whereabouts to anyone. He is trying to protect himself and is very vulnerable right now," Felicity told Judge McCoy and Jade as she prepared to board the southbound stage.

"Don't worry about a thing. We won't speak about you to anyone," Judge McCoy patted Felicity's smooth hand with his wrinkled one. He took her bags from her and handed them to the stage driver. The judge was very sorry to lose this lovely girl but understood her loyalty to her brother.

Felicity smiled through tears as she waved good-bye to the older man and her young replacement. She hoped all would go well for them during her absence. It was hard to leave the man who was so good to her. She straightened her shoulders and patted her hat. Determined to make the best of it, Felicity Parnell would put her best foot forward and do her best to help her only brother through the terrible ordeal of losing his wife. It wasn't the first time in her life she had had to make sacrifices.

Moving to Santa Fe from San Antonio, Texas, Felicity arrived in Santa Fe on Wednesday, June 16th. The city was bursting with activity. Bishop Lamy was being raised to the rank of archbishop amidst scores of banners and cannon blasts. Felicity felt a stirring pride in this raw territory and her pride grew as she watched the city prosper over the next several years.

An attractive woman but not conventionally beautiful, her personality was compelling and her fiery hair drew a lot of attention. Women tended to avoid her, especially the plain, mousy ones. The men, on the other hand, were attentive and Felicity enjoyed herself, attending every dance that was held. She spent many years caring for her drunken father and finally was free.

One night, soon after arriving in Santa Fe, Felicity watched a tall man with distinct Nordic bearing, talking to a distinguished older man in the town square. Lanterns lit up the dark summer night until it was nearly as bright as day. She recognized the older man as Judge Phillip McCoy. She had been introduced to him the week before at a dance. She caught the judge's eye and he nodded at her. The younger man looked to see what distracted the judge's attention. He glared at her. The blond man shook his fist in the older man's face and stomped off angrily in her direction. A small group of people, laughing and talking, stopped in front of the angry man and one look at his furious face made them step aside hurriedly. He brushed past her without acknowledgment and Felicity turned to watch him disappear into the shadows.

Her savings were gone. She had fun while they lasted but it was time for her to settle down and find a job. Pangs of guilt assaulted her as she thought about her father, alone and penniless in San Antonio. Many years of her life were spent trying to help him. She scrubbed floors for wealthy families, learned to cook, took in sewing, and even saved a little money. At night, when she came home, her father would be asleep with a whiskey bottle beside him. She talked to everyone she knew and tried to persuade them not to sell her father any liquor.

Returning from work very late one night, Felicity went to the loose floorboard in her room to put some money in her savings jar. All of her money was gone. When her father returned to their tiny, rented room, filthy and reeking of alcohol, he swore he couldn't remember taking her money. Felicity stayed with him for another year. She allowed him money for a bottle of whiskey a day and sewed a pocket into her petticoat to hide her savings. At night, she lay awake, dreaming about her escape. She wanted to go to Santa Fe. It was far away and mysterious; it must be a wonderful place. One of the families she worked for had recently moved to San Antonio and longed to return to the beautiful high desert. She heard them reminiscing frequently.

Santa Fe wasn't what she expected. Political fever ran rampant and most tried to impress those with the most clout. The blond man Felicity had seen speaking to Judge McCoy was a new resident of Santa Fe as well. His name was Peder Jorgensen and he was a Swedish immigrant. Felicity was fascinated by his dashing good looks and fiery temper.

Judge McCoy interviewed Felicity for the position of housekeeper and soon she was living in his beautiful house, wearing a stiffly starched black uniform, and serving as hostess during the judge's many parties. Jorgensen was present at many of these parties and Felicity observed him. He was coolly disdainful to most people unless they had political ambitions and then he sought to engage them in conversation. It was obvious that the young man loved to argue.

Felicity regretted that Jorgensen seemed to look right through her. Unaccustomed to being ignored, Felicity decided to set her cap for the young man. She plotted how and when she would win his heart. Her plans were unrealized when she received the telegram from Frank. It wasn't fair. She didn't want to leave now that she had plans for her future. She spent several hours wrestling with her conscience.

There must be another way for Frank to get by, why did he need her help? He had spent most of his life alone. Yet he had never asked her for anything before, how could she say no.

It was the most difficult decision she had ever been forced to make. Felicity was tempted to approach Jorgensen to determine if he was truly interested in her or if the electricity she felt in his presence was her imagination. But that would ruin everything and how could she be sure that it wouldn't drive him away. The man was so involved in his career and in making his name well known; he had little time for anything else let alone a lovesick female. A large lump formed in her throat as she stood in the telegraph office. As tears stung her eyes, she wrote telling her brother she would come. *So much for her plans!*

Chapter 19

The stage carrying Felicity to Deming was on time. Frank helped her out. She smiled at her brother, and gasped. "Frank, what happened? Why didn't you tell me?" she cried.

"I'll tell you all about it. First, there is someone I want you to meet," Frank said.

Felicity was so surprised by Frank's empty sleeve, she failed to notice the beautiful child standing behind him. She had large blue eyes, the prettiest eyes Felicity had ever seen and had golden hair curling around her face. Felicity held out her hand to the little girl and Prudence grasped her aunt's fingers.

Frank looked around him. The stage depot was crowded and he overheard snatches of conversation while he and Prudence waited for the stage. Now as he helped Prudence and Felicity into the wagon and retrieved his sister's trunk, he paused. Two cowboys were discussing some railroad in Montana. He thought to himself, "Maybe someday there will be a railroad here."

Felicity sat beside Frank in the wagon and held Prudence. Prudence held Felicity's hand and fell asleep. "She is very trusting. Poor little thing, she needs her mother," Felicity said.

"So do I," Frank admitted, he looked away, because tears began to well up in his eyes.

"It must be hard for you to take care of your ranch and a little girl at the same time," Felicity said, noticing her brother's mood.

"I can't. That's why I asked you to come," Frank said.

"I'm not cut out for this kind of life. I enjoy being around people," Felicity said.

"It can be dull," Frank agreed, "But I expect Pru will keep you busy."

Felicity felt resentful. Why hadn't Frank mentioned his daughter or his injury in his letters? It wasn't fair for him to expect her to be a mother to his child. Remember your promise, put your best foot forward, she reminded herself. "How did Emma like it out here?" Felicity stared at the flat desolation around her. When her gaze was drawn to the majestic mountain range, the Floridas to the east, and three small hills to the west called Tres Hermanas by the locals. She admitted to herself that this land had a raw beauty.

"Emma seemed fine. I think she liked the quiet even though she came from St. Louis and her parents are society people. She liked taking care of our family," Frank said.

"She must have been a special lady," Felicity said as she gently stroked the sleeping child.

Frank shifted on the wagon seat. It was hard for him to talk about Emma. He decided to change the subject. "The house isn't much. It's more like a shack; but its livable. We've got about 30 head of cattle now. I just sold 20 last week at Fort Cummings. I spend most days making sure the cattle don't stray too far. Our well supplies us with all the water we need," Frank squinted and pointed toward the Three Sisters. "If you look over there, you can see John and Betsy's old place. John is the man who got me started here; I guess he and his younguns are in Texas and settled by now."

Felicity couldn't see the house that Frank was pointing toward; but said she could. Out here, so far from town, a little homestead was vulnerable to Indian attacks. The only Indians Felicity had ever seen were in Santa Fe. They were polite with downcast eyes and sullen features. She shuddered when she caught her first glimpse of the shack that was to be her new home. It was so rustic. She was pleased to see that it was at least clean inside.

"This is it. What do you think?" Frank asked.

Frank noticed her hesitation. To Emma and him, their home was perfectly adequate; but now he noticed its shabbiness and felt ashamed.

"It isn't quite what I expected," Felicity admitted. It was hardly the place for a young woman to spend the final days of her life, especially if she had grown up used to luxury. Felicity looked around the small room and noticed the feminine touches here and there. A small print of a waterfall hung on one wall, a crocheted blanket covered the large bed and a smaller pink one covered Prudence's bed.

Felicity had never met Emma but she felt a sense of loss. Grief hung in the room like a shroud. Frank and Prudence's countenances changed when they entered the house. Pru's sunny blue eyes were cloudy and close to tears. There was little furniture and when Frank began to unload her luggage, Felicity noticed a small cot in the wagon. She was busy trying to imagine where they would put her trunks.

"I've cleared out this chest for your clothes and I will put your bags in the barn," Frank said. "I'll sleep on the cot and you can have the bed. I can't sleep anyway."

Felicity smiled when she saw Emma's spinet. She gently touched the chipped keys and played a chord. Frank swung around, glaring at her. "Don't touch it," he yelled.

His tone startled Prudence and she started to cry. Felicity tried to soothe her.

"Frank, you scared her," Felicity scolded.

"I'm sorry. Papa didn't mean to frighten you. It's just, I can't bear it," he mumbled something about seeing to the mule and went outside, slamming the door.

Felicity started to follow him and then decided against it. She rolled up her sleeves and changed Prudence's clothes. Then she set to work to prepare dinner. Prudence stood nearby watching her. Fortunately, the larder was well stocked. Soon the room was filled with tantalizing aromas.

"Mama likes to cook," Prudence said. "She helps me make cookies."

"You can help me now," Felicity said kindly.

"Where is my Mama?" Prudence asked.

Felicity winced. The child didn't understand that her mother was dead, she realized with dismay. "Your Mama has gone to sing with the angels," Felicity told her.

"What are angels?" the little girl wanted to know.

"Angels are beautiful creatures that take care of us. They smile down on us from heaven and take care of us always," her aunt explained.

"My Mama can't sing too good. Maybe the angels would like her to play the piano. Mama likes to play the piano."

"Well, perhaps that is why they called her," Felicity said, patting her head.

"If I call her will she come home?" Pru pushed her hair from her eyes and peered intently at her aunt's face.

"I'm afraid she can't come home. I'm sure she would rather be here with you and your Papa; but she has to stay there."

"Why?" Prudence asked.

"Her time here was over. The angels wanted her to play the piano for them and they decided to take her up to heaven with them."

"Where is heaven? Is it as far away as Deming? Can't she come home so I can say goodbye?"

"Heaven is very far away. If you are good, you will be able to go see your Mama someday. She would want you to be good and help your Papa. You can speak to your Mama anytime you want to you know?"

"How can I talk to her?" Prudence jumped to her feet and grabbed Felicity's hand.

"Just close your eyes and imagine you see her face. Then tell her anything you want to and she will hear you."

Prudence was very quiet for a few minutes. Felicity glanced at her and saw that her eyes were tightly closed and her fists were balled at her sides.

When Felicity saw her relax, she asked, "Did you talk to your Mama, Prudence?"

Prudence smiled, "My Mama is glad you came!"

Felicity felt warm; her arms and hands tingled. She stood silently for a moment. "Are you big enough to set the table, Prudence?" Felicity asked her.

"I'm big enough, my Papa said so," Prudence smiled and went to take the dishes from their box in the corner. Having no experience with children, Felicity was overwhelmed. This was going to be quite a task, helping to raise a young girl in the middle of nowhere.

Streaks of gold and gray hung over the mountain. Frank watched the sun's blazing retreat standing near the barn where his life had changed so drastically. He wondered what would have happened if he hadn't lost his arm. Would Emma have lived longer? His long recuperation and the invasion of their home by the strange man with the knife, seemed to cause Emma's relapse. She was only able to regain part of her strength. He would never be sure if he was at fault; but he felt guilty all the same. He paused to pat Sassy's nose and offered him a handful of hay before he went back into the house. Felicity had finished preparing supper.

"I didn't take time to make any biscuits because Prudence couldn't wait much longer to eat and I wanted her to have something before she fell asleep," Felicity said.

Prudence sat in her chair at the table, her blond head nodding. Her droopy eyelids nearly covered her eyes as she smiled sleepily at her father.

"I'm sorry I yelled at you earlier. I guess I'm still grieving," Frank apologized.

He was heartily sick of his own cooking. Felicity was an excellent cook and very proud of the fact she could make the food she prepared reveal a hint of her distinct personality. "You go ahead and eat, I'll help Prudence," Felicity put her niece in her lap and fed the drowsy child. After only about ten bites, Prudence was tucked into her bed. Felicity went to the pump outside for water and poured it into a large kettle on the stove.

Cleaning up the dishes was a lot of work out here. In Santa Fe, the water barrel in the kitchen was kept filled by servants and wood for the stove was stacked neatly beside it. When she finished and was just about to blow out the light, she heard a scratching on the door. She carefully picked up Frank's rifle; Frank was asleep in his chair. She lifted the door latch and held the rifle ready to fire. Homer trotted in happily, wagging his tail. His scruffy coat was covered with burrs.

"Oh no, you don't," Felicity said as she saw the dog moving toward her bed.

She put down the rifle, picked up the broom and shooed the little dog outside. He crept off with his tail between his legs and his head down. "Frank, wake up," Felicity gently shook her brother.

"What's the matter?" Frank asked rubbing his eyes.

"You didn't tell me you had a dog. It tried to get in the bed. Don't you know dogs carry disease? You shouldn't allow it in your house!" Felicity said, sternly.

"Homer is a clean dog. Emma used to bathe him every week. She let him sleep on our feet," Frank said.

"He is none too clean right now. He has burrs all over him. I'll tell you right now, either he goes or I do," Felicity said.

"Don't say that. I'll make sure he stays outside until you get used to him. I can't give him up. He saved Emma's life once." Frank told her about the night Homer became part of the family.

Felicity shook her head. "I guess I will put up with him for now. But if I ever find him in my bed…" she was interrupted.

"I'll do my best to keep Homer out of your way," Frank mumbled. He picked up his coat and went out to find Homer. Homer patiently allowed Frank to pick the burrs out of his coat. Frank picked up the little dog and opened the door. He was just able to make out Felicity's form in the bed. She didn't stir so he crept in and put Homer on the foot of his cot and undressed in the dark.

The wind blew early the next morning, ushering in a storm from the south. Frank secured the window shutters and brought in a stack of wood in a little cart. Piece by piece, he unloaded the cart, placing the wood in the box near the stove. Then, he went to the barn to saddle his mule. Doing routine tasks with only one arm was tiring and difficult. Fortunately, the mule, Sassy was cooperative and stood still as Frank struggled.

Smoke rose from the chimney, when he led Sassy from the barn. Frank brought the mule to the house and dropped the reins. He stomped his feet and pushed open the door. Felicity's hair, unbound, hung down nearly to her knees. It was a riot of color in the lamplight, gold mixed with red. She was surrounded by a halo of light. Holding Prudence on her hip, she fed chunks of wood into the stove.

"I'll have your breakfast in a few minutes, if you want to wait?" Felicity said.

"I'll just have some coffee for now," Frank said.

The little family group sat around the table for a few minutes while Frank drank his coffee. He told his sister he would be checking on his stock for most of the day. "The weather may get bad. The wind is starting to blow and there are a few clouds moving in. I think you have enough wood and I'll bring in some more water before I leave. Just stay inside today. Tonight, we can make some plans," Frank patted his sister's shoulder and went outside to get the water as promised.

The storm, as Frank predicted, was short lived and most of it blew over. The strange weather left Felicity with an unsettled feeling. Restlessly, she paced the floor most of the day. That night, the air was eerily still. The heat was stifling. Felicity opened the small window and leaned out, anxious to catch a breeze.

"Mama? Mama!" Prudence sat up suddenly in her bed. Her eyes were frightened. Frank and Felicity both rushed to her.

"Mama, where are you?" Prudence sobbed.

Frank said, "Mama had to go away, but your Papa is here and he loves you." He gathered his sobbing child to his chest, and holding her tightly against him, he rocked back and forth. A huge lump formed in his throat. He tried to soothe her but couldn't speak.

Watching their grief, Felicity felt helpless. She stood beside them, stroking Frank's head. It took nearly an hour to resettle Prudence for the night. During the next week, Prudence awoke sobbing uncontrollably three more times. Felicity prayed for guidance. What could she do to comfort Prudence? Lying awake until dawn, she arose at her usual time to start breakfast. Frank's eyes were bloodshot. She saw Homer at the foot of Frank's cot and said nothing. Frank ran his hand through his mussed hair and greeted his sister.

"Good morning," he said.

"Good morning, Frank. Would it be all right for me to use the fabric from one of Emma's dresses to make something for Prudence?"

"Sure, take what you need," Frank said. "I need to gather up her things anyway."

Felicity finished her household chores, scrubbing the worn floor and tidying up. Then she took a chair and placed it in the corner of the room. Earlier, she had taken an old dress of Emma's and some other odds and ends and wrapped them together in a flour sack. She drove two nails into the walls and suspended a piece of rope between them. Then she draped a blanket over the rope. The rope was just below her shoulder level while she was sitting in the chair. The blanket served as a curtain for her hands and lap. In this way, she could watch Prudence but Prudence couldn't see what she was doing.

Felicity told her niece that if she was a good girl and played quietly, she would get a surprise after supper. Prudence tried several times to open the curtain but Felicity insisted it was a secret. Felicity's project took all afternoon and supper was a little late. As promised, Felicity presented Prudence with her surprise after supper. Felicity had fashioned an exquisite doll using Emma's old dress. The doll had wings and a halo. Felicity explained that the doll was "Mama Angel" who was sent to stay with Prudence because her Mama had to go to heaven.

Frank was dumbfounded. When Prudence was asleep with her new doll in her arms, he thanked Felicity.

"Do you see what you have done? Her face was happier that I have seen it since we lost Emma. You will make a great mother, sis!" Frank gushed.

Felicity blushed. Frank felt foolish, excused himself and went outside. He was so touched by his sister's gift to his daughter that he embarrassed himself. He decided he would do everything in his power to repay his sister's kindness. As the weather grew cooler, Frank's phantom pains grew worse. Caring for stock and mending fences took most of his time and had been difficult when he had two arms. Now he drove himself to the point of exhaustion and was unable to complete simple tasks. Frank hated to ask for Felicity's help but had no choice. Felicity tried to harvest what she could from the small garden, do the cooking and cleaning, and read to Prudence but she was exhausted as well. The endless dust wouldn't allow her to keep the floor tidy, and Frank was not very neat, so she seemed to be constantly picking up after him and Prudence. Frank was also accident-prone. His thoughts kept returning to his time with Emma and how happy they had been.

One afternoon, toward the end of September, Frank felt the nip of autumn in the air. It was time to go into town for supplies and after hitching Sassy to the wagon; he lifted up some old gunnysacks in the wagon bed and found a pink ribbon. Feeling his eyes fill with tears, he remembered how the ribbon came to be there.

The summer nights were hot in the desert. Emma opened the window but there was no breeze to cool the house. She took Frank's hand and led him outside. The sky was brilliant with stars; so close that it might be possible to reach out and pull them down. Emma prepared a bed for them in the back of the wagon. She lifted her arms and removed her nightdress, it puddled at her feet. Climbing into the wagon, she helped Frank remove his nightshirt and they took turns bathing each other with cool water. It was a wonderful night, despite the heat.

Felicity watched from the doorway as her brother stopped what he was doing and gazed off into space. This couldn't continue much longer. She felt trapped in an ancient dungeon. Unfortunately, there was no handsome prince likely to find her in this godforsaken place.

"I can't go on like this. Our routine is monotonous and the dust is overwhelming. We never see anyone. I'm afraid I'll have to leave. I know Prudence needs me; but she also needs her father. She hardly spends any time with you."

"You can't leave us. What will we do without you?" Frank asked.

"I have a suggestion but you won't like it," Felicity said.

"I'll listen to anything. Please, what is it?"

"Let's move into town. We could both work and Prudence can start school when it is time," Felicity said, putting her hand on Frank's shoulder.

Frank looked at her with disbelief. Emma loved it here. But did he have a choice? If he stayed it meant they would lose Felicity. Taking care of this place was nearly impossible for him. "We could move to Deming and rent a room," Frank said. "I will go talk to Joe Landrey, he told me a few years ago that he would like to buy this place."

Felicity squeezed Frank's shoulder. "Couldn't we go to Silver City?" she asked.

"Silver City is where Emma's folks live," Frank said, shaking his head.

"I know, but I will continue to take care of Prudence while we think of some way to keep her out of their way," Felicity said. She knew the main reason Frank didn't want to move to Silver City was he was afraid Emma's parents would take Prudence away from him.

Discouraged and tired, Frank went to bed feeling very sorry for himself. It was bad enough to give up his dream; but now he would be living in the same town with two people who must despise him.

Three days later, Frank talked to Mr. Landrey. Landrey offered him a fair price for the land and cattle. Frank wired John his portion of the money and was left with about $150 dollars to start a new life in Silver City. Frank kept his mule and wagon and loaded the family's meager supplies and all of Felicity's trunks and cases. Homer was excited and ran around barking and jumping in and out of the wagon bed. Frank's eyes filled with tears and Prudence cried when Homer was led away by Tommy Landrey, Joe's youngest son. Tommy picked him up and put him in the Landrey's wagon. Even Felicity was upset and she considered the little dog a nuisance.

Homer's barking could still be heard as the family set out for Silver City. The lump in Frank's throat threatened to choke him. He didn't look back. If he did, he knew he could never leave. The Florida Mountains shimmered in the sun and dust coated his dry tongue. He swallowed hard and looked at Felicity and Prudence in the seat beside him. Large tears coursed down Pru's cheeks. Felicity tried to distract her attention, but nothing worked.

"Homer is going to the angels?" Prudence asked in a shaky, little voice.

"No, he is going to live with the Landreys. He will be very, very happy," Felicity assured her.

"That's right, Pru, and so will we," Frank said hopefully.

Chapter 20

Felicity gently stroked the dusty hair of the child seated in her lap. From time to time, she hummed absentmindedly causing the little girl to fidget. The sun set on an endless day, as they entered the outskirts of Silver City. A few minutes later, Frank jumped down from the wagon and reached up with his left arm to take his small daughter. Felicity sighed deeply as she shifted the sleeping child in her lap into his waiting arm.

Frank held his daughter tightly against his chest and walked into the Southern Hotel. Mrs. McAllen, the housekeeper, introduced herself and escorted Frank and his sleeping child to their room. "My sister can sign the book," Frank whispered as he gently laid Prudence on the bed.

"This room is too small for three people. Besides, it isn't proper for a lady to stay in the same room with a gentleman who isn't her husband," Mrs. McAllen sniffed and lifted her nose a little higher as she studied Frank's disheveled appearance.

Frank knew how the situation must seem to the lady, and he tried his best to be civil to her; but it took all the patience he could muster. Mrs. McAllen looked like an avenging angel, standing in the doorway with her hands on her hips.

Frank removed Prudence's shoes and socks and covered her with a blanket. He turned and smiled innocently at the woman behind him. "We haven't enough money for two rooms and have come a long way today. I think the bed will be large enough for my sister and daughter. If you could spare a couple of blankets, I will sleep on the floor," Frank said.

The small blond child opened her eyes and stared at the woman in the doorway. Mrs. McAllen lit the lamp on the dresser and picked it up. She walked toward the child and peered at her. "I must be getting old," she muttered. Turning around, she slammed the lamp down on the dresser and marched out of the room. "Where have I seen that child's face before?" she wondered aloud. Captain Connor wasn't going to like this situation one little bit.

Felicity leaned wearily against the front desk and pulled a used handkerchief from her sleeve. Her red hair straggled from its bun. Wiping her face, she left streaks of dirt on her cheeks. Smiling politely, at Mrs. McAllen, she asked, "Is there a bath?"

Shaking her head angrily, Mrs. McAllen shoved the registration book at Felicity. "There is a tub in the kitchen, down the hall and to the right. You'll have to haul and heat your own water. My help quit yesterday and there aren't many around here who will work for wages. I'm particular!" the older lady replied sharply. "Most of our clientele are men and only want a place to eat and sleep. I don't stand for any nonsense or they'll find their belongings in the street!"

Felicity wondered why the lady was so angry. She had just asked about a bath. It wasn't difficult to imagine why she couldn't keep her help. It was very late when Felicity pumped water into the large kettle. She was so tired she could barely carry it to the kitchen stove. Partially filling an old wooden tub with cool water, she set the large kettle on the still warm stove. She added a few chunks of juniper to the stove and soon the water was ready. There was a rag hanging on a sideboard and she wrapped it around the handle of the kettle and added the hot water to the cold.

"Ahhh…" she slid into the tub and using a large tin cup, poured water over her head. She lathered her hair with a small cake of lavender soap she purchased in Santa Fe. It was hard to believe she had been gone for several months. Through the open window she heard the sounds of night in a small town. The tinkling of a piano from the saloon down the street, the raucous laughter of some passing men, and the braying of a disgruntled mule were strangely energizing after so much quiet.

She bathed quickly and eased her cotton shift over her head. The water in the tub was filthy. It took awhile to dip all of the water out and throw it out the back door. Felicity opened the kitchen door slowly and checked the hall. Not seeing anyone about, she rolled up her discarded clothes and dashed down the hall to her room. Moonlight streamed across the bed, as she tiptoed in and lay down beside her little niece. Frank was on the floor, on his back, snoring gently.

Morning filled the town's streets with freight wagons. Thick clouds of dust choked the high desert air. Frank donned his clothes knowing it would be a difficult day. There should be plenty of jobs, like woodcutting, mining, and ranch hand work but most wouldn't hire a one-armed man. Frank went to get Sassy at the Old Man Corral on Yankie Street where he boarded him the night before. Mr. Goodell, the owner, met him at the door of the stable.

"I fed your mule this morning and noticed that his left front leg is swollen. I'd advise you to leave him be for a few days until the swelling goes down. If you like I can have the horse doc come take a look at him. It doesn't look serious to me; but it'd be a good idea to have it checked," Mr. Goodell said.

"I'd be obliged if you would have the doctor check his leg. But that leaves me without a mule. Do you have any I could rent for a few days? I'm going to cut some wood this morning," Frank said.

The night before, Frank lay awake while Felicity was bathing, trying to decide how to proceed. He knew their money wouldn't last long and he must find a steady income quickly. In a town where all residents cooked on woodstoves, and plenty of men clamoring to be fed after a hard day's work, firewood was in great demand. He decided, just before he drifted off to sleep, he would try woodcutting.

Mr. Goodell grinned when Frank asked about renting a mule. "I don't have any mules available but I do have a burro. It wouldn't be worth your while to rent my burro to use for woodcutting." The stable owner paused and scratched his head, "Tell you what I will do. If you'll cut me a load of wood for free today, I can let you use my burro today and tomorrow."

Frank felt he had little choice but to accept the offer. He shook hands with Mr. Goodell and took the little burro's bridle reins, leading her down the street. On the corner, near Porterfield's Drugstore, a man yelled at Frank. "Hey mister, you don't know much about the little burros, do you?" Frank pulled on the reluctant burro's bridle as she balked and brayed. He was in no mood for a ribbing.

"Hey mister, don't you hear me?"

Frank turned to see where the loudmouth was. He was nearly blinded by the sunlight reflecting off the bright head of the man teasing him. The man was an enigma. His hair was a bright yellow and his skin was a creamy coffee color. The man smiled revealing dirty mottled teeth as he ducked into the shade of the building.

"I ain't never seen nobody looking so funny. That little girl sure has you buffaloed," the large blond man threw back his head and roared with laughter.

Frank bristled feeling the hair on the back of his neck stand up. He thought about it for a few seconds then grinned at the man sheepishly. Frank wrapped the reins around his left hand. Facing the burro, he leaned back with all his weight and the burro refused to budge. Then to add insult to injury, the burro daintily stepped forward and Frank landed on his backside with a thud in the middle of the busy street.

"Oh, oh, oh!" the man had tears rolling down his cheeks and others along the street had joined in.

"I guess you could do better?" Frank yelled.

"Sure, with no trouble at all." The strange looking man stepped into the street and walked toward Frank, who was busy dusting off the seat of his britches. Mario Pedraza reached into his pocket and pulled out a weathered looking carrot. He leaned down and whispered lovingly into the ear of the little burro as he poked the carrot into her mouth. The burro brayed loudly. Mario took the reins from Frank and led her down the street.

Frank was dumbfounded. "How did you do that?" he asked.

Mario turned his head and looked back at Frank. "Rosita, she was my burro, 'til I sold her to Mr. Goodell. Tell you what, since I don't got any plans today, I'll show you how to handle my little sweetheart."

"I need her to haul wood. I made a deal with Mr. Goodell and I have to get started right away. I don't have time to fool around with this stupid burro."

Mario stopped and stroked Rosita's ears. "Oh, *Señor*, how do you expect to cut wood with only one arm?"

Frank was still very sensitive about his handicap. He strode down the street and took a poorly aimed swing at Mario, who easily sidestepped it. "I mean no disrespect, only how can you do it? It is hard backbreaking work. *Mis compadres* and me spend much of our time doing odd jobs around town so we can avoid the aching muscles of the woodcutter. These jobs, they don't pay much but we get by pretty good."

Angrily, Frank pulled the burro's reins from Mario's hand and started off down the street. The burro followed along quietly now. Frank stopped and looked back. Mario stood in the street and he waved happily when he saw Frank looking back at him.

About two miles south of town, Frank stopped. A borrowed ax was tied to the packsaddle and he deftly loosened the rope, using his left hand. He tied Rosita to a sturdy bush and set about chopping the scrub oak and juniper growing on the side of the hill. All around him, other men were similarly engaged.

As the day wore on, Frank's back ached and he experienced phantom pains where his right arm should have been. When the forks of the packsaddle were filled with wood, Frank started back toward Old Man Corral. His pain-ridden trek took him past Wolcott's Saloon. Mario watched Frank's progress up the street and stepped out the saloon's swinging doors just as Frank struggled past.

"To show you that I have no hard feelings, I would like to buy you a drink, *amigo*. Let me tell you, you sure look like you could use one."

Frank grimaced as he stopped to look at the large man standing next to him. "You've got yourself a deal. Sorry I took a swing at you."

Mario clapped him on the back with a large callused hand. The force of the blow nearly knocked Frank to the ground. "Ooof, take it easy!" Frank yelled.

"Sorry, sorry," Mario led the way into the crowded saloon. The acrid smells of smoke, cheap liquor and sweat enveloped Frank as he walked in. "A drink for my new *amigo*, Louis," Mario yelled over the bar.

"I can't be your friend if I don't even know your name," Frank said, his voice edged with disgust.

"Name's Mario Pedraza. Most call me *Guero*. Got this hair from *mi madre* who was a *gringa*. She was a pretty little thing and very popular with the *hombres*.

Me padre was from *Mejico*, I think, but I can't be sure," Mario lifted his beer mug into the air and sloshed foam all over the man standing next to him.

"I figured as much," Frank muttered.

"What did you say?" Mario asked as he cupped his hand around his ear. The noise in the saloon was deafening.

"Oh nothing, never mind," Frank said, a little louder.

"What is your name, amigo?"

"My name is Latimer Jones."

Mario looked puzzled, "What kinda name is Latimer?"

"What's wrong with my name, Mister?" Frank said touchily.

"Nothing, nothing, only it's a strange name. I ain't ever heard it around these parts," Mario said.

Frank sipped his warm beer gratefully. He must remind Prudence and Felicity to use their aliases.

"If you don't mind me asking, how'd you lose that arm?" Mario set down his beer with a careless splash. He dragged his dirty sleeve across his foam-flecked lips.

Frank gulped down his beer and slammed the mug down on the bar. "Buying me a drink don't give you the right to ask personal questions," shoving his battered hat on his head, he stomped out of the saloon. Rosita brayed loudly when she saw him. He grabbed the reins of her bridle and led her to the corral. Goodell met him at the gate and told him where to stack the wood.

When Frank got back to the boarding house, he felt like a bull had trampled him. Too tired to eat, he threw the blanket on the floor and promptly went to sleep. Felicity and Prudence were in the back with Mrs. McAllen. Felicity tried to impress the lady with her skills as a housekeeper. She removed the rugs from the parlor and whacked the dust out of them as Prudence tried to catch grasshoppers in the garden.

Finished with the rugs, Felicity replaced them in their rightful location and took Prudence to dinner at the dining table. The boarders gathered and noisily took their seats.

"Has anyone seen my brother," she asked. No one there except Mrs. McAllen knew what he looked like, so she described him. The hungry men shook their heads and kept eating. Not one of them had stood up when she entered the room. Mrs. McAllen entered and there was a loud scraping of chairs as the men jumped to their feet and wiped their mouths with the linen napkins from their laps.

"That's better," Mrs. McAllen smiled. "I'll have no disrespect in this house. George, will you please seat this lady and her niece? Thank you."

Felicity accepted the chair pulled out for her and filled their plates. She realized Frank was a grown man and perhaps he was eating elsewhere tonight. After dinner, Felicity did the dishes. Mrs. McAllen was glad she helped; but didn't ask her if she wanted a job.

In the parlor, after the dishes, Prudence and Felicity joined the men. They were talking politics and discussing the Pullman strike. There was a consensus of opinion Mr. Pullman was abusing the railroad workers and the government should intervene. Prudence crawled up on her aunt's lap and went to sleep. Felicity felt her own head beginning to nod. She said goodnight and carried Prudence to their room.

Her nostrils were assaulted by the smell of beer and stale tobacco smoke. She coughed loudly and Frank snorted, grumbled a bit, then went back to sleep. After Prudence was tucked into bed, Felicity stuck the toe of her boot in Frank's ribs. "You are becoming an animal, Frank. What would Emma say if she saw you now?"

Frank struggled to his feet and leaned against the wall as he pulled on his boots. "Damned if I know. She'd probably be ashamed of me like you are," he grumbled.

"I'm sorry, I know you're still grieving for her. But you have to pull yourself together or we aren't going to make it." Felicity checked to see that Prudence was still sleeping before she led her brother down the hall to the kitchen. She repeated her labors from the night before as she filled the tub for her brother.

When she closed the door, Frank stood in the sudsy water and cried. He was unable to sit in the tub so he poured tepid water over his head with the tin pitcher his sister provided. Three days worth of beard trapped the suds and made his chin itch like fury.

Bleary sunburned eyes stared back at him as he stood over the table and looked into a small hand mirror. He looked like hell. Raking the straight blade of his razor across his face, he left several small nicks and a large cut on his chin. Satisfied he couldn't do better or feel much worse, he finished his bath and dressed in clean clothes. It was hard to do the simplest tasks anymore. "I've got to quit feeling sorry for myself," he whispered aloud.

Emma was proud of him once. The last time he had been to Silver City was on their wedding day, full of hope and plans for the future. Now the future was swathed in a bleak mist.

Prudence was really all he had now. He knew Felicity would stay for a while; but she was anxious to return to her home in Santa Fe. She missed the fancy balls and political functions at the territorial capital. She wasn't cut out for ranch life or living in a small mining town.

Prudence sat up in bed when Frank came into their room. She rubbed her eyes and smiled at him with her mother's smile. "You smell better Papa," she said giggling.

"Why aren't you asleep? Did I wake you up or did you have a bad dream?" Frank asked her.

"No, I was waiting for you. Where did you go today?" Prudence wanted to know.

"I went to cut wood, I'm trying to make some money for us, little one. Were you good today?"

Felicity slipped out of the room quietly. She went to get the food she kept aside for Frank's supper and some cold milk.

"I guess. Aunt Felicity didn't yell at me, 'cept for one time when I chased Mr. Whiskers up a tree. I only wanted to put a pretty bow in her fuzzy hair and she scratched me. So I chased her and she got up a tree and then she yelled at me. She climbed up even higher and couldn't get down."

"Did you say the cat's name is Mr. Whiskers?" Frank asked, grinning.

"That is what Mrs. McAllen calls her," Prudence said.

"Doesn't Mister mean that the cat is a boy?"

Prudence looked puzzled for a second and then laughed. "Maybe that's why he didn't want a bow in his hair."

"Goodnight, princess, sleep tight and don't let the bedbugs bite," Frank said tucking Prudence into the bed.

Prudence shivered. "Do they got bedbugs here?"

"No, now go to sleep, tomorrow is going to be a big day."

Felicity came in with a tray of food and milk and set it down carefully on the dresser.

Frank kissed his daughter's cheek. Felicity walked over to her brother and sniffed the air. "Pru is right, you do smell better."

Frank grabbed his pillow and proceeded to whack his sister over the head with it.

Felicity shrieked and Prudence pounced on her. There was a loud pounding on the wall. This provoked silent laughter until their sides ached and tears rolled down their cheeks. Frank ate and curled up on the floor to sleep.

Red streaks etched the sky the next morning. Frank went to the corral to retrieve his reluctant helper. Rosita balked and brayed as he attempted to lead her through the gate.

"Just like a woman, don't you think?"

Frank heard Mario's voice behind him and he cringed.

"I feel kind of sorry for you, *amigo*, and I think I can help you. I know of a job, not much money, but enough for a little *hombre* like yourself."

"I don't want or need your help. Now get out of my way!" Frank pulled on the reins with a snap.

Rosita rolled her eyes and lifted her head and brayed. Two dogs came running down the street barking. A baby wailed in the distance.

"Now see what you have gone and done. You have upset the fair Rosita. She will not do what you ask no matter what, now." Mario grinned revealing his grayish teeth.

A string of cuss words broke from Frank's lips and he threw down the burro's reins, pushed Mario aside and stomped up the street. The barking dogs stopped in their tracks and watched him go with looks of amazement. Mario chuckled and patted Rosita on the head. "Do not worry little one. That man is *loco* but he would not hurt a fly."

Frank's head was about to erupt. When he left the corral, he stomped toward the saloon. He needed a drink badly and it was barely 7:30 in the morning. He noticed the saloon was empty except for the bartender, Louis.

"Guero ain't much good fer nuthin. He spends most of his time making people miserable. I saw you in here with him last night," Louis explained. "What'll ya have?"

"Whiskey, please," Frank said politely.

"Kinda early, ain't it? I've got some good strong coffee, no charge," Louis said kindly.

"Yeah, all right," Frank agreed.

Louis reached under the bar and pulled out two large stoneware mugs and set them down on the bar in front of Frank. "Believe I'll join ya myself," Louis said.

Frank sipped his coffee tentatively. It was scalding hot and very strong. Louis looked carefully at the man who appeared to need some food. He reached under the bar and retrieved his own breakfast, some cold biscuits and sausages from his boarding house, he set them down still wrapped in paper in front of Frank who gratefully accepted them.

"Thanks mister. I'm looking for a job, got any ideas?" Frank asked.

"Well, some fellas are workin' in an adobe hole. Can you carry a bucket?"

"Sure thing," Frank said. "Who can I talk to?"

"Name of the foreman is Champion. Just ask fer him and someone'll point him out to ya," Louis drawled.

"Thanks for the breakfast and information. See ya around," Frank picked up his hat and headed for the doors. Frank located Champion easily. A large man with a very ruddy face, his voice could be heard from a block away. This particular adobe hole was for a building under construction on Main Street. Men were working in the hole with pickaxes and shovels, others were hauling dirt out of the hole in large buckets. Another group was mixing straw, water, and mud and pouring the mixture into rectangular shaped wooden forms. The bricks would bake and harden in the desert sun.

Frank approached the foreman and stood quietly until he caught his eye.

"What can I do for you, son?" Champion asked as he eyed Frank's empty right sleeve.

"I need a job, sir," Frank replied.

Champion scratched his head causing his thinning hair to stick up at all angles.

"I could only pay you half what a man with two arms would make. You can only carry one bucket at a time," Champion said.

"I understand. When can I start?"

"Soon as we can get you a bucket," Champion replied.

Frank started working immediately. By the end of the first day he was so tired he could barely move. As he passed Wolcott's Saloon, Frank glanced around, hoping that he would not encounter Mario. Luck was with him, Mario was nowhere to be seen.

On Broadway and Hudson, that particular evening, a large crowd was gathering as Frank approached the Southern Hotel. Filled with curiosity, Frank made his way through the crowd. The entrance, parlor, and dining room were filled with men of all ages. Mrs. McAllen was bustling around yelling orders to no one in particular. Felicity was a culinary genius. Her buttermilk biscuits melted in your mouth and her pies were heavenly. Judge Zachary, Felicity's employer in Santa Fe, really missed his fabulous cook. Now Felicity was in her element. She took over the kitchen and the news of her cooking abilities spread through the town like wildfire.

Forced to elbow his way to the kitchen, Frank stopped to explain to several people, he was not cutting into the line. Felicity was smiling and singing in the kitchen filled with wonderful smells. Mrs. McAllen brought in two local girls to help with the serving and two more to help with the cooking. The small kitchen was a beehive of activity.

"Where's Pru?" Frank hollered over the clanging of the pans.

"Outside in the back," his sister hollered in reply.

Prudence was outside, sitting on an old box. In her arms, she was cradling the biggest, ugliest cat Frank had ever seen. To make matters worse, the poor cat was sporting a baby's bonnet. "What have we here?" Frank asked.

"Papa, you're back! This is my new friend, Mr. Whiskers. He belongs to Mrs. McAllen and I think he likes me," Prudence said, her eyes dancing with delight. "I think he likes the bonnet better than the bow I tried to put on him yesterday."

"A bonnet is much more proper than a bow. Maybe he knows that," Frank said. He reached down and took his daughter's small hand and went to the kitchen to find something to eat."

Chapter 21

The desert sun dropped behind Chihuahua Hill. A chill caught the small hairs on the back of Mario Pedraza's neck. He shivered and mumbled an admonishment to himself. He crept toward the tiny adobe house shrouded in shadows. Gently, he tapped on the door and waited impatiently. When there was no answer, he peered through the tiny pane of glass in the door.

A single candle dimly lighted a grim room. A young woman was bent over a washtub, pouring water from a pitcher over her long black hair. She was naked to the waist and she straightened to apply soap to her hair. Mario shivered again and watched as the woman continued her sensuous ablutions, oblivious to his presence. When she finished washing her hair, she wrapped herself in a filmy shawl and sat in front of her tiny fireplace. Slowly, she began to work the tangles from her hair with her fingers.

Mario was enthralled and breathless. Compelled to watch, the night grew cooler as Mario got warmer. When the woman finished with her hair, she dipped some water into the washtub from the pot hanging in the fireplace. Slowly, she removed her shawl and draped it over the back of the chair. Then she removed the rest of her clothing and stepped into the tub. Standing in the shallow tub and facing the door, she gently soaped her body. From Mario's vantage point, he had an unobstructed view. He sighed longingly.

Finished with her bath, the young woman dried herself and dressed in a long, dark skirt and peasant blouse. Mario grew more uncomfortable. As she started to empty the tub, Mario retreated into the shadows at the side of the house. He heard the door latch being lifted and water tossed outside. The woman's face appeared in the doorway and a small beam of light caught her translucent skin. Mario remained hidden for several minutes and then approached the door. As before, he tapped gently. The door opened a crack and revealed the beautiful, smiling face of the woman. Her smile faded immediately when her eyes encountered Mario's features.

Mario groaned inwardly, as he said, "Nicholas is waiting, Blanca."

Later that same night, Mario walked up the street toward Chihuahua Hill. Beside the road in the shadow, a business partner of Mario's was waiting. Nicholas Oso was notorious in Silver City and being sought for allegedly stabbing a woman. Since the stabbing, Nicholas was keeping a low profile.

Nicholas put a finger to his lips and motioned for Mario to follow him. He led him into a small house. "I am leaving tomorrow," Nicholas said.

"*¿ Por qué?* What happened?" Mario asked.

"The deputies are looking around up here and I think they've been watching my house," Nicholas told him. Nicholas's gear was in piles on the floor in front of them.

"I need you to help me get out of town, Guero. Can you get me two horses?"

Mario grinned, "What's in it for me?"

"*Compadre*, after all we have been through? I am deeply injured," Nicholas said.

Mario licked his lips, "Where did you put that last stuff I brought you?"

"It is safe for now. I tell you what, you get me those horses, then we will talk," Nicholas dusted off the fancy sombrero in his hands with delicate flicks of his fingers.

"It is not easy for me. People, they know me. I do odd jobs; what do I want with a horse?" Mario wanted to know.

"Steal some," Nicholas smiled, revealing beautiful even white teeth.

Mario envied those teeth. The *señoritas* found Nicholas irresistible. He was a cruel man and when he finished with a woman, he usually left his mark on her. Nicholas's knife, in a beautiful hand tooled sheath, was hanging from his belt.

"It is a big price to pay if I get caught," Mario said.

"I told you! I'll share some of the stuff you got on the last job. If that is not enough, I guess I'll have to try something else," Nicholas smiled wickedly and drew his knife from its sheath. Gently, he ran his finger along the length of the blade.

"I will do it. But only because you asked so nicely," Mario eased his way to the door all the while watching Nicholas closely. When he reached the door, he turned and ran out. Nicholas laughed and continued to get things ready for his journey.

Mario returned to his room and applied boot black to his bright hair. It was hard not to get any on his face. Darkening his hair dramatically changed his appearance and gave him an anonymity that would be necessary for tonight's success. He put on a long dark coat, climbed out the window and dropped to the ground. Staying in the shadows, he headed for a nearby livery stable. A black gelding and an old roan mare were noisily chomping oats side by side in the corral.

Mario slid a loop of rope over each one's head and led them quickly to the gate. Looking both ways and seeing no one around, he lifted the wooden latch, and led them into the dark street. He cautiously made his way down side streets and alleys. Once the roan nickered and Mario hastily silenced her by placing his hand firmly on her nose and giving her a carrot. She snorted and snuffled for more. "No *mi hijita*, come along," he whispered in her ear.

Mario lived in the streets, since age nine. He had a way with animals and when he was in his late teens worked in Lordsburg for the Butterfield Stage Company. He was adept at calming frightened animals and could hitch and unhitch teams at record speeds. He discovered liquor in his early twenties and lost his job after an evening of revelry in Ralston City. At the Last Chance Saloon, a young *senorita* smiled at him and he made some unwelcome advances toward her. When she protested, he slapped her and a *gringo* intervened. Drunk, Mario pulled a knife. The unlucky *gringo* lunged at Mario and fell on top of him. Mario's knife was buried up to its hilt in the man's bowels.

A few weeks later, the man died of a bad infection and Mario fled to Silver City. The law would be after him and he was determined to steer clear of trouble. Although Mario was used to hard work, drinking and carousing came more easily. He found a certain unsavory element in Silver City would pay well for his particular talents. He was a smooth talker and a charmer. As a child he grew adept at picking pockets. Stealing was second nature to him.

Nicholas met him at the bottom of Chihuahua Hill. He took the black gelding's rope and led him behind a building where his belongings, saddlebag, saddle, and packsaddle, were stashed. Mario followed leading the roan. Nicholas saddled the gelding and assisted Mario in tying Nicholas's gear on the roan's packsaddle.

"We had a deal, hombre," Mario whispered.

"*Sí*, we did. Things are bad for me here. I'll leave you with this," Nicholas reached into his saddlebag and took out a large bag of coins. Mario gasped loudly. He'd never seen so much money at one time. He dipped his hand into the sack and let the coins slide through his fingers.

Nicholas smiled and nodded. Two men came out of the shadows behind Mario and grabbed his arms. Mario was taken completely by surprise as Nicholas deftly slid his knife under his ribs as the men lowered him to the ground. From the shadows, two more men emerged. They lifted Mario's unconscious body and heaved it over the packsaddle.

"*Un momento*," Nicholas said. He reached down to pick up the sack of coins and Mario's battered hat. Genuflecting, Nicholas made the sign of the cross and mumbled, "*Vaya con Dios, mi amigo*." He scuffed the dirt with his boot to cover any blood on the ground and carefully wiped his knife on Mario's shirt.

Nicholas smiled and mounted the black gelding. One of the men handed him the reins of the packhorse and he disappeared into the darkness.

The next morning, a posse was dispatched to look for the missing horses. Several local people reported seeing the gang and the posse followed some false leads. Three days later, the posse returned never spotting the bandits or the stolen horses. The bandits' hoard was discovered and most of the loot was recovered.

A full moon cast shadows of the trees on the frosty ground. The horses picked their way carefully along the icy trail and chuffed when Nicholas stopped near Bear Creek. Only about a hundred yards off the trail, Nicholas unceremoniously loosened the rope holding Mario's body and allowed it to slide into a pile of leaves. The air was spiced with the smell of pine and a hint of wood smoke. Its crispness held anticipation of snow for the foothills of the Continental Divide. An icy gust of wind blew the smell of frying bacon and coffee to Nicholas. His stomach protested with a loud growl. The mining town of Pinos Altos was only a couple of miles up the trail.

Nicholas would disappear for awhile. So many people were coming and going in Pinos Altos, he figured he could slip in and remain inconspicuous for at least a few days. Removing his pants with the silver conchos and his hand-tooled black leather belt, he donned Mario's clothes and carefully placed his *sombrero* on top of his clothes. As he removed Mario's shirt, he found it was stiff with congealed blood. It was against Nicholas's fastidious nature to wear another man's clothes, let alone blood caked ones. So he satisfied himself that Mario's dark coat would cover his own shirt well enough. Nicholas was relieved to find there was very little blood on the coat itself because it was open when Mario was hoisted across the horse's back.

A little trickle of water in the creek provided him with the opportunity to wash his hands and knife. Using his white linen kerchief, he dabbed at stiffened areas on his coat and pants. Carefully, Nicholas folded his clothes and put them in his saddlebags. His *sombrero* was impossible to conceal with his other belongings so he made a cache of rocks against the side of the hill and wrapped his hat carefully in a blanket and piece of oilskin to protect it. Satisfied his *sombrero* was well hidden, he made a mental note to retrieve it as soon as he was out of danger. He kicked leaves over Mario. Because he needed food, it would be wise to wait until later to bury the body.

In Pinos Altos, Nicholas headed for the saloon. The smell of food penetrated his numbing senses. He dismounted, tied his horses to the rail outside, and trudged up the steps dragging the mud on his boots into the smoke filled establishment. Clinking glasses and murmured conversations continued as he approached the bar. "Do you serve food here?" he politely asked the wizened bartender.

The old man grinned and nodded, "Sure do, what'll ya have?"

Nicholas paused, "I would like a large rare beefsteak, fried potatoes, onions and coffee."

"Comin' right up," the old man's gold teeth glinted in the murky lantern light. He turned and ducked through a narrow doorway behind the bar. Soon he was back and busied himself at the cook stove. He picked up a dented metal coffee pot with a dingy rag, poured a generous portion of the strong brew into a chipped mug, and plunked it down in front of Nicholas.

"That'll be 1 dollar and 50 cents," the man said.

Nicholas grunted and tossed the coins down on the bar. People called *him* a thief!

While the scalding coffee burned his tongue, it restored some of the feeling in his frozen face. He set down the cup, picked up his stool and placed it next to the fire burning in the large stone hearth at the back of the room. He retrieved his cup and went to sit with his back leaning against the wall near the fire. Half closing his eyes, he furtively scanned the room for familiar faces. Not seeing any, he sighed heavily. His feet in their scuffed muddy boots felt as though they were cubes of ice. He slid them as close to the open fireplace as he dared.

When his steak was ready, the bartender seated him at a table near the fireplace. Carefully, Nicholas trimmed the fat from the steak and set it aside. The potatoes were a crisp golden brown, the onions cooked to perfection. His steak oozed juice. Nicholas closed his eyes, chewed slowly, and savored every bite. His stomach calmed immediately. When he was finished, he lit a large cigar and leaned back in his chair, exhaling the aromatic smoke through his lips and nose.

Some "ladies" came down the stairs and Nicholas sat quietly. One scantily clad redhead walked over to him. She leaned forward to give him an unobstructed view of her assets. He smiled at her and shoved her away roughly because she reeked. Nicholas pushed back his chair and walked out into the street. Staying in the shadows of the buildings, he led his horses to the outskirts of town where miners lived in a tent camp. A noisy poker game attracted his attention and he ducked into one tent where rowdy men were drinking and laughingly yelling obscenities at each other.

In less than an hour, Nicholas was the owner of an old Army tent and cot. The miner was not a good loser and was determined to win his stuff back. Fortunately, some of his friends saw the dangerous gleam in Nicholas's eyes and when the miner began to protest, they convinced him to go into town for another drink. When Nicholas claimed his temporary home it was littered with discarded bottles and cans. The man's mining gear was arranged neatly on one side of the tent. Nicholas kicked the cans and bottles outside. It had been an eventful day and he was tired. The temperature outside was very cool for this time of year. Nicholas removed his boots, wrapped himself in three musty blankets and went to sleep.

Chapter 22

Needlelike cold penetrated his skin and felt like insects were scurrying along the frozen hairs on his arms and legs. Sleep beckoned; his aching, pounding head longed for oblivion, but he resisted. He knew if he slept now, he wouldn't survive the night. Lying in the hills near Pinos Altos, Mario was frightened. The leaves cushioned his fall from the horse but afforded little protection from the night's wintry chill. Clouds moved in but occasionally moonlight illuminated nearby rocks and revealed Oso's cache. Mario dragged himself to the small stack of rocks. Wincing in pain, his feet, legs, hands, and buttocks scraped across the cold, rocky ground toward the cache. He pulled out the blanket and oilskin Nicholas used to protect his *sombrero*, wrapped them around his half frozen body and settled himself against the hillside.

The front door of the cabin was stuck. Sadie Calhoun went out the back door and noticed her brothers' hunting rifles leaning against the rear wall of the cabin. Supposed to be out hunting, the young men were nowhere to be seen and their rifles had been left behind, so she supposed they were up to no good again.

The cabin lay in a small valley several hundred yards from the trail up to Pinos Altos. It was difficult to climb up to the trail, especially wearing a long skirt. As it was beginning to get light, and Sadie went to find her brothers. Their meat supply was dwindling quickly and they must stock up for the winter. The chilly wind made ghosts of her breath as she trudged along. A sudden noise startled her. She stopped and listened. It was someone groaning. She patted the pocket of her coat where a derringer was concealed. Her father insisted she carry it when she was alone. Her fingers slid around the grip of the small gun as she crouched down and crept slowly toward the sound.

Near the hillside was a man wrapped in a blanket and oilskin. Shallow gasps escaped from his blue lips. Alarmed, Sadie rushed forward and leaned over the unconscious man. There was a rustling behind her and Sadie pulled the derringer from her pocket.

"Hold on there, Sadie. Don't shoot your own brothers!" her brother Sweeney yelled. Sweeney and Mark, Sadie's brothers, emerged from the brush that had concealed their approach.

"Where have you two been? Oh never mind, help me get him to the cabin," Sadie ordered.

The young men lifted Mario's limp body as Sadie rushed ahead and stoked the fire. She threw some heavy blankets down on the floor. A small shed behind the house served as the family's smokehouse. The door latch was frozen so Sadie went to the woodpile to get the ax. She used the butt of the handle to pound on the board to loosen it. Replacing the ax in the woodpile stump, she opened the door of the shed. Only one piece of cured venison was hanging there. Sadie found her father's knife, sliced off a large chunk of meat and took it into the cabin.

She tossed some wood into the stove and put a kettle of water to boil. She pulled a cooking pot out of the oven and put water in it. On a butcher block, she chopped up the meat with a heavy cleaver and threw it into the pot. When the water in the kettle started to boil, she poured some into a tin mug, added some whiskey she kept in the pantry for medicinal purposes and a dollop of honey.

When the man began to stir, Mark propped him up and Sweeney urged some of the now cooling liquid between his cracked lips. Coughing and sputtering, he awakened completely and looked around the room with wild, frightened eyes.

"¿Adónde estoy? ¿Quién es?" he asked. Then he smiled and closed his eyes. He retained an image, the pretty face of a young woman. As the warmth penetrated his limbs, Mario Pedraza knew he was dead. *Heaven must be a nice place with such pretty angels*, he thought as he drifted away.

Sadie sat beside the strange looking man. His hair was plastered with some sort of black oily substance that left smudges on his face. She considered trying to wash it out but remembered her mother's warning never to wash her hair when she was sick because it might cause a chill.

When Sweeney decided the stranger's color was improved, he removed the dirty oilskin and blanket and found a knife wound. Sadie washed and dressed the deep wound. Fortunately, cold temperatures and pressure from the weight of Mario's body draped over the back of the horse, caused the blood to clot.

The wound oozed a little as Sadie washed it with warm water. She poured some whiskey on it and covered it with a clean cloth. Mark raised Mario's upper body and Sweeney secured the bandage with strips of cloth. Barking dogs announced the arrival of Buchanan Calhoun. Most people who knew him thought he looked nothing like his name. He was a wiry, beanpole of a man. Buchanan, Buck to his friends, stood nearly 6 foot 7 inches in his stocking feet and weighed less than 16 stone. He bent nearly double as he entered the cabin. His skull was creased with many dents, reminders of previous encounters with the unyielding wood of the cabin's doorframe. Straightening up, he turned and patted his trouser leg and two large dogs came bounding into the room.

"Close the door, Pa, you're letting in the cold," Sadie said sharply.

Buck slammed the door and latched it. "Too cold out to do much today. Water's nearly frozen in the creek," he exclaimed as he pulled an old pipe from his pocket and filled it from a tobacco pouch on the table. "Who's that?" he asked as he noticed the still form in front of the fire.

Sadie helped her father out of his coat and hung it on peg near the door.

"I found him this morning while I was out looking for the boys," she replied. "They brought him here."

As Mario dozed, his mind wove a tapestry of past events. *First, he saw himself as a small boy, playing with a stray puppy. Next, he was a youth, harnessing a stagecoach team. Then, unbidden, the face of an angel would appear,* and Mario's past was blotted out.

Sadie placed her hand on Mario's forehead. He was feverish. "Pa, I know you don't want to go back to town today, but this man needs a doctor. Would you fetch Doc Kennon for him? Sadie went to her father who was sitting in his favorite chair, enjoying his pipe. His feet were propped up on a stool near the fire. He was dozing.

Sadie was concerned about her patient. When he regained consciousness, she had her brothers lift his head and she spooned warm broth into his mouth. She wondered what else she could do when Sweeney's voice penetrated her thoughts.

"What do ya suppose that stuff in his hair is?" he asked.

"I don't know, it looks like boot black," Sadie snapped impatiently.

"Why would he put that stuff in his hair?" Sweeney persisted.

"I don't know. Why do you ask so many questions?" his sister wanted to know. Someone had tried to kill this man and taken his clothes, but why? The answer to their questions would just have to wait.

"Mark, take Sweeney and see if you can get us some meat for dinner," Sadie directed the older of the two brothers, nineteen last April.

"Do you think we should leave you here alone with him? What if he wakes up?" Mark asked.

"Pa will be back soon with Dr. Kennon. This man is so close to death that he couldn't hurt me even if he wanted to," Sadie replied.

"Maybe we should tie him up," Sweeney suggested.

"Oh get away with you," Sadie tossed the young men their coats and shooed them out the door.

The doctor arrived with Buck about an hour later. During that time, Sadie made an interesting discovery, the stricken man had blond hair. With warm water and soap, she rubbed some strands until the greasy substance came off.

Dr. Kennon was a fine man. Sadie worked with him from time to time. Not having any trained nurses in the vicinity, he would ask Sadie to look in on sick miners.

"Hmm," the doctor said as he examined Mario's wound, "Hmm."

"Well, Dr. Kennon, will he live?" Sadie asked impatiently.

After a lot of prodding and poking, the doctor cleaned and redressed Mario's wound. "Lucky fellow," he said. "Whoever did this knew what he was doing. The knife was slipped under the ribs and directed at the heart, but it just missed."

"He has a fever, does that mean an infection? Will he live?" Sadie wanted to know.

"I wish I could say for sure, Miss Sadie," the doctor admitted, "I think with proper care he should be just fine. But time will tell. When he wakes up, give him a teaspoon of laudanum for the pain. He can have some every four hours. This powder can be mixed in water. It is for the fever. Keep his wound clean. If you see any redness or pus, send your Pa or one of your brothers to get me. I'll come back in 2 days. If he isn't any better, we might see about taking him to Silver City. I understand they have a hospital now."

"Thank you, I'll take good care of him," Sadie said.

"I'm sure you will. You have a natural gift," Dr. Kennon said as he gathered his supplies and put on his coat and gloves. He smiled at Sadie and her family and went outside into the chilly afternoon.

Sweeney and Mark excused themselves after the doctor left and came back about a half an hour later with two fat jackrabbits. Buck settled himself in his chair and propped up his feet. The boys were taking a long time to clean the rabbits so he decided to go outside and see what they were up to. The two were hard at work, removing the bark from some logs. Buck watched as they smoothed the wood and built a frame. They stretched an old piece of canvas across it and secured it with ropes. Mark tested the bed to see if it would hold his weight.

"It ain't bad. At least the poor man won't have to sleep on the cold floor," Mark offered.

Sweeney grinned. "It could be prettier, but it'll serve its purpose." He went to the cabin door and knocked.

Sadie answered the door. "What have you two been up to? I've had supper ready for nearly an hour," she said.

Sweeney and Mark grinned sheepishly. "We've made something for you," Mark said.

"You'd better come inside before the food dries out," Sadie answered crossly.

"Just a little while longer," Sweeney grunted as they carried their invention into the room.

"Is that what you have been doing?" Sadie asked.

"What do you think?" both boys asked simultaneously.

"I think it will be a nice piece of furniture for the cabin," she said.

Sweeney and Mark blushed. Their sister handed them each a steaming bowl of stew and freshly baked bread set to rise before her morning walk. Buck was already at the table. He bowed his head and said Grace as was his custom. They ate in silence.

It was Sweeney's job to clear the table while Sadie washed the dishes and put them away. The family put a heavy blanket over the canvas, gently lifted Mario, and covered him. His eyelids fluttered and he groaned but did not awaken.

"If I can get more canvas and rope, maybe we could make us all some beds like that." Buck was thinking out loud. He was very proud of his young sons. They were fine, thoughtful young men. Sadie was "the apple of his eye." She assumed the household duties of his late wife without a murmur. Though nearly twenty years old, she looked much younger. Her round rosy face was kissed with tiny freckles and her baby fine hair framed her face like a halo.

"What happened to those rabbits you shot? I thought you were going to clean them," Sadie asked.

"Oh, we did. They are hanging in the smoke shed," Mark said. "Do you have any pie left from yesterday?"

"You just ate two big bowls of stew. Do you ever get full?" Sadie laughed.

"Not very often," Mark admitted.

Buck grinned and went back to his chair by the fire. Sadie sounded like her mother when she talked to the boys. Her voice was stern as she scolded them. She'd make a fine wife and mother someday.

Chapter 23

A red mist floated in front of his eyes. The fever drenched his skin, parching his lips and mouth. *Somewhere, someone was calling his name. He couldn't see her. He tried to answer but couldn't make a sound.* His breath came in short gasps, choking and gagging, he swirled toward consciousness only to be sucked back into the red mist. He tried to scream as the burning pain increased. *She stood before him, naked to the waist, her long raven hair was wet. Blanca's smile was tender, then it faded and her face was creased with concern.*

"You must go now, Guero. He will come for you. You are not safe!" she urged. The red veil shrouded Blanca and soon hid her from his sight. He reached for her but she was no longer there.

Then the angel's face appeared. She smiled and dissolved into wave of white hot pain.

When the veil was gone, Mario could see his surroundings for a few moments or maybe it was a dream. He saw a light suspended over a round table, a group of people, three men and a woman, speaking in low voices. The oldest man held a large book. The words the man read were soothing.

Death hovered for several days. Dr. Kennon cautioned Sadie the man was too sick to move. They would have to do the best they could for him at the Calhoun cabin.

Blanca visited Mario often, stepping through the red mist, begging him to leave.

Eight days after Sadie discovered him, Mario, wearing only long johns, left the cabin. He took some of Sweeney's clothes from the clothesline and an old pair of boots near the back door.

The large book, he had seen the people reading, was a Bible and might be valuable, he paused to look at it. But something else caught his eye, a silver hairbrush. He could get enough for that to live comfortably for several weeks. He knew Nicholas would find him soon and harm this kind family.

The wound in his chest ached so badly Mario could scarcely breathe and it took him several hours to get to Pinos Altos although it was a short distance from the Calhouns's cabin. Luckily, there was thick brush along the side of the trail and it was very dark in the early hours before dawn. Resting frequently, he hid from anyone who came along.

Near the Pinos Altos Mercantile, Mario spotted a cart full of burlap sacks. The horse pawed in its traces. Mario shrugged; it was pointed toward Silver City, his destination. He crawled under the moldy bags, and covered himself completely. Exhausted, he slept in less than 5 minutes. He stirred slightly when the driver set out. The wagon jerked to a sudden halt, sending a mind-numbing pain through Mario's chest and a loud groan escaped from his lips.

A scuffling sound above him caused him to hold his breath as he heard Nicholas's voice.

"*Hola,* Señor. I am looking for a friend of mine. He is a rather funny looking *hombre*," Nicholas described Mario.

The driver chuckled, "I ain't seen no one like that. Are you gonna rob me of my sacks?"

"Oh Señor, I am not a thief. Just an honest man searching for his friend," Nicholas smiled, his teeth flashing. "I am most grateful for your assistance." Nicholas poked at the burlap sacks in the wagon with a long stick, barely missing Mario.

"Well, I can't help ya. If ya don't mind, I'll be on my way," the driver flicked his reins and the wagon lurched forward.

Mario held his breath for what seemed like hours as the wagon continued to move along, slowly winding its way down the rocky trail. He thought about the angel and her kindness. Never in his life had anyone been as gentle towards him. He recalled watching her face through half-closed eyes and never saw distaste, only compassion, on her well-scrubbed face. Somehow, he sensed that she'd never experienced any pain or loneliness.

Given a little glimpse of heaven, he vowed he would try as hard as he could to be a better man. Mario prayed, as he lay in the wagon, to a God with Whom he had only a passing acquaintance. "Please, Señor God, if you will let me live, I will try to be an honest man and work hard," he mouthed silently as he lay hidden under the shroud of burlap sacks.

He remembered the hairbrush and was ashamed. The sun was well up into the sky, when the driver discovered Mario and shook him awake. Mario rubbed his eyes and looked around. He was back in Silver City. The wagon stopped in front of Miner's Mercantile and he was in luck. His friend, Juan Hernandez, lived nearby.

Juan was an old retired miner living in a small shack in the midst of the infamous houses of Kate Stewart. When Juan was sober, he served as a handy man for the friendly madam. Kate saw to Juan's meals and gave him a little money.

Juan told Mario it was his sincerest wish to die in the arms of a beautiful young woman. Juan's home was his earthly paradise. Mario approached the house cautiously. Hanging in the window was a pair of greasy long johns, serving as curtains. The door stood ajar and Juan was sprawled on a cot in the middle of the room. The dirt floor was littered with discarded whiskey bottles and the odor of sweat and decay permeated the dimly lit room. Mario pushed the door open and edged inside. The old man was snoring loudly, sputtering as he opened his bleary eyes.

"Who the hell is in my house?" he yelled. He picked up an empty bottle by the neck and brandished it like a sword.

Mario shuffled forward. Suddenly, pushed from behind, he sprawled in the middle of the filthy floor, unable to breathe because something heavy was on top of him. The pain in his chest was excruciating. A large woman laughed and after several rolling attempts, managed to pull herself up. Mario lay on his side and she smiled broadly, offering him a hand. She staggered slightly, as she pulled him to his feet.

"Mercy, that gin sure does pack a wallop!" she chortled. The woman's makeup made her look like an oversized clown.

"Juanito, who is your friend?" the drunken clown asked.

"I don't know. I was asleep when he came in. What are you doing here, Georgie?" Juan asked suspiciously.

"Miss Kate sent me to fetch you. We're having a party tonight and she wants you to come."

Juan leered. He loved Kate's parties. There was free food and drink, and young girls to fondle. Kate Stewart liked to dance and Juan could be depended on for at least a couple of two-steps. Mario cleared his throat and Juan squinted at him again.

"Who are you, Señor? What do you want here?" Juan asked, still clutching the empty bottle.

Georgie sat down unceremoniously on the floor. Reaching into the front of her dress, she pulled out a flask.

"It's me, Guero, Señor Juan," Mario stammered.

Juan shook his head vehemently. "No! Guero is dead! You do not even look like Guero! What do you want here?"

"Let's invite him to our party," Georgie suggested, puffing and panting as she struggled to her feet. "It will be getting started soon. As Mrs. Stewart always says, "The more the merrier."

Juan's head was pounding. He could use a drink to clear his brain. Georgie yanked Juan up and grabbed Mario's arm and shoved them through the door ahead of her. The odd looking trio entered the bordello through a side door. The parlor was filled with half-dressed women in all shapes and sizes, lounging suggestively on velvet couches and chairs. In the glow of the gaslights and candles, there was a palatial air of a Middle Eastern harem. The royal purple drapes with gold pull ropes were drawn tightly against the outside light.

Two guitarists provided lively music for the gathering. As men arrived, the atmosphere was redolent with sin. Mario's head was pounding. He needed a place to lie down. Unsteadily, he saw Juan surrounded by four, exceedingly plump women, and being fed grapes. The smell of greasy food being prepared in the kitchen, made Mario gag. Slowly, he made his way through heavy draperies that concealed a large staircase. He ascended the stairs one slow step at a time, leaning heavily on the banister. At the top of the landing, a door stood open, and Mario staggered toward it. The pain in his chest made breathing difficult. He peeked into the room and seeing that it was unoccupied, he went in and bolted the door.

It was a feminine room sparsely furnished with only a dresser and a large, rumpled bed. A large hipbath, filled with water, sat in one corner of the room. The water was warm and obviously used only once. Oh, the luxury of a bath!

Running his fingers through his greasy, blackened hair, Mario undressed and slipped into the soothing water. He lathered his hair with some flowery smelling soap.

Blanca was smiling at him and beckoning to him. He reached for her and buried his head against her naked breasts. Her dark hair covered him. Succumbing to the pain and watery caresses, he slipped into unconsciousness.

A loud pounding at the door, caused him to jerk and pain drove through his chest. It took several seconds for Mario to become aware of his surroundings. Black, greasy beads floated on the surface of the now cold tub water. Mario used the soap jar to rinse himself and hastily picked up a towel hanging on a chair next to the tub.

"Jessie, are you in there? You'd better not be in my room without my permission. Remember what happened to you the last time? Come out right now!" the shrill voice demanded. "Right now girl! Do you hear me?"

Mario unbolted the door. He draped the towel around himself.

A young woman shoved on the door. "You're sure not Jessie. Why are you in my room?" she wanted to know.

Mario was embarrassed. He held the towel in place as he scooped up his discarded clothing. "I am so sorry, Señorita. I was very tired and looking for a place to lie down. I saw the bath and I was so dirty. The water had already been used and I thought it would be all right."

The woman smiled coquettishly and reached up to stroke Mario's cheek. He tried to smile; but all he could manage was a grimace. He clutched his clothes to his chest and the toe of his boot was pressing hard against his healing wound.

"Please Señorita, turn around so that I can dress," he begged shyly.

"As you wish," the woman complied.

Mario went to a corner of the room and dressed quickly. He looked up and saw the young woman had positioned herself so that she could observe him in the dresser mirror. He could see that underneath her thick coat of garish makeup, she was little more than a child. Her prepubescent, small boned shape was girded into stays. The beginnings of a real beauty she had long, curly, dark hair and smoky eyes. Mario recalled Kate liked to hire very young girls to cater to the tastes of some of the older gentlemen. He pretended he wasn't interested in her advances and stooped to kiss her on the forehead as he left her room.

The party was going strong. Dimmed lighting revealed couples and threesomes involved in familiar activities. Many of the women appeared attractive and anxious to display their charms. A statuesque redhead approached him and held out her hand coyly. It was time to leave, he decided.

Weakly, Mario managed to drag himself to the door of Juan's hovel. His pride prevented him from staying in the warm house in the arms of the redhead because he knew he would be unable to do anything but sleep. In a shabby trunk stashed under dusty rags in the corner, Mario located some clean blankets. He draped them around him, kicked some of the empty bottles out of the way, and curled up on the floor.

Near morning Mario awoke to wind howling under the door and moonlight streaming through the window. His teeth were chattering and his stomach ached. With nothing to eat or drink for over a day, he was so hungry. Summoning his remaining strength, he crawled to Juan's cot. There were about four swallows of whisky left in a dusty bottle. Mario helped himself. Tears sprang to his eyes as the fiery liquid scalded his raw throat. He must find something to eat. He waited until the whisky began to take effect. Slowly, raising himself to his feet and holding on to the walls, he edged toward the door.

Mario opened the door to the bordello and the harsh morning light pierced its gloom. Various patrons and hostesses sprawled around the room like dirty laundry, stained clothing in disarray. No one noticed Mario greedily shoving leftover chunks of meat into his mouth. Instantly he was sorry and relieved his stomach into a large potted plant. As his nausea subsided, Mario cautiously ate a few bites at a time, allowing his body time to adjust.

Chapter 24

Nicholas clucked to his horse and shifted in the saddle. He turned back up the trail toward Pinos Altos. The night before he went to bury Guero's body and retrieve his own stylish clothes. When he arrived, his beautiful *sombrero* was lying in the dirt and ruined. Nicholas searched for Guero for hours, before returning to his tent outside of Pinos Altos. That morning, as he headed out to search, he saw the wagon leaving town and followed it. Now, he would scour the mountain and finish the job.

This was out of character for a *bandito* of his caliber Nicholas refused to allow Guero, that hideous giant, to win. He must find and kill him.

Nicholas returned to the place he left Guero, scouted around and found tracks. Following them, he discovered the Calhoun cabin, in a little valley near the trail. Dismounting, he tied his horse to a small scrub oak. Carefully dusting off his coat, he walked up to the cabin and knocked on the door. Sadie heard the knock and thought it was Sweeney. She shook her head, it was time for them to go into Silver City, to visit some relatives. Sweeney liked to tease, knocking at the door, and pretending to be a gentleman caller to see her. She was dressed in her best clothes, a long fawn colored skirt and striped bodice.

The stranger she had been caring for, disappeared during the night and despite a long search, Sweeney and Mark were unable to find him. Several weeks ago Sweeney promised to take her to Silver City. Sadie opened the door and swept into a curtsey.

Nicholas's eyes widened in surprise.

Sadie blushed and stuttered realizing the man standing before her was not her younger brother but a stranger. "G-good day, sir. May I help you?" she asked.

"*Buenos días,* Señorita. My name is Nicholas Marcos," Nicholas lied. He removed his ruined sombrero and swept into a bow. "I am looking for a good friend of mine. I believe he may be injured and I would like to help. He was in a bar fight and the man he fought is looking for him. I would like to find him first and warn him to be careful," Nicholas smiled revealing his pearly teeth.

Sadie shivered, she sensed this man was evil. He was probably the one who had inflicted that awful wound. Instinctively, she started to close the door.

"I am so sorry, Señorita. It is a bit cold today. I should come in to speak to you," Nicholas purred as he pushed his way inside. It took a few seconds for his eyes to adjust to the darkness of the room but he knew she was alone in the cabin. There were five beds in evidence, and one was in front of the fire. His oilskin was folded neatly at its foot.

Sadie shrank against the wall. Nicholas blocked the front door, her only chance was to escape through the back door. She decided to make a run for it. Unfortunately, Nicholas was too fast for her. He grabbed her arm and dragged her toward Mario's bed.

"You are not very polite, Señorita. You do not wish to stay and keep me company?" he whispered, pressing his lips to her ear.

Sadie shivered and stiffened. "Your friend is not here. There is no reason for you to stay. Please leave before my father and brothers return," she croaked, her voice deserting her.

Nicholas caressed her cheek with the back of one hand while maintaining a firm grip on her upper arm with the other. He liked what he saw. "You are all alone. I am not a stupid man. I find you very attractive and would like to spend some time with you. But first, you must tell me where my friend, Guero, has gone."

"I know nothing about anyone called Guero," Sadie said fearfully. Nicholas pushed her down on the floor and straddled her. She pounded at his arms and chest with her fists. Her legs were pinned under the man against the cold floor.

"Oh, but you do. I recognize my oilskin there on the bed. It has a torn edge and Guero borrowed it from me," Nicholas said. "Now let us not waste any more time, tell me where you have hidden him."

"I—I don't know where he is. When I woke up this morning, he had gone," Sadie gasped.

Nicholas smiled. "I believe you, I don't know why, but I do. I must find him before he notifies the sheriff. But I think I have time for a little fun first." He kissed her roughly and seized her hair, when she struggled he pulled it so hard that she could feel blood trickling from her scalp. Then he let go and pulled his knife out of its scabbard.

"I love women, especially the young pretty ones. I will not be angry if you struggle, it will make it more fun for me," Nicholas groaned.

Sadie choked as bile rose in her throat. She turned away but he jerked her head around and kissed her again.

"You are so lucky, Señorita. I am a good lover," he murmured.

"Please, don't..." Sadie gasped.

"That's right, little one. I like it when women fight me. It makes lovemaking more enjoyable," Nicholas grunted.

Sadie bit her lips until they bled. A loud noise caused Nicholas to jump. Sadie's ginger cat knocked a can of beans from the shelf. It landed on the floor beside them with a loud crash. Sadie caught Nicholas off-guard suddenly hitting him full force in the stomach with both her fists. Nicholas fell back, Sadie hit him again, and freed her legs. She gathered up her long skirt and pulling it up toward her waist, she ran for the back door. Nicholas was stunned for a moment. He reached the door and saw the girl disappearing into the brush away from the trail up to Pinos Altos.

He crashed out the door after her. This was getting more and more interesting. Perhaps she would lead him to Guero. Maybe she thought the odd looking giant would protect her.

Sadie headed for her father's claim. It wouldn't take her long to reach him if she could stay on the path. The brush scratched at her and the long skirt was cumbersome. She paused for a moment and heard the stranger crashing behind her hidden by thick scrub oak.

Quickly, Sadie slid out of her skirt and dropped it in a heap in the middle of the path. Now she could move her legs and run. The man was getting closer and she heard his heavy breathing in the thin high mountain air. She must get to her father.

Nicholas could see her up ahead. Her auburn hair straggled out behind her as she ran. She looked back over her shoulder and tripped but managed to regain her balance. Nicholas smiled. "Now is my chance," he thought, lunging for the girl. But she evaded his grasp. He fell, lying face down in the dirt as he stood and brushed himself off, he paused to admire her shapeliness in the tight chemise.

Buck heard Sadie before he saw her. He swung a pick and dropped it when he heard a noise behind him. He grabbed his rifle and was prepared to fire when he found himself face to face with his half naked daughter. "Sadie, what's wrong?" he yelled as she flung herself into his arms.

"Pa, there is a man after me. He forced his way into the cabin looking for the injured man we found," she gasped.

"Calm down. I'll take care of this," Buck said. "I'll have a surprise for him when he gets here. Sit down on that rock. Pretend that you have hurt your foot."

Sadie nodded. She sat down facing the path. Her shoes weren't meant for running so her feet did hurt. Leaning forward, she pretended to examine her right foot. She was badly shaken. Nicholas stopped and leaned against a tree, watching Sadie. The scrub oaks had given way to large Ponderosa pines as the path climbed up the mountain. *"Something isn't right,"* he thought suddenly.

"Put your hands on top of your head and turn around slowly, mister," a voice behind him, ordered.

"I have done nothing wrong, Señor. The little *señorita* misunderstood my intentions. I just wanted to speak to her for a few moments," Nicholas said politely, doing as he was told.

Buck looked at the *bandito* suspiciously. He looked familiar.

"What's your name, mister?" he asked.

"My name is Nicholas Marcos, as I told the *señorita*. The man I am looking for is called Guero. He is a good friend of mine and I only want to help him," Nicholas smiled.

"Well, let's see what the sheriff has to say about all of this," Buck said.

Nicholas obediently led the way back down the path to the Calhoun cabin. Buck kept his shotgun pressed against his back and Sadie followed, stooping to retrieve her discarded skirt.

When they reached the cabin, Buck handed Sadie the shotgun. He got a long piece of rope and after tying Nicholas's hands securely, he hitched up their horse to the wagon. Sadie put her skirt back on and tidied her hair, preparing to accompany her father to Silver City. When Mark and Sweeney showed up a few minutes later, the small group proceeded down the winding road toward the county seat and sheriff's office.

At the bottom of the mountain, six armed masked men blocked the road. Waving a gun at the family, the leader demanded they release their prisoner. "You must turn that man loose. If you do not, there won't be enough left of any of you for even the coyotes to find," the man demanded in a heavily accented voice.

"This man is going to see the Sheriff. He tried to hurt my daughter," Buck replied.

"Nicholas Oso is the greatest *bandito* in all of Mexico. A pitiful specimen will not be his undoing," the masked rider told him. "Let him go at once or I can promise that I will hurt your daughter."

Badly outnumbered and outgunned, Buck untied Nicholas. Nicholas grinned and bowed at the family. He leapt from the wagon and jumped up behind one of the riders in the group. "I will find Guero and when I do, I will tell him that you sent your regards. Just before I kill him," Nicholas sneered.

The band of men was on their way to Pinos Altos to meet Nicholas. They planned to meet him there and head for Mexico. Buck Calhoun and his family were luckier than most. If the men hadn't been in a hurry, they would have been killed. Buck continued on to Silver City and told the sheriff the story of the injured man and the *banditos*.

Sheriff Murphy scratched his whiskery face as he listened to Buck's tale. Sadie told him about the man the outlaws called Nicholas Oso and how he forced his way into their cabin and chased her up the mountain.

"Nicholas Oso is a wanted man. Too bad you couldn't bring him in. There is a reward for that no good son of a bitch and you could have claimed it. Pardon my language, Miss," Murphy said. "Now what can you tell me about the injured man?" The sheriff listened patiently as Buck told him all he knew.

Chapter 25

Frank shifted his aching muscles into a more comfortable position. Tomorrow, he would ask Mrs. McAllen for a cot or mattress. Working in the adobe hole was harder than anything he had ever done. His body felt bruised and battered. Since sleep was elusive, he rose quietly and got dressed. The lobby was deserted and as the huge clock in the corner chimed 3:00, Frank went outside. He inhaled deeply and gazed up at the night sky. The stars were so close he could almost touch them.

After a long walk, Frank's tight muscles relaxed and when he lay down on the floor, fully clothed, he slept instantly. What seemed like moments later, Prudence shook him gently.

"Aunt Felicity said it's time to go to church."

On Sundays, Frank's boss, Howard Champion required his men to report to work at 1:00. Frank and his family attended St. Vincent's Catholic Church services regularly. The day's sermon was presented by Archbishop Bourgade who expounded on the virtues of the Holy Roman father. Felicity daintily covered her yawns with her gloved palm and Frank was unceremoniously elbowed when he dozed. Only Prudence was enthralled by the Archbishop's service and didn't fidget as usual.

After church, they ate lunch in the Southern Hotel dining room. Felicity excused herself and went to plan the evening meal for hotel guests. Frank changed his clothes and reluctantly left for work. It would be nice, he thought, to spend some time with Prudence. Lately, he sensed his daughter's loneliness and it made him feel guilty. Mr. Whiskers, Mrs. McAllen's huge tabby, was her only playmate.

Later that night, Frank walked up Broadway toward the courthouse. Something isn't right, he sensed. There was no breeze and no activity at all on the street. A shot rang out and then another. Frank ducked behind a tree. Suddenly, men came rushing into the street from all directions.

"FIRE, FIRE," they yelled. One stout man rushed by blowing a whistle.

Smoke belched from J. O Campbell's drugstore. Men with axes chopped their way into the front of the store. A few carried buckets of water and tried to douse the encroaching flames. There was no hope for the drugstore and as the walls collapsed into twisted rubble, the men saw the adjacent building was burning as well. Frank saw Mr. Champion, dressed in his nightshirt and boots rushing toward the group of volunteer firemen.

"We need to stop the fire from spreading," he paused, "We have to blow up the saloon!"

"Are you crazy? Blow up the saloon?" a soot-blackened man grabbed Champion by the collar of his nightshirt.

"Calm down, it's the only way to stop the fire. He's right," Frank said. "Where do you keep your explosives, Mr. Champion?" Frank asked.

"Behind the blacksmith shop in the shed," Champion told him.

Frank hurried to get the dynamite and several men followed. When they returned, Champion was talking to Sam Eckstine, the owner of the Miner's Saloon.

"There ain't no other way to stop this fire?" Eckstine was visibly stunned.

Champion shook his head emphatically. As they discussed their options, flames licked the saloon roof and Eckstine nodded and turned away to hide the emotion on his face.

Curious onlookers gathered to watch so Eckstine and others warned everyone about the impending blast. When they were certain no one was inside any of the buildings. Frank and Champion placed sticks of dynamite in strategic places so the building would collapse inward and lessen the chance of stray sparks setting off more buildings.

The explosion rocked the entire section of town. Plate glass windows shattered. Shards of glass flew toward people removing store goods from adjacent buildings in the hope of saving some of them from destruction. All would be lost if the fire wasn't contained soon. Several buildings were destroyed; but so far no one had been killed or severely injured.

Champion clapped Frank on the back. "Looks like we did it, son." The powerful flames shrank into ash-choked darkness. Frank thought his bed on the floor would feel pretty good right now. But he and Champion stayed to help shopkeepers gather what they could salvage.

Martin Maher, a prominent Silver City resident, announced it was time to have a formal fire department. Later that morning, he was circulating among Silver City merchants and townspeople, trying to raise money to outfit a fire department.

"What's the matter with you? Can't you see that it is only a matter of time until a fire will come around and wipe us out? We don't even have enough buckets for a fire brigade, let alone a fire truck!" he protested loudly.

The electric lights on Bullard and Broadway were out and the Town Council was struggling to obtain assistance from El Paso.

"Mr. Maher, the townspeople are up in arms because we're unable to restore the electric light service. The lights take priority right now. Let's meet again in a couple of months about starting a fire department," the mayor told him.

Maher couldn't believe it was more important to have electric lights than a fire brigade. Their priorities were certainly misplaced! Angrily, he left the Town Council chambers and returned home. When Maher asked for volunteers to attend the Town Council meetings and express their opinions, Frank declined. Although Frank agreed with Maher, he was determined to maintain his anonymity.

As a new century approached, Silver City was experiencing growing pains.

Chapter 26

The night of the fire, Frank and Howard Champion became friends. They maintained a respectful working relationship during the day and played poker three nights a week.

"What have you done with your life? Champion asked Frank while they were sitting in the corner of the saloon one evening.

Frank shrugged. "Not much I guess."

"What kind of work experience do you have? I know you haven't always wanted to tote buckets of dirt out of a hole," Champion chuckled.

"I worked for the government and did some tracking. After I was married, I took up homesteading. Then I lost my arm and my wife. I couldn't continue doing what I loved and decided to move to town," Frank confided.

"The sheriff is looking for men with tracking experience," Champion clapped Frank on the shoulder. "We should let the sheriff know you're interested."

"Hold on a minute. I don't recall saying I was."

"Well, you should be. Our job ain't going to last much longer. The posse work won't be steady but it's pretty good money," Champion insisted.

"I've been doing my best not to bring attention to myself and my family." Frank needed someone he could trust. He told Champion about his relationship with the owners of Miner's Mercantile.

"I think you should talk to them and tell them they have a granddaughter," Champion leaned forward and squeezed Frank's shoulder.

"You don't understand. Jensen is a powerful man, he'll take Prudence away from me."

"Do you really think that it's fair to keep your daughter a secret?" Champion asked, leaning back in his chair and taking a long drag from a fat cigar.

"Do you know the Jensens?" Frank asked.

"Only by reputation. Mrs. Jensen is interested in civic affairs and Robert Jensen is a political force to be reckoned with and owns shares in many of the mining interests hereabouts."

"Exactly what I mean. He's a determined man. I'm sure he'd feel I'm a bad influence on my daughter," Frank confided.

"I guess you're right. But it's too bad they won't know their daughter's child," Champion said with a wink. "You think about tracking for the sheriff?"

Frank shrugged. He felt better having talked to Champion about his situation. He decided to talk things over with Felicity and see what she thought.

Temperatures dropped; but there was no rainfall to speak of. The adobe hole closed up and the men sought other forms of employment. Briefly, Frank worked for the Silver City and Fort Bayard Telegraph Service, delivering telegrams around town. In the vicinity of Miner's Mercantile, Frank pulled his hat down over his eyes and walked with a limp.

Felicity thrived on the compliments for her superb culinary achievements. The Southern Hotel became high on the list of places to stay for visiting dignitaries. Florence Jensen and Beatrice Farnsworth came for lunch on several occasions. Felicity kept Prudence out of sight, in the kitchen or tiny fenced yard in the back.

When Prudence was lonely, she climbed up to the hotel balcony and watched people going by on Hudson Street. She made up stories about the people she saw and imagined the ladies in nice carriages were queens with lots of pretty jewels. The men were desperadoes with six-shooters on their way to shoot up a bank and steal gold.

At bedtime, Felicity told Prudence stories and read borrowed books. Prudence's imagination was very active.

On the balcony, with her chin in her hands, Prudence watched some children playing below her in the street. She imagined they lived in a regular house with a mother and father. They had a lot of toys and brothers and sisters. They could go anywhere they wanted and didn't have to wear an ugly bonnet that kept the sun from shining on their faces and people from seeing them smile.

"Why can't I play, Papa?" she asked Frank as he tucked the covers around her.

"I watched you playing with Mr. Whiskers today," Frank smiled.

"I can't play with Teensy and Carmen. Aunt Felicity told them to go home when they came to see me," Prudence complained.

"She doesn't know them and I told her to keep an eye on you while I am working," Frank said sternly. He disliked Prudence's tone and had very little patience with whiny children.

"They could stay here and play," Prudence persisted.

"You'd make a lot of noise and disturb the guests. No more about this now, it is time for you to go to sleep." Frank kissed her on the forehead.

"But, Papa..." Prudence began.

"I said go to sleep," Frank interrupted, "We will talk about this tomorrow."

But Frank would not discuss it with her. He always changed the subject when she asked when she would be allowed to play with other children. Prudence talked through the fence with Teensy and Carmen. The girls were friendly but lost interest when they were told Prudence couldn't play with them.

Late in October, Frank delivered a telegram to R.D. Farnsworth at Miner's Mercantile. He pulled his hat down over his eyes and limped through the front door. Inside, he stared at the floor when he told the clerk he had a telegram for Mr. Farnsworth. Robert Jensen was standing in front of a large display of rifles, speaking to a well-dressed gentleman.

"I think you will find these are the finest rifles available in the territory," Jensen asserted, pointing to some gleaming Winchester 44s.

"I'm sure they are but they're a little rich for my blood," the man drawled.

"Looking at you, sir, I'd say you like quality. I'm telling you, these are the best," Jensen said. He glanced around and saw Frank standing near the counter. Something about Frank drew his attention for a moment.

The customer coughed. He was holding a pistol in his hand and aiming right at Jensen's midsection.

"Well, sir, you've convinced me. I'll take one," the man laughed.

Robert Jensen gasped. He tried to get the clerk's attention but he'd gone in the back to get Farnsworth. The only other person in the store was the telegram man with one arm and he was studiously ignoring him.

Jensen grinned sheepishly and carefully removed the Winchester from the gun rack and handed it to the thief.

"I like a man with good sense," the stranger said. He shouldered the rifle and walked out the door into the street without a backward glance.

"That man stole a rifle," Jensen yelled at the one-armed man standing at the counter.

Frank threw the telegram down on the counter and ran out the door, just as Farnsworth emerged from the back of the store. The clerk looked frightened when Jensen told Farnsworth about the robbery.

After the partners left the mercantile to find the sheriff, the clerk reached under the counter. Glancing around to see if anyone was looking, he pulled out an old revolver buried in a box of rags. He opened and rolled the cylinder and stuck the loaded gun in his belt. He wasn't taking any chances.

Frank waited until he saw Jensen and Farnsworth leave the Sheriff's Office. He offered his services as a tracker. Sheriff Murphy nodded at the one-armed man. He reached into his desk drawer and picked up a tin star. He tossed it to Frank who caught it deftly with his left hand.

"We're leaving in twenty minutes, meet us out front," Murphy grunted.

"I'll be here," Frank assured him. He rushed to the Southern Hotel to tell Felicity and gather up his gear.

Chapter 27

Mario stayed near the bordello during the day and ventured out only at night. Mrs. Stewart was a generous patroness. Pleased with Mario's handiwork, she paid him to fix broken furniture and care for her carriage and horses. She was surprised he kept his hands off the girls, but said nothing.

Juan bought him an occasional bottle of *mescal*, so Mario stayed out of saloons. Nicholas would come after him and he had no idea where Nicholas was. Letting his guard down could prove fatal. At night, when shadows of the trees shrouded his features, he would put on a shabby hat and pull it down low over his eyes. Sometimes he watched the street dances. Envying the handsome men holding the pretty *señoritas*, he'd go back to Juan's shack and drown his sorrows in some mescal or Juan's whisky.

One night in November, Mario sat on Juan's filthy floor. He was flicking cards into a hat a few feet away and taking occasional pulls on his bottle. Juan staggered in accompanied by a blast of frigid air.

"Hey *hombre*, good news! I hear that *bandito* that stabbed you has been caught. He and his *amigos* stole some sheep in *Méjico* and the *Federales* captured them," Juan said excitedly.

"How do you know this?" Mario wanted to know.

"It was in the newspaper," Juan answered.

"*Hombre*, you can't read," Mario snorted. "How can you be sure?"

"Alberto Castillo told me. He went to school and can read and write pretty good. He says that Señor Oso will never return to Silver City," Juan patted Mario on the shoulder. "This calls for a celebration, *mi amigo*. *Vamos a la cantina por cerveza!*"

"I don't want any beer. But I would like to get some air. Let us take a walk."

Juan laughed and shook his head. "Why should I want to do that if I'm not going to get some beer?" he laughed.

"*Bueno*, I'll see you later," Mario stood and picked up his hat.

The wind was blowing and Mario held his hat to prevent it from being carried away. For the first time in several months he could hold his head high. Juan was right, it was time for a celebration. Mario wanted to enjoy his newfound freedom and not dull his pleasure with alcohol, at least not yet.

Lost in thought, Mario realized he was walking up Chihuahua Hill past the house where Blanca had lived. If only he had warned her about Nicholas, she might still be alive. The pretty angel in Pinos Altos was also on his mind. She was a real lady and would make a fine wife and mother for some lucky man. Mario's face burned with shame. He was still a tough *hombre* but something inside changed forever when he was stabbed. Feelings of guilt about his past were his constant companions now.

Walking down the hill, he heard shouts and laughter coming from the saloon but he continued along Bullard Street at a leisurely pace. Two young lads rushed past him and disappeared into an alleyway. Mario watched as two older gentlemen ran to the front door of the New York Clothing House and began kicking it. When the door gave way, Mario smelled kerosene. A drunk staggered by and reached out to grab Mario's arm to steady himself but Mario evaded him. The drunk regained his balance, straightened his coat and proceeded to the nearest saloon. While Mario watched, the men got the clothing store fire under control. Outwardly, the building seemed to have sustained little damage.

It was time to make plans for his future. When he returned to Juan's house, Mario sat quietly for several hours. He had few options so decided to try his hand at gold mining. He pictured himself with a pick and shovel; ripping the earth wide open and gold spilling out to cover his boots. He'd become a rich man and find the Mother Lode. Or while panning, he would find a nugget the size of his fist.

Once an old prospector confided to him that most gold miners died as poor or poorer than when they started but when one prospector died, there were usually two to take his place.

No, silver mining would be smarter. He'd work hard and save his money. When he had enough, he could buy a *ranchito* and raise some cattle. Maybe someday, he'd find a *señorita* to share his life.

The next day, he bade goodbye to Juan Hernandez, Kate Stewart and her girls. He used his sparse savings to buy Rosita from Mr. Goodell.

"That stupid burro has been nothing but trouble. You're welcome to her," Goodell told Mario as he tossed him a worn bridle.

Mario went to Camp Fleming. Several of the crew frequented Mrs. Stewart's establishment and were friendly enough. Bursting with pride when he received his first paycheck, he accompanied some miners to a dance in Silver City. Mario was teased and told he thought he was too good to dance. Mario took the ribbing good-naturedly. He didn't know how.

Chapter 28

"What's the matter *hombre*? Can't you read?" Paco Grijalva chortled. "You really are as dumb as they say, aren't you?" He jabbed Mario in the ribs with his bony elbow. Mario swung hard, slugging him in the jaw. Paco's head snapped as he slammed into the wall of the foreman's office.

A large sign had been posted on the office door earlier that day. Mario stood around listening to bits of conversation, hoping to find out what it said. His pride wouldn't allow him to ask. The bold, black letters nearly leapt off the paper and Mario cursed himself because he couldn't read.

Paco wasn't laughing as he shook his head and lunged, grabbing Mario around the throat. Mario snarled punching the smaller man in the gut. Paco's breath reeked of stale tobacco and stung Mario's eyes.

"You stink," Mario caught a handful of Paco's hair and shoved his head into a water trough. Paco flailed and struggled. As Mario pulled Paco to his feet, the door to the foreman's shack burst open.

"What in the hell is going on out here?" the foreman, Donald Greer, demanded.

"Nothing boss, just fooling around," Mario said. Paco was sputtering and shook like a wet dog.

"Get out of here both of you or you won't have a job in the morning," Greer shook his fist and muttered under his breath as he stormed back inside and slammed the door.

Paco rubbed his aching jaw. "This isn't over, Guero," he growled. Grijalva shared a tent with Mario and two others. Now, Mario would be forced to watch his back again. The black letters of the sign mocked him. They were clear to his eyes but he couldn't understand them. If he could see them, why wouldn't they speak to him as they did to others?

Father Reynaldo, a priest from Silver City, visited camp weekly and brought holy water and communion wafers. Many of the miners were Catholic, so he prayed with them, heard confessions, and even read and wrote some letters. His rich voice reading Bible passages was pleasant and soothing. Mario greatly admired Father Reynaldo but hesitated to ask for his help.

"Is something troubling you, my son?" Reynaldo asked him, one cool afternoon in April as Mario saddled the *padre's* mule for his return trip to Silver City.

"Why do you ask?" Mario shrugged.

"No reason, except you seem to be avoiding me lately," the kind priest patted Mario's shoulder.

"*Sí*, Padre, you are right. I have been wanting to ask you something, but don't know how," Mario admitted.

The priest's benevolent face was suddenly lit with a radiant smile. Mario smiled back.

"Father, I can't read. I want to learn but there is no one to teach me. I'm an old man, nearly twenty-three and I can't go to school," Mario whispered.

"Why do you wish to read?" the older man asked.

"The letters are proud. They speak to some, but not to me. I'd like to know what they are saying."

"Well, good!" the priest reached into his saddlebag and pulled out a small package wrapped in brown paper and string and placed it in Mario's hands.

"By the end of the summer, you will be able to read every word in this book. Next year, we can begin on the classics! After that, who knows?" the priest rubbed his hands together in delight.

Mario's hands shook as he put the package inside his shirt. He went up the hill and sat behind a small juniper tree. Father Reynaldo promised to return in two days to begin his reading lessons. Fumbling with the string, Mario discovered it was a new book. Bound in blue leather, the cover had writing and even pictures of two children and a dog. Reverently, he examined the pages. Even the smell of the paper and ink made him tingle with anticipation.

"Very soon," he told himself, "I will be a smart man."

Chapter 29

"The hotel will be closed soon. You and your family should look for other accommodations," Mrs. McAllen told Felicity early one morning as she was preparing breakfast.

"The Southern is closing?" Felicity gasped.

"I'm afraid so. I hoped that Mr. Abraham would change his mind. I'm sorry, my dear."

"Where will we go?" Felicity asked. "Frank wants to buy a house but hasn't saved enough yet."

"I'm retiring. I've worked a long time and have a little nest egg. My feet and legs are worn out," Mrs. McAllen sighed, "It will be nice to sleep late once in awhile."

"Is Mr. Abraham planning to sell? Maybe I could speak to the new owner," Felicity said hurriedly. "There must be something I can do!"

"I believe he has already sold it, to Mr. G.T. Reid. Mr. Reid wants to remodel it and close the dining room."

"You can't be serious? People come from miles around to eat here. Why would he want to close the dining room?" Felicity clapped her floury hand over her mouth.

Mrs. McAllen smiled at the younger woman.

"I'm sure I don't know. I guess he just doesn't want to have to worry about feeding his customers. There's a lot of competition out there. I understand that the Broadway Hotel is going to be managed by Ah Den, the Chinaman."

"Our business is wonderful," Felicity said, as she dabbed at her face with a wet dishtowel. "I've got to speak to Mr. Reid!"

Later that night, Frank tried to calm his distraught sister. "Don't talk to Mr. Reid about the dining room. It is a good way to get us booted out of here. Right now, I'm not making enough money to buy a house."

"But Frank, the dining room is bringing in a lot of money. He would be foolish to close it down," Felicity retorted. Anger crept into her voice despite her efforts to stay calm.

"I agree, but it's his establishment and we're his guests."

G.T. Reid allowed Frank and his family to stay in exchange for their help with the remodeling. The Southern Hotel was reopened to the public without a kitchen and dining facility early the following year. Felicity was made head housekeeper and received a small salary and did not have to pay rent.

Reid was appalled by the condition of Hudson Street. He approached the Town Council about the ruts and sea of mud that patrons had to wade through, and was told Main Street was in as bad or worse shape.

When a skating rink opened nearby, Felicity took Prudence to watch the skaters. Prudence loved the piano accompaniment. Nearly bouncing off the bench, Prudence wanted to skate. Felicity told her she'd have to wait until she was a little older.

"Those bigger children can barely keep their balance. Look those two just crashed into each other," Felicity pointed at two children, both about ten, sitting on the floor looking around dazedly.

Prudence enjoyed the outing so much she begged her aunt to take her with her when she went on errands. Frank relented but insisted Prudence wear the oversized bonnet.

Chapter 30

In the sweltering heat, Silver City people prayed for rain but it didn't come in early July. Lightening and thunder teased in the distance. The thunderheads built up, but the wind blew them away. Florence sat on her front porch and watched the street. Li Soo was late coming back from the market and Robert would be home soon.

The news of Emma's death, nearly two years earlier, had aged Florence. Florence's letters to Emma were put in a trunk tied with the Emma's blue hair ribbon. Every night, Florence knelt beside Emma's bed to pray.

As Robert grieved, he hoped Florence would forgive herself. Emma's portrait hanging above the fireplace reminded him every day she was gone. Today, he trudged up the road toward his house wishing things were different.

Li Soo watched him walking ahead of her. It seemed a shame that a man with all of his money had to walk back and forth to work, instead of riding in fine carriages like his neighbors.

Robert felt someone watching him and turned to see the slight figure of his housekeeper hurrying toward him carrying two large canvas bags.

"Let me help you with those, they look heavy," Robert offered kindly.

"No sir, I can manage, thank you," Li Soo smiled and lifted the sacks a little higher.

Robert shrugged and continued on. His sweat soaked shirt was chafing his neck and wrists. The slight breeze of the morning had changed to gusts. Little dust devils whirled in the street ahead of him. He found himself longing for a cold beer.

Having spent the morning looking for Chan Cho, Li Soo's head was full of worries. She sensed her father was right, she should stay away from Chan. But she'd loved him for so long.

Every week, Li Soo visited all of Chan's favorite haunts. Shivering, she recalled the waxy yellow skin and dead eyes peering through a small hole in a door. Long bony fingers grasped her money and slammed the shutter in her face. Why would anyone go inside, she wondered? Yet the opium den on Yankee Street seemed the most likely place to find Chan Cho. Li Soo looked in her tiny purse and found she had a few coins. A woman hurried past and brushed against her arm. The coins flew from her fingers and were scattered in the dust of the road.

"Allow me, Señorita," Li Soo heard a voice say as she stooped to pick up her money. A blond man towered over her. He knelt to help.

"Thank you," Li Soo said politely. She stood and brushed the dust from her hands. The man handed her the money and tipped his hat. What a strange looking man, she thought.

Li Soo put her hand on his arm. "Please sir, you seem like a kind man. I was wondering if you might do me a very large favor?" Li Soo asked timidly.

"I would be happy to be of assistance," Mario said smiling at the pretty girl and careful not to show his teeth.

"My childhood friend is in trouble and I would like to help. I am a woman and cannot enter an opium den. His name is Chan Cho," Li Soo admitted.

"I don't go into those places. I hope your friend is not inside. That is a very bad place. I've seen the fiends in this street at night, dirty, smelling like rotting flesh," Mario shuddered.

"I am so frightened for him. Please, sir, help me find my friend," Li Soo pleaded.

Mario looked at the tiny woman; she didn't dare enter the opium den. "I'll see if your friend is inside. Stay on the other side of the street near that tree and don't bring attention to yourself," Mario ordered.

Li Soo smiled and pressed her remaining coins into Mario's hand but he wouldn't accept them. "No Señorita, I'll ask about this man, but I won't pay for information. Do as I say, stand over under that tree," Mario pointed across the street.

Li Soo trembled as she watched the man enter the opium den. She waited a long time for him to reappear. Florence would be angry if she was much longer.

The door creaked open and the man came out into the street. He blinked several times and seemed dazed. Li Soo rushed over to him. "Are you all right, sir?" she asked.

"It's much worse inside than I imagined. Your friend hasn't been seen in several days. I was told that he owes a lot of money to some very bad men and they're looking for him. I think you should go home little *señorita* and forget about him."

Tears sprang to her eyes as she nodded numbly and thanked him. She had to finish her shopping and get back to the Jensen's. Hurrying to the mercantile, she made her purchases and started for home.

When Robert finally reached the porch, he stopped to lean against the post and was perspiring profusely. Li Soo rushed around him and came back with a large glass of lemonade.

He sat down heavily in the rocking chair next to Florence who handed him a clean handkerchief. Robert sipped the cool drink; it wasn't beer but it was wet.

Several weeks later, Li Soo walked past the opium den on a cold, windy night. The building hulked in the shadows. A cloying smell permeated the dank air as Li Soo wished she'd chosen another route home.

In her parent's home, Li Soo could truly be herself. Her parents' values were strict, old-worldly, and difficult to understand but she knew of their love and faith in her. Her mother didn't offer her any advice about Chan Cho. She stood beside her silently with her hand on Li Soo's shoulder while her husband counseled their daughter. It wasn't necessary for her to say anything because whatever Lan decided, Mai would agree.

"I have heard you still seek Chan Cho and you went to an opium den to find him. I am very troubled that you have disobeyed me. I ask you to leave this house and not return until you have given up on this quest," Lan's voice shook with emotion.

This was worse than being slapped.

"My father, if I may speak?" Li Soo whispered.

"Of course," Lan answered.

"I have taken your advice and am no longer searching for Chan. I am sorry my father, if I have distressed you and hope that you will forgive me," Li Soo murmured, looking down at her feet, respectfully.

Lan paced, his hands clasped behind his back. He paused and walked over to his daughter. Cupping her chin in his hand, he tipped her head gently, until she was looking into his eyes.

"It will be as though it never happened. You are welcome to stay as long as you wish."

Lan lit his pipe and shuffled over to sit in front of the fireplace. It would devastate him to lose his daughter's respect but he remained firm in his resolve to keep her safe from the baser members of their race.

Li Soo stayed with her parents for a few days. After living in a Western household, she felt like a lost soul. The rituals, so much a part of her childhood, seemed foreign to her now. She grieved silently for innocence and youth. Now she was aware that her parents, she'd once believed immortal and imminently wise, were really only middle-aged people entrenched in Old World customs.

"You are so quiet, my daughter, is something troubling you?" Mai asked, the following morning.

Li Soo shook her head and said nothing.

"Very well, we will speak of it when you can put your feelings into words," Mai walked away, appearing more fragile than Li Soo remembered.

It was unkind to compare the Soo household with the Jensen's. They were much different. The Soos were not wealthy but sent a large portion of their income to relatives in Canton. The atmosphere at the Jensen's was calm and uncluttered. No rituals took up a good part of their day. Meals were prepared and served at certain times but other than a prayer before eating, and a weekly excursion to church, Robert and Florence Jensen were not obvious about their religious beliefs.

"Mother, I am trying to adjust to living with this Western family," Li Soo admitted later as she helped her mother prepare the meal.

"It must be very difficult for you. Remember to allow yourself time for the process. Take some from the old ways and combine them with the new. In this way, you can truly be yourself," Mai recommended.

In the past several months, Li Soo thought about some of the old Chinese traditions. The ones she felt strongly about were incorporated into her new life. She was learning to eat with a spoon and fork because it helped her fit in better. Li Soo thought wearing Western-style clothing might help her feel less foreign but it was a difficult decision. It made her feel strange when visitors to the Jensen household stared at her when she entered the room.

"A time will come when all of the questions you have will be answered. Don't strive for change too quickly, take your time with decisions that will affect you for the rest of your life," Mai counseled.

"Thank you, my mother. You are very wise."

Li Soo went back across town following the same route. She felt lighter because she had cast aside her burdens and could explore and embrace this New World and all of its wonders and mysteries.

Chapter 31

Nearly half the town turned out to watch the long procession. O. S Warren had been a well-respected man. The black hearse, pulled by a matched black team, led the way down Main Street, past his home and his newly completed office. Dr. Slough and John Miller escorted Elizabeth Warren and her children to the cemetery. The last few days had taken their toll on them and they all sat in the coach dry eyed and pale.

Florence and Robert were in the funeral procession. Florence wanted to offer condolences to Elizabeth at the funeral. The only thing that she could think of was "I'm sorry".

Elizabeth smiled at her and nodded, "It happened so suddenly." She blinked several times and her eyes sparkled with tears behind her spectacles. "He was a good man."

Florence nodded and Robert bent to kiss Elizabeth's cheek.

"It will be so hard for her now," Florence whispered as she and Robert neared their coach.

"It will indeed. But she can go to her family if she decides not to stay in Silver City," Robert answered. "She's a spunky little thing, she might stay and give the people around here a run for their money."

"Oh, Robert, don't be silly, she's a woman. There is only so much she can do."

"Whatever you say, dear," Robert chuckled. He recalled seeing Elizabeth working in the lamplight, late in the evening, in her husband's office. Influential people talked and Elizabeth's name was mentioned almost as much as her husband's, during political discussions.

Dinner was late being served because Quetta was angry. Florence and Robert heard her in the kitchen banging pans and jabbering away in Spanish. Li Soo served the soup and main course almost simultaneously.

"What's wrong with this household?" Robert demanded a large vein pulsed in his temple.

"I'll speak to her as soon as we are finished, dear," Florence patted his arm. "Now eat your food before it gets cold."

Robert grimaced when he tasted his soup. "Is she trying to poison us? What is this slop? He threw his napkin on the table and scrapped back his chair. Stomping into the kitchen, he demanded to know what was going on.

"It is not a good day for me, Señor. Li Soo went to the gardens and brought me back some vegetables. Some of them were rotten. They were buried under some good ones and I did not know they were bad until I was preparing your dinner. The milk was spoiled. The dinner wasn't good and I am ashamed," Quetta blurted out, all in one breath.

"I won't have this kind of behavior in my house. Dinner is to be served on time and should be well planned and prepared. My wife is upset; go to the dining room and apologize to her, at once," Robert demanded angrily. His complexion matched his temper. His brows were drawn together tightly and his face was suffused with blood.

Quetta nodded meekly and curtseyed. She ducked her head and scurried for the dining room. Florence rose from her chair and smoothed her dress. "I am very disappointed in you. You have never behaved in this manner before and I warn you, it must never happen again," Florence hissed through clenched teeth.

"*Sí*, Señora," Quetta whispered meekly. "Will that be all?"

"You may return to your duties now," Florence sniffed. The funeral had tired her and she wasn't about to quarrel with the domestic staff tonight.

Robert's head was throbbing as though it would explode. The doctor warned him about getting so angry. Sometimes it happened suddenly, without warning. Dr. Woodville told him to pay more attention to his health and advised him to walk to work and back every day. Unfortunately, the good doctor informed Florence and she demanded that Robert do it.

Since then, Robert lost a little weight and lost his temper less frequently.

Emma's picture over the dining room table smiled down on him when he returned to finish his dinner. Perhaps he would feel better tomorrow. It was Saturday and he could relax with a book in front of the fire.

Florence, seated across from him, watched with concern on her face. "I think you should get more exercise. Tomorrow we will take a stroll downtown to watch the skaters. It will be good for both of us," Florence insisted.

Robert shrugged. "Yes dear." Perhaps he would have time to read when they returned from the skating rink. His eyes sought his daughter's picture, and she smiled at him reassuringly.

Chapter 32

"Have you lost your mind?" Felicity demanded. Her red hair stuck out at odd angles from her head. She pulled at it as she screamed at her brother.

"No, I don't think so. I have to go somewhere to make some fast money. The prospectors have been pulling gold out of Kingston for at least eight years and there doesn't seem to be any end to it. I know a man that owns a rich claim up there and he needs someone to watch out for his interests while he is away. He is a friend of Champion's and offered me the job. It is only for about two months," Frank asserted.

"I suppose that means that Prudence and I will stay here while you are off gallivanting around the country. I'm not your daughter's mother, I love her but she isn't my responsibility and the sooner you realize that, the better," Felicity stormed around the room flinging clothes out of her trunk onto the floor and bed.

"Let me explain. I'm almost out of money and I'm not making enough to support us. If I take this job, we can stay here and have a little money to put aside in case of an emergency," he continued calmly. "I just want to do what's best for us, that's all."

"The money I bring in isn't enough for us to live on but when you are working, we get by," Felicity cried, tears streaming down her face.

"Please understand me, I'm not deserting you. I want us to have some security. The jobs in Silver City don't pay much and although the sheriff said I could do some tracking for him; I can't depend on the money because it isn't steady work."

"I don't think it's good for Prudence to be away from you for so long. She needs her father," Felicity swiped at her cheeks with the corner of one of her petticoats she had thrown on the bed. "Maybe we could come with you."

"I've thought about that and it's not a good idea. There aren't many women there and I'm not sure I could protect you. You have to understand, I only want what's best for all of us," her brother said calmly.

Felicity shook her head, fighting a fresh onslaught of tears. It wasn't fair! She'd abandoned her life to help her brother, found that she would be responsible for his child and now he was leaving them to go up into the mountains to protect a gold mine. She turned to face him and shrugged her shoulders. She knew that look, he'd already decided to go and nothing she could say would dissuade him.

"What if I said I would just pack up and leave; what would you do then?" Felicity demanded.

"I'd hire someone to look after Prudence and go anyway."

"I'm not surprised. You're the most stubborn man I have ever met!" Felicity gave the clothes she was holding a toss and stomped out of the room, slamming the door.

Frank grinned. He knew his sister would stay and look after Prudence. He picked up a worn canvas Army bag and began to pack. He'd leave for Kingston tomorrow morning early.

Felicity stood on the porch of the Southern Hotel. The chilly wind plucked at her thin shirtwaist and she shivered. The tingle down her spine was partly premonition and partly an illogical fear; if Frank left, he might never come back. The mountains around Kingston were full of bandits, rustlers, and outlaws. Apaches raided the camp and took what they could carry. Frank was right; it wasn't a good place for a woman and child. It wasn't a good place for a one-armed man either.

Frank felt guilty leaving them, even for a short period of time. Prudence followed him around as he gathered his clothes. Taking one look at his daughter's sad face, he stopped to pick her up. As he sat down on the edge of the bed, he hugged her until she begged him to stop.

"Papa, Aunt Felicity and me don't want you to go," Prudence said.

"Pru, do you remember your Mama at all?" Frank asked.

Prudence's eyes filled with tears as she nodded.

"What I remember best about your Mama was how much she loved us. Remember when she used to hold you on her lap and you would both play the piano?"

Again Prudence nodded.

"I made a promise to your Mama that someday I would give something to you that was very, very special to her. I think this is the time," Frank reached into his shirt pocket and pulled out a small package and handed it to Prudence.

"When I leave in the morning, I want you to open this package and remember that no matter where I go, no matter how far away, your Mama and I will always be with you. Can you do that for Papa?" Frank kissed the top of Prudence's head as she nestled up against his chest.

"Yes, Papa."

Early the next morning, Frank kissed Prudence and hugged Felicity. He assured his sister that he'd be back by the middle of March. Mounting old Sassy, he swung the mule's head around and headed north, out of town.

Prudence saw that her aunt was crying and began to cry.

"Papa will come back to us won't he?" Prudence asked in a tiny voice.

"I hope so, Pru, I hope so," Felicity said soothingly.

Prudence went out to the small yard behind the Southern Hotel. Some crates were stacked against the fence. She crawled underneath them. A small chink of light shown down on the package she held in her hands.

It was cool but not cold for late January. The trail was well traveled and it only took Frank three days to get to Kingston. The smell of meat cooking over a campfire was Frank's introduction to the town he'd heard so much about.

A wagon approached stacked with furniture and several trunks. A tiny woman sat perched on the seat beside a disgruntled looking older man. Even at a distance, Frank could hear the obscenities the woman was flinging at him. When the wagon stopped suddenly, it appeared the whole load was about to crash down on top of the occupants.

Frank kicked Sassy causing the mule to bray loudly and sidestep. He kicked him again and headed over toward the teetering load.

"Get out of the way, that furniture is about to come down on top of you," Frank yelled.

The man looked up at the load, "Damn Sarah, he is right! Get down, quick!" he shoved the tiny woman off the seat and she barely managed to land on her feet. He jumped off beside her and the man and Frank struggled to keep the furniture from falling.

"I guess I should have tied them ropes tighter. Much obliged," the man said. "Name's Orchard, my wife, Sarah," the man held out a calloused hand to Frank.

"Nice to meet you. My name is Latimer Jones. I'm here to work for Calvin Harrington. Do you know him?"

"Sure, I know of him. We're moving from Hillsboro. Plan to set up a stage business here," Orchard said.

"Mr. Jones, I believe that is your friend Mr. Harrington coming out of the hotel," the woman said in a lilting British accent.

"Thank you, ma'am, so it is. Sorry to be rude but I need to catch up to him," Frank said hurriedly.

"Thanks again for your help, young man," Orchard said.

"Anytime, sir," Frank said as he grabbed Sassy reins and ran to stop Harrington before he entered a noisy saloon.

Chapter 33

The crisp spring morning was perfect for planting. Li Soo gathered her gardening supplies and put them in her canvas bag. She started early to be back before the Jensens left for church.

Very few people were about as she made her way down Black Street. It was planting time and she knew she would see her family already there, working in the cool of the day. "Trees of Heaven" lined the road near the Gardens. Li Soo's mother, Mai brought seeds from the Old Country and planted them around their garden plot. They lent color and mystique to the landscape. Li Soo believed they were like ancient Chinese spirits watching over the Chinese Americans.

Mai was bent over a furrow poking seeds into the moist earth. "I am so happy to see you, my daughter. I was afraid you could not come," Mai smiled.

Li Soo saw the lines in her mother's face. Mai's life was hard, she worked all week in the laundry, kept house, cooked, cleaned, and worked on Sundays in the garden. Others had garden plots to supplement their incomes by selling their produce to the locals.

"Mother, you look so tired. Please, try to get more rest. I can come help at the laundry on Tuesdays, my day off," Li Soo said with concern.

"You need your rest as well. What would I do if I didn't work?" Mai smiled again as she returned to her planting.

"How is my family?" Li Soo asked realizing her mother would continue to do as she pleased.

"They are well. Your father is at home today. A dignitary from China is visiting in the area and your father hopes that he might come to Silver City." She paused for a moment. "What of Chan?" Mai asked.

Li Soo looked at her hands, "I have done as my father asked and am no longer searching for him. Sometimes I feel as though I have no one left to care about, other than my family."

"Your heart is good. The great Confuscius said, "To hear in the morning that The Way prevails is to die without regret in the night"," Mai said.

"Thank you my mother," Li Soo said quietly, a lone tear slipped from her eye and rolled down her cheek. She reached into her canvas bag for her gardening tools. Working in the moist pungent soil always made her feel better.

Time passed quickly, when Li Soo packed up her things and started for the Jensen house, the church bells tolled and the birds chirped in the trees. Li Soo felt alive and young with her whole life ahead of her. The burden of trouble that Chan had laid upon her was going to slip away.

Florence and Robert climbed into their carriage when Li Soo arrived.

"You're very late," Florence admonished. "I've left a list of chores for you on the table. Please see that they're done and lunch is prepared by the time we come home." She flicked her fingers at Li Soo as she dismissed her. Li Soo sighed and went inside.

Chapter 34

Summer storms hit with a vengeance. Sodden streets were clogged with all manner of refuse. The City Fathers were outraged and demanded citizens be more careful with their disposal of garbage. Many demanded a wagon be hired to pick up and haul waste out of town.

Churning mud welled up and seeped into cracks in building foundations. Florence refused to visit Miner's Mercantile, after getting stuck in her carriage just outside, one afternoon after a heavy rain.

"You must take the horse to work while it's raining so much," Florence said to Robert during breakfast the next morning.

"What about needing to walk? A little rain won't hurt me," Robert said, sipping his coffee. He loved to tease Florence unmercifully.

"You know very well the streets are in disrepair and without a horse you may not get to work," Florence informed him indignantly. She knew Robert was teasing her and she was not in the mood for it!

"Very well, my dear. I'll take the horse." He folded his newspaper and leaned over to kiss her on the cheek. "I'll be off then."

Robert stepped onto the front porch and took a deep breath. The acrid rain-washed air smelled wonderful and a light mist caressed his cheeks. The bay horse nickered when Robert entered and snuffled his coat for carrots. Robert hadn't forgotten and he pulled a carrot from his pocket. "I knew she would tell me to ride today, I just knew it. She thinks I'm lazy," he patted the horse and bridled her. A big shipment of mining equipment was arriving at the train depot and he wanted to be sure that it was delivered and on the shelves before payday.

The Miner's Mercantile was conveniently close to the depot and made the deliveries easier for them than most other area businesses. In some cases, the heavy delivery wagons bogged down in the mud and had to be unloaded before they reached the stores.

Robert saddled the mare and led her to his mounting stump. It was difficult to climb on, so he used a large stump in the yard. "Ugh," he groaned as he struggled to gain his seat in the saddle.

Florence watched from the upstairs window. She must consult the doctor again. All of the walking did little to decrease his girth. There must be something else she could do. She opened the window in the front bedroom and watched as Robert trotted up the street on the bay mare. She worried so much about him.

Florence sighed, went downstairs, and out into the garden. The roses bloomed in riotous colors. In the corner of the yard was Emma's favorite, the coral rose. It looked a little bedraggled the week before but Florence lavished a lot of attention on it and restored it to its former glory.

She paused, as she heard the tinkling laughter of a little girl close by. Closing her eyes, she sat down on the garden bench and listened to the little voice singing a nursery rhyme. An idea came to her. Florence went into the house and sat down at the piano. She played the simple song the girl had been singing. She smiled and thought about Emma.

Outside the singing stopped as the little girl and her aunt listened to the piano music. Felicity drew a sharp breath. Prudence pressed her cheek against the fence and thought about her mother. In her tiny fingers, she held a silver locket with the name, *EMMA,* engraved on it.

Chapter 35

Frank's two-month job in Kingston lasted closer to four months. He knew being gone that long was not fair to Felicity but he needed the money and had corresponded regularly with "his girls" as he liked to refer to them. Felicity admitted that the money Frank sent made her feel more secure. She opened an account at the Meredith Ailman bank. Mr. Ailman, co-owner and a prominent man in the community, had assisted her with the paperwork.

Frank rode into Silver City, the end of April. His demeanor was different. He felt a sense of pride in himself again and it was obvious to everyone he met. Sheriff Woods knew Latimer Jones was a good tracker. Frank met Woods outside the County Jail the day after he returned.

A few weeks earlier, when Frank was still in Kingston, the Sierra County sheriff, J.W. Allen was killed, under very suspicious circumstances, while trying to disarm a drunk. "Glad you're back. Truth is, I could use your help. J.W. Allen was a friend of mine. We can't trust some of our law enforcement people. It seems Deputy Belt and Mr. Gillett chased Nick Ware into Mexico after it was discovered that he and his bunch had been rustling horses. Ware was a Texas Ranger and Silver City deputy." Wood admitted.

"What can I do to help?" Frank alias Latimer Jones, asked.

"I'd like to deputize you. I know you like to keep a low profile and I'm not sure why. I doubt it's because you're dishonest. I pride myself in being able to tell what a man is made of after meeting him a few times. You'd be a real asset to Silver City law enforcement. I'd call on you whenever we needed a tracker for a posse. We can't pay much but can manage a small retainer fee, if that's agreeable."

Frank didn't know what to say. He was flattered but also concerned that his duties might keep him away from Prudence and Felicity for long periods of time.

"Let me think about it, sir," Frank said.

"Sure, let me know as soon as you can," Woods nodded.

A few weeks later, Sheriff Woods and Deputy Belt waylaid and shot a man running down an arroyo east of town. The man was ordered to stop by the sheriff and continued to flee. The man had a badly crippled hand and partially severed fingers. He was in the possession of an expensive Winchester rifle. The serial numbers matched the one taken from Miner's Mercantile. Woods and Belt suspected that he might be involved in the murder of Deputy Hall, who had been ambushed by Sheriff Allen's killer. The fugitive gave the name of Manuel Gonzalez and was a hardened criminal from Mexico.

Frank decided to take Sheriff Woods up on his offer, and for several months was kept busy, tracking leads. Deputy Hall had been killed about a mile above town on his way back from Pinos Altos. By the time Frank started investigating the case, the trail of the killer was extremely cold. Nevertheless, Sheriff Woods insisted that he do everything he could to bring Hall's murderer to justice.

Frank's inquiries led to several dead ends. Discouraged, Frank reported what he had been able to discover.

"The wood-haulers reported seeing a man leading a horse with a woman astride. It looked to them like the man had a rifle. That was all they saw. I have questioned others known to be in the vicinity at the time but no one reports having seen anything suspicious or hearing gunshots.

I located and spoke to the young woman, Miss Alvarez. She admitted a man named Pilar shot Hall in cold blood when he asked too many questions. Pilar went to a settlement near the San Francisco river. I found two men who saw someone who met his description, about a week after Hall's murder. They both believe Pilar went back to Mexico."

Sheriff Woods grunted. What could he expect? It seemed that Hall's murderer would never be caught. He marveled at Jones's ability to get the young woman to talk. She'd been extremely reluctant to speak at the coroner's hearing and seemed to be terrified that Pilar might retaliate.

Woods propped his feet up on his desk and leaned back in his chair. Frank shook his head and left the office. The threat of Indian raids was gone since Geronimo's capture. There must be a way to get a grip on the criminal elements in Grant County, if only Woods could muster enough indignant citizens. But how?

Chapter 36

Frank smiled as Prudence showed her aunt the picture of her mother inside her locket. Before giving the memento to his daughter, Frank carefully removed the picture of Emma's parents. He didn't know why but he put it inside a small box hidden among his clothes.

"Do you think I look like her?" Prudence asked her aunt for the hundredth time.

"Yes, you look exactly like her," Felicity repeated. "I'll bet when you grow up you will be able to play the piano just like her too."

Frank sighed, causing both of "his girls" to look at him. It bothered him he couldn't afford to buy a house, piano and lessons for Prudence but it wasn't possible. Despite his search, a lucrative job in Silver City continued to elude him. So far, all he could find were poor paying temporary positions. He'd bartended, chopped wood, worked as a janitor, anything to keep them fed and clothed. He and Felicity were determined not to touch their savings.

Tracking with a sheriff's posse brought in some extra money but the retainer was so small it didn't help much with their expenses.

Frank went outside for some fresh air as Felicity and Prudence continued their needlework. Felicity was teaching Prudence some basic stitches. Very coordinated for such a little girl, Felicity praised her attempts.

On the front porch of the Southern Hotel, Frank met up with Tiny Torkelsen. Tiny was the biggest man Frank had ever seen and had one of the gentlest dispositions of anyone of Frank's acquaintance. The two men decided to go have a beer at the Centennial Saloon. Supper wouldn't be ready for a few more hours. Just as they stepped off the porch, the ground seemed to rise up in front of them.

"What the hell??" Tiny yelled.

Frank reached back to steady himself with the banister. The ground jerked and a low rumble rose from beneath their feet. His first thought was Prudence. Leaving Torkelsen standing in front of the hotel, Frank bounded up the shivering steps two at a time, and crossed the lobby. As he started up the stairs, the building began to vibrate violently.

Prudence and Felicity huddled in the corner of the room on the floor. Frank crashed in.

"What happened?" Felicity shrieked as she clutched sobbing Prudence to her chest.

"I'm not sure but I think it might have been an earthquake," Frank replied in as calm a voice as he could manage.

Robert was dozing in his chair but he let out an abrupt snort as he was hurtled into a standing position. Loud screams emanated from the kitchen. He made a dive for the kitchen as the floor gave another sudden lurch. Robert was forced to grab the doorframe to keep from falling.

Li Soo and Quetta were standing in the middle of the kitchen and both were completely covered with flour. The tremor caused a large bag, stored on a high shelf, to shift suddenly and dump its entire contents on the two terrified women.

Robert tried very hard not to laugh. But he burst out with a loud, rude guffaw as both women glared at him.

Florence ran in through the back door. Outside cutting roses for the dining table when the tremors hit, her roses were crushed beyond redemption and her hands were bleeding. Robert picked up a tea towel and rushed to his wife. He took the mangled bouquet from her and threw them on the counter, lovingly wrapping the towel around her hands.

"It's all right. I think it's stopped," he said reassuringly. He sniffed several times trying to regain his composure. "It must have been an earthquake," he said matter-of-factly.

Chapter 37

Felicity gathered her cloak around her and held it with one hand as she reached to grasp Prudence's hand with the other. The little girl could barely see and reminded Felicity of a horse with blinders. Whenever Prudence went outside the Southern Hotel, Frank insisted she wear the oversized bonnet.

Felicity was grateful her niece wasn't allowed to play with other children because she knew they would tease the little girl unmercifully. Hurrying along with her head down against the wind, she bumped right into Mr. Ailman, co-owner of the largest bank in town.

"My deepest apologies, madam. I'm afraid I wasn't watching where I was going," Mr. Ailman said politely.

"That's quite all right, I'm afraid I wasn't either," Felicity said, smiling.

Mr. Ailman looked at her uncertainly for a moment and smiled back. He looked dreadful, with dark circles under his eyes and an unhealthy pallor.

Felicity asked, "Are you all right?"

He shook his head sadly. "I seem to recall you have some money in the bank."

"Yes, s-sir, a small savings account," Felicity stammered.

"I would advise you to withdraw it immediately," Ailman whispered.

Felicity watched as the man continued down the street, his shoulders sagged and his step faltered. Ailman's whole demeanor indicated despair. So the rumors were true! Lately, there had been gossip that the Meredith Ailman Bank was in financial trouble. Felicity tugged Prudence's hand and hurried across Bullard Street to the bank.

"Where are we going?" Prudence wanted to know.

"Just be still and be a good girl. Aunt Felicity has something she has to do," Felicity said quickly dodging a muddy hole in the street.

Felicity went up to a teller's window and withdrew their entire savings amounting to $290. The teller looked at her suspiciously when she closed out the account. Felicity smiled and told him she'd been saving for a dressmaking business and was getting ready to start buying equipment. It seemed to satisfy the man and Felicity hurried Prudence outside. She stood for a moment and gathered her resolve. Miner's Mercantile was her next stop. She paused for a moment to refasten Prudence's cloak and pull up her hood over the bonnet. Dark clouds scudded across the sky and the cold wind was piercing.

The mercantile was bustling. Several customers were housewives with children in tow; there were miners with heavy boots clunking across the wooden floor. Two old men sat in the corner playing checkers. Prudence watched a young mother, with two toddlers, order supplies from a flustered clerk.

"No, I said ten pounds of flour, not five! I want to have enough to do some Christmas baking," the young woman explained loudly.

"Sorry, ma'am," the poor clerk apologized.

Felicity guided Prudence to a corner near the stove. From there she could watch the checker players.

"Stay here for a few minutes, Pru," she instructed her niece.

Prudence nodded enthusiastically. One player, a grizzled old man with a long white beard, winked at her, as she passed. She smiled and winked back. The old-timer laughed and slapped his knee.

"Watch me wallop this young punk here," the man said.

Prudence grinned and nodded. The other player looked only slightly younger than his opponent. The younger man paused, moved a checker on the board, and aimed at a nearby spittoon. A trail of tobacco juice escaped his mouth and beaded on his chin. Prudence looked at the floor, stained by attempts of the less practiced.

The older man scratched his chin, causing his beard to bristle.

"Con-sarn it, looks like you skunked me again!" he grumbled.

"I told ya, I can beat anybody, anytime," the younger man boasted, wiping his chin with his handkerchief.

Felicity waited until a clerk was available and asked to speak to Mr. Jensen.

"I'm afraid he is very busy at the moment, Miss. New stock has arrived and he's doing inventory," the clerk informed her.

"It's of the utmost importance," Felicity said politely.

"I'll see if he can speak to you." The clerk left his position behind the counter and went through a narrow door into the back of the store.

After a few minutes, Robert Jensen came out of the same door, the clerk was following close behind him. "May I help you, young lady?" Robert asked.

"I want to discuss an important matter with you," she replied.

"We can speak in my office if that's agreeable to you," Robert said politely. He stepped aside and directed Felicity to his well-appointed office at the end of a narrow hallway. Felicity managed to catch Pru's eye before she left and motioned for her to stay put. Pru nodded and watched the opponents prepare for another game of checkers.

Felicity caught her breath when she saw a small family portrait hanging on the wall of Robert's office. She was making a huge mistake bringing Prudence here. Looking at Emma's likeness, she knew Robert Jensen would recognize Prudence immediately. The picture in Prudence's locket was by the same artist but the image was fading, Felicity had no idea until that moment, that the mother-daughter resemblance was so striking.

Struggling to regain her composure, Felicity toyed with the strings of her bonnet as Robert reached into a box on his desk and removed a fat cigar, which he promptly lit. Felicity coughed delicately, placing a gloved hand over her nose and mouth.

Robert apologized as he quickly stubbed it out. "I should have asked if it was all right. My wife protests whenever I smoke so I limit my cigars to working hours only," he coughed.

"I'll get right to the point, sir," Felicity said. "I've been told you and your partner are unable to keep a driver for your Pinos Altos freight wagons."

Robert looked at her in surprise. "That's right. How does that concern you, young lady?" he wanted to know.

"My brother is an excellent driver and looking for just such a position," she boasted.

"If your brother is looking for work, why didn't he come himself?" Robert asked, chuckling at the young woman's tone.

"My brother has only one arm," she explained. "He can do nearly anything anyone else can do and is very trustworthy."

Miner's Mercantile owned four freight wagons that made regular deliveries. The Pinos Altos run was very difficult due to marauding bandits. R.D. Farnsworth, Jensen's partner, hired six new drivers only to discover all but two of them were miners. When a new vein of silver was discovered up north, four of the men collected their pay and took off.

Robert sensed the attractive young lady seated in front of him was uneasy about something. But her courage impressed him. He paused for effect and then said, "I will speak to your brother, Miss...ah?"

"My name is Felicity Jones," Felicity stood and quickly extended her hand which surprised him. As he accepted her proffered hand, Felicity went on, "I can't thank you enough and I promise you won't be sorry."

"Miss Jones, I'll meet your brother here tomorrow afternoon at two o'clock. I'm not promising anything, mind you," Robert asserted as he escorted her to the front of the store.

"Thank you again, Mr. Jensen," Felicity said.

The checker game was still in progress but Prudence was no longer interested. She watched the clerk removed a long black licorice whip from a shiny confectioner's jar. He placed it on a thin piece of waxed paper and deftly rolled the paper into a cone. He poured a scoop of hard candy into it as well before handing it to a little boy who held out a penny.

"Don't eat it all, Joey," the clerk laughed. "Your mama said you have to share it with your sisters."

The little boy frowned and nodded. He skipped out of the store clutching the wrapped candy tightly to his chest.

Felicity waited for the clerk to finish and when it was her turn, she purchased some cloth, buttons, thread, and a packet of needles. She whispered something to him and he opened the confectioner's jar again and presented Prudence with her own licorice whip.

The pretty child thanked the clerk. He looked at her strangely for a moment then smiled and said, "You're very welcome. You come back to see us soon."

Savoring her first bite, she chewed it slowly. There was a loud hissing sound as a coffee pot boiled over on the stove. The checker players had been sitting close to the stove and jumped up sending the board and checkers skittering across the floor.

The door banged loudly behind Prudence and Felicity. Making ghosts with their breath, they trudged toward the Post Office. Just inside, Prudence stopped. She liked the musty paper and ink smells. As her aunt tended to her business, Prudence studied the yellowing wanted posters. Some bare nails held only torn corners. Bounty hunters ripped the posters down and took them along as reminders of what the desperadoes looked like, her Papa told her once.

Felicity was elated. There was a letter from Santa Fe. She folded it carefully and placed it in her reticule. Impatient to read her letter, she took Pru's hand and pulled her toward the door. They had been gone too long and she needed to dust the furniture in the lobby.

Later that night, Felicity looked out over the frozen street from an upstairs window of the Southern Hotel.

"What's the matter? You look sad," Prudence asked from the doorway. She was carrying her mama angel doll.

Felicity knelt in front of her niece and took Pru's chin in her hand. "It's hard to explain. A woman needs her own time and place. She might only find these things in her head but it's important she find them and hold on to them for all she's worth. Do you understand?" Felicity spoke slowly with emphasis.

Prudence nodded. She had no idea what her aunt meant but wanted to please her. Felicity nudged Prudence toward the door and closed it behind them. The room was inspected and ready for the next guest.

Back in their room, Prudence sat quietly with her doll in her lap and held her mother's locket. The delicate chain had broken after catching on a tree branch. She was afraid to tell her Papa because she had been warned several times not to climb the tree in the backyard. Maybe, Papa could fix the chain but he might be angry because she had disobeyed him.

Frank entered the room quietly. He dropped his coat on the chair and sat down heavily on it to remove his boots.

"Why are you back so late?" Felicity picked up his discarded coat, dropped it in his lap, and pointed to the coat hook on the wall.

Tired and cross, Frank snapped back at her, "What are you, my wife?"

Felicity's eyes flashed, he'd gone too far. She flew into a rage. "How dare you talk to me like that!" she shouted. "I take care of your child, *your child,* all day and work as well. All I ask in return is that you get in at a decent hour!"

Frank reached for her arm as she brushed past him. She slammed the door when she left the room, the blood rushed to her face, and her eyes glistened with tears.

Instantly sorry, Frank shoved his feet back into his boots and jumped to his feet. "I'm sorry if we frightened you, little one. Stay here for a minute, I want to talk to Aunt Felicity," he said.

"But wait Papa. I haven't had my supper yet and I broke my necklace. Can you fix it, please?" Prudence cried. She held out her hand holding the necklace. Frank felt a surge of sorrow when he saw the delicate broken chain.

"I'll take a look at it later. Just wait right here, I'll be back in a few minutes," Frank handed her back the locket.

"Can you fix it? Mama would be unhappy if I broke her necklace," Prudence said desperately.

"Your Mama would understand. I'll fix it so you can wear it. Please stay here so I can talk to Aunt Felicity," he said as he patted his daughter on the head.

Felicity was on her knees scrubbing furiously at a spot on the lobby carpet. "I gave up my life in Santa Fe to come help you. How do you repay me? You leave us for days, tracking bandits and renegades, for nearly nothing. Then you and your pals spend your nights drinking in the saloon. Well, I've had just about all of this kind of treatment I can stand!"

Frank knew she was right. He was suffering a lot of pain. Most of it was emotional but some of it was physical as well. Yesterday, while laying brick, he was seized by the most excruciating pain he'd ever experienced. The brick he was holding shattered when it fell on a large rock. Starting to rub his arm, he suddenly realized that it wasn't there. He slumped against the wall and slid to the ground. He remembered an old Confederate army officer he knew as a boy. Carleton Hicks was a young man when he fought in the War Between the States. Hicks lost his leg because of an infected saber wound. The leg was removed in a field hospital without benefit of so much as a drop of whiskey. Hicks described the recurring pain he felt as phantom pain and swore it was like reliving the nightmarish experience of the amputation.

Frank had been unconscious and feverish during his own amputation and was unable to recall any of it. But his "phantom pains" were occurring more frequently and with greater severity.

"I'll try to do better," Frank told his sister as she continued to scrub at the stubborn spot. "Please try to understand."

Felicity stopped scrubbing and threw the brush into the bucket of soapy water.

"Understand what? You lost someone you loved? You lost your arm, your homestead, and all you have left is your little girl?" Felicity stopped to catch her breath and force herself to calm down. "I don't understand," she continued more calmly, "How can I? I haven't lived through your experiences and you don't confide much in me."

Frank shook his head sadly.

"My life isn't in Silver City, I belong in Santa Fe. How will you manage when I'm gone and you're forced to care for Prudence? That's right, I won't stay forever. My life isn't over, I came to help and I have," Felicity covered her face with soapy hands.

"You've been a godsend," Frank paused, "Has something happened?"

"I wanted to tell you later but I guess now is as good a time as any," Felicity said, wiping her hands on her dress. "I went to Miner's Mercantile today to ask your father-in-law to give you a job!" she said proudly.

"You didn't! Tell me you didn't," Frank pleaded.

"I didn't tell him who you are. I told him that I knew he was looking for freight wagon drivers. He said he'd talk to you."

"How can I talk to him?" Frank asked impatiently. Why had she gotten involved in this? Felicity took her brother's arm and led him toward a large gilt mirror hanging near the fireplace.

"Take a good look at yourself. Do you honestly think he could recognize you?"

Frank winced as he saw what others saw. Thinning hair straggled down to his shoulders, his beard was liberally sprinkled with gray. Bloodshot eyes were dulled by hopelessness and his clothes hung loosely on his emaciated frame. He looked nothing like the man who met Robert and Florence Jensen on the stage from Deming to Silver City.

"When do I see him?" he inquired, dully.

"Tomorrow at two o'clock," Felicity informed him.

Chapter 38

Around midnight, Frank stood on the porch of the Southern Hotel. Speaking silently to Emma comforted him. Before he met her, Frank spent many days and nights alone with only a horse or Army mule for companionship. Now he felt loneliest in a town full of people. A sudden plunge in temperature caused Frank to shiver and he trudged upstairs to bed.

At dawn he awoke and rubbed his swollen eyes. His throat felt dry and painful. When he arose the morning sky was streaked with cold silver light. He went to the washbasin, washed his face and attempted to smooth his hair.

He shook his head in disbelief, this couldn't be happening. His worst nightmare would come true today. Many years ago, Frank and Emma discussed their marriage. Emma wanted to elope but Frank wanted to speak to Robert, face him, man-to-man. Emma pleaded with him, asking that he not attempt it.

"My father is a good man but extremely protective, if he even suspected that we planned to marry, he might shoot you," Emma whispered for dramatic effect.

Frank had laughed. "I should speak to your father," he insisted.

"You have no idea what you are saying. He'd be furious. Please, for my sake, say nothing to my father," Emma cried.

In the end, Frank complied with her wishes because it was the only way he and Emma could be together.

Felicity was putting up her hair and Prudence was still asleep as Frank put on his coat and went to have a quick breakfast. There were several buildings on Main Street getting a new façade. Red brick leant an air of permanence to the town. No longer just a mining camp, Frank was proud, knowing he had done a lot of the work himself.

Blake Nester, Frank's foreman, was studying blueprints, when Frank arrived. During the past few weeks, Frank had been a bricklayer. Nester was unhappy when Frank told him that he was considering another job.

"Don't want to see you go, Jones. You're a good worker but can't say as I blame you for wanting better pay," Nester said. He agreed to let Frank off early to go for the interview.

At exactly 1:00 pm, Frank went back to the Southern Hotel. He got cleaned up and changed his clothes. Miner's Mercantile wasn't very busy so the clerk ushered him to an office in the back. R.D. Farnsworth, Robert's partner, stood as Frank entered. Automatically, R.D. extended his hand and then looked embarrassed when Frank extended his left hand.

"Your sister made quite an impression on my partner. We're looking for a reliable man to haul freight to Pinos Altos. I'll be honest, it's a short run but a difficult one. Four times in the last three months, bandits have attacked a driver and stolen supplies. Only one man was killed, the rest quit. It's been a very costly endeavor."

Frank barely heard him, he was so relieved that Robert wasn't present.

"I understand that you're at a disadvantage," R.D. said, looking at Frank's partially empty sleeve. "Jensen and I discussed it and we've decided to hire someone to ride shotgun. If you want to drive, we'll give you a try. The job pays $1.50 a day. You will be hired on a two- week trial basis. If, after that time, your work is satisfactory and you are willing to continue, we will give you an additional 50 cents a day, a discount at the mercantile, and a six month contract."

Frank was stunned. He swallowed hard, unable to speak.

"Well, sir, do we have a deal?" R.D. asked.

"Yes, sir, thank you!" Frank jumped to his feet and extended his left hand. "When do I start?"

"Do you think you could make a trip tomorrow? I realize it's short notice but we need to get supplies up to the Ancheta Trading Post. We already have a man to ride shotgun. On your way out, please speak to Paul, our clerk, and he'll take down some information," R.D. smiled and shook Frank's extended hand.

Frank went to find Nester and tell him of his opportunity. Nester whistled.

"It must be a dangerous job, to pay that much. You be careful, you hear?" Nester warned him.

Frank went to the barber and got a haircut but only had his beard trimmed. He wanted to look good for his new job. Feeling like a new man, the next morning he dressed and arrived early at Miner's Mercantile. Behind the store, a freight wagon was being loaded. Frank entered through the rear entrance, as the clerk, Paul instructed. R.D. stood when Frank entered the room and introduced him to Martin Caldwell, his new partner. Caldwell was well known in Silver City having recently won a sharp-shooting contest in Georgetown. Men from all over the territory had entered the contest and Martin, a young man of twenty-three, was the undisputed winner.

R.D. was pleased when Caldwell accepted the job and was certain he could provide excellent protection for the freight wagons bound for Pinos Altos.

"You men get acquainted. I'm going to supervise the rest of the loading. Once you get to Pinos Altos, proceed to the Ancheta Trading Post. There'll be some young men there to unload the wagon," R.D. said, lighting a cigar and inhaling deeply.

Frank decided he liked Caldwell. The younger man was nondescript with dark eyes and hair. Frank appreciated his politeness and respectful attitude. On his own for several years, Martin's manner held none of the cockiness seen in most young men.

The freight wagon rolled out of Silver City at 8:00 in the morning, pulled by two large black mules. Transporting a huge load up the mountain, they arrived at 4:30 in the afternoon, without incident.

There were two young men waiting at the store to unload the wagon. The storeowner, Trolius Stephens, was glad to see them arrive unscathed. Frank sensed his partner, Caldwell, was a little disappointed that they hadn't encountered any trouble.

Sweeney and Mark Calhoun assisted Stephens with odd jobs and when they weren't busy, they amused themselves, trying to lasso the hitching post out front. Inside the store, Sadie Calhoun was buying supplies for the week. She smiled shyly as Frank and Martin Caldwell entered to have some coffee. The men nodded and tipped their hats. She finished her business and went outside to keep an eye on her roguish brothers. Unsupervised, they'd get into mischief.

Chapter 39

Frank sat beside Prudence's bed. Moonlight streamed in through the window and made her hair look like a golden cascading waterfall. She was delicate, like her mother, and he feared he might lose her, too.

His new job was proving to be more demanding than he imagined. His dealings were with R.D. and fortunately he hadn't encountered Robert Jensen yet. The Jensens, Robert and Florence, left for St. Louis two days after R.D. hired Frank and hadn't returned. They were expected back this week and preparations were being made for a welcome home party. Families of employees were invited but Frank told Felicity that he would go alone. Felicity was angry.

"I want to go. I work all the time and never attend any parties or dances. You're being very selfish, Frank," she said.

"No, I'm being careful. I don't know if I'll be recognized. I'd like to postpone this meeting indefinitely; but that would look suspicious, so I'll take my chances. But I want to know that you and Pru are safe. Please listen to me," Frank pulled his sister's shoulder, turning her to face him. "It isn't that I don't want you to go. It's just that it might be dangerous. I don't know what Jensen might do if he discovers who I am," Frank said as he stroked his sister's cheek.

"I'm sure there won't be any trouble at a party. I bought a new dress for the occasion. Please Frank, let me come with you," his sister pleaded.

"If it's that important to you, but don't say I didn't warn you," Frank growled.

The party was a quiet affair with just employees and their families. R.D. and Robert put in an appearance but they seemed preoccupied. Robert looked very tired and excused himself shortly after dinner. Frank left soon afterward, Felicity stayed and visited with some of the women. She was asked to dance several times and enjoyed herself immensely.

Oversleeping the next morning, Felicity was awakened by a loud knock on the door. A young freckle faced boy stood grasping an official looking paper.

"Telegram for Miss Felicity at the Southern Hotel. A lady downstairs told me to come to this room. Are you Miss Felicity?" the boy asked shyly noticing her disheveled appearance.

"Yes, I am. Just a moment," Felicity retrieved a coin for the boy.

"Thanks, Miss," he grinned and tipped his hat. He handed her the telegram and closed the door.

Felicity's fingers shook as she read the brief note.

REGRET TO INFORM YOU JUDGE MAY BE DYING STOP HE IS ASKING FOR YOU STOP PLEASE COME WITHOUT DELAY STOP JADE FINDERLEY

Felicity sank to the floor. What was she going to do? Frank had just signed a rent agreement for a row house on Cooper Street. The Southern Hotel was a nice place but nowhere for a little girl to grow up. Determined to raise Prudence in a real home, Frank decided that a move was in order. Next week, Prudence would start school and Felicity wouldn't be there.

Felicity owed Judge McCoy a lot. She came to him with no references and he gave her a position of authority in his household. It was unthinkable that she would ignore his dying request.

Prudence was downstairs talking to the old cat, Mr. Whiskers. Felicity straightened her hair, brushed off her dress and went to look for her niece.

"Doesn't Mr. Whiskers look wise? Don't you think he could go to school too?" Prudence asked smiling.

Felicity smiled back and patted her niece's head.

"I'm sure Mr. Whiskers would be a very good student; but cats aren't allowed to go to school," she said.

"Why are you crying, Aunt Felicity?" Your eyes and nose are red," Prudence observed.

"I have to go away for a time and I don't know when I'll be coming back. You and your Papa are moving and you'll be starting school next week. I don't know what to do!" Felicity sobbed.

"Did I do something bad?" Prudence whimpered.

"Of course not, silly. I have to go because a good man is very sick and I need to see him."

"Is he going to die like my Mama?" Prudence asked, patting her aunt's shoulder.

"I don't know. He's very sick and needs me to take care of him for awhile."

Prudence put her arms around her aunt. She sat quietly for a few minutes. "If he's very sick, you have to go Aunt Felicity. Then maybe you can make him better and come back to us," Prudence said wisely.

"Thank you, Pru. You're a very nice little girl. I have to tell your Papa tonight. I'll ask Mrs. McAllen to come stay with you downstairs for awhile. Is that all right with you?" Felicity asked, carefully drying her tears with her handkerchief.

Prudence nodded and said nothing.

The evening was clear with only a thumbnail of a moon. The saloon piano tinkled merrily and was accompanied by many off-key voices. A dog barked incessantly as a horse tied to the hitching post in front of the saloon snorted and shook his head as if in protest to the noise.

Fried onions and wood smoke perfumed the air and Frank's stomach rumbled noisily reminding him it had been over five hours since he'd last eaten. Prudence was in the lobby, sitting by Mrs. McAllen, with a pile of yarn at her feet. Frank sensed something was wrong. Felicity must want to discuss something with him alone.

He greeted his daughter and Mrs. McAllen and went upstairs. Felicity met him at the door. Frank took one look at his sister's face and knew she was fighting tears. "What's wrong? You look terrible," he said as he took off his dusty hat.

"You always know just how to make me feel better," Felicity dissolved into a weeping mass.

"There must be something seriously wrong," Frank observed sympathetically. When he put his arm around her shoulders, she pressed her face against his chest. It took several minutes for her to stop crying.

"I saw Pru downstairs with Mrs. McAllen. She looked very worried. Did she do something to upset you?" Frank asked.

Felicity shook her head and continued to cry.

"Moving is difficult, if you really want to stay here, we can manage I guess," he said still unable to determine why his sister was so upset.

Felicity sputtered and choked, then blew her nose and took several deep breaths. "Judge McCoy is dying and has been asking for me. I have to go to him," she blurted between sobs.

Frank was stunned. It never occurred to him that Felicity would leave them. When she came to stay with them at the homestead outside of Deming, she said she would leave some day. But times were better and now the three were a family. This couldn't be happening!

"Say something Frank. Don't just sit there. Tell me what to do. I still have to pack and Pru needs new shoes before she starts school next week," Felicity stood wringing her hands.

Frank was determined to put on a brave face for his sister. She meant so much to him and Prudence. "The train leaves tomorrow at 7:20 am. You should go to the station now and get your ticket. I'll tend to Pru's supper," Frank offered kindly.

"No, I can't just leave with nothing ready to move and Prudence isn't ready for school. She needs me!" Felicity sobbed.

"We both need you, but so does the Judge. He helped you when you needed it the most. You can't let him down now."

Felicity nodded and bit her lower lip as she went to wash her face in the basin. Looking in the little mirror, she frowned. She was a wreck and needed to pull herself together.

"I gave Mr. Reid my notice this morning. He was very understanding; but I think it upset him. I seem to be making a muddle of everything," she lamented.

"None of this is your fault. Now get down to the station and get your ticket," Frank helped her with her shawl and led her to the door.

Downstairs, Felicity slipped out while Frank went to speak to Mrs. McAllen. Prudence held yarn between her hands as the lady rolled the yarn into a large ball. Mr. Whiskers watched from under the chair and occasionally reached out to swat the moving yarn with a furry paw.

Prudence dropped the yarn and ran to Frank. She saw the look on his face and knew Aunt Felicity was leaving.

"I'm a big girl, Papa. I'm old enough to go to school, so don't worry, I'll take care of you," Prudence said, her large blue eyes sparkling with tears.

"I know you will, Kitten," Frank said. Frank called her Kitten because she loved the old cat so much. Prudence liked the endearment and would sometimes pretend to purr when he used it.

Difficult to imagine life without Felicity, Frank decided to ask Mrs. McAllen for advice. She was a busybody but loved children and had a good heart.

"Felicity is going on a long trip. An old friend of hers is dying and she needs to go to him," Frank explained.

Mrs. McAllen raised one eyebrow questioningly. She knew Felicity was bound to have a man friend somewhere. The pretty young woman was in Silver City to escape some kind of scandal. She dropped the ball of yarn into her bag and snapped it shut. Leaning forward, her eyes gleamed as she waited for Frank to continue.

"As you know I've rented a row house on Cooper Street and planned to move by the end of the week. Do you know anyone in that area who could care for Prudence while I am away?"

Mrs. McAllen smiled. *So he needed advice. Didn't that just take the cake?*

"My goodness, young people can sure get into a fix. Let me think…" Her voice trailed off. "My friend Margaret Flaherty lives in one of the row houses. She has three growing sons and would probably be glad of the extra income," she said smugly, feeling very proud of her solution. "Now tell me about this man of Felicity's. Are they very close? Does she write to him?" She seemed to recall seeing several letters addressed to a Judge McCoy in Felicity's neat handwriting, on the lobby table. She assumed that the Judge was either a relative or an old lover of Felicity's. This was her chance to find out all about the relationship.

Frank smiled. "She worked for him once and he is asking to see her before he dies."

Felicity hurried in clutching her train ticket and paused a moment before going upstairs. Mrs. McAllen sniffed with disapproval.

"Thank you for watching Prudence for us, Mrs. McAllen," Frank stood and reached for his daughter's hand. "Felicity will need some help with her packing."

The next few weeks were going to be tough but they'd manage. He was supposed to haul freight to Hillsboro in four days. In the meantime, he'd finish packing and move them into their new house. Only one part of his plan worried him, the Jensens would be living right around the corner.

Chapter 40

School started in early September. The last few days were spent moving their belongings to the little row house on Cooper St. It was very cozy and Prudence decided she'd like living there. Apprehensive about starting school, Prudence wondered if the other children would like her. She had never played with anyone her own age and worried that there was something wrong with her.

Frank left for Hillsboro the Friday before school started. Mrs. McAllen's friend, Margaret Flaherty, was a grandmotherly sort. She and Prudence became great friends. Mrs. Flaherty could be trusted to take excellent care of his daughter while he was gone. He started to tell her about his relationship to the Jensens but decided against it. It would be best not to let anyone know.

Prudence cried herself to sleep the night before school started. Aunt Felicity and Papa were gone. She would have to get through tomorrow alone. Even her friend Mr. Whiskers had been left behind at the Southern Hotel.

Mrs. Flaherty combed and braided Prudence's hair and put a huge oversized bonnet on the little girl's head. It seemed a shame to cover her pretty hair and face with such an abomination; but Mr. Jones, the little girl's father insisted.

The Flahertys arrived in Silver City during the coldest weather ever recorded. Snow blanketed the little town. To the Irish immigrants, the cold seemed relatively mild compared to the fierce Indiana winters they had endured before coming to the New Mexico Territory. Mr. Flaherty worked for a construction company and was home every night for supper. The Flaherty boys were a wild bunch and attracted trouble wherever they went.

Mrs. Flaherty would chuckle indulgently and say, "Boys will be boys."

Prudence wasn't sure what that meant, but smiled and nodded. The boys weren't bad, just mischievous.

"Now young missy, you're ready to go. Here's your lunch. Be sure to pay attention and mind your teacher," Mrs. Flaherty wiped her large red hands on her apron and smiled at the little girl. Margaret Flaherty wanted a little girl and God had seen fit to give her three rowdy sons instead. *Ah well*, she sighed heavily and kissed Prudence's cheek. "You know the way. Be careful and go straight to school," she added.

"Yes, ma'am," Prudence said politely.

"Why don't you call me Meggie, dear," Mrs. Flaherty suggested, hugging her.

Prudence wondered if Meggie could hear the thundering she was feeling in her chest. She clutched her lunch pail tightly as she walked out the door into the early fall sunshine.

On the hill to school, Prudence clutched her mother's locket in one hand and her lunch pail in the other. Holding her mother's locket was something she always did when she was frightened or unsure of herself. She was glad Frank had replaced the broken chain with a leather cord.

As she neared the school, Prudence heard someone walking behind her. A little girl smiled shyly, revealing a space where a tooth was missing. "Hi, I'm Callie," she said. "You're Prudence, aren't you?"

Prudence nodded and asked, "How did you know my name?"

"Your Aunt Felicity is my mother's friend," Callie replied, "I'm sorry she had to go away, I liked her."

"You must be the girl Aunt Felicity told me about. I'm so glad to see you." Prudence confided, "I'm scared."

Callie giggled, "Me too. Maybe we can be best friends and help each other not be scared?"

The two girls held hands and went to line up outside the door to the school.

"What are you holding?" Callie asked.

Prudence smiled and showed her new friend her locket.

A teasing voice behind her jeered, "I think that is about the ugliest locket I've ever seen. Look, it's on an old, dirty cord." The voice belonged to an older girl standing behind Prudence in line. Pru didn't know what to say or do. Tears streamed down her face. This is just what the older girl expected.

Triumphantly, the girl continued. "Look at the crybaby with the ugly necklace." Her remarks caused some of the older girls to laugh. Prudence closed her eyes and held the locket tightly. She stopped crying and held her breath.

"Now, let's proceed in an orderly manner to our classes," chirped a cheerful voice.

Prudence opened her eyes and saw a pretty woman standing directly in front of the steps leading into the new school building. Callie and Prudence were in the "Baby Class" which meant they were just beginning their first year. Both girls resented being called babies because they were nearly grown but pretended not to mind. They were delighted to find their assigned seats were next to each other. Hardwood floors gleamed in the early morning sunlight filtering through the large windows. The oak desks in the large, airy classroom had ornate wrought iron legs. The desktops could be raised and their slates and books put inside. How wonderful!

Miss Percy, their teacher, told them this was her first teaching position. She was anxious for the children to like her and seemed so excited the children were caught up in it and chattered like magpies. "Please, we must get to work," Miss Percy said sternly, her dimples deepened as she admonished the children for their unruly behavior.

When recess arrived, Miss Percy asked Prudence to stay in so she could speak to her, having overheard the older girl's rude comments about Prudence's locket. "May I see your locket?" Miss Percy asked.

Prudence nodded shyly and held it up for her teacher to see.

"It is very unusual, where did you get it?"

"It was my Mama's. My Papa gave it to me when I was big enough to take care of it. It even has a picture of my Mama inside. It had a real pretty chain but it broke when I was playing and Papa fixed it with this cord," Prudence told her.

"Where is your mother now?" Miss Percy asked.

"She died when I was little. I don't remember her very much. Papa said that she loved me a lot," Prudence opened the locket and held it out.

The features of the young woman in the picture inside were faded and difficult to make out but Miss Percy didn't say so. "Your mother was very beautiful," she said kindly. "You should take good care of your locket. I am sure that your mother would be very proud of you."

Prudence was radiant as she bid her teacher good-bye that afternoon. Taking Callie's hand, the girls skipped down the hill together. Prudence knew she was going to like school.

Wind blew whirls of dirt as they made their way home. Near the bottom of the hill, the trees, dressed in autumn colors, spilled piles of gold at their feet. The two chattered like old friends. Prudence was more animated than usual. In her haste to join her friend, she forgot her oversized bonnet.

Robert Jensen puffed along the road toward home. He still ate the rich food he enjoyed but complied with Florence's wishes that he walk to and from work at least twice a week. It was a nice day but a busy one at the store and he was very tired. He focused his attention on the ground in front of him and heard noisy children passing him on their way home from school. A shipment was due tomorrow and he concentrated on planning a new display. Nearly home, he raised his head and breathed a loud sigh of relief. His bones were aching and there was a creeping numbness in his right arm. His head pounded and his eyes watered.

"Oh bother," he muttered as he felt a shooting pain in his right eye. He leaned heavily against a cottonwood to catch his breath and waited for a wave of dizziness to pass.

Some schoolgirls went by and stared at him curiously. His vision blurred and he thought momentarily of sending them for his carriage. As the girls approached he heard them saying something unintelligible. He blinked hard and stared at the little girl standing in front of him. It was Emma! No, it couldn't be, Emma was a woman. He slid down the trunk of the tree and lapsed into unconsciousness.

Prudence and Callie were frightened. They ran quickly to a nearby house to get help for the unconscious man. A tall man told the girls to go along, he'd make sure his neighbor was cared for. The girls waited until the sick man was lifted into a cart, before continuing.

Bits of conversation drifted into Robert's mind through the fog. He thought he heard Florence speaking. What was she saying? Her words made no sense, no sense at all. It was easier to slip back into the blackness than to pry open his heavy eyelids.

Florence Jensen saw a vehicle coming up the road. She was standing by the front gate because Robert was late. He arrived home at five, leaving R.D. to close up at six. It was 5:30 and still no sign of her husband.

"Mrs. Jensen, send your maid for the doctor immediately. I fear your husband has suffered some kind of attack!" a tall man driving the cart yelled, as he jumped out.

Robert's face was suffused with color and he was unconscious. She guided the men into the house, to the guest room downstairs.

"Li Soo, Li Soo, come here!" Florence screamed.

Li Soo came running from the kitchen.

"You must go quickly and bring Dr. Woodville, Mr. Robert is in trouble," Florence bustled around trying to think what to do to make her husband more comfortable.

The tall man, Albert Johnson and his neighbor, Carl Witherspoon, stood quietly and waited to see if they could be of further assistance.

"Sit down gentlemen and stay until the doctor arrives. I sent Li Soo because she can run very fast," Florence said.

Robert moaned. His right arm and hand were limp and lifeless and the right corner of his mouth drooped.

"I fear it might be apoplexy," Florence began to sob, holding Robert's limp hand against her cheek. "I should never have made him walk so far."

"Sometimes these things look a lot worse than they are, Mrs. Jensen. Wait until the doctor comes, I'm sure he will soon sort things out," Mr. Johnson remarked.

Li Soo found Dr. Woodville at his clinic and begged him to rush to the Jensen house.

"I will need to examine him thoroughly before I can offer a diagnosis. Please step outside and close the door so that I can have absolute quiet," Dr. Woodville ordered.

"Please doctor, please help him," pleaded Florence hysterically.

Mr. Johnson placed his hand under her elbow and led her from the room, closing the door behind her. The little group waited in the parlor. Li Soo and Quetta stood in the parlor doorway in case they were needed. Time seemed to stand still until the doctor joined them. They looked to him expectantly, anxious, yet dreading what they were about to hear.

"It is as I feared," the doctor said shaking his head sadly. "Your husband has suffered an apoplectic seizure. He is conscious now. With time, he may recover completely. I must warn you, he is suffering from aphasia or the inability to talk. It may be some time before he is able to express himself. He is very weak and will require constant nursing care for a few weeks. I am very sorry."

Florence crumpled to the divan and waved away everyone who tried to comfort her. After several minutes, she composed herself enough to speak.

"Li Soo, please send for Mr. Farnsworth. Tell him that it is urgent," she said.

Dr. Woodville offered Florence a sedative but she refused. It was imperative she be fully alert to handle this crisis. R.D. arrived in his buggy and wanted to see Robert. R.D. and Dr. Woodville conferred with each other in the corner of the parlor for a few moments, speaking in hushed tones.

Lying on his back with his eyes wide open, Robert attempted to sit up when R.D. and Florence approached his bedside. He looked confused and frightened as he opened his mouth to speak. Nothing came out except a series of snoring sounds that continued as he tried to breathe.

"Don't worry, dear," Florence said sitting down beside him and taking lifeless hand. "Dr. Woodville thinks that this weakness and inability to speak are only temporary and that you'll soon be yourself again." She looked at R.D. for encouragement.

All R. D, could manage was a blink of his eyes and a nod of his head. A huge lump in his throat prevented him from saying anything. For twenty years, Robert had been his closest friend. Now he was lying weak as a kitten before him. R.D. fought to master his voice and managed to speak with only a slight tremor, "I will get someone to help Florence with your personal care. You must rest and regain your strength."

Florence nodded and looked at R.D. closely. Intuitively, she sensed his desperation. Faced with his own mortality, it scared him. As soon as R.D. was able to come to grips with his friend's illness, he would be more of a comfort to Robert. She knew all R.D. wanted was to leave the house as fast as he could.

Late that night, Prudence struggled in her sleep. Her blankets enveloped her like a cocoon. She thrashed and moaned; flailing her arms and legs. Margaret Flaherty, staying in Frank's room while he was gone, heard the commotion in the next bedroom. She rushed to see what was the matter. Her long, graying hair straggled from its loose braid as she touched Prudence gently on the shoulder.

"What's the matter, wee one?" she asked, her voice thickened with a sleepy Irish brogue.

"The man, the man was trying to tell me something! I couldn't hear what he was saying," Prudence sat up in bed. Her eyes were wide with fright until she realized the comforting presence of Margaret.

Flickering shadows danced across Prudence's pale countenance as some high clouds drifted across the moon.

"The man you saw today, the one who was sick?" Margaret asked as she picked up the little girl and cradled her against her ample bosom.

"Oh, Meggie, I think he wanted to say something but he couldn't talk. When he opened his mouth, I was so scared," Prudence's shoulders were shaking.

Mrs. Flaherty's brothers and sisters had called her Meggie and she missed them. Hearing her old nickname helped ease the loss she often felt in this land so far away.

"Perhaps you can hear what he wanted to tell you with your heart instead of your ears. Were you frightened because of the way he looked or because of what you thought he was trying to say?" She believed that souls often communicated with one another.

"I don't know why I was scared. He looked at me like he knew me and I was supposed to do something. He was really big but he didn't look mean," Prudence said.

Meggie reassured her. "Maybe we can make more sense of it all in the bright light of day." She put the little girl down on the bed and covered her with a patterned quilt. Stroking her forehead, Meggie sang an old Irish lullaby.

Chapter 41

Prudence and Callie walked down the road on their way home from school. Prudence stopped mid-sentence when they reached the spot where the man had fallen. She held her breath for a moment; someone was playing the piano. It was far away but she could hear the familiar melody. To her surprise, she felt her eyes fill with tears.

"What's the matter, Pru? Why are you crying?" Callie asked.

"I'm not crying, I just wish Papa was home. My Mama played the piano. I thought I heard someone playing but I don't hear it anymore."

Callie paused and turned her head to one side. She didn't hear anything.

"Come over to my house and my Mama will play for you," Callie said.

"I'd have to ask first. Meggie and I are going to bake some cookies. Papa is coming home tomorrow and we want to give him something nice. But I'd like to hear your Mama play the piano," Prudence said wistfully.

The girls joined hands and skipped the rest of the way to Prudence's house.

Charles Mills was a medic in the War Between the States with the Confederate forces. He wanted to continue his medical training but without money or resources left, he was forced to work his way west, doing odd jobs. A position with Dr. Woodville enabled Charlie, as he liked to be called, the opportunity to do the work he loved.

R.D. spoke to Dr. Woodville and they decided a man like Charlie was just what Robert needed to recuperate. A perpetual optimist, Charlie possessed the gift of being able to buoy people's spirits. Very slight in build, Charlie possessed remarkable physical strength. Even Dr. Woodville was amazed when he saw Charlie lift a grown man and move him around as though he weighed no more than a sack of flour. With graying kinky hair, a ruddy complexion and a merry twinkle in his eye, Charlie liked everyone and everyone liked him.

Florence was amazed at how Charlie took charge. He went in to meet Robert and quickly assessed the situation. Talking a mile a minute, Charlie told Robert about himself and how the two of them would become great friends. During this one-sided conversation, Charlie went about plumping pillows, arranging the furniture, and generally making the room more efficient. Florence watched this little whirlwind of a man and listened to him chatting merrily, feeling instantly comforted. She watched Robert's amused eyes following Charlie around the room.

Leaving Robert in Charlie's capable hands was a relief. R.D. was looking out for their welfare. Beatrice came to visit and brought some food for Florence. Now R.D. was forced to assume Robert's duties in addition to his own at the mercantile.

Frank was stunned when he heard about Robert. The man seemed larger than life. How could he be stricken with such a devastating illness.

Florence wrote to her parents:

Dear Mother and Father,

I hope this letter finds you well. Robert is ill, he returned from our visit with you anxious to return to work, yet very tired. Shortly after our return, he suffered an attack of apoplexy. He's unable to speak and can barely sit up.

I was worried about his lack of exercise and told him to walk more. It was during a walk home from the mercantile that he collapsed. R.D. hired a wonderful man to care for Robert while he recovers.

I'm well despite everything. I'll write more when I have some news.

Your loving daughter,
Florence

She sealed her letter with wax and placed it in her reticule. Robert kept accounts for the store. Tomorrow Florence planned to speak to R.D. about assuming some of Robert's responsibilities.

Early the next morning, Florence assisted Charlie with Robert's breakfast. The gruel dribbled out the side of Robert's drooping mouth. Charlie showed her that by turning Robert's head slightly and putting the liquid in the unaffected side of his mouth, Robert was able to swallow more of the warm cereal.

When Robert was fed and bathed, Florence headed for Miner's Mercantile in her buggy. Her eyes filled with tears and she brushed them away impatiently. A man like Robert shouldn't have to be fed like a baby.

"How are you?" R.D. asked leaping to his feet when his partner's wife came into the room. "Is Robert all right?"

"He is improving I think. It's hard to say. Dr. Woodville said I must take things one day at a time. I'm here to discuss something of great importance to both of us," Florence spoke quietly. She explained the purpose of her visit.

"It's admirable of you to want to help with the accounts. But you should be with Robert now. He needs you. I hired a bookkeeper yesterday and he seems quite competent," R.D. patted her hand, "I'll keep you informed about the business."

Florence, feeling dismissed, went out through the back of the mercantile into a large freight loading area. She watched as a one-armed man loaded sacks of grain into a wagon. The man's hat covered most of his face. He glanced in her direction once, adjusted his hat and returned to his task. Lost in thought, Florence barely noticed him after standing there for several minutes. It was quieter outside and she needed time to think before returning home.

Frank noticed Florence immediately. Carefully, he kept his face in the shade and his hat down close to his eyes. With luck, she wouldn't come any closer and perhaps recognize the man who had eloped with her daughter.

When Florence went back inside, Frank breathed a loud sigh of relief. It was time for lunch and he made himself comfortable in the shade of the wagon. His meat and bread was wrapped in brown paper and another piece of paper held the homemade cookies Prudence and Mrs. Flaherty lovingly baked for him.

The next trip would take him to the Mormon Settlement. He sensed something was bothering Prudence because the night before she tossed and turned a lot and wasn't her usual cheerful self. Maybe she missed Felicity. Suppertimes were very different without Felicity chattering away about town gossip. Frank tried several times to get Prudence to talk to him about school. She looked at him with her enormous blue eyes, murmured something, and continued to look very sad. He felt guilty being gone so much. But what could he do? It was the best job he could get and he needed to make a living.

A cool morning mist soothed Frank as he went next door to speak to Mrs. Flaherty. She was in the kitchen kneading dough for biscuits when he knocked. "Sorry to bother you so early, but I'm on my way and I needed to ask you about Prudence," Frank apologized.

Mrs. Flaherty was surprised Frank had noticed anything amiss. In her family, men were not in tune with the feelings of others. "Well sir, she had a bad experience on the way home from school. A man was taken ill and the poor colleen was frightened by it all. I've been keeping her close to me and I take care of her like she was my own. Go on with you now, else you'll be late," Mrs. Flaherty smiled and shooed Frank out the door with her apron.

"What man was taken ill? Where did it happen?" Frank felt the blood drain from his face. He'd heard Robert collapsed in the street near his home.

"I don't know too much about it. The poor colleen seems better when she doesn't think about it too much. Now don't worry, sir, I'll be taking good care of her." Mrs. Flaherty gently closed the door.

Frank knocked on the door again. Mrs. Flaherty looked concerned. "Please be sure Prudence comes straight home from school," Frank said. "I must go now. We can discuss this more when I get back. Tell her I love her when she wakes up. Will you do that for me?"

"Sure, and I will, sir. Now you'd better be going," Mrs. Flaherty reassured him.

Prudence didn't tell Callie about her dreams. She was afraid her friend would think she was silly. Every time the girls passed the tree where the man fell, Prudence heard the faraway strains of piano music. The music sounded familiar and made her feel sad.

Prudence neared the top of the hill on Cooper Street. Kicking leaves with her feet, she twined the ribbons of her bonnet around and around her fingers. She tried to hum the song she heard near the tree but it got all mixed up in her head. Mrs. Flaherty was hurrying toward her wringing her hands.

"There you are little miss. I must go see Mrs. McGrath. She took ill and her doctor is delivering twins. I told him I would stay with her until he could come back. Be a good girl and stay here with Mr. Flaherty until I come home."

Meggie Flaherty rushed down the hill as fast as her chubby legs could go. Prudence looked into the Flaherty's small sitting room. Himself, Mrs. Flaherty's name for her husband, was sprawled in the big chair, his hands folded across his ample stomach. His mouth was wide open with some very disturbing sounds issuing forth. The Flaherty boys weren't at home so it was very quiet except for Mr. Flaherty's snoring.

After sitting quietly for several minutes, Prudence left the house. Some cottonwoods were perfect cover for the little girl. A tingle ran down her spine but she continued through the trees until she reached the back of the house. Lamplight streamed from one window as Prudence cautiously approached it hoping for a glimpse of the sick man who had haunted her dreams for so many nights, she had to be sure he was all right.

Pressing her cupped hands to the glass, the little girl peered into the room. The man lay on his back in a huge bed. His eyes were wide open, staring at the ceiling. One side of his mouth was turned down making him look like a picture book clown. The man was concentrating, Prudence watched as he lifted one of his fingers and then another. The door of the room opened and instinctively, Prudence drew back. A woman entered, adjusted the man's pillows and eased him over on his right side, facing the window. Kissing him on the forehead, the woman turned down the lamp and left the room, closing the door behind her.

Prudence watched as the man closed his eyes. Not seeing him move for several minutes, Prudence became concerned. She pressed her face against the window and could see his chest was rising and falling. Calmer now, Prudence observed the details of the room. The pretty flowered wallpaper, the thick cushions on the chair near the window and other finery were unlike anything Prudence had ever seen. The Southern Hotel had been comfortable and elegant but it was not like this place. This was a home.

A gust of cold wind tugged at Prudence's bonnet, nearly jerking it off her head. The man's eyes opened and he stared at the little girl standing near the window. He seemed to be struggling to say something to her. *Just like in her dream.* Startled, she stepped back tangling her foot in a fallen tree branch. She regained her balance and ran for home.

Although only a short distance to her house, Prudence felt like she had run for miles. Her chest burned and her eyes were wet. She dabbed at them with her bonnet strings when she reached the Flaherty's front door. Mr. Flaherty was still snoring. Feeling frightened and alone, Prudence sat huddled in the corner. A loud tapping on the door caused Mr. Flaherty to jump and rumble. Prudence opened it a crack and was surprised to see Mrs. McAllen, the retired housekeeper from the Southern Hotel, with a large covered basket on her arm.

"Don't just stand gawking, girl. Let me in," Mrs. McAllen said crossly.

"Mr. Flaherty is sleeping and I'm not to disturb him. Meggie went to help Mrs. McGrath," Prudence whispered.

"Oh very well. Then come outside, it was you I came to see anyway," Mrs. McAllen said more softly.

Prudence picked up a lamp near the door and went out on the porch. Mrs. McAllen sat down on Meggie's porch chair. Knowing Mrs. McAllen tended to be very gruff, Prudence felt like crying.

"Margaret told me that you haven't been sleeping very well. I remember when you would sneak out and sleep with old Mr. Whiskers. He seems to miss you and I decided that even though it will be hard for me, he belongs with you," the lady said, almost kindly.

She opened the basket and Mr. Whiskers's head popped up. Throwing her arms around Mrs. McAllen and the basket, the rocking chair nearly fell over backwards.

Meggie puffed around the corner, "What's going on here?" she demanded. When she saw Mrs. McAllen and Prudence trying to keep from falling off the porch, she hurried to help them.

Embarrassed by such a display of emotion, Mrs. McAllen stood up and carefully straightened her hat.

"It's getting late, I must get back. Take good care of that cat," she said sternly.

"Oh thank you, Mrs. McAllen. I'll take very good care of him," Prudence assured her.

Meggie Flaherty shook her head. Would people never cease to amaze her? She'd never seen Maude McAllen ever do something so unselfish. Earlier in the week, she met Mrs. McAllen at the post office and told her Prudence was lonely and not sleeping. Never in a million years did she expect her to give the little girl her beloved cat.

"Let's go inside now, colleen. We'll give Mr. Whiskers some milk," Meggie helped Prudence inside with the heavy basket.

"And can you believe it Margaret? The British Ambassador is trying to get the Irish Americans to vote for Grover Cleveland. Ha! That'll surely lose the election for him," Mr. Flaherty shouted. Oblivious to what was happening, he picked up his paper from the floor.

Mrs. Flaherty patted her husband's shoulder. "To be sure, dear, to be sure. I'll be getting your supper now."

"You poor child must be wanting your supper. Just you come with Meggie and she'll get you fixed up good and proper," Meggie patted Prudence on the head, took her hand, and led her into the kitchen.

The kitchen was cool so Meggie quickly stoked the stove. Prudence shivered, not so much from the cold but from her experience. Something kept drawing her back to that house.

That night, Prudence held Mr. Whiskers tightly as Meggie tucked her into bed. "I don't think you should sleep with that cat but I know that having him close by makes you feel better so I'll allow it," she whispered as she bent to kiss Pru on the forehead.

Prudence lay awake, staring at the ceiling. That man needed her, she knew it, but she wasn't sure why. She closed her eyes tightly and wished Aunt Felicity would come back. She'd know what to do. Tears rolled down her cheeks and made little puddles in her ears. The puddles tickled and she giggled. Mr. Whiskers rubbed his head against her cheek and purred. Soon, Prudence was fast asleep.

The trip to Mormon Settlement took much needed food supplies to the settlers and miners. Frank and Martin passed the Old Man Mine, traveled across the Mangus Valley, and forded the Gila River. The water level was low and the heavily loaded wagon could easily become mired in the mud at the bottom. Frank was a skillful driver and managed to avoid getting stuck. They camped near White House on the first night. As the night grew chilly, the moon was surrounded by a halo of soft light. The fire blazed as Martin stirred it and added more wood.

"I think we're in for a cold winter. The trees are shedding leaves quicker than in most years and the fresh wind has a nip to it," he observed, pulling his coat up around his neck.

"Could be. It does seem cold for this time of year," Frank agreed.

"We'll likely make it by noon tomorrow, if we get an early start. I'll check the load in the morning to be sure it won't shift much. The draws between here and Lone Pine are steep. We don't want to cause the mules any more work than necessary," Martin said as he unrolled his bedding.

Frank started clearing an area and dug a shallow trench. He rolled up his coat for a pillow and covered himself with a wool blanket. Martin kept the first watch. Promptly at midnight, he awakened Frank for his turn at watch.

Frank groaned; he'd been dreaming about Emma. She was standing next to him wearing her favorite dress. He could even smell her rose perfume. Just as he reached up to stroke her hair, Martin gently shook his shoulder. Reluctantly, Frank struggled to his feet and went to stand by the fire. He added a few chunks of wood and took some deep breaths to clear his head. Carelessly, he brushed his hair out of his eyes and went to check on the mules tethered to one side of the wagon because there were no trees in the vicinity. The men had to bring wood for their fire with them.

An hour elapsed and the mules grew restless. Frank noticed a light some distance to the east. He picked up his 50 caliber Remington and checked to be sure it was loaded. The light disappeared for a time only to reappear again. Frank decided that it was perhaps a campfire or the light from a cabin. It didn't seem to be coming closer.

Streaks of greenish light filled the early morning sky and the flat area known by locals as Cactus Flats was soon awash with colors ranging from deep brown to purple. Frank roasted some green coffee beans, preparing them the Army way. As the sun peaked over Wild Horse Mesa to the east, he strained the coffee into two mugs. Going over to Martin, he prodded him with the toe of his boot, playfully. "I think you should get up now, it's nearly noon," Frank said.

"What? Whaaa…? Martin sputtered as he swatted at Frank's foot.

"I'm just having a little fun with you," Frank said, handing Martin a cup of his special coffee.

Martin sipped and nodded appreciatively, "That's what I call coffee!"

Frank picked up a large iron skillet out of their supply box and set it on the fire. Dropping some thick strips of bacon into the pan, he let them sizzle awhile, before using a fork to turn them over. Martin was surprised how well Frank managed with only one arm. Frank never volunteered any information about how he'd lost it and Martin hadn't asked.

"I know it is none of my business but…" Martin began.

"I wondered when you'd get around to asking," Frank interrupted.

"Asking what?" Martin feigned innocence.

"You want to know about my arm, right?"

"You never told me how you came to lose it. I figured you might sometime but you haven't."

"Nothing much to tell. I had a homestead once. I was working on the roof of my barn when the wood gave way. When I fell, my arm got caught on a nail. A bad infection set in and the arm had to be taken off," Frank related.

Martin accepted a large slice of bread and bacon from Frank. He sipped his coffee and waited to see if Frank would continue. Frank started eating and offered no further information. Martin thought it strange that a man would give up a ranch in favor of driving a freight wagon, but said nothing.

As the freight wagon crunched down through the draws and creek beds it rocked violently from side to side. The men were aware of the autumn colors that enhanced the landscape. The scent of wood smoke filled the crisp air as they approached the settlement of Pleasanton. Only a few miles ahead, as the crow flew, lay Mormon Settlement. A large hill lay between them and their destination. To take some strain off the mules, they decided to go along the San Francisco River.

A recent influx of miners into the area increased the demand for supplies. R.D. was shrewd to land a contract with a mill builder, John Graham. Scattered Mormon homesteaders tried to make a living raising vegetables and hay for livestock. There weren't any women on the street when the freight wagon stopped in front of the newly built General Store.

After unloading the wagon, Frank decided to satisfy his curiosity about the town. It didn't take long, there was a main street and a few hastily erected miner's shacks. Whitewater Creek supplied the settlement's water. The surrounding mountains sheltered the little community from fierce winter winds. It would undoubtedly be very pretty in the summer when the large trees were surrounded by lush grass.

John T. Graham was very gracious and invited Martin and Frank to stay the night after providing them with a steak dinner. Frank declined. He was anxious to get home to Prudence.

The rare steaks were tough. But the men lost no time polishing them off with large tumblers of whiskey. Martin, a little disappointed that Frank wanted to leave right away, didn't argue.

The trip back to Silver City was accomplished in record time. The mules were energized by the lightened wagons.

Frank was home late the next evening. He was surprised to see a large washtub in the middle of the sitting room. Mrs. Flaherty was boiling water.

"I know what it's like to go for days without a bath. It can't be helped sometimes but when there is plenty of water and soap we should use it," she said smiling. "You take your time and when you are finished, I'll have your supper ready."

After pouring several pots of heated water into the tub, she set some more water in buckets nearby. Clean clothes and towels were on the table next to a large cake of soap. Deftly, Mrs. Flaherty stropped Frank's razor and laid it beside his shaving mug. Then she tested the tub water with her elbow before adding some cool water.

"I'll leave you to it then," she said. "Your little girl is a treasure. Sure and I love looking after her. She's tucked up nice and snug in her bed. Mrs. McAllen gave her that old cat, Mr. Whiskers. I didn't think you would mind. Prudence and I spent the afternoon making you some special cookies and we have cold milk."

Before Frank could thank her, she was gone. Wearily, he removed his dusty, smelly clothes and piled them on the floor. He tested the water with his elbow. It was perfect! Easing his tired body into the tub, he sighed thankfully as his tightened muscles relaxed.

Chapter 42

"What did you say, Father?" Mario asked not believing his ears.

"I've found you a job as a typesetter at the Silver City Enterprise newspaper," Father Gerard repeated, smiling benevolently.

"I can't believe it. You got me a job at a newspaper," Mario looked dumbfounded.

"It is on a purely trial basis. But I think you're up to the task."

Since Father Gerard only visited Camp Fleming once a month, Mario's reading lessons were severely curtailed. He was determined to learn everything he could about reading and writing from the priest. After grueling hours of working in the hot sun, he would perch under the shade of a small juniper tree on the hill and struggle with the written words.

Sometimes, he went to town solely for the purpose of seeking answers for his numerous questions. Father Gerard was a very busy man and but always made time for his pupil. Mario's self esteem grew in leaps and bounds as the mysterious letters began to "*speak to him*". There was no more teasing when Mario began to read and answer letters from home for many of the miners.

Father Gerard brought old newspapers, discarded books that were rare, and anything written he could find, so Mario could practice. To his surprise, Mario was an excellent speller and found misspelled words in the newspaper. He marked them with his pencil and showed the priest.

Earlier that week, Father Gerard had passed the Enterprise office and seen the sign in the window advertising for a typesetter. Without hesitation, he inquired about the job and explained about his pupil. The editor insisted on an interview with Mario before making a final decision. The priest prayed about it and knew in his heart the job would be his if he had the courage to take it.

Mario stood for a long time staring at the priest. His mind couldn't grasp what the good man said. A typesetter for a newspaper was typically a well-educated man by modern day standards. Mario barely resisted the urge to fall to his knees. God had answered his prayers and made him a smart man.

"What must I do, Father?" he whispered, almost reverently.

"The editor wants to interview you tomorrow afternoon. You must take a bath, put on your best clothes and be on time," the priest smiled, noting Mario's excitement. "Now, I must go prepare for Holy Communion. Later I'll speak to your foreman and explain for you. In the meantime, pack your belongings and you may ride back to town with me." Father Gerard added, "Don't forget Holy Communion, my son."

Mario grinned and rushed off.

Father Gerard lifted his eyes up and felt warmth and a tingling sensation starting at his scalp and gently enveloping his body. He wasn't sure what caused the familiar feeling but his faith told him it was the Holy Spirit. It was his sincerest wish mankind would benefit from his having been here on earth. Even though it sounded prideful, he did feel, every once in awhile, like he made a difference.

Mario was present at Holy Communion and ready when the priest was prepared to leave for town. Donald Greer, Mario's foreman, didn't seem too surprised when Father Gerard told him about the interview at the Enterprise.

"He's a good man and we'll be sorry to lose him. I had a feeling he would be leaving when he started getting so interested in books. I've never seen anybody get so excited about a newspaper!" Greer laughed. "I wish him luck."

The ride to town was uneventful; but Mario couldn't remember when the birds sang so loudly or the breeze smelled so clean. Floating in a cloud of dreams, he barely heard the priest's conversation and only grunted from time to time in response.

Mario rented a room at the Timmer House and sent out his clothes to be washed and pressed. He knew it was an extravagance he could ill afford but wanted to look and feel his best the next day. Unfortunately, sleeping was out of the question. He tossed and turned and ended up sitting at the table reading until nearly 5:30 in the morning. Just as the sun rose, his eyelids began to get heavy.

He crawled into the disheveled bed and slept soundly for nearly three hours. There was a loud crash outside the door of his room. He fumbled for the pistol he always kept under his pillow and ran to the door. Gently, he eased it open and looked out into the hall.

A young maid was down on her knees in the middle of the floor, scrambling to pick up the remains of a tray full of dishes. "I'm so sorry if I disturbed you, sir," she apologized, "I tripped on the carpet and lost my balance."

Mario laid his gun down on the washstand inside the door and bent to assist the girl. She looked grateful. "I am going to be in a lot of trouble for breaking all of these dishes. I was asked to pick up a breakfast tray and thought I could carry it," she explained as she tried to put some of the pieces back together.

Mario helped her to her feet and finished picking up the tray of mostly broken china. Then he set the tray in her arms. "Maybe I should carry it to the kitchen for you," he offered.

"Oh no, sir," the little *señorita* exclaimed, "I would lose my job. *Muchas gracias* for helping me." The girl paused for a moment and looked at him with a strange expression on her pretty face.

"*De nada*," he said. He watched her carefully balance the heavy tray and retreat down the hall.

Mario went to the dining room for a late breakfast. His appetite, eating two eggs and a good-sized portion of ham, surprised him. The barbershop was his next destination. He got his hair cut and a shave and paid two bits for a hot bath. Donning his clean clothes, he felt like royalty. It was nearly noon and a warm day. A cold beer would really taste good, he thought.

As badly as he wanted the beer, he wanted the job more and decided it wouldn't be a good idea to go to his interview smelling like alcohol. He went back to the Timmer House and had some cold lemonade instead. After eating some lunch, he went to the Silver City Enterprise office to wait.

The editor saw him promptly at 1:00. He noticed Mario's carefully groomed appearance and shined boots. He gave him a sheet of paper to read with several misspelled words on it. Mario quickly identified them. They proceeded to the printing shop where he was introduced to Stephen Hill, the chief typesetter. Hill showed him what typesetting entailed. Mario admired the man's ability to work so quickly and said so.

"Come back tomorrow at 9:00 and I will let you know my decision," the editor told Mario.

Mario nodded and thanked him for his time. He went back to Timmer House and found Father Gerard in the lobby waiting for him.

The priest looked tired, Mario noticed. "How did your interview go?" the older man asked.

Mario sat down heavily on an ornate settee across from the priest. "I am not sure, Father. I am to go back tomorrow at 9:00 to be told if I have the job," Mario leaned forward resting his elbows on his knees. "Do you think I have a chance?"

"I have every confidence that you will get that job. I must warn you though, the editors will not tolerate tardiness or drunkenness. A parishioner of mine lost his job there because he showed up drunk one morning."

"No need to worry about that," Mario assured him, thankful he had skipped the beer.

"Let's have a good dinner and discuss your plans," Father Gerard suggested kindly.

"I'd like that very much," Mario rose to his feet and helped the priest from his low chair.

The next morning Mario was in front of the Silver City Enterprise building before it opened. He sat on the front steps and waited. Stephen Hill noticed him and went out to speak to him.

"We had a long talk yesterday after you left and have decided to give you a week's trial. If things work out, we will hire you for six months and discuss a more permanent arrangement after that," Hill told him. "If during those six months, we don't feel like you are performing well, we will let you go."

Mario thanked Fred Hill profusely and offered to start right away.

"That's all right, tomorrow is soon enough," Hill assured him.

Chapter 43

R.D. stopped in front of the Jensen house. Robert and Florence, accompanied by Charlie Mills, had been gone for nearly eight months. When Robert's ability to speak failed to return, R.D. did some research and found a doctor by the name of Samuel Potter who achieved great success in working with speech disorders. Florence had lost no time in arranging for train tickets and finding lodging accommodations in Philadelphia where Dr. Potter practiced.

From time to time, R.D. heard from Florence and was not surprised Robert was making progress. She regretted not taking Robert to see Dr. Potter sooner but knew Robert had to be strong enough physically to make the trip.

R.D. missed his friend and realized that he might never come back to Silver City. He knew Florence would rather stay in St. Louis because her parents were there.

It was R.D.'s habit to stop at the Jensen home once a week to pay Li Soo and Quetta their salaries and be sure that they were taking care of everything properly. Li Soo met him at the door and ushered him into the dining room. He sat in Robert's chair and his attention was drawn to Emma's portrait. What a pity she was gone.

R.D. took out his leather pouch and gave Li Soo money for household expenses and their salaries. "I expect to hear from Mrs. Jensen by the end of next week. I'll let you know their decision," he told her.

"Yes, thank you, sir," Li Soo said politely.

R.D. grunted and returned his pouch to his pocket. "I will be back next Friday," he said. When he returned to Miner's Mercantile a telegram was waiting for him. It was dated that morning.

Emma had a child. Stop. Is living in Silver City. Stop. Must find. Stop. Will be home as soon as can arrange. Stop. Florence

Emma had a child? R.D. was very perplexed. Still, if Florence said it, she must know something she didn't when she left town. That must mean Robert had told her. R.D. was elated; they were coming home! Bright and early on Monday morning he would go to school and try to find the Jensens's grandchild. It would help if he had a name or even knew if the child was a boy or girl.

"I might need your help, dear," R.D. told Beatrice that evening. "If the school will cooperate, I shouldn't have any trouble locating the child. Otherwise, we may have to begin a search around town."

"I'm sure the school will cooperate, why would they not?" Beatrice asked. "After all the Jensens are prominent people in the community and might show their gratitude by donating money."

R.D. was at school on Monday morning. He climbed the hill and waited on the steps as the children paraded past after the bell was rung. Hoping to catch a glimpse of someone who looked familiar, he waited and waited. No one resembled Emma, Robert, or Florence.

Meggie was worried because Frank had been gone for five days and Prudence was sick. The doctor visited and said it was nothing serious but she should stay in bed for the next few days. Meggie rushed to the druggist to get some medicine the doctor prescribed. Prudence wasn't able to keep it down and was still feverish.

Prudence's cheeks were flushed and her lips were very dry. Meggie gave her sips of cool water while supporting the child's head with her hand. "There, there little lamb. Meggie will make you all better. You just lie back and rest now," she said soothingly.

"Can Mr. Whiskers stay with me?" Prudence asked.

"If you like," Meggie said as she picked the big cat up and set him on the bed.

"I'm cold," Prudence whimpered, sitting up. "Can I have another blanket?"

"I'll put some more wood in the stove. Now be a good girl and lie down."

"When will my Papa be home?" Pru asked when Meggie returned with a blanket.

"He should be back tomorrow," she told the little girl. "You must go to sleep and get better as fast as you can."

"All right, Meggie," Prudence closed her eyes. Mr. Whiskers purred as Prudence snuggled down under the covers, feeling comforted.

Meggie closed the door and went to make herself a cup of tea. It would help her think what else she could do to get the child through her illness. Not having any little ones for awhile, she was out of practice.

The wind was so cold his bones ached. Twenty more miles and he could sit in front of the fire to thaw out. Frank kept his eyes open due to reports of a band of outlaws in the area. They were carrying the freight payment back from Georgetown.

Clouds darkened the late afternoon sky. Martin was up ahead on the road watching for any signs of trouble. Frank kept the mules at an easy trot. With the wagon unloaded, they were able to make good time.

Martin came at a gallop. "Just up ahead, I saw some tracks leading off the road toward the hill. I think we might be in for trouble."

"How many horses?" Frank asked.

"I can't be sure but I'd say about five or six."

"Is your rifle loaded?" Frank reined the mules to a stop.

"Sure, I've got three rifles in the wagon and this one," Martin assured him.

"Let's camp over there behind those rocks," Frank pointed to several large boulders about twenty yards away.

"You don't think we should try to make a run for it?" Martin asked, cocking his pistol.

"We wouldn't stand a chance in hell of out running men on horseback. It'll be dark in about two hours. We can build a fire and set up camp, acting like we don't know they're around. Then we can hide and start shooting when they come to get us."

Martin frowned and looked disappointed.

"Believe me, we're a lot better off waiting for them than having them wait for us," Frank assured him as he urged the mules toward their planned campsite.

Martin gathered wood as Frank dug a fire pit. The wind was really beginning to blow and the men had difficulty getting the fire started. They piled wood on the flames and crouched beside it for a few minutes to soak up some heat before taking defensive positions in the brush.

Martin fixed their bedrolls to look like they were in them and disappeared into the darkness to wait.

Frank's phantom pains were so severe, he could barely breathe. His rifle was propped and aimed at the fire. Fighting discomfort, he prayed they wouldn't have to wait too long.

His prayers were answered. Dark figures approached stealthily. He held his breath as he watched one stoop to check his bedroll.

"There's no one here, Sheriff," he heard a voice shout.

"Sure they're here. They saw our tracks and are hiding in the bushes. Jones! Are you out there?" the sheriff yelled.

"Is that you, Sheriff?" Frank yelled back.

"I heard you were out here and wanted to let you know that we caught those bandits and are on our way back to town. Thought we might ride with you."

Frank emerged from the darkness and Martin joined the others near the fire. The outlaws were tied together and members of the posse took turns guarding them. The rest huddled around the fire drinking hot fragrant coffee.

Frank and Martin unrolled their blankets under the wagon as a light snow fell. Breaking camp at sunrise, the large group of men headed for Silver City.

Chapter 44

"Guess what, Prudence? Guess what?" Callie yelled excitedly, when she met her friend on the way up the hill to school.

"What?" Prudence was immediately caught up in her friend's excitement.

"My grandmother sent me a whole fifty cents and my mother said we could go to the store after school and spend a nickel each on candy. If it's all right with your papa," Callie was jumping up and down and so was Prudence.

"My Papa is gone, but I'm sure Meggie wouldn't mind," Prudence's eyes sparkled. A whole nickel for candy!

The girls ran the rest of the way to school and were breathless by the time they reached the line. Hours dragged by. Finally, school was over for the day and the girls grabbed their coats and rushed down the hill toward Prudence's house.

Bursting through the door, Prudence nearly knocked Meggie down.

"Sure and what's your hurry, colleen? You nearly knocked the wind out of me," Meggie smiled as she saw the look of joy on the girls' faces.

"Callie's grandmother sent money for us to buy some candy. Can we go to the store now and get some?" Prudence pleaded.

"Well now, it just so happens that I need to go to the post office. If you will give me a minute, I will go with you," Meggie was pleased to see Prudence in such good spirits.

"Oh, please hurry, Meggie!" Prudence begged breathlessly.

Soon the three were on their way to town. Meggie left the girls at Miner's Mercantile and told them to wait there for her. Prudence and Callie stood for a long time in front of the candy counter. The store was very warm and after the running she had done, Prudence was uncomfortable. She took off her large bonnet and tied the ribbons around her neck so she wouldn't lose it. Now, she could really examine those mouthwatering temptations. She'd never seen so many different kinds of candies. How would she be able to choose?

Robert and Florence had returned to Silver City by train three days before. Charlie Mills had decided to stay in St. Louis. Nearly completely recovered from the effects of his apoplexy, Robert unexpectedly appeared at the mercantile that morning and was working with the new bookkeeper, R. D hired.

After examining the ledgers for nearly two hours without a break, he decided to get up and walk around. He was wearing spectacles for the first time and although they made the numbers clearer, he was beginning to get a headache. Removing his spectacles, he rubbed his eyes and polished the lenses with his handkerchief.

Some children were laughing and he smiled as he walked toward the sound. Two little girls were standing in front of the candy counter. His eyes blurred suddenly and his breath caught in his throat. He staggered toward R.D.'s office and walked in without knocking.

R.D. took one look at his friend's face and thought he was having a seizure. Alarmed, he jumped to his feet, poured a glass of water from the tumbler on his desk and shoved it into Robert's hand.

"My God, you look like you've seen a ghost. Are you all right?" R.D. stuffed his arms into his greatcoat getting ready to run for the doctor.

"She's here!" was all Robert could manage to say.

"Who's here? You aren't making any sense," R.D. admonished him. Suddenly, he understood and ran out into the store.

Prudence and Callie made their candy purchases and paused near a perfume display. Prudence carefully picked up a pretty cut glass bottle and removed the stopper. She was just bringing the bottle to her nose when R.D. burst into the store. Startled, she turned to see him pointing at her and yelling for her to stop. Without thinking, Prudence dropped the bottle and ran from the store. Callie was right behind her.

Meggie met Mrs. McAllen in the post office. The two were catching up on gossip and failed to see Prudence running up the street with R.D. right behind her. Terrified, she didn't even think about Meggie, she knew she must get home. Callie ran in and grabbed Meggie's coat.

"Just a minute, young lady. It is rude to interrupt when grown-ups are talking," Mrs. McAllen scolded.

"I'm very sorry, ma'am but Pru's in trouble," Callie apologized and started to cry.

"Gracious, child. What kind of trouble?" Meggie asked biding Mrs. McAllen a hasty goodbye. Callie dragged her out into the street.

"There's a man chasing her. I think she's going home. We didn't do anything bad. The man scared Pru and she dropped a bottle of perfume. She didn't mean to but he yelled at her and now he's chasing her."

"Oh, my! The poor colleen she must be frightened out of her wits," Meggie exclaimed as the two started running toward home.

Frank brushed some of the dirt from his trousers before entering the house. He was anxious to read Felicity's letter. After a long trip to Alma, he was ready to sit in a comfortable chair and relax. Prudence was in town with Meggie and would be back soon, Mr. Flaherty told him. He fed a few chunks of wood into the stove, stirred the fire, and lit the lamp. Felicity's letters were long and chatty. She wrote much like she talked and he enjoyed reading them over and over.

Dear Frank and Prudence,

You'll be glad to know that the judge is much better and has even been talking about working again. Of course, he can't for a while yet but he enjoys thinking about it.

I'm very happy because I've decided to come for a visit to Silver City and I'm bringing a surprise. You can expect me sometime in late April or early May.

Frank paused, he knew Prudence would be thrilled. Hearing a commotion outside, Frank went to the window to look out. His boss, R.D. Farnsworth was standing on the porch with Prudence. Frank's knees turned to jelly, as he opened the door.

R.D. looked at his employee in surprise. "This is your daughter?" he asked.

Frank managed a nod and a weak smile.

"Well, sir, I think you and your daughter need to come with me," R.D. commanded. He escorted them directly to the Jensen house.

Florence noticed some people approaching the house in the dwindling light and thought Robert had suffered another attack. Panic stricken, she rushed to the door and threw it open. Falling to her knees and sobbing, R.D. helped her to a chair. He ushered Frank and Prudence into the parlor and asked them to wait while he went to get Robert.

The icy wind pierced Robert's greatcoat as he walked toward his home. R.D. rushed out of the store following a little girl, the clerk told him. Robert must get home to tell Florence. A wagon clattered by and Robert was so lost in thought, he nearly stepped into its path. Numbly, he proceeded in the direction of home.

R.D. asked Li Soo to stay with Frank and Prudence and make them comfortable while he went back to the mercantile to get Robert. He harnessed the Jensens's horses and hitched up the trap. He went about half a mile and encountered his friend walking. Bundling, Robert into the trap, R.D. clucked to the horses and rushed back to the Jensen house.

Li Soo stared at the little girl in amazement. She looked exactly like the picture of Miss Emma hanging in the dining room. Florence recovered from her near faint and was staring at the man and little girl in front of her. She opened her mouth once or twice to say something and then shut it abruptly. Even her mistress was at a loss for words.

Robert and R.D. came in and sat down. Frank shifted in his chair. He hadn't bathed for three days. Clearly, he was in for a difficult confrontation. R.D. formerly introduced their employee, Latimer Jones, to Robert and Florence.

"My name is Frank Parnell and this is my daughter, Prudence," Frank corrected him. His mouth was so dry he could barely speak.

Robert noticed Frank's discomfort. Slowly, he rose from the chair and walked over to the liquor cabinet. "Would anyone like a drink?" he asked.

"I'd like a drink of water," Prudence said timidly. Her papa had told these people their real last name!

"Of course, dear. Let's you and I get acquainted and leave these men to talk. Is that all right?" Florence asked Frank, who nodded.

Mr. Flaherty heard the man demand Frank and Prudence accompany him. When his wife came home, he told her what happened. Meggie took Callie home and explained to Callie's mother that Callie was entirely blameless.

Meggie fretted and stewed all evening. Prudence would not break the perfume bottle on purpose. Would the man arrest the child and her father? Surely not, she reasoned. She should never have allowed the two girls to go into the mercantile unattended.

"Nonsense, my girl," Mr. Flaherty said. "It was none of your doing. Don't get so steamed up. I'm sure the girl and her father are on their way home already. They can take the cost of the scent out of her Pa's pay."

Florence reached for Prudence's hand and guided her into the dining room. Florence lit the lamps watching Prudence's face. The little girl was in awe of her surroundings as she looked around the room. When she saw the large portrait of Emma, her eyes widened in amazement.

"That's my Mama!" she gasped. Her hand went to the locket around her neck and she opened it showing the faded picture to Florence.

"Yes, dear. That's my daughter, Emma. I'm your grandmother and Robert, the man you helped, is your grandfather." Florence choked as she reached for her clean handkerchief to dab at her eyes. "We're very glad to have found you."

Prudence gazed at her mother's portrait. The sick man seemed familiar because he was her grandfather. She felt a lump rise in her throat. Her Mama tried to tell her with the enchanted tree and piano music. Prudence put her arms around her grandmother's shoulders. "I am glad that you found me, too," she whispered, as tears slid down her cheeks.

Chapter 45

Florence went into the parlor, after asking Quetta to serve supper. Li Soo helped Prudence wash up. It was well past the dinner hour and Florence decided they should eat before entering into what might prove to be a very long discussion. She was surprised to see Robert, R.D., and Frank sitting in front of the fire, sipping whiskey. She could see the telltale artery in Robert's temple pulsing and knew she must do something to diffuse the situation.

"Gentlemen, I think we should all have something to eat before talking. Quetta laid three more places at the table and dinner will be served in about ten minutes. Finish your drinks. I'd like to speak to you alone, Robert, if you gentlemen will excuse us for a moment?" Florence asked politely.

Robert sighed and slowly rose to his feet. Hesitantly, he followed his wife outside to the veranda.

"What are you going to say to him?" she asked her husband.

"I'm not sure," he replied. "I can't imagine why he didn't contact us when Emma became ill!"

"Don't allow yourself to get angry, dear. It will serve no purpose and only cause Frank and Prudence to be driven away from us for good. I want our granddaughter in my life and no matter what Frank may have done, she is blameless!" Florence insisted.

"You're right, I'll stay calm. After we eat, have Li Soo look after the little girl and we'll discuss the situation like adults," Robert agreed.

Dinner was tense. Feeling extremely uncomfortable, Frank watched the large clock in the corner of the dining room. Its ticking was deafening in the silence that ensued during the meal.

His eyes were drawn to the face of Emma in the large portrait. Robert, Florence and R.D. noticed the expression on Frank's face when he first saw the portrait upon entering the room. The love he had for Emma was apparent to everyone.

Prudence was very sleepy and disturbed by the adults' silence. She squirmed in her chair but didn't say anything. Li Soo watched from the doorway and when Pru was finished eating she came in and took her by the hand, announcing to the group that she had prepared a bed upstairs for Prudence. Frank and Florence nodded.

Quetta served coffee in the parlor and closed the door. Frank cleared his throat. He would be expected to account for the past and he was unsure how to begin. "I know this will be hard for you to hear but I loved your daughter. She was my life. When she died, I had only Prudence and I couldn't face losing her," he began.

"Why would you lose her?" Florence asked.

"Emma led me to believe that you might try to take my daughter away from me if you knew of her existence."

Robert sputtered and started to rise from his chair. Florence threw him an admonishing look. Grunting, he sat back down.

"Why weren't we informed she was so ill?" Florence asked calmly.

"She was afraid that you might insist she leave me and come home with our daughter," Frank replied sadly. "She wanted to visit you when she recovered; but her illness got worse and she was too weak to make the trip. I wanted to tell you, but she pleaded with me."

"She must have thought we were monsters!" Robert cried.

"No sir, she loved you both very much. She was unsure how you would behave toward me. I was afraid you would insist on taking our child knowing Emma was so ill. I was so taken in by her fears that when we came to Silver City, I was determined not to let you know of Prudence's existence."

Frank told them about their courtship, marriage, and experiences on the homestead. They listened carefully and Frank observed the play of emotions on their faces. After nearly two hours, he felt drained and empty, not caring what happened to him, just wanting it to be over at last. He would keep Prudence at all costs, even if it meant running.

Florence was the first to speak when Frank finished his story.

"I am so sorry! You must feel terribly alone. Robert and I want Prudence to be a part of our lives. Emma loved you and you were her family as you are now ours. We would never take your daughter away from you. Please allow us to be her grandparents and love her, our only daughter's child," Florence pleaded.

Frank smiled and reached for his mother-in-law's hand. She grasped his hand firmly, feeling the rough calluses. "Of course, there is nothing I'd like better," he assured her.

Robert stood as Frank jumped to his feet. The two men shook hands and R.D. clapped them both on the back. Florence dabbed at her eyes with her kerchief. Her chest ached with happiness. She would never have Emma back; but at least she could watch her granddaughter grow up. How she looked forward to loving her daughter's beautiful child.

PART II
NEW BEGINNINGS

A well-heeled traveler once wrote to family back East about the strange weather in the southwest territories of New Mexico and Arizona. He compared the summer rains to the monsoons of India and the word monsoon stuck. He wrote:

The desert writhes under a blistering sky and casts ropy dust devils toward oblivion. Acrid breezes rustle down arroyos; stirring cupped cottonwood leaves.

A ghostly specter rises behind a craggy cliff, its pale tentacles embrace the rocks and mold billowing turrets, as it festers. Shadows shroud the land as an eerie silence prevails. Then a low rumble from a giant's throat spews forth an arsenal of fiery spears. Roaring, the behemoth flicks spittle from its huge maw. Fine pockmarks riddle the pristine powder of a mountain trail left scoured by relentless winds.

After an emission of explosive groans, there is a crescendo and deafening bullets pelt the earth; the monster liquefies. Moisture congeals in patches and tiny rivulets trickle down chapped rocks. Soon, a deluge of mud and splintered stone rips through the sun-scorched gullies, shredding and devouring living and dead flora, in its maelstrom.

Gouging, with its glistening teeth, it surges toward a small town near the foot of the Rocky Mountains. Its menacing, muddy roils erode the streets and dreams of the townspeople.

Then, as if by magic, the hush of an elusive rainbow, strokes the swollen sands.

Chapter 1

Frank looked at his father-in-law skeptically. Robert's idea of putting him in charge of ordering and stocking Miner's Mercantile was unsettling. It was a big step and one Frank would like time to consider.

"It would mean a large pay increase, of course," R.D. assured him.

Frank grinned, slightly embarrassed. It really wasn't about the money. "I guess I could try it for awhile. Could I think about it for a couple of days?"

R.D. and Robert smiled at each other and then at Frank. The two cooked up the plan together over the last week. Florence pleaded with them to find Frank a position that would insure his safety. Driving the freight wagon was much too dangerous.

The two men spoke to Frank on several occasions and casually questioned him about his past. They were pleasantly surprised to discover that Frank, known to his employers as Latimer Jones, could read and write legibly. There was a consensus of opinion that Jones was a reliable, hard-working man.

R.D. and Beatrice came for supper, one night in late August. Beatrice and Florence discussed the latest project of the Ladies' Aid Society while R.D. and Robert spoke in hushed voices near the fireplace. Florence looked up sharply when she heard Frank's name. Beatrice was rattling on and on about a quilt she was making.

"Wait just a moment, my dear. I must find out what those two are talking about," Florence told her friend. "I get the feeling they're talking about something that concerns our son-in-law and I want to know what it is."

Beatrice stopped in mid-sentence. She knew of Florence's concern and ignored her rude interruption. She was more than a little curious herself about the partner's decision regarding the Jensens's newly discovered son-in-law. Florence rose from her chair and crossed to her escritoire, pretending to retrieve a writing paper and pen.

Robert and R.D. stopped their conversation and looked guilty.

"I realize what you decide to do about Frank is your business but I'd like to be included in this conversation, if you don't mind," Florence said.

"Very well, my dear. You have a right to know what we've decided," Robert agreed.

Robert and R.D. invited the two women to join them near the fire and told them about their decision to offer Frank an office job. Florence doubted it would be as easy as the partners predicted. She felt Frank might be hesitant about accepting an indoor job. He was a rugged outdoor individual by all appearances. She kept her opinion to herself and let the men continue with their plans.

It was dark when Frank arrived home after R.D. and Robert had insisted in discussing the details of his new position. He finally agreed to try it for at least six months.

Prudence was helping Meggie clean the pantry. She met him at the door with a large towel wrapped around her dress and a rag tied around her hair. A large smudge of dirt across her nose made her look like a little street urchin. Frank chuckled as he brushed at the smudge with his finger.

"Why are you so late, Papa? Supper was ready hours ago," Prudence admonished him.

Frank knelt down in front of her. "Your grandfather and Mr. Farnsworth gave me a new job. They wanted to discuss it with me. I won't be driving the freight wagons any more, I'll be staying home and working at the mercantile. Now I'll have time to spend with my best girl."

"Oh, Papa!" was all Prudence could say as she threw her arms around him and smothered his face with kisses.

Mario sat looking out of the second story window of his room in Timmer House. He was far away, marveling at his good fortune and making plans for the future. He heard a commotion in the street below.

Juanita, the little maid, stood in the street below, her hands on her hips, speaking loudly to a woman standing in front of her, "But I didn't get any of my paycheck this time. It all went to cover breakage. It's not fair, I try so hard to do my job!"

"Don't worry, you will do better. Just give yourself some more time. You've worked at this job for a year and this is the first time you didn't get at least some of your paycheck," the older woman said trying hard to soothe her.

Juanita tended to be overly dramatic and dabbed at her eyes with her handkerchief.

"You couldn't possibly understand, Quetta. Mama says you're perfect and never make mistakes," Juanita sobbed.

As Mario sat hoping for a cool breeze, the older woman caught his attention. He caught his breath. She was beautiful!

Not wanting to be caught eavesdropping, he pulled his head in. He glanced in the mirror and straightened up his clothes. He wanted to meet this woman. Rushing downstairs, he nearly knocked down an elderly couple approaching the landing. The gray haired man shook his cane at him and muttered something, the lady just smiled. Mario smiled back and didn't slow down.

By the time he reached the street, Juanita and her sister were nearing Main Street. He coughed loudly causing Juanita to look back. She smiled and waved and motioned for him to catch up.

Quetta looked embarrassed. She slapped at her sister's hand.

"It isn't proper for a lady to behave like that," she admonished a wickedly grinning Juanita.

Mario rushed up and extended his hand to Juanita. "H-How are you today, little Señorita?" he stammered.

"I'm fine, Señor Mario. This is my sister, Enriquetta. She is the cook for the owners of Miner's Mercantile. She isn't married," Juanita giggled.

Quetta was shocked at her sister's behavior. "I am very sorry, Señor. I don't know what is wrong with my sister to behave like this. We must go on about our business. *Mucho gusto*," Quetta grabbed Juanita's arm and pulled her toward the dressmaker's shop.

Mario started to protest but saw Enriquetta was upset and didn't want to make things worse. He watched silently as the women entered the shop and closed the door. His heart was beating rapidly and he could barely breathe. Enriquetta was the most beautiful woman he'd ever seen. Even her voice sounded like the wind in the trees.

"Bah, now I'm getting sentimental," he chided himself. But try as he might, he couldn't forget Quetta's unique beauty.

"What a fool I am, to fall for a pretty face!" he thought the next morning as he went downstairs for breakfast in the dining room. Juanita was there, dressed in white and serving coffee from a silver pot. She approached his table smiling.

"What did you think of my sister?" she didn't wait for him to reply. "I told her that you are an important newspaperman. I think she was impressed."

"I am not a newspaperman, I am a typesetter. There's a big difference, little one," Mario smiled.

"Not to me. I'll bet you could write for the paper. Every time I see you, you're reading something. You must know a lot from all of those books."

"I thank you for your confidence in me. Your sister is very pretty. I would like to get to know her better but it wouldn't be proper for me to approach her. Do you think you might help me meet her and perhaps talk a little?" Mario asked. He couldn't help feeling a little self-conscious. It wasn't proper for him to ask Juanita to help him.

"I happen to know that she will be attending the street dance tonight. You could ask her to dance because I did introduce you," Juanita grinned, feeling very superior. For weeks, she tried to think of a way to get her sister and the nice Señor Mario acquainted and now it was going to be easier than she expected.

Chapter 2

Prudence brushed her hair carefully and Meggie helped her braid it. Buttoning her shoes was impossible; Pru's fingers were shaking so badly. Frank put on his good suit and they were on their way to meet the train. Felicity was coming today and bringing a surprise.

Frank finished reading Felicity's letter to Prudence for the hundredth time, when the train roared into the station. A tall blond man with wintry blue eyes stepped onto the platform and turned to help his companion, Felicity! Felicity grasped the man's arm and hurried over to where Frank and Prudence were standing.

"Frank, Pru! It is so good to see you! I've missed you so much!" she hugged them both. Then she turned her head to smile at her companion. "I would like to introduce you to my husband, Peder Jorgensen."

Frank blinked several times and his jaw dropped. Prudence smiled shyly at the handsome man. There was warmth in his eyes when he smiled back. Frank shook Peder's hand. Unable to find his voice, he went to get their luggage.

"Sorry, you caught me off guard. Congratulations, I am very happy for you both," he said struggling with Felicity's bag.

Felicity looked hurt. Prudence reached for her aunt's hand.

"It's a nice surprise, Aunt Felicity," she said sincerely.

Judge McCoy advocated statehood for New Mexico as Peder Jorgensen worked long and hard to see that dream become a reality. Just when it seemed statehood might be imminent, the judge died one night in his sleep. Felicity was heartbroken; the poor man just couldn't recuperate from several long bouts of pneumonia. Peder continued but his heart wasn't in it anymore.

During Judge McCoy's illnesses, Jorgensen often visited his house to consult the older man. Felicity made sure that the two were fed and comfortable during their long meetings.

Peder Jorgensen sought out Felicity at the Judge's funeral. When he saw her reddened eyes and pink nose caused by hours of crying, his heart ached. He visited her later that evening and the two found solace in each other's company. Peder brought her flowers and candy. Felicity had a beau! She couldn't believe her ears when he asked her to marry him a few short weeks later.

After they were married, Felicity started a letter to Frank, and decided she'd prefer to tell her brother in person. She persuaded Peder to take a break from politics so that they could visit her family in Silver City.

On the way home, Prudence sat silently clinging to Felicity's arm. It was hard to keep from telling Felicity how much she had missed her. Her pretty aunt had her own life with her new husband, Prudence thought.

I mustn't let her think I'm a baby, she told herself.

Peder and Frank discussed Peder's favorite subject, statehood. Frank admired the man's ability to speak candidly about his passion for politics. Peder liked Frank's opinions. Felicity breathed a sigh of relief. She couldn't stand it if the men in her life didn't get along.

"You're awfully quiet, Pru. What do you think of my new husband?" Felicity whispered.

"He's nice, I guess," Prudence whispered back.

"Let's go to your room and have a talk," Felicity said, taking Prudence's hand. She led her to the tiny bedroom and gently closed the door. "Just because I'm married doesn't mean I don't love you anymore. When you were a baby, you needed someone to take care of you. Your papa asked me to come because he had no one else. I stayed until you were old enough to go to school. I realized what I had been missing after spending time with you," she paused, "I'm not happy living in a small town. I want a family of my own," she noticed the stricken expression on Prudence's face. "I know I'm not explaining this very well."

Prudence looked forward to Felicity's visit because she thought she might be coming home to stay. Now she knew her aunt would never live with them again. It was hard to breathe as a huge lump formed in her throat. Felicity's heart ached, she put her arms around her niece's small shoulders and rocked her back and forth.

Chapter 3

Robert stood looking out his office window with his back to Frank. He sensed something was wrong. "You're doing a great job, son," Robert said.

He was unable to see the play of emotions on Frank's face but turned around when Frank did not reply. Frank didn't know what to say so he sat quietly staring at his hand. Six months of paperwork made the calluses disappear, the skin was smooth and even his fingernails were clean. During all these months, he never really looked at his hand. Now he almost didn't recognize it.

Not sure what to make of his son-in-law's silence, Robert continued crossing over to stand beside Frank's chair. "We'd like to make your position permanent. R.D. and I like things legal, so we will draw up a contract and get your signature. Your raise will go into effect at that time," Robert clapped Frank on the back with enthusiasm. "By the way, Florence and I would like to invite you and Prudence to supper tonight. She has something she'd like to discuss with you."

Frank looked up at his father-in-law. "What time sir?" he asked.

"Around six. We can talk before we eat," Robert replied.

Frank nodded and rose to his feet. "I guess I'll get back to work, if that's all?"

"Sure son, see you at six," Robert said. He went over to sit down in his chair. Steepling his fingers, he leaned forward and rested his elbows on the desk. Frank didn't seem very excited about his job. What was the problem?

Frank went to the supply room and sat down on an old wooden bench. "How am I going to tell them?" he wondered aloud.

Felicity and Peder's visit lasted only two weeks. From Silver City, they were going to Denver. Peder wanted to explore Colorado. A born politician, he knew some people who could introduce him around. If things looked promising, the newlyweds might settle there.

Soon after they left, Frank realized how dissatisfied he was with his new job. In some ways, a jail cell would be easier to tolerate. The work wasn't so bad, it was just confining. His entire life, Frank worked outdoors. Working day after day, at a little desk by a tiny dusty window facing the loading dock, was his idea of hell. To make matters worse, Martin and his new partner enjoyed swapping yarns and laughing right outside. Frank wanted to join them.

The job had its good points, too. It was nice going home to Prudence every night. She enjoyed herself in school and was taking piano lessons three times a week from her grandmother, Florence. When sleep eluded him, Frank sat in the

Silver City Roils

rocking chair in Prudence's room, watching her sleep. Several hours later, he was stiff, cold, and sore. Returning to his room, he'd lie awake and stare at the ceiling.

Something had to be done, he couldn't continue like this. Reluctant to let Robert and R.D. down, he struggled to figure out a way to tell them.

Frank finished up his work and started for home. He tucked his hat under his partial right arm and went to the hitching post outside. Sassy was waiting, his graying chin raised in a greeting as his master approached. Frank smoothed his own graying hair before putting on his hat.

Robert and Florence welcomed Prudence and Frank into their family. Every Sunday, the four of them attended church and returned to the Jensen home for dinner. Florence gave Prudence piano lessons on Monday, Wednesday, and Friday afternoons after school.

Frank explained to Robert and Florence he didn't want Prudence to be spoiled. Before they gave her presents, they needed to discuss it with him. The first thing Florence bought for her granddaughter was a silver chain to replace the leather cord around her neck. Prudence was delighted with the gift and Frank didn't have the heart to tell her the cord was more practical. He put the beloved locket on the chain for her. Prudence was so proud, she rushed right over to show Meggie.

It was very unusual for the Jensens to invite them over for dinner in the middle of the week. Frank hoped he would think of some way to bring up the subject of his job while he was there tonight.

Prudence was sitting on the front porch holding old Mr. Whiskers. She sang a lullaby while the cat purred loudly.

"Your grandmother invited us for dinner tonight. Run along and wash your face and hands and change your dress, we don't want to be late," Frank said as he dismounted.

Prudence and Frank arrived at the Jensen's promptly at six. Greeted at the door by Li Soo, Prudence began chattering as soon as she saw her. Li Soo and Quetta were Prudence's special friends and she loved to visit with them. Li Soo took them into the parlor where Florence was waiting.

"Prudence, Quetta would like to see you in the kitchen for a few minutes. Would you please go and see if you can help her?" Florence asked.

"Is it all right, Papa?" Prudence wanted to know.

"Go ahead. I'll see you at dinner, Kitten," Frank agreed. He sat down in his favorite chair, anxious to find out what this was all about.

As soon as Prudence left, Robert came in and sat down. The two older people sat on the settee facing Frank. Florence didn't waste time with small talk.

"My father is very ill and my mother fears he's dying. It is his greatest wish to meet Prudence," Florence told him. "Robert and I feel it would be a good time, now school is nearly over, for me to take Prudence to St. Louis."

Frank started to reply, and Florence held up her hand. "Before you speak, let me finish. I know this will be a difficult decision for you to make but please consider your daughter. She has never been back East or even to a city. It would be a wonderful opportunity for her to see more of the country as well as a chance to meet her great grandparents."

"I don't know what to say. It's dangerous to travel across the country and I wouldn't even be there to protect her. I'm sorry but I don't think it is a good idea."

"I don't want to argue with you, Frank, but my father is not going to live much longer. He has been so good to us and asked for very little in return. I'd love to be able to grant his dying wish," Florence said softly with emotion.

"I understand how you must feel but I don't want my daughter exposed to any danger. She's very young."

"I would never allow anything to happen to her as long as there is breath left in my body!" Florence assured him. "We'll travel by train and be in St. Louis in less than a week. Please think it over and tell me on Sunday what you have decided."

The adults were very quiet during the meal. Prudence noticed and tried to draw them into conversation to no avail. On the way home she asked, "Why are you so sad, Papa?"

He kissed the top of her head. "I'm not sad, Kitten, I'm just thinking."

"Grandmother and Grandfather acted sad too. Did I do something wrong?" she asked.

"Of course not. We discussed something while you were in the kitchen and we couldn't agree on what was to be done. Sometimes adults have problems talking things over. It wasn't anything you did."

"What were you talking about? Maybe I can help," Prudence said, precociously.

"You may be right," Frank paused and considered discussing the trip to St. Louis with her. "Your grandmother would like to take you to visit her parents, your great grandparents, in St. Louis. I wouldn't go; it would be just the two of you. Your great grandfather is very old and sick and wants to meet you."

"Oh Papa, couldn't you come too. It would be fun to go on a train and see St. Louis. Grandmother talks about it all the time," Prudence was seated in front of Frank on the saddle and nearly bounced off.

"I couldn't come, Pru, I have to stay here and work. But maybe you should go. I am being selfish and thinking only about myself."

"Papa, I promise to be good and do everything that Grandmother tells me. I would really like to go."

"Let me think about it a little more and I'll give you my answer," Frank said.

Frank helped his daughter down from the saddle and led Sassy around the back to the corral. He was being selfish and not considering what the experience would mean to Prudence. It was just so dangerous!

Chapter 4

On a sunny summer morning, Frank felt icy fingers crawling along his spine. After several days of deliberation, he agreed Prudence should have the opportunity to meet her great-grandparents. As they approached the train depot, Prudence gently took his hand.

"Don't worry, Papa. I won't be gone very long. Please take good care of Mr. Whiskers, he'll miss me."

"Be a good girl, Kitten, and mind what your grandmother says," Frank grinned weakly.

"Oh, I will. Thank you for letting me go, Papa," Prudence jumped up from the wagon seat and kissed his cheek. Frank kissed her back; his chest felt tight.

Later he watched until the train was out of sight, before leaving the platform. When he reached Broadway, Martin, his old partner hurried over to him and shook his hand. It was obvious he was excited about something and didn't notice Frank was upset.

"You won't believe it. It's finally happened! I found a girl I want to marry," Martin said proudly.

Frank listened as Martin rambled on and on about his wonderful Judith. He praised her so highly; Frank began to doubt he was speaking about a real woman.

"I really want you to meet her and tell me what you think," Martin insisted.

"Maybe, we could all go to dinner," Frank said quietly.

"No, I have a much better idea. There is a dance tomorrow night in Pinos Altos. We'll ride up tomorrow and come back on Sunday and live it up for a change."

"I'm not up to socializing right now." Frank explained Prudence was on her way to St. Louis with her grandmother.

"Don't you see pal? Socializing is just what you need right now. Your girl is growing up. You need to worry about yourself for a change. I'll meet you in front of the store, after work," Martin grinned exuberantly and hurried away before Frank could reply.

Frank shook his head. Martin's enthusiasm was unusual and maybe there was something in what he said. There would be a time when Prudence would get married and have children of her own and he would be a lonely old man.

Late summer afternoons in the southwest are uncomfortably warm. The next day as Frank and Martin entered the foothills of the Continental Divide, they were greeted by a cool breeze. Frank rode old Sassy and had difficulty keeping up with Martin astride his young mare. Sassy's white muzzle belied his age and he no longer had his youthful enthusiasm for outings. Despite Sassy's reluctance, the men settled in at the Palmer House in Pinos Altos by seven. Ancheta's Barber Shop was open late so there was time for a bath, shave, and haircut before the dance.

The new Pacific Hotel was having their grand opening. Flowers were abundant in brass vases and great quantities of food were prepared for this summer festivity.

Martin was taller than most, and stood with his back against a wall while scanning the room. Judith Watson promised to meet him here tonight. He knew she was one of the hostesses for the event and already there. It didn't take him long to spot the prettiest girl in the room. Her black hair gleamed in the lamplight.

"Uh, I've got it bad," he groaned, clutching his abdomen.

"Did you say something?" Frank asked.

"Er, no, I see Judith speaking to those ladies. Come on, I'll introduce you," Martin led the way through the thickening crowd.

After introductions, Martin led Judith away to dance. The musicians had started and soon her hostess duties would occupy most of her time for the rest of the evening. Frank looked around him and spotted Trolius Stephens, owner of Ancheta Trading Post General Mercantile. Stephens raised his arm in greeting and beckoned for Frank to join his group.

Several fiddle players stood on a platform in the corner and two of the men had a contest to see who could play the fastest. The dancers' feet flew and breathless laughter rang from the rafters. When the song was over, everyone including the onlookers, gasped for air.

Frank saw her. Standing amid a throng of young men, she looked up suddenly and smiled at him. Laughingly, she fanned herself with her hands. Sadie Calhoun was even more beautiful than Frank remembered.

"Don't you agree, Jones…I mean, Parnell?" Stephens asked.

"Uh, yes…I mean, I'm sorry sir, I didn't hear what you asked," Frank stammered.

Trolius Stephens's eyes narrowed as he followed Frank's gaze to the other side of the room. "It wasn't important. Why don't you ask Sadie for a dance?"

Frank turned to look at the older man. "She has a number of beaus. I don't think she would even consider dancing with me."

"Son, you've got a lot to learn about women. Sadie has known most of those fellas her whole life and she hasn't fallen for any of them yet. Don't count yourself out so easily," Stephens paused to light a large cigar and puffed smoke up toward the ceiling. "Go on now, ask her for a dance."

"If you really think I should, I guess there's no harm in asking," Frank laughed with a confidence he didn't feel. He caught Sadie's eye and saw a flicker of interest as he approached but before he could reach her, a handsome young cowboy took her hand and led her toward the dance floor.

"Just a minute, Sam, I promised this dance to an old friend. I'm sure you don't mind," Sadie withdrew her hand and turned to Frank whose face was wearing a look of pure disappointment.

The sudden smile on Frank's face touched something deep inside Sadie. Her fingers trembled as she grasped his hand. She'd always known he was someone special. When he and Martin drove the freight wagon to Pinos Altos, Sadie tried to show "Latimer Jones" that she was interested in him but although polite, Mr. Jones seem disinterested. Tonight, he seemed different, more confident. She could tell he was attracted to her.

The tired fiddlers eased into a slow waltz tempo. Frank held Sadie at a respectful distance but as the dance went on, the floor became so crowded Sadie was pressed closely against his chest.

Frank hadn't danced with a woman since Emma. Sadie was so soft, his arm tightened around her. He couldn't see her face but he sensed Sadie was smiling.

The dance was over and the musicians called for a break. Dancers rushed to the dining tables to refresh themselves. Frank escorted Sadie back to her group of young men who had been joined by some ladies. Frank realized he was much older than Sadie's friends and he felt out of place. He thanked Sadie politely and started to walk away.

"Mr. Parnell, don't you remember? You promised to take me to supper," Sadie asked sweetly. *Oh, my! What on earth possessed her?*

Sadie knew his real name? Frank turned around. Her pretty face was flushed with embarrassment. Of course he hadn't asked her to supper, he hadn't seen her in ages. Was it possible she felt something for him?

"Of course, Miss Calhoun, I'd be honored to escort you to supper, I mean, I forgot," Frank added hastily. Sadie looped her arm through his, leaving her friends looking on with disbelief.

Chapter 5

Prudence spent most of the train trip to St. Louis looking out the window. The long, flat prairies and badlands would have been boring but for an occasional glimpse of wildlife and small rugged towns and settlements. Near the end of their trip, the landscape was so green her eyes ached. It was a different world, like nothing she had ever seen.

Even the style of dress was different. Women boarded the train in beautiful colorful, if impractical outfits. More than once, Florence chided her for staring.

Although the train ride was full of new experiences, Prudence was in awe of life in St. Louis. When they arrived at the train station, they were escorted to an elegant carriage. Impressive buildings lined the streets on their way to a stunning mansion near the outskirts of the city.

"When my father built this house, it was a country manor. Now, the city is moving out to it and soon it will be just another town house," Florence shook her head sadly.

Prudence jumped out of the carriage and was about to run to the house when Florence laid a restraining hand on her granddaughter's shoulder.

"Remember your manners. In St. Louis "Children are to be seen and not heard". You must never address an adult unless you are addressed and then you must answer politely, sir or ma'am. I'm sorry I didn't take the time to teach you proper behavior but I've been so worried about my father…" Florence's voice trailed off.

"I'll be a very good girl, grandma and make you proud of me," Prudence assured her.

"Oh, I know you will, dear. Please call me grandmother, if you would, it sounds more proper," Florence sniffed and dabbed at her eyes with her kerchief.

"Yes, grandmother," Prudence obeyed.

The footman opened the door and winked at Prudence who rewarded him with a big smile.

Jennie Renard, Florence's mother, swept down the staircase, as they entered the mansion.

"Oh, my darlings, you have finally arrived," Jennie gushed, as she engulfed the newcomers in her lilac scented embrace.

"Mother, it is so good to see you. How is Father?" Florence felt dusty and unkempt next to her immaculate mother.

"He's much the same, my dear. I am so glad you're here. You must be very tired. Why don't you freshen up and eat something? I'll take you up to see your father when you've had a chance to rest," Jennie shooed away the maid hovering nearby.

"I will attend to them. Just see that Helga prepares lunch soon. We will be dining it the conservatory in an hour."

Jennie showed Florence and Prudence to their rooms. Prudence longed to flop down on a bed but when she entered the pristine white bedroom with lacy curtains and matching coverlet, she was dismayed. What if she got them dirty?

Florence was being escorted to her own room by her mother and deeply engaged in conversation. Prudence took off her cinder blackened gloves and dusty bonnet and placed them on the floor in the corner. She looked around the room for a washbasin and was dismayed to find no water. She opened what she thought was a closet door and looked inside. Richly scented bubbles rose from hot water inside a huge tub standing near a tiled wall. On the far side of the room, sat a strange looking contraption with a chain hanging above it. Prudence examined it closely. Being a lover of fairy tales, she decided it must be some kind of wooden throne.

She heard a noise in the bedroom and went to the door. A nicely dressed young woman was unpacking Prudence's clothes. When she opened an upright chest, Prudence took a deep breath, as a rich woody smell filled the room.

"Did you find your bathroom, young lady?" the lady asked with a distinctly foreign accent.

"Yes, ma'am. Is the water in the tub for me?" Prudence asked timidly.

"Of course. The water closet is also for your use, little one," the lady smiled.

"What does the water closet do?" Prudence wanted to know.

"I am sorry, I forgot you would have no experience with one. Let me show you," the lady said kindly.

Charlotte was Prudence's personal maid. She explained the indoor plumbing to Prudence. The little girl's eyes grew wide with disbelief. After bathing, Prudence went with Charlotte to the conservatory for lunch. Unable to eat more than a few bites, Prudence went to sleep in her chair. Florence awakened her and told her she must go upstairs to meet her great grandfather. She reminded Prudence to be on her best behavior.

Prudence looked around in wonder as they ascended the huge staircase and approached the sick man's room. She wrinkled her nose at the medicinal smell and took a deep breath before entering the darkened room, feeling frightened. She couldn't see anyone but as she approached the bed she heard breathing. Her eyes became adjusted to the shadows. She gasped and stepped back. Large folds of skin hung under the old man's eyes. The colored portions of his eyes were milky and his pupils were very dark. His face wore a haunted expression.

He reached out his hands for Prudence. Large knuckled hands covered with blue veins hung tentatively in the air and then dropped to the dark coverlet.

"Florence, you're home. Now I can die in peace. I wanted to see you one more time," he whispered in a deep, raspy voice.

He wheezed loudly several times before he continued. "This must be Prudence. She looks exactly as her mother did at her age. A delightful child, I'll wager." He tried to smile but it looked more like a grimace, revealing large yellowish teeth.

Prudence hid behind her grandmother's skirts.

"Don't be afraid of me. Your grandmother is my daughter," the old man explained.

"I'm sorry father, I can't imagine what's gotten into her," Florence reached for her father's hand as Prudence bolted from the room.

"Don't worry my dear. She and I will soon be good friends. I do look rather frightening, I'm sure. Don't scold her, just explain to her that I've been ill and haven't always looked this way."

Prudence fled down the hall toward a staircase. She was lost! Desperately, she opened doors searching for something or someone who looked familiar.

Chapter 6. St. Louis

"What is this now?" a kindly voice asked. A tall young gentleman with kind brown eyes, towered over her.

"I'm lost," she sobbed.

"How can you be lost when your family lives right here in this house?" the man asked her.

Prudence looked bewildered as she studied the young man. His dark hair was rather unkempt as if he had briskly run his fingers through it several times. His eyes though kind, seemed sad too. Prudence decided that he was someone she could trust.

"I've been bad and I don't know how to find my room," Prudence gulped, trying not to cry.

The young gentleman tapped his lips with long tapering fingers. "Allow me to introduce myself. I am Dr. Landon A. Beale, a recent graduate of Missouri Medical College and your great grandfather's physician." He reached out his large well-manicured hand.

Prudence curtsied as she had been taught and held out her hand.

"Very prettily done, indeed. You are quite the young lady," Dr. Beale smiled.

"Allow me to escort you to your room, young miss."

"Oh thank you doctor. My grandma…mother will be very cross with me," Prudence said.

Florence met them coming up the hall. After introductions, Dr. Beale excused himself and went to check in on his patient.

"I must say, I was surprised that you would behave in that manner," Florence scolded.

"I am truly sorry, grandmother, but he frightened me," Prudence's chin quivered.

Remembering her father's words, Florence continued. "Don't worry dear, I understand you were frightened. But my father is a wonderful, kind man and needs your love. I'm afraid he will die soon and you'll never have the chance to know him. Please try harder not to be afraid," Florence said softly, putting her arms around her trembling granddaughter.

"I will go see him now, if you will go with me," Prudence said after a few moments.

"No dear, tomorrow will be soon enough," Florence patted her back. "I'll come back in a little while and we will join my mother for dinner. Put on your pretty blue dress with the flowers on it. I must take you shopping while we are here."

Prudence smiled. Grandmother loved to buy new clothes. Before leaving Silver City, Florence purchased several new outfits for both of them. None of them compared to the clothes in St. Louis, and Grandmother would never be outdone.

The next morning, Florence and Prudence went for a walk after breakfast. When they stepped outside, Prudence could barely catch her breath. She hadn't noticed how heavy the air was while inside but outside it felt stuffy. Prudence felt like running away as far as she could without stopping. Florence noticed her reaction.

"Don't worry dear, you will get used to the heat. It is very different from Silver City. Here the summer heat is moist, there it is very dry," Florence explained. "That is the reason why your grandfather and I moved to Silver City with your mother. She couldn't breathe well in this climate and we were told she would get better if we took her somewhere where the air was drier and she could get more sunshine."

"Papa said she loved our homestead near Deming. She didn't like the wind but she loved the country," Prudence told her.

"I'm sure she did. She wouldn't have stayed there if she hadn't. We had better get back before my mother wonders what has happened to us."

"I'm afraid I must insist, Mrs. Renard. Your husband is not getting enough nourishing food. He is slowly starving to death." Dr. Beale knew his place and resisted the impulse to put his arm around the older woman.

"I'm trying to get him to eat but he refuses. I have special meals both brought in from nearby restaurants and prepared by my staff. After just one or two bites, he says that he has had enough," Jennie Renard studied the young doctor's face hopefully. "There must be something else we can do, Dr. Beale. Claude will die if he is put in a hospital."

Dr. Beale shook his head sadly from side to side. Florence and Jennie looked so crestfallen, he hadn't the heart to tell them that Mr. Renard might improve in the hospital where he could receive round the clock medical attention.

"What if we hired a nurse?" Florence asked.

"His appetite is the problem not his care. He could stay at home if we could get him to eat more. Just a minute, I have an idea. Watch after him for a few hours and I will be back, hopefully with some good news," Dr. Beale rushed from the room but was back a moment later for his medical bag and equipment. "Wish me luck," he said.

"That was rather rude. What did he mean by good news, I wonder?" Jennie asked her daughter.

"Mother, we have to face the fact Father may have to go to the hospital. I don't want him to go either but if he won't eat or cooperate, we must do what is best for him."

Jennie sighed loudly. "I will go up to speak to him now. Stay down here awhile, my dear. We need to discuss this alone."

Florence was worried. "I understand, Mother. I will take Prudence for a walk."

Where had the years gone? It seemed liked yesterday when Claude took her for a ride in the park in their new carriage. They laughed so loudly that people stopped what they were doing to stare at the old couple behaving like young people.

Slowly, Jennie ascended the steep stairs up to the first landing. She paused to lean against the wall for a few moments before she continued. For the first time in weeks, Claude was awake when she entered the room, as if he was expecting her.

"Ah, there you are. I missed you," Claude whispered hoarsely.

"I'm here. We have to talk," Jennie murmured as she bent to kiss his forehead. She sat down on the edge of the bed and took his hand. Gently, she traced the blue veins with her finger.

Claude watched her face. How he loved this woman. He knew he would leave her soon and she would continue on without him. "What is it, Jen? Did the doctor tell you something?" his rheumy eyes searched her face.

"He wants to put you in the hospital. He says that you don't eat enough nourishing food. We could hire a nurse but he didn't think it would help," Jennie told her husband.

"I try to eat but everything seems to taste bad." He stroked her hand. "I'm truly sorry for putting you through this."

"Dr. Beale will be back soon and in case he decides to put you in the hospital, I should prepare your things," Jennie sighed in resignation.

Florence tapped on the bedroom door. "May I come in?"

"Yes, you may," her mother answered. "I thought you were going for a walk.

I am going to prepare your father's things to take to the hospital. Stay with him while I get his trunk from the attic."

"It is beginning to rain. Shouldn't we wait to see what Dr. Beale has to say before you start packing? He said he would be back later."

"I refuse to sit here and wait. What for? He said there wasn't anything else we could do for him here," Jennie dabbed her nose with a filmy kerchief.

"I don't like to disagree but he said he might have an alternative. Shouldn't we wait to pack until we hear what he has to say?"

"You're right, as always, my dear. I will wait. In the meantime, do you think Prudence might play the piano. I had it brought upstairs so your father could listen to music once in awhile when he feels up to it."

"What a wonderful idea, she can get in some practice."

Prudence stared at the ornate piano in the upstairs sitting room. "Did my mother ever play this piano?" she wanted to know.

"As a matter of fact, she learned to play on it," Florence replied.

Prudence suddenly remembered an old battered spinet in a small room. She wasn't sure but she thought it must be the one from the homestead. *Why had her grandparents taken her Mama so far away from all these beautiful things? Mama had died anyway. At least she would have been happier here with all of these nice things and her life would have been much easier. She closed her eyes wishing her mother could be with her right now.*

Meggie's kind face appeared in her mind's eye. *My little colleen, having pretty things doesn't make you happy. Loving people and having them love you back is what is important.*

Timidly, Pru approached the instrument as blood pulsed in her ears. Her fingers rolled across the keys fluidly, unusual for a child her age. Jennie and Claude held hands in the next room beginning to darken in the twilight. They smiled at each other when she finished playing. She was indeed Emma's child!

Later that evening, Dr. Beale smiled as he left the Renard home. He nodded to Florence and Prudence as they entered through the garden gate but swept past them without uttering a word.

"The impertinence of that young man. He was very rude not even speaking to us as he passed," Florence muttered.

"Perhaps he was thinking about something important, Grandmother," Prudence made an excuse for her new acquaintance.

"Nevertheless, dear, he should always acknowledge his betters," Florence informed her. "We must look in on Father after we freshen up."

Prudence winced but didn't let her grandmother see her do it. She knew she would be angry with her.

Jennie met them at the door. "Wait until you see your father, it is a miracle!"

"Mother, what are you talking about," Florence untied her bonnet strings and removed her gloves as she entered the foyer. She assisted Prudence to do the same and then turned to face her mother who was chattering away incoherently.

"What has happened?" Florence began but her mother interrupted.

"Dr. Beale got your father to eat today. He brought some kind of a "dietary supplement" to improve your father's appetite and it worked, it really worked."

"What is a dietary supplement?" Florence asked, catching her mother's excitement.

"Something that is supposed to improve his appetite. He offered to let me taste it but I couldn't, it's a messy brown paste made from peanuts. He left some of it here to give to your father this evening and he also wanted you and Prudence to try some."

Florence was tempted to make a face but thought better of it. Instead she smiled and agreed to taste the concoction some other time. Prudence was hungry and was willing to taste it. Jennie asked the cook to apply the paste in the center of two pieces of bread and gave Pru a big glass of cold milk to go with it.

"Ooo." Prudence said as she took her first bite, "This is good!" She held up her sandwich for her grandmother to taste it.

Florence looked skeptical, shrugged, and took a bite. "It is good, no wonder Father likes it." The rest of the afternoon was spent discussing what could be eaten with the interesting new "dietary supplement" invented by a St. Louis physician to improve his patients' appetites.

Over the next few weeks, Claude Renard gained strength and was able to go outside in a wheelchair and be propelled around the garden by his great granddaughter. He told her stories by the hundreds about the early days of St. Louis and the changes he had seen in his lifetime.

Florence and Prudence boarded the train back to Silver City on the last day of August. Prudence got home in time to start school in September and Frank was elated to have her home again.

Chapter 7.
New Mexico Territory

It was beginning to snow as Juanita left the Timmer House and started for home. Her walk was uphill and facing into the wind. Shivering, she gathered her shawl around her more tightly. The family was gathering tonight for *Tío Tómas's* fiftieth birthday celebration. With any luck all of the brothers, sisters, aunts, uncles, and cousins would be gathered in her parent's tiny home on Bennett Street. Her sister, Quetta, promised their Mama she would prepare the red *chili*. Juanita made *empanadas* but she must hurry to help her mother prepare for the large gathering.

Leaving the Silver City Enterprise office, Mario was on his way to the train depot to pick up a load of paper. He wanted to get back before it began to snow more heavily. A woman was approaching, tears streaming down her face. Wearing only a light shawl, he wondered why she would be dressed like that on such a cold day. Suddenly, he realized it was little Juanita, from the Timmer House.

Turning the wagon around in the middle of the rutted road, Mario snapped the reins, and trotted toward Juanita. She looked up in alarm when she saw the horse and wagon headed toward her.

"Don't worry, little princess. I came to offer you a ride home," Mario reassured her.

Juanita looked up at the large blond dark-skinned man and smiled. "Oh, Señor, thank you so much. I'm afraid I'm not dressed for the weather," Juanita gave her hand to Mario and he pulled her up into the wagon seat. Gallantly, he wrapped a large blanket around her that was kept under the seat.

Juanita wrinkled her nose, the blanket smelled like a horse, but at least it was warm and dry. She gave Mario directions to her house and they started off as big fat snowflakes began to fall. When they reached her house, Juanita didn't wait for assistance but removed the blanket and jumped down quickly. She thanked Mario and asked him in.

"I'm sorry but I must be on my way, I have a load of paper to pick up. Say hello to your sister for me," Mario tipped his hat and snapped the reins.

Juanita yelled, "Wait, Señor, I forgot to ask. Can you come to a party tonight? There will be a lot of good food and you can meet the rest of my family."

Mario pulled up on the reins. "I would be honored, Señorita."

Juanita rushed inside and was greeted by her mother and Quetta.

"*Mi hija*, why didn't you wear your heavy cloak this morning?" her mother asked as she dragged her daughter over to the woodstove rubbing her child's arms briskly with her own hands in an attempt to warm her.

"Don't worry, Mama. I was given a ride home in a fine wagon."

As the three women were reminiscing happily in Spanish they prepared a beautiful meal for *Tío* Tómas and their large family.

Mario went to the depot, loaded the paper into the wagon, and took it to the back of the Enterprise office. Two apprentices came out to help him stow the rolls of paper in the shed. Snow was sticking in clumps to the vegetation around the office. Mario glanced down at his hands; he needed to remove some of the ink before going to the party.

At the Tovar home, Mario raised his hand to knock on the door. From behind he was grabbed by both arms and nearly lifted inside. "Welcome, you must be Señor Mario. Little sister thinks highly of you. Make yourself at home," the older of the two men said.

Colorful woven rugs hung from iron hooks on the walls and a woodstove stood in a kitchen corner. Heavenly aromas of spicy food combined with the smells of damp wool. In another corner, several small children played with crudely carved animals. Older children were gathered around a young boy with a battered guitar trying to play a song. People of every age, shape and description were crammed into the small house.

Tío Tómas was being regaled with laughter and toasts to his aged condition. Mario felt a huge lump form in his throat. Never having a family, Mario felt like an outsider. Then a small hand grabbed his elbow and guided him toward the stove.

Quetta and her mother were dishing up huge plates of food and Quetta didn't see Mario come in. She looked up and he caught her eye as she handed him his plate. He smiled tentatively and was relieved to see her smile back and nod. Mrs. Tovar chattered away to her guests and placed her warm hand on Mario's arm as he looked around for some place to sit.

"We are happy to have you as our guest tonight and hope you will come back often." She added in Spanish, "You are a good man, my Juanita tells me and are always welcome."

Mario felt a warm glow inside. He conversed easily with the family and discovered one of Juanita's brothers worked at the Enterprise office. Juanita's father, Domingo, asked Mario to propose a toast to his older brother Tómas and Mario quickly agreed.

"Señor Tómas, it is easy to see that you are a happy man with a fine family. I wish you many years of health and prosperity. I would like to thank all of you for allowing me to come to your party. ¡*Salud!*" Mario tipped back his tequila and drank it in one big gulp.

It made him cough and he was clapped on the back enthusiastically. It was a wonderful evening.

Chapter 8

Sheriff Lockhart was angry. Not just upset, downright mad. William Walters, alias Bronco Bill, had escaped from the county jail and it was up to him to find him and bring him back. This would go against his spotless record. Lockhart was breaking in a new guard, Justin Chalmers, and the kid wasn't bright enough not to know Bill's visitors should be searched.

Frank knew Lockhart was blaming himself but no one had been hurt during the jailbreak and that was unusual. Poor Chalmers was held at gunpoint and dumped outside of town. The kid was so frightened he could barely talk.

Lockhart's booming voice had Chalmers cringing; Frank laid his hand on Lockhart's shoulder.

"Just you stay out of this, Parnell. This kid has no idea what he's done!" Lockhart roared. "It took a long time to bring Bronco in and just when it was about to be all over, this numbskull kid lets him walk out of here. I've a mind to…"

"Just a minute. He's a kid who made a mistake. We're wasting time, we should go after him," Frank interrupted.

"Which way did they head, Chalmers? Do you at least know that?" Lockhart asked, sarcasm dripping from his voice.

"Toward Mexico, s-ssir, I think," the young man stuttered.

"You THINK!" Lockhart bellowed.

"Toward Mexico, yes sir!" Chalmers quaked.

"Okay, Parnell, round up a few men and get going. Send word back to me as soon as you pick up his trail," Sheriff Lockhart ordered.

"I'll get Perfecto and Tómas and get started right away," Frank spent a few minutes at the jail looking around the hitching post and then around the back of the jail. He found Perfecto Rodriguez and Tómas Martinez coming out of the saloon on his way to Miner's Mercantile.

"Lockhart wants us to go after Bronco Bill. How soon can you be ready to go?" Frank asked when he got close enough to shout.

Passersby stopped to listen to the exchange. Perfecto Rodriguez grinned and wiped the top of his boot on the back of his pant leg. He was a small handsome man with an eye for the ladies. An excellent lawman when he was sober, he managed to hold his liquor for weeks at a time, then stay falling down drunk for an equal number of weeks. Tómas Martinez was itching for some action, Silver City was entirely too tame for him.

"We can meet up with you in half an hour. Just need to get our gear, *hombre*," Perfecto told Frank.

"I'll meet you at the end of Main Street in 30 minutes!" Frank jogged off in the direction of the store.

Robert took stock of the situation when he saw Frank rush in. "Go on ahead, son. We'll look after Prudence, don't you worry. Be careful, I hear Bronco Bill is a wild one."

Frank nodded. Lockhart told him that Bronco Bill was armed with a 38-caliber revolver.

Frank shook Robert's hand. He had stashed supplies and his rifle in the storeroom so he could be ready to go to work, as a tracker at a moment's notice. Sheriff Lockhart frequently needed a tracker and Frank was the best one in these parts.

By the end of an hour's time, the three men were headed for Central City. In two hours, Frank picked up Bronco Bill's trail and Martinez was headed back to Silver City to report to Sheriff Lockhart. Frank was able to discern from the tracks that a horse with a worn front shoe was tied outside the county jail earlier that day. Now, he and Rodriquez discovered hoof prints matching the previous ones about three miles outside of town headed in the direction of Mexico. They were in luck the slick thief was doing just what they expected.

The men tracked until dusk and bedded down in an arroyo, where it was a little cooler, for the night. Tómas Martinez was back before morning and the three set out again as soon as it was light. Frank lost the trail five times before they reached Deming. Two days later, they were questioning Henry Holgate who had just had his prize stallion stolen and a horse with a worn front shoe left in its place.

Holgate was sure Bronco Bill was headed for Palomas, Mexico. Frank, Perfecto and Tómas were sorely tempted to follow him but had orders to contact Cipriano Baca and let him pursue the bandit into Mexico. Known to his friends as Cipi, Baca had a good reputation with the Mexican authorities. He was a jolly fellow and his round face shone with delight when Frank told him what Holgate related.

"This will be quite an *aventura*. I will enjoy this very much," Baca told him. "You, *hombres,* wait here for me and I will bring him back very soon."

Frank and the two deputies waited in Columbus for three days. True to his word, Baca returned on the fourth day with Bronco Bill. Baca located Bronco Bill quickly and told the bandit that he was in Palomas to "collect bills". Baca knew Bronco Bill liked pretty *señoritas* and the two of them decided to give a dance with Baca paying for it all and sparing no expense. After drinking for most of the night, Bronco Bill liked the sound of the proposal, and the two set off in search of a fiddler to be sure that the dance would be a success. Baca failed to tell him the fiddler lived just on the other side of the border. By the time Bronco Bill figured it out, Perfecto and Tómas had him.

Chapter 9

Sadie passed the cemetery on her way to see a sick miner. The sun was setting, the trees rustled and clouds cast shadows on the headstones. The pungent smell of newly turned earth reached her nostrils and she remembered there had been another funeral today. Nellie Watson became ill a few weeks ago and now she was dead. Leaving behind her husband, four year old Dorothy, and two year old Harry. So many women died young in this country.

She didn't want to think about that. Minding her step so as not to break the earthenware jug she carried, she watched the ground carefully for loose rocks and debris. For the past several weeks she had been seeing Frank Parnell and now his daughter was home from St. Louis.

The miner's shack looked deserted. Ragged curtains hung in the doorway and the smell of sickness permeated the air of the tiny room. "Joshua, it's Sadie. I've come with some birch bark tea to help with your infection. Doctor Kennon said you must drink some every few hours so I made enough to last you through the night."

Joshua was lying on a blanket on the floor. Sadie gently laid the back of her hand against the sick man's forehead. It was warm to touch but not hot. She lit a candle stub and uncovered Joshua Black's feet and legs. They were swollen and red. The infection seemed to be spreading. Without adequate medical attention, he might die. Dr. Kennon saw as many people as he could during the course of a day and at night he was up delivering babies and patching up men who had been fighting in the saloons. The wear and tear of living in a mining town was catching up with him and he was suffering from double pneumonia.

Sadie knew she couldn't care for all of Dr. Kennon's patients but would do her best to help those she could. Joshua had some sort of kidney ailment and the birch bark tea was usually an effective treatment. She poured some of the tea, brewed earlier at home, into the cleanest cup she could find and searched for a spoon. Finally, she located one in a dirty boot in the corner of the room. She rinsed the spoon with some of the tea and wiped it on her dress. Lifting the man's head with one hand, Sadie carefully ladled some of the liquid into his mouth. Choking and sputtering, Joshua tried to knock the spoon away but Sadie was resolute and succeeded in getting most of a cup into him. She poured some more into the mug and set it nearby.

"Do you hear me, Joshua?" The poor man nodded his head. "You must drink some more of the tea in a couple of hours." He nodded again.

"Thank you, Miss Sadie," he whispered through his cracked bleeding lips.

"You're welcome, I wish I could do more for you. I'll be back in the morning."

The wind crept along the ground and blew bits of tree branches and leaves down on the path. It was fully dark and passing by the cemetery made Sadie uneasy. Perhaps it was the stories the old ladies told to the children that made her wary of the place. The ghost of *La Llorona* was a favorite nightmare tale. The ghostly woman was said to weep inconsolably while searching for her lost children. Sadie shook her head and tried to concentrate on pleasanter things. Frank would be back next week. He wasn't sure how to tell his daughter about Sadie. Did he love her enough to risk his daughter's affection and the alienation of his in-laws?

Passing the last headstone, Sadie felt better. Continuing along the road, she neared the trail to the Calhoun cabin. She should go see old Pete tonight but his cabin was clear on the other side of town. Thunder rolled across the tops of the mountains and fiery lightening spears pierced the pitch-black sky. Quickening her step, she reached the familiar path. She could walk it blindfolded. Large drops of rain splashed on her face blinding her momentarily, there was a loud crash as a tree split and fell at her feet. Her dress tangled in the branches and she fell, striking her head on the ground. *La Llorona* was beckoning to her and everything went black.

Chapter 10

The storm wreaked havoc during the night, leaving trees and branches strewn across seas of mud. Frank slogged his way through the sodden streets on his way to work as numerous unpleasant smells assaulted his senses. A large wagon loaded with supplies tilted precariously, two of its wheels on one side were up to the axles in mud. A burly rancher stood nearby cursing and slipping as his young son held the reins in front of the horses and tried to coax the team forward. The boy, about ten years old, was covered from head to toe with mud. His father tried, in vain, to right the wagon.

"You'd probably have better luck if you'd unhitch the team and unload the wagon," Frank told him.

"What do you know about it? I don't recall asking for your advice!" the rancher growled.

Frank shrugged, winked at the boy, and kept walking. By the time he reached Miner's Mercantile, he was covered with mud. There was no avoiding it. He retrieved a rag from the storeroom and wiped the worst of it from his boots and trouser legs.

The door of the mercantile burst open. A wild-eyed Buck Calhoun crashed into a display knocking pans to the floor. "Sadie's gone missing. I looked for her all night. I found a piece of her dress on a fallen tree near our cabin. The rain destroyed any trace of footprints. You've got to help me find her! I've sent telegrams to Mark and Sweeney. Some of the folks in Pinos Altos are already looking for her."

Frank rushed to tell the clerk back in the storeroom he had to leave. The clerk, Mr. Murphy nodded, his slightly pointed ears quivered as he leaned forward hoping to discover what happened. When Frank and Buck left, poor Murphy's curiosity was unsatisfied. Disappointed, he picked up the fallen pans and restored the display.

Frank's new bay mare would come in handy today. After renting horses for years, he decided to make his life easier and have one available whenever he wanted to go to Pinos Altos or was needed as a tracker. Sassy was semi-retired now.

Buck's horse was tired and muddy, so the two men walked to the Old Man Livery and Feed on Arizona St. They got Frank's horse and went to see Margaret Flaherty about caring for Prudence while Frank was gone.

"Sure, it will be like old times, it will," the cheerful lady agreed.

"I've been called away on urgent business. I haven't told Mr. Jensen, would you please let them know that I'll be back as soon as I can," Frank asked.

Margaret wondered at Buck's appearance. He was a stranger to her but from the look of him, he was in some sort of trouble. He was lucky that Mr. Frank was going to help him.

Frank and Buck went up the mountain toward Pinos Altos. When they reached the fallen tree Buck showed him the cloth torn from Sadie's dress; Frank searched carefully for signs of blood and footprints. Buck went back to the cabin for supplies, and to get Sadie's dog, Dutch. Buck felt entirely responsible for Sadie's disappearance. Sweeney purchased Dutch for Sadie on her last birthday. Dutch usually accompanied Sadie on her rounds but Buck asked her to leave the dog with him so he could use him to help pull some stumps. In a harness, the large heeler shepherd mix dog was nearly as strong as a mule and a lot less stubborn.

When Buck got back to the fallen tree he asked, "Where should we start looking?" Dutch snuffled along the ground but did not appear to be picking up anything.

"You said she was going to tend a sick miner. Let's start there and see if he can recall anything," Frank suggested.

"That's a good idea," Buck agreed. He whistled for Dutch, still sniffing without results.

Along the trail past the cemetery, Joshua Black's desolate shack dripped despondently in the rain-chilled air. Frank brushed aside the sodden rag hanging in the doorway. Joshua's vacant eyes peered from a bloated, mottled face. Frank groaned, knelt down, and gently closed the miner's lifeless eyes.

Chapter 11

Quetta was dreaming. *Josefa Benavidez, Quetta's best friend since childhood, was walking down the aisle at St. Vincent's Church dressed in a snowy white gown. A man, whose face she couldn't see, waited at the altar. The picture faded. Then she saw Josefa sitting in front of an old house, her belly swollen with child. In her arms, she held a child of about 2 years of age. Her face was careworn and sad.*

Quetta awoke, sobbing. From Quetta's earliest recollections, many of the elders held the belief that Josefa was a *bruja* because she seemed to cast a spell over men. Of course, Quetta knew that her friend was not a witch. Josefa was a beautiful woman with an uncommon zest for living and enjoying life. Quetta knew how much anguish Josefa's impetuous and loving nature caused.

Rising from her bed, Quetta lit a stubby candle. Still raining, the roads were so muddy that travel was being discouraged but she must get to Josefa. Mrs. Jensen agreed to loan her the trap to visit her friend last week before the rains came. Now she must figure a way to sneak out.

A mist gathered outside. Inside it was deathly quiet, there was blood everywhere. Josefa was ashy white, her lips transparent blue. A white owl sat outside the window and tapped on the pane with its beak, gently at first, then more insistently.

"AARgh!" Quetta sputtered. She had gone back to sleep. Now, a grayish light entered the small attic room. Shivering from the moisture that settled in her bones, she was tempted to crawl back under the quilt and snuggle into its depths.

Rubbing her eyes, Quetta realized the candle was out. She carelessly raked her fingers through her hair, pulled on her clothes and tossed some others into an old cloth bag. She pulled an old shawl from the hook by her door and wrapped it around her head, neck and shoulders.

Across town, Josefa sat in an old wooden rocking chair. The pains had started several hours ago. Her brother, Eusebio, would be up soon to go to work at the lime plant. She eased herself to her feet and hobbled slowly to the dresser. Inside a large drawer, her beautiful angel Rumaldo, was sleeping. She bent slowly to kiss his cheek. His baby face smiled and his mouth puckered. Placing her hand on the corner of the dresser, she straightened and examined her face in the cracked mirror. Raven black hair, thick and lush, surrounded her thin face like a halo. Her facial features were small and well proportioned. Everyone told her she was beautiful but right now she felt like a huge, pregnant cow.

On a small cot in the corner, Rafaela, her eldest slept. Untamed, riotous curls covered her face. She was a wonderful child and such a help to her mama.

Rafaela had more responsibility than any other child her age. Josefa smoothed Rafaela's hair from her face with her fingertips and bent to kiss her face. Seized by another labor pain, she held her stomach and limped back to the rocking chair. *If only Quetta was here*, she thought.

Quietly, Quetta descended to the Jensen's kitchen. Prudence was staying in the guest room on the second floor and was a very light sleeper.

A family emergency had called Mrs. Flaherty away. The day before, Quetta watched as Mrs. Flaherty knocked on the front door of the Jensen house holding Prudence's hand tightly.

"Me oldest son, Aidan, was in a mining accident in Bisbee," she hurriedly explained to Florence. "I promised Mr. Frank that I would watch over the dear little colleen but I must go to my son. I left a note so he will know where she is, I must be goin' now."

Florence started to ask where Frank had gone but decided it was fruitless to question the distraught woman. Florence had sniffed haughtily and Quetta knew poor Mr. Frank would get a piece of his mother-in-law's mind, when he returned.

Quetta harnessed the horse and readied the trap for her visit to Josefa. It occurred to her that some food would be welcome at her friend's home, so she went back inside to pack a basket.

Prudence heard Quetta getting ready to leave. Thinking about another day stuck in the house with Grandmother, she decided to sneak out and go with her. A box situated behind the seat of the trap would be the perfect place for her to hide. She crossed her fingers hoping Quetta wouldn't decide to put the basket in the box.

Quetta placed the basket of food and her sack of clothes on the seat. She hoped the cover over the trap would block at least part of the rain. The muddy roads caused Quetta to nearly upset the trap on her way across town but she was determined to reach Josefa and she finally made it.

Chapter 12

Choking and coughing, Sadie struggled to breathe. Her eyelids fluttered and when she opened her eyes, she was frightened. Surrounded by smoke, she tried to crawl but found it impossible to move. *What was happening?* She couldn't reach the small revolver she always carried but sensed it was gone.

"Don't move," a hoarse voice cried out.

"Cccan't breathe," she gasped and began to gag.

"It'll be all right in a minute. Just lie still."

"W…where are you?" Sadie whispered, still unable to catch her breath.

"Over here. Breakfast caught fire. I'm trying to open the door. Never have been much of a cook, never have been," the voice cracked and wheezed with laughter.

A burst of cool rain-washed air struck Sadie. Gulping and hiccoughing, she squinted her burning eyes straining to see who had spoken to her. After a few minutes, most of the smoke was gone but a severe headache and fine haze combined to make objects appear to dance about magically. Near a tiny fireplace sat a wizened gnome-like creature with a long white beard, stirring a huge pot with a long stick. "Good morning. I hope you slept well," the gnome said pleasantly.

"Who are you? Why am I here?"

"Name's Barabas Featherstone. Found you last night after you'd hit your head. Didn't knowed where you lived, so brought you to my place. Yer welcome to stay 'til you get better."

Sadie felt very odd. She didn't know what to say to the elderly man and was frightened and confused. *What was wrong with her*, she wondered?

The old man hobbled over to her and leaned toward her face. "I told ya what my name is, now how's about you tell me yourn?" the old man grinned revealing blackened teeth.

"Uh, my name is…" Sadie swallowed hard. "My name is Sadie, Sadie Calhoun."

She felt sick and dizzy. The old man sensed her discomfort.

"Well, it 'ppears we'll have to eat stew fer breakfast. Was out huntin' last night when I found ya but had to leave the rabbits I shot behind so's I could carry you." Barabas told her.

Barabas dipped some stew into a cracked dirty bowl and handed it to Sadie. Sadie accepted it politely and tried hard not to gag when she saw the large lump of grease floating on top of the unidentifiable mixture. Smiling weakly, she lifted a spoonful to her lips.

Watching with his guest with anticipation, Barabas ate his own meal. Sadie was surprised it wasn't too bad. She carefully maneuvered her spoon around the lump of grease and was able to eat most of the meal. Very tired when she finished she managed to thank Barabas before curling up on her side and falling asleep.

Barabas sat up that night trying to decide what to do. An old man used to living alone never faced problems like this. He sat by the fire stirring it with a stick. He decided to keep the young woman to cook and clean for him. All he needed to do was figure out the dose of Winslow's Baby Syrup that contained some wonderful stuff called laudanum, to put in her food. He wouldn't want her too sleepy to work just unable to think clearly. Finally, his eyelids grew heavy and his chin fell down toward his bony chest.

Chapter 13

Quetta approached Josefa's house slowly. The trap and horse were covered with mud and it was raining hard. She pulled her shawl around her more tightly and picked up the basket and sack of clothing on the seat next to her. The cover over the basket and the sack were drenched, and she wished she had remembered to put them in the box behind the seat before she left the Jensen's. She went to the door and knocked sharply.

Rafaela's tousled head appeared. "*Tía* Quetta, Mama is crying for you. I'm so glad you have come at last. I was just about to send someone to get you."

Quetta patted the little girl's shoulder. Rafaela called her *tía* or aunt, even though they were not related. It was because Josefa wanted Rafaela to know Quetta was special. Josefa and Quetta were such close friends since childhood; they considered themselves sisters.

Rafaela clutched Quetta's hand and led her to her mother's room. Quetta asked the little girl to fix something for her little brother to eat. Rafaela smiled at her and left the room.

In the kitchen, Rafaela put on her mother's flowered apron and started making *tortillas*, like Mama taught her, for her little brother Rumaldo. Uncle Eusebio had already left for work at the lime plant and didn't even know Josefa was in labor. She added some water to the beans from last night's supper and put them on the stove. Steam fogged the kitchen window. Rafaela took a corner of the apron and wiped the glass.

Rafaela watched as the box behind the seat of Quetta's trap opened and a girl, about her own age and size, climbed out and looked around cautiously. Remembering the *tortillas*, Rafaela hurried back to the stove and deftly flipped them over using only her fingers. She ran back to the window and looked for the girl but could no longer see her. Just then, Rumaldo toddled into the kitchen. Rafaela put him in his chair and tied a towel around his neck.

Rafaela put some beans on a small plate and carefully mashed them with a wooden spoon. She removed the tortillas from the stove and waved one in the air to cool it.

"Here is your breakfast, *mi hijo*. Sit up straight and I will get you some milk," Rafaela said in her most grown-up voice. Carefully, she poured milk into a tin cup and set it beside her small brother.

Burning with curiosity about the girl, Rafaela busied herself near the window. Rumaldo was happily blowing bubbles in his milk and spilling most of it on himself. Mama said it was just what babies do when they learn to feed themselves, so Rafaela ignored her brother. She went to the front door and looked outside. The girl was standing in the doorway, wet and shivering. Without a word, Rafaela grabbed the girl's arm and pulled her inside. "You came without *Tía* Quetta knowing, didn't you?" Rafaela whispered.

Prudence nodded miserably.

"Come with me."

Rafaela led Prudence to the kitchen and handed her a worn but clean towel. Prudence thanked her and started drying her hair. Rafaela pulled a chair over to the stove so Prudence could get warm.

"Would you like some *tortillas* and beans? It isn't much but it is hot."

"Thank you, I would like something. I left before eating breakfast," Prudence admitted.

"You shouldn't have come. My *tía* will be very angry when she finds you here. She came to help my Mama have her baby and might be here for a long time. Your Mama will be angry with you too," Rafaela scolded.

"I don't have a mother. But my grandmother will be angry. I don't care, I never do anything exciting," Prudence said with a defiant flounce.

Rafaela wasn't sure what Prudence meant. She had very little time to spend with girls her own age and was anxious to talk to this *gringa*. It was sad the girl had no mother. "Do you live with your grandmother?"

"No, I am staying with her while my father is away," Prudence told her.

"You have a father and no mother and I have a mother and no father."

Prudence held her precious locket in her hand. Her grandmother promised to have a new picture of her mother made for it because the one she had was so old and faded. She was envious, Rafaela had a mama and she didn't.

Chapter 14

"Hold on to the bed posts while you push," Quetta told Josefa. "It will make it easier."

"I remember now, ooo, I wish it would all be over, I can't stand the paaa eeen!" Josefa yowled.

Frightened by her mother's yells, Rafaela followed closely by Prudence, ran to the bedroom door.

'*Tía*, is my mama all right?" Rafaela shrieked. She shoved the door open and ran into the room. There was blood everywhere. Gasping, Rafaela sank into the rocking chair. "MAMA, don't die!!" the little girl wailed.

"Your mama is not going to die. Calm yourself. Go to the kitchen and bring me some hot water. Hurry now, soon you will have a new brother or sister," Quetta said calmly. Her reassuring words helped Rafaela remember she was supposed to perform certain tasks during her mother's birthing process.

Rafaela smiled tremulously and went to her mama's side, patting her hand. "I'm sorry, Mama. I will get the water," the little girl assured her.

Prudence stood just outside the bedroom door. Her face was pale and she looked as though she was about to faint. Rafaela took her hand and led her back to the kitchen. Getting a cup reserved for guests out of the cupboard, Rafaela pumped a glass of water for Prudence and urged the girl to sit down.

"Would you watch my little brother for me while I boil the water and prepare the scissors and twine for my *Tía*?" she asked Prudence.

Prudence nodded. She was frightened by what she had seen. Once she asked an older classmate at school where babies came from and the older girl assured her the stork brought them. Prudence liked to read and knew that there were no storks in the New Mexico territory. When she told the older girl she laughed and said, "That just shows what you know."

It appeared the older girl didn't know where babies came from after all.

"Have you seen babies be born before?" Prudence asked Rafaela.

"I have seen baby goats born and once some kittens but not a real baby," Rafaela smiled. "It is very simple really. My Mama says when two people fall in love they decide to have a baby. After a while God puts a baby in the mama's stomach, when it is time He lets the baby come out and the mama and papa are happy."

"What about all of the blood?" Prudence wanted to know.

"I didn't know about that. Mama said that there is a little scab where the baby is attached to the mama and it sometimes bleeds when the baby is being borned. That's what Mama said," Rafaela's eyes were misty. When she spoke about her mama her face looked reverent. It was easy for Prudence to see Rafaela adored her mama. Prudence watched as Rafaela wiped her little brother's messy chin and helped him out of his chair.

"I would like to show you something. Come with me," Rafaela took Rumaldo by the hand and Prudence's hand and led them to a small room about the size of a closet, just off the kitchen.

Proudly, the little girl showed Prudence a dress her mama was making for a wealthy lady. It was made of shiny silver material and trimmed with tiny pearl beads. It looked like the dress a princess would wear, Prudence thought.

"Does your mama always make clothes?" Prudence asked as she stroked the beautiful dress.

"Oh, yes. She makes dresses for all of the ladies in Silver City. Mrs. John Fleming is one of her best customers," Rafaela smiled.

Prudence was interested in the dress form, collection of threads, buttons and trims as well as several bolts of gorgeous material arranged neatly on built-in shelves.

"Now I will show you something you have never seen before," Rafaela whispered secretively. She whipped off a sheet covering something in the corner.

"Oh, it's beautiful. What is it?"

A shiny black machine with gold letters sat on a wooden chest with drawers. Underneath the chest was a black wrought iron contraption. Prudence was impressed.

"It's a sewing machine. There aren't many of them in Silver City. A friend of my mama's bought it for her. She hasn't had it very long but she said it helps a lot not having to sew everything by hand."

"I think that the water is ready for *Tía* Quetta. I had better take it to her."

Prudence watched as Rafaela carefully covered the sewing machine with the sheet.

"I'll help you," Prudence told her.

"I'm very glad that you came today," Rafaela said.

The girls took Rumaldo back to the kitchen. Prudence found a toy for him to play with and both girls took the boiling water, scissors, and cord Josefa instructed Rafaela to have ready, to the bedroom.

Quetta motioned for them to set the water down on the table and waved them out the door. The girls obeyed. Quetta shook her head when she saw Prudence but said nothing. Her arm was hidden beneath the blanket covering Josefa. The two girls watched from the doorway as Josefa gritted her teeth and strained with all her might. Her face turned red and a small vein stood out on her forehead. Then with a loud yell, Josefa suddenly went limp. Quetta smiled as a mewling noise came from under the blanket. As if by magic, a tiny perfect baby girl emerged from under the mound of counterpane.

"Oh…" Prudence and Rafaela said in unison.

When the new baby, called Felecitas was cleaned up and given to her mama, Quetta scolded Prudence. "Your grandmother is going to be very angry. She is probably very worried about you."

Prudence hung her head. She knew grandmother would be mad at her but she hadn't been so excited in a long time. The new baby was beautiful and she had made a new friend.

Rafaela helped Quetta unpack the basket of food she brought for them. Quetta cleaned up the bedroom, gathered the dirty sheets and towels, and put them in a large washtub she filled with cold water.

"Rafaela, you must take good care of your mother, brother, and baby sister for the next few days. As soon as it stops raining you must wash the sheets and towels in very hot water and lye soap. Let them boil over the fire for at least five minutes, allow the water to cool and rub them on the washboard to remove the blood," Quetta instructed. "I brought enough food for your dinner tonight and tomorrow night. All you will have to do is heat it up." She kissed Rafaela on the forehead and wiped Rumaldo's face with a wet cloth. "I wish we could stay a little longer but I must get Miss Prudence home before it gets dark." Quetta winced. The murky sunlight was nearly gone. She picked up the large empty basket and took Prudence by the hand. Señor Morales, who lived next door, hailed them when they opened the door.

"Señorita Enriquetta, I took the liberty of putting your horse and trap in my barn. Has the little one come yet?"

Quetta waved and smiled. Mr. Morales was a nice man but liked to gossip.

"*Sí*, the little one was born, a girl called Felecitas. She looks like her mama. Thank you so much for seeing to the horse and trap, it was very kind of you."

Señor Morales liked Quetta and had for many years. A very attractive young woman, he knew she would never have anything to do with an old man but he still had hopes that she would at least admire him.

Quetta was aware of Señor Morales's affection and did nothing to encourage it but was kind to him because he was a good man. He led the horse and trap out of the barn and over to Quetta and Prudence. Tipping an imaginary hat, he handed the reins to Quetta after assisting her into the trap.

Navigating across town through the boggy streets was more difficult because of a cold wind coming from the south. The rain drenched both Quetta and Prudence and by the time they reached the Jensen house, they were nearly frozen.

Florence was standing at the door when they arrived and hurried out to meet them. "I suspected as much. Shame on you young lady! Your father has gone off to who knows where and you run away and worry me to death. It is obvious to me you need more discipline and I must take more responsibility in your upbringing."

"I'm sorry, Grandmother but I met the nicest girl. Her name is Rafaela and her mother just had a baby. I got to watch it be born," Prudence clapped her hand over her mouth. She knew that her grandmother would be furious.

"You what?" Florence looked as though she was about to faint.

When Quetta came back from the stable, Florence grabbed her by the arm and dragged her into the kitchen. "I am giving you your notice, Miss Tovar. My granddaughter is a young lady, she had no business witnessing childbirth. It was bad enough for her to go to that part of town but allowing that to occur, I'm sickened."

Quetta pulled away from her employer. "I have worked for you and Mr. Jensen for a long time and have served you well. I did not know Miss Prudence was hidden in the box in the trap. I was assisting my friend Josefa with her childbirth. Miss Prudence came into the room just as the babe was being born. I would never do anything to hurt her, I love her like she was my little sister," Quetta declared indignantly.

Florence stood in the warm kitchen facing her cook. Angry as she was, she knew Quetta was telling her the truth. She had no reason to lie. Florence felt helpless.

In a tight voice, she said, "I'm sorry. I can see you're telling the truth. My granddaughter is very headstrong, just like her mother. Please go put on some dry clothes and get Prudence into a hot bath. I'll deal with her later."

Quetta reached down, took Pru's hand and squeezed it gently. "I'm very sorry Quetta, I didn't think," Pru whispered when they reached the stairs, "I knew I'd get into trouble but I didn't think about you."

Quetta smiled, "Don't worry, you are a little girl and little girls don't always think before they do something."

Chapter 15

Buck and Frank covered the miner's face with a blanket. "We can notify Doc Kennon when we get back to town," Frank told Buck.

When they reached the fallen tree where Buck had discovered the cloth torn from Sadie's dress, Frank spotted some dead rabbits hanging in a tree. The rabbits had been snared, skinned, and cleaned. Frank pointed them out to Buck.

"Maybe the hunter stumbled across Sadie lying injured and left the rabbits here because he couldn't carry them along with Sadie. I think you should stay here in case the hunter comes back for the rabbits. I'll go on up the mountain and see if I can pick up the hunter's trail."

Sadie's eyelids felt like lead, her arms and legs didn't respond when she tried to move them. She couldn't recall what had happened to her. Staying awake was nearly impossible but she had to find a way to get home. Struggling with every ounce of strength her body could muster, she was able to sit up. In the very dim light of the fire, Sadie saw Barabas was sound asleep with his mouth wide open.

She crawled to the door of the hut and reached up to open the latch. Her fingers crept up the roughhewn door until she felt metal. But she couldn't push it up. Then she remembered seeing a walking stick propped against the wall near the door. With her bare big toe, she bumped the stick and it fell to the floor with a clatter. Barabas jumped but didn't awaken.

Holding her breath, she scooted the stick as close to her hand as she could with her toes. As soon as she grasped the stick, she used it to push up the latch. She used it as a crutch to get to her feet. The moonlight lit up the mountain, as her eyes grew accustomed to it, Sadie searched for familiar landmarks. She was startled by a noise behind her. Something cold bumped the back of her hand. It was Dutch, her dog. His big tail thumped against her leg. Weak with relief, she sank to the ground.

The door of the hut burst open, Barabas squinted for a moment. He yelled out, "Where do you think you are going, little missy?" Chuckling and wheezing, the old man hobbled toward her then stopped dead in his tracks.

A huge dog, its teeth bared and hackles raised, slinked toward him. The old man edged back inside the door of his hut and dropped the latch.

Sadie sat on the damp ground with her arms wrapped around her faithful dog. Her father must be nearby but Barabas had a gun. "Come on boy, help me up and we'll hide in the trees so that mean old man can't find us," Sadie whispered into the dog's ear.

Dutch braced himself beside her and stood still while she used him and the walking stick to stand. The two walked slowly toward the nearby Ponderosa pines along the trail down the mountain. Periodically, Dutch looked back toward the hut, keeping an eye out for the man who threatened his mistress. When they reached the trees, Dutch started to growl. She looked back toward the shack and saw the doorway gaping like a black hole.

"Be still Dutch," she whispered, "Maybe he won't see us."

"You had better pray your dog doesn't bother me, I'd be happy to shoot him. As a matter of fact, I think I'll do it anyway." The grizzled hermit raised his scattergun and fired before Sadie could say or do anything.

Dutch yelped loudly and fell to the ground. There was a loud buzzing sound in her ears; Sadie's eyes swam as she fell to the ground.

Barabas kicked the dog as he hobbled past. He dropped his scatter gun nearby and grabbed Sadie's arm. It would take most of his strength and both hands to drag her.

Chapter 16

Sadie blinked several times and groaned when she moved her stiff body. *Where was she?* She looked around the dark room.

A cold nose sniffed her face. *Dutch?* "Pa?" her dry throat croaked.

"Right here," a familiar voice answered.

"What happened?" she whispered. Her father's concerned face hung suspended in front of her.

A loud noise and a gust of wind, and Sadie heard, "Is she awake?" *It sounded like Frank's voice.* Sadie sobbed and shivered with relief. Sweeney, Mark, and Frank were standing beside her Pa. She was at home, in her bed, with people who loved her.

Dutch moaned and laid down heavily on the floor.

Sadie remembered the loud report of the rifle. "Is Dutch all right?" she asked.

"Shot up some, but he'll recover. Don't waste your strength," her father admonished her. "That old man won't bother anybody again. The sheriff has him in jail and he'll go to trial for kidnapping next week."

Pots and pans banged near the woodstove, as Mark and Sweeney prepared the evening meal. Their sister was alive and would need some tending awhile. They wanted to make sure she had something to eat and were hungry as bears themselves, so it was time to rustle up some grub.

Frank leaned over and kissed Sadie's smudged cheek. It was a miracle he and Buck were able to find her. *Dutch had picked up the trail of the old man and bounded off into the trees. The horses couldn't proceed through the woods quickly because of the rain soaked ground and fallen branches. It took some time for them to find the dog. The gunshot nearly killed Dutch but led the men in the right direction. The old man was easy to capture and tie up. Dutch was in bad shape but had cornered the old man. They found the enraged animal crouched, near Sadie's unconscious form, growling menacingly at the old man.*

Frank and Buck fashioned a stretcher out of some green pine branches and old blankets and tied it to the back of Frank's mare. They put Sadie on it with Dutch at her feet. Buck rode double with the smelly old hermit back to the Calhoun cabin.

Frank escorted the kidnapper to Pinos Altos, meeting Sweeney and Mark on the way. It took a lot of persuading to prevent Sadie's two brothers from stringing up the culprit before they reached the jail.

Feeding Sadie was a sloppy process but Frank had the foresight to tuck a rag under her chin to keep her from being totally drenched. Sadie giggled. Men, so big and strong, were clumsy when it came to taking care of someone. But they tried.

Chapter 17

The last week of confinement after Felecitas's birth dragged on and Josefa found herself entangled in Juanita's scheme to match her big sister Quetta with the strange looking Mario.

Before her baby's birth, Juanita pointed out the unusual looking man to Josefa while they were downtown. Juanita was positive he was the man who would make her sister happy.

"I had a dream when I was little," Juanita said, breathlessly. "Quetta lived in a big house on a hill, surrounded by trees. A little creek ran in front of it and there were a lot of children playing in the yard. A large man sat on the porch and smiled as Quetta poured lemonade into glasses. He had blond hair and very dark skin. When Quetta turned to look at him, I saw adoration in her eyes. I am sure Señor Mario is that man!"

"¡*Dios mío*! I had no idea," Josefa exclaimed. "I see why you're so interested in getting the two of them together."

"If you will help me, I know I can do it. It will take a lot of planning but since you aren't allowed out of bed yet, we can think up some ways to help Quetta see that Señor Mario is the man for her," Juanita clasped her hands together over her heart and sighed.

Josefa stifled a giggle. Quetta was in big trouble.

"Okay, little one, what can I do to help?" Josefa leaned forward, eager to be part of the conspiracy.

"Li Soo, the housekeeper for the Jensens, is a good friend of Quetta's. Recently, I overheard Quetta telling my mother Li Soo is considering becoming more Western in her ways and manner of dress. At the time, I didn't think to much about it but now…" Juanita paused for effect.

"Don't tease me, tell me what you are planning," Josefa's impatience was evident in her tone.

"We always attend the street dances. A big one is coming up next month, in new dresses made by your talented hands, we would make quite an impression. While shopping for material for the dresses, there is an accidental encounter with Mario, we ask him to tea and casually explain what we are doing. What do you think?"

"Hmm," Josefa smiled. "I think you may have come up with a pretty good plan. A few details need to be worked out, but there is plenty of time."

"We'll have to let a few people in on this scheme or it won't work," Josefa tapped her nose with her finger.

Juanita squealed and hugged Josefa. "I knew I could count on your help."

Li Soo stood in front of the little mirror in her bedroom and examined her features. In comparison to her friends, she looked so foreign. Quetta's friend, Josefa, was a professional dressmaker. Josefa promised Li Soo a dress designed just for her. Li Soo was really looking forward to this dance.

It wasn't hard for Quetta to determine Juanita was up to something. She knew her sister. Juanita was spending a lot of time with Josefa and confessed she adored baby Felecitas. Quetta was surprised when Josefa offered to make them new dresses for the dance and even more so when her friend professed an interest in helping Li Soo.

"I know your friend, Li Soo, is lonely. Please allow me to make her a dress that will make her beauty shine," Josefa said poetically.

"I can get some time off for the two of us next week," Quetta told her. It would be fun to include Li Soo.

The morning of the shopping trip, Li Soo and Quetta prepared breakfast for the Jensens before their departure. Florence heard them giggling in the kitchen and went to see what was going on. The two young women were draped in dishcloths and dancing around the room when she entered. They crashed into each other and fell in a heap on the floor. Florence shook her head, muttered something, and left the room. The two picked up the cloths and tidied the kitchen. Arm in arm, they picked up the shopping baskets and ran out into the warm spring sunshine. Looking forward to an adventure, they met Josefa and Juanita on Main Street and went to one of the best dry good stores in Silver City. But finding suitable material for the kinds of dresses Josefa envisioned proved to be difficult.

Li Soo was in awe of Quetta's friend. Josefa had a regal bearing and upon entering a dry goods store or general mercantile, busy clerks stopped what they were doing to assist her. Josefa addressed each by their name and smiled coquettishly.

At Miner's Mercantile, Mr. Murphy perspired profusely. "Good afternoon, l-ladies," he stammered, mopping his dripping brow with his apron. "What may I h-help you with today?"

"We are looking for some dress fabrics, Señor Murphy," Josefa described what she had in mind as the clerk licked his lips and nervously plucked at his clothes.

"I think I know what you have in mind. We just received a new shipment of dress goods yesterday. I'll go to the storeroom and see if any will suit," Murphy smiled nervously.

"My friends and I will come back in a few minutes, thank you," Josefa smiled.

"Certainly, Miss Benavidez. I'll have our new clerk, Ernest watch the counter while I look for your fabrics personally," Murphy watched as the ladies walked to the door.

"Ahh," Murphy sighed. Shaking his head sadly, poor Mr. Murphy, who would never stand a chance with a woman like Josefa Benavidez, went to the storeroom to begin his search.

Three enterprising youngsters stood behind a large wooden crate directly across the street from the Silver City Enterprise office. The ground around them was littered with bits of lemon rind and a large sack marked SUGAR sat on another crate just behind them. Some tables were set up in the shade and the chairs around them were empty. A crude board was tacked to the front of the first crate, it read: *"LemINaid Fer SeL 5 cens"*.

As Li Soo and Quetta sat down and fanned themselves, Josefa approached the gangling boys and smiled prettily. "Hello, Billy. I would like three glasses of your very best."

"Yes ma'am," Billy said seriously. Wiping his sticky hands on his pants, he poured three large glasses of lemonade. Josefa winked and handed him a quarter. Billy grinned happily.

It was obvious that the glasses were borrowed from Louis, because the saloon's name was prominently displayed on them. At least they are relatively clean, she thought.

Billy watched admiringly as Josefa deftly picked up all three glasses to carry to the table. He snapped his fingers and his two younger assistants scurried over to assist her.

Quetta's eyes were trained expectantly at the front of the Silver City Enterprise building, when a bright haired man emerged from the front door. Carrying a small package in one hand, he shaded his eyes with the other and looked right at her. She ducked her head and covered her face with her fan but kept one eye on Mario. He shook his head and walked around to the side of the building; there was little shade this time of the day.

Quetta realized Mario was looking for a cool place to eat his lunch. Josefa sat down and the two little boys handed Li Soo and Quetta their glasses of lemonade. One of the boys had a moist rag and carefully wiped the table. Josefa patted him on the head and gave him a penny. His eyes widened and he swept into a gracious bow. He looked so comical, the three young women laughed.

Mario looked up from his lunch but the shade hid the women's faces from his view. Their musical laughter caught his attention for a moment until he saw a bony puppy approaching him its nose sniffing the air. He held out some meat, with a faint woof, the puppy swayed toward him. After a second of hesitation, the tiny animal came closer and gulped it whole. Mario quickly gave it another piece of his lunch and it was consumed as quickly as the first.

Quetta watched as the puppy ate most of Mario's food. After its meal, it leaped up on Mario's lap and licked his face. Mario stroked it gently with one finger. Most men would have kicked the puppy away, but he displayed an unusual tenderness.

No need for putting Juanita's plan into action, this was much better, Josefa thought.

When he folded up his lunch package and went back inside to work, the three women returned to Miner's Mercantile. Proudly, Mr. Murphy displayed the fabrics he had managed to locate matching Josefa's description for two of the dresses, her own and Quetta's.

After another hour of looking for material for her own dress, Li Soo invited Josefa and Quetta to meet her mother. Mai Soo, Li Soo's mother, smiled as the young women explained they were looking for material for dresses and Li Soo was the only one unable to find what she liked. Mai Soo excused herself and left the room. She returned a few minutes later carrying a large package. She placed it gently in her daughter's lap.

"What is this, my mother?" Li Soo asked, lapsing into her formal way of speaking to her parent.

"I have been saving this for a long time knowing one day I would give it to you. Open it and see," Mai said softly.

Li Soo carefully unwrapped the parcel covered with delicate rice paper. She gasped when she saw the gold and red silk material inside.

Josefa rushed over to examine it. "It's perfect!" she exclaimed.

Chapter 18

Eusebio Benavidez, Josefa's brother, worked for Felecito Esquivel in his lime plant. Eusebio owned a small house and lived there with his sister and her three small children. Too shy to try to meet women, the arrangement suited Eusebio but he was worried about Josefa. Their aging parents lived in Georgetown and expected him to find a husband for their daughter.

If she married a solid respectable man he could tame her wild streak and provide well for her and the children.

Esquivel, a widower in his fifties, at least twenty years older than Josefa, was still a handsome man, who was kind and fair. While out repairing a fence alongside his employer, Eusebio decided to bring up the subject of marriage. "You were married for a long time. Have you ever thought of getting married again?" Eusebio asked Esquivel.

Esquivel stopped wrapping wire around the wooden post. Looking off into the distance dreamily, he smiled. "I've always had my son to consider. I knew he needed a mama but not just anyone could replace my Adelina. Now I'm too old," he grimaced and went back to his task.

"My sister, Josefa is a fine mama. She has two girls and a son that need a papa. You might consider her as a new wife," Eusebio swallowed hard, amazed at his courage.

"I've seen your sister. She's a fine looking woman. She wouldn't want an old man like me," Esquivel laughed.

"She needs to settle down and raise her children. Even though she loves them very much, she spends a lot of time looking for a husband. She's a good Catholic girl and needs someone to look after her," Eusebio confided.

"I'll think about it," Esquivel said giving the wire a final twist.

Eusebio watched as Esquivel went to shovel lime into the flash furnace. He admired the older man's involvement in all aspects of his business.

Josefa was fixing dinner for her small family when Eusebio went home. "*Hola, hermano.* Do you want to eat with us tonight? I made some corn *tortillas* this afternoon and they're still warm," Josefa said as she wiped her hands on a ruffled blue flowered apron.

Eusebio nodded and watched his sister finish preparing the meal. She was flushed from standing over the hot stove and small moist tendrils of hair clung to her face. Even in the stifling kitchen, Josefa appeared poised and graceful. Her eyes sparkled and danced as she teased her brother. "I've been told a certain *señorita* has her eye on you. She is very young and her papa is not too happy about having you as a son-in-law. He's a very good shot, so be careful," she warned in a serious tone.

"I want to speak to you seriously for a moment, Josefa. My parents are worried about you. You must find a husband soon and stop all the gossips in town. I think Señor Esquivel might marry you. He's a good man and has money," Eusebio told her.

"Señor Esquivel is a fine looking man. I think he is shy because I never see him speak to women. I think he'd make a fine husband. Bring him to the dance and you can introduce him to me," Josefa said.

She scooped a large bowl of beans from the cooking pot and added several spoonfuls of red *chile*. She stirred them together and added some salt. The fresh corn *tortillas* were placed on the table and Josefa went to call her children.

Eusebio knew Señor Esquivel didn't attend dances because he couldn't dance. Somehow, Eusebio must convince him to take some lessons so he and Josefa would have something in common. Josefa was dancing as soon as she could walk. Esquivel was so involved in his small lime plant he found little time for socializing. His idea of a good time was riding horseback through the rugged hills behind his sprawling adobe house.

Eusebio had done his homework. A dancing school opened on Bullard Street and was popular among the *gringos*. Mr. LaMont Girdeau introduced his students to new Midwest and Eastern dances as well as some from Europe. He taught a variety of older styles and his fees were reasonable. His teachers consisted of seven beautiful, sophisticated young ladies and three urbane handsome young men.

Eusebio ate in silence and observed his niece. Little Rafaela talked about school as Josefa smiled proudly. Her little *hija* was growing up so quickly. Her thoughts drifted back to Felecito Esquivel, Eusebio's *jefe*. Since her baby's name, Felecitas, had been selected by Josefa's mama and she had never met Señor Esquivel, this might be a good sign. Perhaps this was the man who could make her happy.

When Eusebio rode back to the lime plant that night, the sky was sprinkled with bright stars and a slight breeze stirred the cottonwoods. Tomorrow, they had a big order to fill for the smelter. It promised to be a long, backbreaking day. Smoke from the lime furnace, rose like a spiral into the cooling air of late summer. Esquivel allowed the younger men to do most of the shoveling of the wet lime into the drying furnace, as he stood to one side. Deftly, he rolled a cigarette between his tobacco-stained fingers and cupped his hand around its tip as he lit it from a stick that Eusebio held up for him.

"I have been thinking about your *hermana*," Esquivel told him. "I'd like to get to know her. What do you suggest?"

Eusebio was pleased; he'd been trying to think of a way to suggest the older man take dancing lessons. It would be easier than he thought.

"Josefa loves to dance. She goes to all of the street dances and is very popular," Eusebio replied.

"¡*Hay Dios*! But I cannot dance at all. This may not be such a good idea," Esquivel grunted and turned to walk away from his foreman.

"There is a dancing school in town. They might be able to help you."

Esquivel paused for a moment. He thought about Josefa, she would be worth the effort. A woman like that in his bed would make him feel like a young man.

Esquivel flicked ashes into the air. He paused to consider. "All right, tomorrow have Gerardo ask about this school. I'll go so that I may have something in common with *la bonita mujer*," Esquivel announced, sounding more confident than he felt.

The next morning, Eusebio told Josefa he would bring Esquivel to the dance. He didn't mention the dancing lessons thinking it best for his sister to believe Esquivel had been dancing for years.

Esquivel liked school and looked forward to seeing his teacher, Mademoiselle Monet, a beautiful dark haired Frenchwoman. She smelled of expensive perfume and held him tightly as she taught him intricate dance steps. He forgot about Josefa when he was dancing with his teacher and entertained thoughts of courting the Frenchwoman.

Chapter 19. Silver City

Mai Soo, Li Soo's mother, held her five-year old granddaughter in her lap.
"Grandmother, will you read me a story?" the child pleaded.
Mai Soo hugged her tightly. "I read you a story already."
"Yes, Grandmother, but that was in Chinese. Read one in ING-lish."
Mai Soo winced. It was a touchy subject. She couldn't read English. Despite the pleading of her husband and children, she hadn't learned to read and write in the language of her new country. Perhaps she was too old to learn something new.
"Let us go see what Grandfather is doing. He will probably be ready to eat soon," Mai Soo held the tiny hand and they went into Lan Soo's office.
He was bent over a large ledger and writing tiny characters into little squares. Lan Soo paused and squinted through his spectacles. He smiled at them and leaned back in his wooden chair. Mai Soo looked at the large book. None of the marks on the book looked familiar to Mai Soo. Flooded with a sense of shame, she realized even her little one knew what those marks meant.
Li Soo visited her parents every Tuesday afternoon. Mai Soo prepared her favorite foods and waited to speak to Li Soo alone. For the last several years, Li Soo recruited students for Mr. Coates, a Methodist minister, who held English classes at his own home every evening. Li Soo was one of his first students. She gained so much confidence that she made it a point to contact every newcomer of Chinese descent. When she was able, Li Soo helped Mr. Coates with his classes. Li Soo was frustrated but hadn't given up on convincing her mother.
Li Soo came in and Mai Soo's heart quickened. Li Soo appeared radiant and joyful. Her news would further elate her daughter, she thought.
Li Soo noticed her mother's mood. Sensing she had something important to discuss, Li Soo sat down and began to eat the delicacies her mother put before her. After several minutes of silence, Li Soo couldn't wait any longer.
"Mother, when are you going to tell me?" Li Soo asked impatiently.
"Tell you what, daughter?" Mai Soo looked at her innocently.
"I have known since I arrived that you had something to tell me. You have never been very good at keeping secrets, my mother," Li Soo lapsed into the formal English of her childhood whenever she was with her parents.
"I wanted to tell you right away but am having difficulty finding the words."
When Li Soo leaned forward in her chair expectantly, Mai Soo smiled. She was enjoying this immensely. "I have decided to attend Mr. Coates's English classes so that I may learn to read and write ING-lish, as our little one calls it."

"Oh, my mother! This is wonderful news. I have spoken to Mr. Coates about you many times. He will be very happy to assist you. When can you begin?"

"I would like to begin tonight. I am afraid if I wait too long, I will find some excuse."

The two women spent the rest of the afternoon discussing plans. Li Soo promised to find a way to spend extra time tutoring her mother. Mai Soo felt a huge weight lift from her shoulders. It had been a long time since she had felt so good about herself. If all went well, within a few months, she would be able to read a story to her granddaughter.

That afternoon, Mai Soo and Li Soo dressed in traditional clothes and walked to the Methodist Church. Mr. Coates was in his study, Li Soo knocked at the door softly.

"Please come in," the kindly minister said loudly. He smiled broadly recognizing Li Soo in the doorway. Li Soo took her mother's hand and drew her into the room behind her.

"Reverend Coates, I would like to introduce you to my honorable mother, Mai Soo. I have told her a lot about your school and she would like to attend some of your classes," Li Soo informed him.

"Wonderful, wonderful," Reverend Coates congratulated her. A large, ruddy-faced man, his presence overwhelmed tiny Mai Soo. "We're just beginning a new reading and writing class and have just enough pupils for a class. Your timing couldn't have been better. The first meeting will be tomorrow evening at six. You'll need to supply your own slate and chalk. We are a poor parish."

Li Soo and Reverend Coates worked out the financial agreement as Mai Soo watched quietly. When they were finished, Reverend Coates offered the two ladies some tea. Mai Soo wasn't sure she had made the right decision. The more she saw of the church, the more uncomfortable she became. Li Soo sensed something but didn't acknowledge it until they were on their way home.

"My mother, you were very quiet when we were with the Reverend Coates. Did he frighten you?" Li Soo asked respectfully.

"Yes, my daughter, how did you know?"

Li Soo laughed. "I felt exactly the same way when I first met him. My mother, he is one of the kindest men I have ever met. He is very large and "Western" but you have nothing to fear from him. Reverend Coates is very spontaneous but an excellent teacher who speaks Chinese almost fluently."

"Why did he not speak to me in Chinese out of respect?" Mai Soo wanted to know.

"Reverend Coates believes if people want to learn English they should practice and practice. It probably did not occur to him that it would be respectful to speak to you in Chinese. I am sure he meant no disrespect," Li Soo assured her. Continuing in a low tone, Li Soo bent close to her mother's ear. "I will attend the classes with you until you feel comfortable, my mother."

Mai Soo felt tears in her eyes. She patted her daughter's hand and squeezed her fingers. "Thank you, my daughter."

Chapter 20

"I won't allow it!" Eusebio Benavidez glowered angrily.

"I'm not stealing, you fool, only borrowing. Besides that old man has it coming. He treats his workers like *peons*. No one but you respects him. I need those parts for a job I am doing for the sheriff," Maximiano Najera sneered.

Eusebio shook his head, "You steal from the man who pays your salary and give what you steal to the sheriff?"

"You don't understand how it is with me. I work hard all day, every day of the week and yet I have nothing. Esquivel does nothing but get in the way here at the lime plant and he has so much money he buries it in tin cans. What is the harm in taking a few things?" Maximiano Najera lived by his wits. He was handsome with dark heavy-lidded eyes and curly black hair. His oily charm was self-seeking and women tended to avoid his company.

Earlier in the day, Najera ran afoul of Frank Parnell. Frank was doing inventory and some new hardware was missing. After questioning Mr. Murphy, he learned Najera examined the missing items before Frank came in.

"Did he ask anything about them?" Frank wanted to know.

"No sir, but he seemed very interested in them," Murphy gulped.

"Do you know where this man works?" Frank asked insistently.

"I believe he works at the lime plant. He comes in to order supplies. I thought it odd he placed no order today just went right to the hand drills," Murphy was becoming increasingly annoyed with Frank's tone. But Robert Jensen was his boss and as Robert's son-in-law, Frank Parnell held power over him.

Frank slammed down his ledger and stormed out of the mercantile. "He allows people to steal right from under his long nose," Frank muttered under his breath.

The lime plant was in full production when Frank arrived. The first person he encountered was Felecito Esquivel, coming out of his office. Esquivel recognized Frank Parnell, the only one armed man Esquivel had ever met. Esquivel walked up to him and extended his hand.

"Mr. Parnell what can I do for you?" Esquivel asked politely.

Frank extended his hand, he had no problem with the plant owner. "I believe you have a man called Najera working here," Frank stated.

"Yes he is here now. Did you need to see him?" Esquivel asked pleasantly.

Frank nodded, "As soon as possible." Frank told Esquivel of his suspicions.

"That sounds like Najera. I think he has been stealing from me but I haven't been able to prove anything. Some of my men are watching him. I'll have Lopez go get him. You can use my office if you like."

After waiting several minutes, Frank began to pace. When the door opened, he turned to face the sullen Najera accompanied by a younger man, presumably Lopez. Lopez ducked his head and shut the door on his way out.

"What did you need to see me about?" Najera asked, innocently.

"You stole something from Miner's Mercantile this morning," Frank stated menacingly.

"Me, steal? Why me? I go to order supplies for this plant all the time, why would I steal? That would be stupid."

"No one said you were smart. Anyway, I want that hand drill back," Frank grabbed the front of his shirt.

"Oh, am I supposed to be afraid of you?" He grabbed Frank's arm and yanked his hand away. He threw back his head defiantly. "Where is your proof? I suggest you leave here and let me get back to work. I wouldn't be surprised if you took the drill yourself and are trying to blame me," Najera snarled.

"Why, you..." Frank growled.

Just then, Esquivel came into the office. "I'm sorry, I didn't realize you were still here," Esquivel apologized.

Frank stomped out. Najera was grinning.

"GET BACK TO WORK!" Esquivel roared.

Najera strutted from the room. It was impossible for anyone to prove he had stolen anything because he was very careful. He was smarter than any of these men and if his plans worked out he'd be able to sit back and laugh at all of them.

Chapter 21

The temperature dropped rapidly when the sun sank. Esquivel dressed carefully and polished his boots. Dressed in black pants and boots, he added a maroon short coat and bolo tie. Despite his age, he carried himself well and drew stares from younger women. With darkness approaching, the street lamps came on and provided the onlookers with a better view.

Eusebio saw him coming and took Josefa's arm. He led her over to meet his boss. Esquivel was very polite and Josefa was impressed by the attention he drew. He bowed slightly and asked her to dance. Josefa grew breathless as he guided her through a series of polished dance steps. He was magnificent and she was ecstatic. She allowed him to hold her tightly as they continued to dance. People stopped to watch them.

Esquivel's hands kneaded Josefa's back and sides. He was pleased to find she was well built and trim. So many women became plump as they aged and although still attractive, seemed to lose their interest in the delights of the bedroom. He watched her face as he felt her body but Josefa pretended not to notice.

Eusebio watched the couple thinking they were very well suited for one another. His face hurt from smiling as he watched the crowd and how they responded to them and was very pleased. Then he saw Najera.

Najera had arrived late and was obviously upset to see Esquivel dancing with Josefa. Eusebio knew Josefa was once involved with Najera but after discovering the man was dishonest, his sister let Najera know that she was no longer interested. It was obvious Najera still cared about Josefa.

Maximiano Najera approached the couple and tapped Esquivel on the shoulder. Esquivel frowned but did not step aside. Najera was furious, taking the older man's attitude as a direct insult. No one had ever done that to him before. He tapped Esquivel's shoulder again. Again, Esquivel refused to step aside. Najera grabbed Esquivel's shoulder and jerked him around to face him. Esquivel pushed Josefa out of the way and took a poorly aimed swing at the younger man. Josefa retreated into the crowd. Eusebio stepped between the two men and grabbed Najera's arm before he could hit Esquivel. Najera was ready to fight anybody and everybody. It took two men to escort him away.

The music stopped and the dancers stood aside to watch the commotion. When Najera was removed, the music started again. Esquivel straightened his clothes and tie and looked around for Josefa. She stood alone near the end of the street and appeared to be badly frightened.

"Are you all right?" Esquivel asked putting his arm around her shoulders. She nodded and shivered. Gallantly, Esquivel removed his jacket and wrapped it around her shoulders. "I'm sorry that you had to see that. The man is rude and had no business behaving in that way. He'll find himself without a job when he reports to work next week. I can't understand why he was so angry."

Josefa shook her head. Esquivel admired the way her hair gleamed in the lamplight. "He and I were seeing each other at one time. I didn't like him very much and said I didn't want to be with him anymore. He was so angry that he slapped me across the face. I never told Eusebio, he would have killed him."

Esquivel was furious as he took Josefa's arm and led her into the trees. He put his arms around her and held her tightly. Taking her chin in his hand, he tipped her face toward his and kissed her gently. She responded with a small sound from deep in her throat. Esquivel felt as though he was on fire. He gasped for several seconds after the kiss ended.

"We must be married soon. You shouldn't be at the mercy of men like Maximiano Najera. I will love and protect you always if you will consent to be my wife."

Josefa looked at him, most of his face was hidden in shadow. It was what her family expected and what her children needed. "Please kiss me again and then I will give you my answer," Josefa responded. This time she initiated the kiss. She wrapped her arms around Esquivel's neck and pressed her lips against his. She leaned against him wanting to see if her body responded to his; it did. "I will marry you, Felecito Esquivel. I am honored that you would ask me. My brother speaks very highly of you and I trust his judgment," Josefa sighed heavily. She wanted to kiss him again but was afraid she would not be able to contain herself. It had been a long time since she had been with a man who made her feel so desirable.

Eusebio returned to the dance after he and the other two men escorted an intoxicated Najera home to sleep it off. He stood on the wooden sidewalk searching the crowd for his sister and Esquivel. When he saw them coming out of the trees, Josefa appeared slightly disheveled and was wrapped in Esquivel's coat. Before he could reach them, they were dancing again. Eusebio smiled contentedly. Another man had succumbed to Josefa's charms. This time, she had made a good choice.

Chapter 22

"He was supposed to be here over an hour ago. I'm telling you, I won't stand for it. He's through. I'm going to send the sheriff to get him," Esquivel was adamant and angry. He was late for an important meeting with John Fleming.

Eusebio, Esquivel's foreman and new brother-in-law had tried for the last several months to keep Najera out of trouble. First there was the scene at the street dance. Then Najera showed up at Josefa and Esquivel's wedding, uninvited and drunk. Eusebio had escorted him home. Yesterday, a laborer in the lime plant saw Najera put some tools in a box and leave the warehouse. Enough was enough.

After a short nod to Esquivel, Eusebio made his excuses to Fleming who was waiting in the next room. His boss was not in any mood to argue. The last thing Eusebio wanted to do was to confront Najera. He still felt guilty about Najera's failed relationship with Josefa.

By the time Eusebio reached Najera's house, he was very angry. Najera answered his knock. "Whaada ya want?" Najera slurred. He peered at Eusebio through bleary eyes and thick mussed hair.

"You were supposed to be at that meeting with the boss today. You didn't show up so he is going to the sheriff with his suspicions about you. If I were you, I'd get out of town right away," Eusebio warned him as he pushed Najera out of the doorway. He dragged an old trunk out of the corner of the room and threw the man's belongings into it haphazardly.

"Whaada are ya doing? I'm not leaving. Whaada about Josefa? I can't leave her, she loves me," Najera groaned and fell down on the disheveled bed.

"She doesn't love you. She married Esquivel."

Najera covered his face with his hands and sobbed.

Eusebio felt sorry for the fool. Najera had nowhere to go; but he had to leave town now. Esquivel was going to speak to the sheriff as soon as he finished his meeting with John Fleming. As soon as he had collected Najera's belongings, Eusebio dragged the trunk to the stage depot and purchased a one-way ticket to Tucson.

Najera was on the stage when it left but not entirely aware of what was happening. Eusebio returned to the lime plant and met his brother-in-law coming out of his office.

"Where is he? I see you couldn't convince him to come. I'm on my way to the sheriff now. He's not going to get away with stealing from me and he will leave Josefa alone," Esquivel growled.

"I put him on the stage to Tucson. He won't trouble you again. Najera is a sick man, he isn't right in the head. Putting him in jail will only anger him and make it more likely that he will make trouble for you and Josefa. Now he'll be far away and with no money, it's unlikely he'll come back," Eusebio said quietly.

Esquivel grabbed the younger man's arm. "You stupid #*#!!"

"Is that any way to speak to your brother-in-law?" Eusebio asked lifting his chin up. He wasn't afraid of Esquivel.

"I'm going to the sheriff anyway. He threatened me last night and I won't tolerate it. He is a dangerous man." Esquivel changed the subject. "Fleming wants to increase his order next month and we'll have to step up production."

Eusebio said nothing. Esquivel was a force to be reckoned with. The sheriff was very busy but might consider sending someone to get Najera. Somehow, he had to change Esquivel's mind about pursuing his complaint. It wouldn't be easy because Esquivel was as stubborn as they come. Eusebio decided to enlist his sister's help.

That evening, after Josefa put her children to bed; she sat in front of the stove with a large basket full of old clothes. She had received them from the sisters at San Vicente. They were preparing for their annual bazaar and she promised to go through them and determine which could be refurbished. Esquivel wasn't home yet; he was meeting with some businessmen about funding for his lime plant expansion.

Eusebio sipped some strong coffee. Josefa was a reasonable woman but guileless. It was impossible for her to be dishonest. Josefa sat quietly as her brother talked.

"I will persuade my husband to leave Max Najera alone. It is the least I can do. I had no idea that I had hurt him so badly."

Chapter 23

"I must speak to you about Prudence," Florence told Frank as he was preparing to leave Miner's Mercantile for the evening. He was surprised to see his mother-in-law at the store so late.

"How are her piano lessons coming along? I understand she's been studying with the Warren girl. Prudence really likes her," Frank smiled as he removed his apron and hung it on a hook on the back of the door.

"Yes, yes," Florence said impatiently. "But that isn't why I needed to speak to you." She coughed suddenly, her face reddened, and she gasped for air.

Frank frowned at his mother-in-law. "What's the matter?" Frank wanted to know.

Florence snorted impolitely. "You're never home. You work here at the mercantile, ride all over the countryside chasing criminals and you spend time in Pinos Altos. You pay no attention to your daughter."

"I'm doing the best I can to take care of her. I realize I've been gone a lot lately but she knows I love her and want what's best for her. What are you trying to tell me?" Frank demanded.

"Robert and I would like to adopt her. I could be sure she continues with her piano lessons and she would have a stable home."

Frank shook his head angrily, "I knew this would happen! You promised you'd allow me to raise my daughter and not interfere. I should have known you wouldn't keep your word."

Florence grabbed her chest and slumped forward against Frank. He tried to steady her then realized she had fainted. Half dragging, half carrying Florence, he put her in a chair near the pot-bellied stove in the corner of the large showroom.

"Murphy, get me some smelling salts," Frank shouted as he struggled to keep Florence upright. He had seen Murphy, the clerk, crouched behind the counter, eavesdropping on their conversation.

"What happened, Mr. Parnell?" Murphy asked, nervously. "Did you hit her? I heard you shouting."

"Of course I didn't hit her!" Frank snarled. "Go see if Mr. Jensen is in his office and get back here."

Murphy went to the PHARMACEUTICAL SHELF and obtained the requested smelling salts. With shaky hands, he struggled to remove the stopper.

"Here you are, s-sir," Murphy stammered backing toward the doorway leading to the offices.

Frank held the smelling salts to Florence's nose while bracing her with his shoulder. The smelling salts caused her to gasp and choke but didn't arouse her. Murphy burst into the room.

"Mr. Jensen isn't in his office or in back. I'm not sure where he went."

"Fetch Dr. Woodville and be quick, use my horse. Tell him to bring his carriage," Frank said urgently.

"I'll be back as soon as I can," Murphy assured him. He had never seen Parnell so upset.

No customers entered Miner's Mercantile. Frank watched the large clock above the cash register. He considered putting Florence down on the floor but hadn't thought to ask Murphy to help him before he left. Ten minutes went by, then twenty. Florence's eyelids fluttered a couple of times and her breathing was raspy and labored. Alarmed by her failure to regain consciousness, Frank started to talk, partly to himself and partly to Florence. It made him feel better and less helpless.

"Listen, Mrs. Jensen. I know we've had our differences but we both care about Prudence and want what's best for her. Although someday she may be a great pianist, right now she is a young girl. I think she needs me and I sure need her. I am gone a lot; but I'm trying to make a living for us. It'll be up to you and Mr. Jensen to see she becomes a lady; but let me be her father."

Dr. Woodville rushed in with Murphy right behind him. "What happened, Parnell?" Dr. Woodville asked breathlessly. He dropped his medical bag on the floor and motioned for Murphy to relieve Frank. Woodville dug in his bag and grunted with satisfaction when he found and extracted his stethoscope. Carefully placing its bell on Florence's chest, he moved it around a few times and then listened to her back. He thumped and prodded, mumbled something and shook his head ominously.

Frowning, Dr. Woodville listened to Frank's description of the argument as he and Mr. Murphy carried Florence to the doctor's buggy outside. "I've warned her about becoming overwrought. She should go to the hospital but there aren't any beds. The best we can do for her is to take her home and find a nurse to care for her."

"What's wrong with her, Doc?" Frank wanted to know.

"She has pneumonia. It's quite common in older folks this time of year. That's why there aren't any beds in the hospital. She should be all right, having a strong constitution and a lot of fight in her. Still she'll need proper care and rest. Where is Mr. Jensen?"

"I'm not sure. He was in his office a few hours ago but I've been busy out here and didn't know he left," Frank replied. Robert would blame him for Florence's condition, when he learned of the argument. It didn't matter how much money they had, he would never let them have Prudence, not while he had breath left in his body.

Dr. Woodville had a bed in his carriage for transporting the sick and injured. Once assured Florence was situated comfortably with her head elevated to help her breathing, Woodville climbed into the driver's seat and grabbed the reins. Frank mounted his horse and followed close behind. Woodville proceeded down Bullard and his vehicle took a sharp left turn on Kelly and disappeared from Frank's view. Frank kept his eyes open for Robert and spotted him coming out of Johnnie Ross's Wine and Liquor Store. It was a good thing the doctor hadn't seen him; Robert had been warned repeatedly to give up cigars.

As Frank tied his horse to the hitching post, he caught Robert's attention. The older man was alarmed when he saw the look on his son-in-law's face. "Something's wrong, well, what is it, my boy?" Robert asked, impatiently.

"Mrs. Jensen collapsed at the mercantile. Dr. Woodville is taking her home. You can take my horse. I'll follow on foot and be there shortly."

Robert needed help to heave his bulky frame onto Frank's rangy mare. The mare groaned as he shifted his weight but responded when he snapped the reins. Frank followed quickly and arrived at the Jensen house as Dr. Woodville was preparing to leave.

"I gave Miss Soo and Miss Tovar instructions on how to administer Mrs. Jensen's medications. I'll look for a nurse and send one over as soon as I can. In the meantime, try to keep her in bed and quiet. Her lungs need a chance to fight the infection. Don't allow your daughter near her for a few days until she starts to get better."

Frank shook his hand and thanked him. Robert stood in the doorway and watched the exchange between Frank and the doctor. It occurred to him suddenly that he could lose Florence. Robert went outside and stared up at the sky. It wasn't fair. He couldn't go on without her. Covering his face with his hands, he was startled by Frank's hand on his shoulder.

"I'm sorry. We had an argument just before it happened and I feel responsible," Frank admitted in a somber voice.

"I told her it was wrong to take Prudence from you. She wouldn't listen; she thinks she can make up for Emma's unhappiness by raising her child."

Frank was surprised. *Emma's unhappiness, Emma was never unhappy, was she? How could she be unhappy, with parents that loved her?*

"Why was Emma unhappy, Mr. Jensen?" Frank asked, tentatively.

"I wasn't aware she was until Flo told me. Emma was disappointed and disillusioned when we moved west because of her health. She wanted to continue with her musical studies and had to give them up. Then to make matters worse, we were unable to bring her piano. Emma didn't know but there was one on the way from St. Louis that arrived a week after she left."

Frank patted the older man's shoulder. "Emma was never unhappy here. She loved you both very much and it nearly broke her heart to leave you. I think she knew we wouldn't have much time together. Now, all I have left of her is Pru and I'll do anything to keep her with me."

Robert sighed. "I'd better check on Florence."

Frank nodded, "I'll be back later after I tell Pru what happened."

Robert was relieved to see Florence awake and sitting up in bed. "Dr. Woodville told me that I have to stay in bed for at least two weeks," she began. "I have to organize the Charity Bazaar; Elizabeth Warren and Beatrice are counting on me. Prudence will miss her lessons if I'm not there to see to her. This is terrible, absolutely terrible. I gave that doctor a piece of my mind."

Robert smiled indulgently. "I'm sure they can manage without you. Besides it's only for a short time. I'll send Quetta with a bit of broth for you. Now, you just rest."

"Just rest indeed," Florence folded her arms across her chest. "I don't want any broth, I'm not hungry."

"It'll be all right, dear." Robert went out and firmly shut the door. Quetta came around the corner with a large bowl of broth, Robert shook his head, "Keep it warm; she's in no mood right now."

Chapter 24

"A pack of filthy lies!" Barabas jumped to his feet in the middle of the Silver City courtroom. Two deputies pushed him back into his chair. That didn't prevent him from shaking his fist at his accuser.

With his elbows poking through the sleeves of his ragged shirt and his scraggly hair standing on end, Barabas Featherstone looked like a scarecrow. "I found that youngun face down in the mud, barely breathin'. Her head was bleeding, bashed in by a fallen tree. I didn't know where she belonged so I took her to my shack to tend to her wounds."

The trial had been postponed for several months due to Sadie Calhoun's injuries. The day before, Sadie had given her testimony. Her recollections had been vague and it was evident to everyone in the courtroom. Today she wasn't present because she didn't want to see Barabas Featherstone.

"Why did you lock her up?" the judge asked. He leaned forward and peered at Barabas through his smudged spectacles.

"I always lock my door at night to keep out trespassers. There's no law agin it!" Barabas leaned forward and squinted at the judge.

"The young lady said you tried to hold her prisoner and shot her dog when he tried to protect her," the judge squinted back at him.

"That there dog tried to attack me. All I was trying to do was help that youngun and that dog snapped and snarled at me. I was protecting myself from being chewed up!" Barabas spit on the floor.

Sighing, the judge leaned back in his chair. The old hermit's story made sense. The girl, Sadie Calhoun, wasn't able to tell him much. Dr. Kennon, from Pinos Altos, had examined Miss Calhoun and determined she had probably sustained a slight skull fracture. Judging from the bleeding from her ears and nose, Kennon admitted the injury could have affected Miss Calhoun's judgment.

Judge Avery addressed the court. "This whole thing seems to be a big misunderstanding. If there is no other evidence, I'm afraid I'll have to let this man go," the judge concluded.

Buck Calhoun jumped to his feet. "Your honor, this man tried to hold my daughter against her will. He shot her dog because it was trying to protect her. He is guilty of a crime, you can't set him free."

"I can and I will, case dismissed!" the judge banged his gavel. When Judge Avery left the courtroom chaos broke loose. Barabas hopped up on a table and spun around crazily and then began to cackle and dance. He shook his fist at the

Calhoun family. Mark and Sweeney struggled to hold Buck to keep him from going after the old man.

"That judge is loco. He didn't even listen to Sadie when she told him what that old feller did to her." Buck roared. He was horrified.

"Be reasonable, Mr. Calhoun. Sadie was pretty banged up and not herself. It's possible she misunderstood the old man's intentions." Frank followed as Mark and Sweeney, still holding their father's arms, went outside.

"My Sadie would never lie and you know it!" Buck retorted angrily.

"No, she wouldn't lie, but she might not have realized he was trying to help her," Frank insisted.

Buck straightened his shoulders and shrugged off his sons' hands. He stomped his feet and strode off down Broadway toward the Southern Hotel. The family had been staying there for the past three days. Mark and Sweeney grinned sheepishly at Frank.

"Pa's got quite a temper when he gets riled. Sadie will settle him down, she's the only one who can when he gets like this," Sweeney assured Frank.

"Let's have a beer and wait awhile before going back to the hotel," Mark said, wiping his lips with the back of his hand.

"I'm for that. How about you, Frank?" Sweeney asked.

"I think I'll stop in to see Sadie. I'll see you tomorrow before you leave," Frank said. The brothers were seeing their father and sister safely back to Pinos Altos in the morning. Nodding in unison, Sweeney and Mark headed toward the saloon.

Frank arrived at the Southern Hotel a few minutes later and Sadie answered the door.

"I'm on my way home. Is there anything I can get you before I go?" he wanted to know.

"No, we'll be fine. Pa's just angry; he'll be okay. Thank you for everything," Sadie told him. She was referring to the room at the hotel and his emotional support of her family during the trial.

Frank grinned and nodded, as he pulled her into the hall and kissed her. He still had one stop to make before going home. A friend promised to keep an eye on old Featherstone. Frank patted his pocket containing the money they had agreed upon and headed for San Vicente Street.

Chapter 25

"Doc says Flo needs bedrest but she won't stay in bed. She can barely stand but gets up and dressed every day. Doc Woodville told her she was not to work on the Charity Bazaar project, and she does it anyway. I can't get her to listen to anything I say," Robert massaged his forehead with his right hand.

The two men were in Robert's office at Miner's Mercantile, the day after Barabas's trial.

"What happened to the nurse you hired to take care of her?" Frank asked as he finished tallying a row of figures.

"Mrs. Tinker quit," Robert shook his head in disbelief, "Actually, Flo fired her. She said she didn't like people hovering and ordering her about. The woman was following the doctor's orders, but Flo would have none of it."

"Hire another nurse," Frank told his father-in-law. "Find someone who can stand up to her." A smile crossed Frank's face. He'd have to hurry to catch the Calhouns.

Robert eyed him suspiciously. *What was Frank grinning about?* He was unusually impatient and testy due to several sleepless nights caused by Florence's behavior.

"I have an idea, Mr. Jensen. Just leave everything to me," Frank told him. He put away his ledger and rose to his feet. "I'll be back in awhile, I think I know someone who can help."

Robert watched Frank ride up the street. One more night spent like last night and he might have another stroke.

When Frank reached the Southern Hotel, he was told the Calhouns had checked out 30 minutes earlier. Going toward Pinos Altos, he spotted Buck and Sadie's wagon near the edge of town. Mark and Sweeney accompanied them on horseback. Frank told the family of his plan.

"Oh, Frank. It's a wonderful idea. I suppose Pa can get along without me for a little while," Sadie admitted enthusiastically. For the last several months, Frank and Sadie discussed how he would introduce Sadie to the Jensens and Prudence. He knew the Jensens would not approve of her. With Sadie as Florence Jensen's nurse, the family would discover what a wonderful person Sadie was and accept her for herself. It was foolproof. He knew Prudence would like anyone who made him happy.

Buck turned the wagon around back toward Silver City. *His daughter was good enough for anyone!* Buck kissed Sadie's cheek as she leaned over to hug him when they arrived at the Jensen home.

"Take care of yourself, little girl," Buck's voice was hoarse.

"Don't worry, Pa, I'll be home in two weeks," Sadie assured him. She was excited but apprehensive. *What if the Jensen's, especially Florence, didn't like her? Would they throw her out in the middle of the night? How would she get home?*

Frank sensed Sadie was worried about her reception. He knew the Jensens well enough to understand the kind of people that they liked. Sadie was well spoken, attractive, and polite. She was the kind of person Emma was and in some ways, Sadie reminded him of her.

Frank went to find Dr. Woodville, after leaving Sadie with Quetta. It was essential that Dr. Woodville assist him with his plan. He'd be able to justify Sadie's presence and assure Robert he could trust Sadie's judgment. Dr. Woodville was locking the door to his office when Frank arrived.

"Doctor, may I speak to you for a moment?" Frank asked politely.

"Make it fast, I'm on my way home for the first time in three days. I've had a terrible week," Dr. Woodville groaned.

Briefly, Frank outlined his plan to the physician and by the time he was finished, Dr. Woodville was grinning delightedly.

"That just might work. I'm impressed Parnell. I'll go with you right now and speak to Mr. and Mrs. Jensen. I know what a good nurse Miss Calhoun is, Dr. Kennon and I consult periodically and he speaks very highly of her."

Dr. Woodville loaded his medical bag into his carriage and proceeded to the Jensen home while Frank went to Miner's Mercantile to get Robert.

Chapter 26

"Oh, what is it now?" Florence muttered as she opened one eye to see who was touching her. It had been four days since she collapsed at Miner's Mercantile and she felt no better.

"Grandmother?" Prudence took a step back when her grandmother spoke.

"I'm sorry, I didn't mean to sound so cross. I'm tired of Quetta and Li Soo pushing broth and medicine down my throat. How can anyone get better when they have to endure that?" Florence's voice sounded congested.

"Papa brought someone, she's in the parlor, shall I bring her to meet you?" Prudence asked, hesitantly.

"I'm in no condition to meet anyone, doesn't he know that I'm ill? What's he thinking?" Florence broke into a violent coughing fit.

Prudence quickly poured her grandmother a glass of water from the pitcher on the nightstand. Florence held her breath and gulped it down.

"Thank you, dear," Florence gasped. "Tell your father I'll have to meet this person some other time. Now run along, my dear." Florence shooed her with the hand.

Prudence left the room and closed the door behind her. Florence closed her eyes but felt someone looking at her. Frank's head was just inside the door.

"I'm not to be disturbed. Can't you see that I am very ill? Dr. Woodville insisted that I spend the day in bed. Quetta and Li Soo have been tormenting me all afternoon. I'm in no mood for company. Please leave right now!" Florence growled.

"I brought a young lady to help you. Her name is Sadie Calhoun. She works with the doctor in Pinos Altos and has a lot of experience with pneumonia," Frank told her.

Dr. Woodville pushed past Frank and entered the bedroom. His scowl made Florence cringe.

"Now see here, Mrs. Jensen, you must follow my instructions in this matter. Pneumonia is a very serious disease. This young woman will be sure you are well attended and are able to make a complete recovery. You will listen to her and do what she says. Is that clear?" Dr. Woodville addressed his patient in an admonishing voice.

Florence nodded dumbly. She wasn't used to people speaking to her authoritatively.

Sadie came into the room with Frank and Florence liked what she saw. The young woman was modestly dressed but had a good bearing. Sadie Calhoun, despite her red hair and freckles, reminded her of Emma. Florence frowned. *What was there about this young woman that made her think of her daughter?*

Sadie held out her hand and grasped Florence's giving it a gentle squeeze. "I'm very pleased to meet you, Mrs. Jensen. I'm sure we'll get along very well." Sadie efficiently plumped Florence's pillows and straightened the counterpane.

"I'm sure we will, my dear," Florence smiled and reached up to touch Sadie's face, "I'm sure we will."

Chapter 27

Florence had been in bed for nearly two weeks; her cough was much better and she was no longer running a fever. Sadie sat up for two nights while Florence's temperature soared. An old remedy, prepared by Quetta following Sadie's instructions, had helped tremendously. Florence sat in an armchair by the window and considered how much she had improved since Miss Calhoun had come to take care of her. Sipping the hot mixture, she felt the discomfort in her chest subside.

There was a soft tapping on the door, Robert came in and sat down on the bed. "You look wonderful, my dear. I'm so glad; I've been worried."

"That young lady is a miracle worker. My chest pain is almost gone and I'm able to breathe," Florence told her husband.

Sadie looked in on her patient; when she saw Robert sitting there, she smiled and closed the door behind her. She was very hungry but told Quetta to wait to serve her meal until she could come to the kitchen to eat. Used to fresh air, sunshine, and the smell of pine, the odors of the sick room were overwhelming Sadie but she reminded herself that she was doing it for Frank.

Frank was in the kitchen, drinking a large mug of coffee, when she arrived. He smiled broadly at her. Quetta and Li Soo smiled at her as well and Quetta winked.

"What's going on?" Sadie asked suspiciously.

"I've been confiding in these two young ladies. They want to help us convince the Jensens we're meant to be together," Frank set down his mug as Quetta brought Sadie's food that she had been keeping warm for her.

The two women made her feel welcome and accepted. She took a bite of the delicious food Quetta gave her. Robert saw the four standing together in the kitchen as he opened the door looking for a snack. The look on Frank's face while gazing at Sadie confirmed Robert's suspicions. Frank was in love. Robert wholeheartedly approved of the young woman who had been in his home for the past two weeks. He gently closed the door.

Robert went to his wife's bedroom. She was still in the chair looking out the window.

"I need to discuss something with you, my dear," Robert hesitated, momentarily.

"If it is about Sadie and Frank, I already know," Florence smiled. "I'm delighted."

"You are?" Robert gasped.

"Of course. She's perfect for him. She'll make an ideal wife for Frank and a good mother for Prudence. I realize now that Prudence needs a young woman to be her mother. I am old, with old-fashioned ideas."

Robert sat down on the side of Florence's bed. He was silent for a few minutes. A big load had been lifted from his shoulders and he sensed Florence felt the same way.

"Should we speak to them about it? I think they are worried about how we will accept her."

"Yes, dear. Bring them in and let's have a long talk. Is Prudence here yet?" Florence adjusted the blankets around her shoulders.

"No, she hasn't come home from school yet."

Robert patted Florence's shoulder again and went out to find Prudence. He walked slowly up Black Street. Prudence was bent over adjusting her shoe. Leaning against the tree, where so long ago, he had collapsed, Robert realized his good fortune.

"Grandfather, what are you doing out here?" Prudence dropped her books, threw her arms around her grandfather, and kissed him on the cheek.

"I wanted to talk to you for a moment before you came home. Do you feel like taking a short walk with your old grandfather?"

"Sure, Grandfather. What is it?" Prudence asked, a note of concern crept into her voice.

"Well, my dear, how you feel about Miss Calhoun?" Robert put his arm around Prudence's shoulders.

"I like her. You know, Grandfather, I think my Papa loves her. I hope he asks her to marry him!" Prudence said enthusiastically.

"Wonderful, we're all in agreement. Your grandmother and I wanted to discuss things with you, to be sure you approved, before speaking to your father and Miss Calhoun."

"I'm glad, I want my Papa to be happy. Let's go talk to them now," Prudence hurried her grandfather back to the house.

Chapter 28

More than anything else, Prudence wanted to play the piano. Her grandmother had taught her everything she could and Frank was opposed to sending her back East to take more lessons. Prudence had an opportunity to prove herself, not only to her father but also to the whole town of Silver City. Judge and Mrs. Newcomb's new grand piano would arrive at the train depot in the morning and would be transported, unloaded, and installed in the Newcomb's upstairs apartment above the Silver City Enterprise office. The Judge, Mrs. Newcomb, and their young son, Henry, were unable to play the piano, so Prudence would demonstrate the piano's beautiful tone in a recital. Many prominent townspeople were invited so Prudence was nervous.

Florence and Laura Newcomb were friends and for years, the judge's wife dreamed of learning how to play a piano. She sat in awe when Florence played some classical pieces for her when she visited in the Jensen's home. Mrs. Newcomb convinced her husband that she and Henry should take lessons. Judge Newcomb insisted they should have the best, so he ordered a grand piano from Miner's Mercantile, and was soon as excited as his wife.

When Mrs. Newcomb asked Florence to come play it when it arrived, Florence smiled. "I have a better idea, Laura, why not have Prudence give a recital? She has never played to a large audience. It would be wonderful practice for her. I'm trying to convince her father she should attend the Academy of Music as her mother did, when she is older," Florence confided.

"Oh, that's a capital idea, Florence. Of course our apartment is too small to hold many guests but we can put chairs and tables outside. Now, let me think," Laura Newcomb paused for a few minutes. "I know! The piano will be lifted in through the large window overlooking Main Street. While the window is off, we'll have the recital."

Florence told Robert and Prudence but said nothing to Frank. He was to direct the crew delivering the piano, and the recital would be a surprise. George Stuckey, the piano tuner, would be on hand to inspect and tune the piano and the recital would begin. Invitations had been sent.

Frank was at the train depot to supervise the unloading of the grand piano. It was loaded into a freight wagon and delivered to the Newcomb apartment. A construction crew removed the window frame; a winch was rigged up and the crate was lifted and set in place. It was a major event, with hundreds of onlookers.

Frank was amazed, everyone knew what he was supposed to do and within two hours, the whole task was accomplished. Mr. Stuckey unpacked his tools and reported that the piano required very little tuning despite its long trip across the country. As he was loading up the crate pieces to take to Miner's Mercantile, Frank saw a large number of people assembling outside the Newcomb residence. Tables and chairs had been set up and Quetta and Li Soo were serving refreshments. Prudence, dressed all in white, sat down at the Newcomb's piano. Her hands went to her mother's locket around her neck and she closed her eyes. Then she smiled and started to play.

The music rippled over the hushed crowd. They were transfixed by the magical sounds. When she had completed her first piece, everyone stood and clapped loudly. Frank's eyes filled with tears but he dashed them away with the back of his hand. *Florence was right; Prudence was gifted, just like her mother. She deserved the opportunity to attend the Academy of Music. He was thankful it would be at least five more years before she was old enough to attend.*

He climbed into the seat of the freight wagon to listen to the rest of Prudence's performance, so proud he could barely breathe. Several people even congratulated him. Prudence came downstairs and was surrounded by admirers. Even from a distance, Frank could see she was embarrassed. He elbowed his way through the crowd and went to stand next to his daughter. One of her hands held the locket at her throat. Prudence linked her arm through her father's and felt comforted. *Her Papa was proud of her, and it was wonderful.*

Chapter 29

"Let's have a small wedding. A big reception is all right but I would prefer the ceremony be just family," Sadie said gently.

"But my dear, the whole town will want to attend. I'll manage everything," Florence pleaded.

Sadie laid her hand on the older woman's shoulder. "I really appreciate everything but I'm from a small town, and not used to big functions. Frank and I are simple people. If you would like to plan a big reception, that would be fine."

Florence hid her disappointment with a smile. She hadn't been invited to Emma's wedding and wanted to see Sadie married in a luxurious ceremony. Maybe a big wedding was a bad idea, she agreed. Sadie hugged Florence and thanked her.

Quetta was waiting outside in the wagon to take Sadie to her friend, Josefa for a fitting. The dress had been designed by Sadie, Quetta, Li Soo and Josefa and they were anxious to see how it looked. Josefa's house was a flurry of activity. Felecitas, the baby, crawled around getting into things, Rafaela chased her and her younger brother Rumaldo around trying to keep them away from the pins and bits of material that littered the sewing room.

Quetta and Sadie examined the delicate lacy gown with seed pearls sewn on the bodice. Josefa told them her son, Rumaldo, was going to be sent to live with her parents in Georgetown. He was an active, noisy child and was getting on her new husband's nerves.

Sadie looked sad and sighed loudly.

"What's wrong, don't you like it?" Josefa asked anxiously.

"I love it, it's beautiful. I wish my mother could see it. She adored beautiful clothes," Sadie whispered.

Josefa clapped her hands together, causing Sadie and Quetta to jump. "Your mother can see it. She's looking down on you right now. I believe that with all my heart," Josefa clapped her hands again. "Don't be sad, this is a happy time."

Quetta and Josefa had their mouths stuffed with pins as Sadie stood poised on a chair, holding her breath. Felecito Esquivel came home and found a lot of giggling and excitement. The children, rounded up by Rafaela, had been taken outside to play under the large cottonwood tree.

Esquivel was a little upset because no food was prepared for supper until Josefa told him she had left him a snack on the stove. He took himself off from this flurry of feminine activity. Delighted with his young wife, Felecito Esquivel was a happy man. Josefa was young, beautiful, and skilled in ways to please her husband. But it was her intelligence that surprised him. She was able to speak about nearly any subject.

While occupied in fixing up her new home, Josefa told her husband she would like to invite his grown son, Carlos, to supper every night, so that he would feel like part of the family. Esquivel's son, Carlos came to supper and was polite to Josefa but very aloof.

Esquivel disliked Josefa's exuberant children and wasn't the slightest bit interested in them. Tolerance was never one of his strong points and he struggled not to lose his temper when they disturbed him. Sometimes, when she thought she was alone, Josefa would hold Rumaldo and cry. The girls were bad enough; but Rumaldo, Josefa's son, must go to Georgetown to stay with her parents.

As he ate his snack, Felecito Esquivel congratulated himself. Life was good with a young wife in his bed.

Chapter 30

Maximiano Najera disliked the Arizona Territory and missed his Josefa. He believed without a doubt that Eusebio had tricked his beloved into marrying Esquivel. At night, Najera dreamed about making love to Josefa in her new husband's bed.

Tucson was too tame and not for him. When his last employer caught him stealing he didn't report him to the Pima County Sheriff, he just ran him off. Josefa was pulling him back to Silver City. Late one night, he left Tucson and headed for home.

Two weeks later, Max Najera stood in a grove of trees near the Esquivel house watching his Josefa sitting on the porch, sewing. Her young daughters were playing with some kittens. He knew that she really loved him. Josefa married Esquivel for his money. If he could speak to her alone, he was sure he could convince her to leave her husband and go with him to Mexico to start a new life.

Najera saw his rival, Esquivel riding up the road toward the house. His horse was pure black and spirited; it pranced along tossing its head. Josefa stood, carefully placing her sewing on the chair. She waved a greeting to her husband. He waved back. Najera burned with jealously as he watched Esquivel dismount and walk over to his wife. Esquivel leaned down to whisper something to her and his hands cupped her breasts. Josefa said something to the girls and the couple went into the house alone.

Najera mounted his horse and rode back to town. Images of Esquivel and Josefa making love rose unbidden in his imagination and he knew he must act quickly. The rest of the afternoon, he sat in a saloon and plotted his revenge. Just as darkness descended over Chihuahua Hill, Najera mounted his horse and headed for the Esquivel house. Najera climbed through a rear window and walked through the dark house looking for Josefa's bedroom. Positive he could convince Josefa to run off with him, he boldly entered the room. Esquivel awoke just as Najera approached the bed; Esquivel and Josefa had been wrapped in each other's arms.

Enraged, Najera threw his Winchester rifle against the foot of the bed and pulled a knife from his belt. Esquivel was tangled in a sheet and Najera took advantage of his helplessness. He stabbed the older man several times as Esquivel instinctively tried to shield Josefa. Najera shoved the wounded Esquivel out of the way and picked up his rifle.

His true love looked at him accusingly. "Max, why have you done this terrible thing? What is it that you want?" Josefa shouted, pulling up the bloody sheet to cover her naked breasts.

"I have loved you for a long time and told you so many times. Yet you married this *viejo* and sleep with him in his bed. You disgust me!" Max Najera's voice broke, tears streamed from his eyes. Najera pointed his Winchester at the only woman he had ever loved, and pulled the trigger. Rafaela crashed into the room behind him. Najera spun on his heel and fired. Hearing loud voices outside the house, Max Najera stepped over the unconscious girl lying in the doorway and ran.

His legs felt like lead and threatened to give way as he crawled out the window. Choking and stumbling toward some rocks, bullets exploded in the dirt around him. All he wanted was for Josefa to love him. She betrayed him but he didn't mean to kill her. Once he reached the rocks, he started shooting toward the gunfire, unable to see anyone.

Marshal Kilburn was among the men shooting at the dark form scrambling up the hill. Kilburn heard the shots and grabbed his pistol. Now he regretted that he hadn't taken the time to get his rifle locked in the gun cabinet. Kilburn was glad that the darkness of the night covered him while he was in the open. The fugitive was in the rocks behind the Esquivel house. He directed his deputy, John Baxter, to keep firing toward the rocks as he tried to circle around behind.

Stealthily, Marshal Kilburn edged along the side of the Esquivel house. Kilburn came up even with the right side of the boulders where Najera was sitting. Najera's attention was on what was going on in front of him. Kilburn raised his pistol to aim it at his shadowy target and stepped on a twig. The resounding snap caused Najera to spin around and fire wildly. The bullet ricocheted off a rock and imbedded itself in the dirt. Kilburn shot at the same time and his bullet glanced off one of Najera's ribs.

Najera grabbed his side and fired at the marshal running along the side of the hill. Kilburn returned fire until he was out of ammunition. Kilburn retreated to get more ammunition as Guadalupe and Manolo Garcia, neighbors of the Esquivels, came to his assistance. Marshal Kilburn pointed as Najera disappeared around the back of the hill and the brothers followed him in hot pursuit. Guadalupe, the faster of the two, fearlessly sprinted off in pursuit.

Warm sticky blood covered Najera's fingers. The bullet caused a sharp burning pain to spread through his torso and into his legs. Hearing someone behind him, he took aim at the dark form and fired. His rifle slipped but he wounded his pursuer in the leg. Manolo reached his brother and knelt beside him. All he had to stop the bleeding was an old bandanna.

Sheriff McAfee and two of his deputies crawled up beside them. "Where is he?" McAfee whispered tersely.

"He went toward the railroad tracks," Guadalupe gasped.

Several men pursued Najera as Guadalupe draped his arm around his brother's neck and allowed Manolo to help him down the hill toward the Esquivel house. Manolo shoved open the front door with his left shoulder and deposited his brother in a chair.

Soft weeping from a room in the back of the house, drew Manolo's attention. He tightened the bandanna on his brother's leg.

"Señor Esquivel, are you in there?" he asked.

His question was answered by continued weeping and a low moan, his fingers trembled as he lit a candle sitting on a dresser just inside the door. The entire room was saturated with blood. The weeping was from the girl, Rafaela, lying on the floor beside the bed, holding her mother's lifeless hand. It was evident to Manolo that the girl had crawled across the floor from where she herself had been shot to her mother's bedside.

Esquivel was lying on his side, his face buried in his wife's hair. Josefa was dead with a gaping wound in her chest. Her stricken husband, who was covered with blood from his own wounds as well, gently closed her staring eyes.

Manolo heard a noise in a dark corner of the room. Josefa's sewing machine was draped with a dust cover and the cover appeared to be moving. Manolo approached quietly and pulled aside the cover. Little Felecitas was sitting behind the sewing machine, her arms wrapped around her knees. He picked her up, shielding her eyes from the gruesome sight, and ran out of the room. Guadalupe was groaning, Manolo stopped to tell him he was going for the doctor.

Clutching the frightened child in his arms, Manolo ran down the road toward town. Manolo grabbed a folded blanket on a bed when he burst into the doctor's office and wrapped it around Josefa's shivering child. The doctor came out from the back, dressed but his thinning hair was tousled and his glasses were smudged. Manolo didn't know this doctor but he was the closest to the Esquivel house.

"What's the trouble here?" the elderly man asked.

"I think that she is all right, but you must go to the Esquivel house, there are many injured people there," Manolo told him.

"I know this child," the doctor quickly examined Felecitas. "How many people are injured?"

"*Mi hermano* and three others, I think," Manolo told him.

"I'll get my bag and some supplies. You take this child to Mrs. Fleming and fetch my assistant Timothy," the doctor scribbled his assistant's address on a piece of paper and shoved it into Manolo's hand. "You can read, can't you?"

Manolo nodded.

"Tell Timothy to meet me at the Esquivel's. Well, get going, man," the doctor shouted hurriedly shoving bandages and instruments into his bag.

Manolo didn't want to disturb important people like the Flemings, but he did as the doctor instructed. Felicitas was given a spare room in the Fleming house and watched over by Mrs. John Fleming herself.

Manolo found the doctor's assistant at home. As he was leaving, he heard shouts from the lawmen gathered on Main Street. Manolo spread the word a posse was being gathered. On the way back to the Esquivel residence, he made detours to the Timmer House and Southern Hotel.

Sheriff McAfee, his deputies, and Marshal Kilburn weren't able to track Najera in the darkness so they rounded up a posse in the middle of Main Street. Frank was having a drink with G.T. Reid, proprietor of the Southern Hotel, when Manolo burst in. Reid quickly saddled his horse and went back to the lobby to remove his old 45 caliber Colts from their wall mountings and pick up some ammunition, as Frank tightened his mare's cinch and loaded his rifle and pistols. Then the two men hurried to the gathering place.

Chapter 31

It was dawn when the posse was finally assembled. Najera's trail led them across the railroad tracks and southeast, toward Lone Mountain. The posse lost the trail several times during the day but continued to search for Najera until daylight faded. After setting up camp, the men ate all of the food they brought with them. Frigid night air penetrated their coats and at midnight, it rained.

The rain completely obliterated the fugitive's tracks; so the discouraged posse went back to town. Marshal Kilburn and Sheriff McAfee left trackers to continue the search and told the posse to remain on stand-by in case any leads turned up.

Two travelers, Colonel Martin and Samuel Sloan were in a buggy headed toward Silver City from the Munson Ranch, when they spotted a man armed with a Winchester rifle, standing in some bushes near the road to Oak Grove. He warned them to continue on their way and not to look back. With his rifle trained at their backs, they proceeded into town.

Frank was at the marshal's office when the two men told Marshal Kilburn about a bareheaded man who had held a rifle on them as they passed along the road. Kilburn looked down at a dusty bloodstained item on his desk, discovered by one of the deputies, on the floor of the Esquivel bedroom. It had been stepped on and kicked under the bed. Esquivel said that the hat didn't belong to him; so it was believed to be Najera's.

Kilburn sent Frank to notify the posse to gather in front of his office. By late afternoon all of the men were assembled and supplied with food and ammunition. Dark clouds gathered and it started to rain. When they reached the outskirts of town, it was pouring. Undaunted, the posse galloped down the road, anxious to apprehend the murderer. The horses plowed large furrows in the road as they thundered toward Oak Grove. Marshal Kilburn wished for the bloodhound he had recently ordered from back east because the dog would be able to track in all kinds of weather.

The posse arrived at Oak Grove and scouted the entire area and were unable to find Najera. McAfee and Kilburn suspected someone was supplying the man with food so they sent some deputies to check around Silver City for clues. Then a coroner's jury, convened by Justice Givens, delivered the verdict that Josefa Benavidez Esquivel had died as the result of a gunshot wound inflicted by Maximiano Najera.

Frank hated to tell Sadie about Josefa's death. The two women were good friends and Josefa was making Sadie's wedding dress. Robert Jensen asked Frank to take a freight shipment to Pinos Altos because the regular driver was a member of the posse and still absent from work. On the way up the mountain, Frank encountered a local rancher. The man's horse was lathered and panting when he pulled up alongside the freight wagon.

"Aren't you one of Marshal Kilburn's deputies?" the man asked Frank. Quickly, the rancher introduced himself.

"Yes, sir, I am," Frank answered, politely. Frank pulled the horses to a stop; the reins were wrapped around his left wrist and hand. His shotgun partner, Michael Talbot, had stopped behind some trees. Talbot always rode 50 yards behind the wagon so he would be in a position to defend it.

Frank signaled to Talbot who approached, still holding his rifle.

"*Hay Dios.* Thank you for not shooting me, *señor.*" The rancher, Guillermo Maynes, gasped and wiped his brow with the back of a calloused hand.

"State your business, mister, then get going," Talbot said, gruffly.

"I am on my way to get Marshal Kilburn," Maynes explained breathlessly. "There is a strange man watching my house."

Frank nodded. "The marshal is pretty busy right now. A young woman was murdered and he's looking for her killer. I'll let him know when I get back to town."

"It can't wait that long. He was outside my bedroom window this morning; then I saw him near my corral. My wife and children are alone. I can't leave them for much longer even though my wife is a crack shot. Will you inform the marshal while I go back to my home and protect my family?" Maynes pleaded.

Frank hesitated. It was his duty to be sure the wagon made it safely to Pinos Altos.

"Give me your horse, Jake. I'll go tell the marshal," Frank said. Jake Talbot was glaring at him.

Maynes thanked him profusely, tipped his hat, and galloped off down the road.

"Now just a minute. These supplies are needed up in Pinos Altos. You can't just go off and leave everything to me. That *hombre* might just decide to hold me up. Then how would you feel?" Talbot complained.

"I can't allow Señor Maynes to leave his family unprotected. Here, take the reins and get going!" Frank climbed out of the wagon.

He stretched out his hand as Talbot dismounted, grumbling under his breath. Frank swung up on Talbot's saddle and nudged the horse into a gallop. Talbot shook his head in disbelief. He flicked the reins and continued up the mountain toward Pinos Altos.

In front of the marshal's office, Frank slid off the saddle. He crashed into the room just as Kilburn was pouring himself a cup of coffee from the pot on the stove. "What the...?" Kilburn yelped as the hot liquid scalded his hand.

"Sorry, Marshal. Guillermo Maynes, up by P. A, says there is a strange character on his ranch. He said the man is up to no good and he wants you to come up and get him," Frank explained as Kilburn bathed his hand in cool water from his canteen.

"That could be a lead. Najera's trail petered out up by Pinos Altos, the posse is scouting around trying to find something. It's just possible it's Najera or the skunk helping him. I'll fetch Rodriguez and Montes and we'll go get him," Kilburn handed a freshly poured cup of coffee to Frank. "You look like you could use something stronger, but this will have to do for now."

"I'll go with you, Marshall," Frank gulped the coffee, savoring its warmth.

"No, sir. You sit down and catch your breath. Get yourself a drink and thanks for the information. I'll let the rest of the men know what's going on."

Frank sat down on the marshal's desk and finished his coffee. He arrived home much earlier than usual and Prudence feared something else was wrong.

"Papa, are you sick? Did you tell Sadie about Mrs. Esquivel?" Prudence's face reflected her deep concern.

"No, Kitten, to both questions. There was some trouble and I had to report it to the marshal. I wanted to take Sadie something. One of the ladies that went to clean the Esquivel house after the uh…" Frank stopped.

"I know what happened, Papa. You don't have to protect me from the truth. I really liked Mrs. Esquivel and her girls and Rumaldo. What were you going to say?"

"One of the ladies found Sadie's wedding dress in a box with Sadie's name on it. I was on my way to see Sadie when a rancher stopped me. There was a stranger hanging around his property and he needed me to notify the marshal. So Talbot took the wagon and I came back to tell the marshal."

Prudence smile wavered as she patted her father's hand. "I'm glad you're home. I worry about you so much," Prudence hugged him tightly.

"I know and I'm sorry but your old man can still do an honest day's work and earn enough money to keep this family going," Frank told her.

"I know that Papa. I'll go fix supper." Prudence's hand went to the locket around her neck.

Frank smiled. She was so much like Emma, protective and kind. After eating until he was uncomfortable, Frank settled into his chair in front of the fire. He knew he should go to Sadie but he was exhausted. A loud pounding on the door caused him to jerk. His head ached unbearably.

"Parnell, are you in there?" a man's booming voice penetrated Frank's drowsy brain.

Yawning, Frank staggered to the door. Jóse Montes strode past him into the room and stood in front of the dying fire. "We've got us a prisoner down at the marshal's office. Kilburn is asking him a lot of questions. The *hombre* has a Winchester like Najera's and was carrying a lot of food. The marshal thinks he's the one supplying Najera," Montes explained.

Frank made arrangements with Mrs. Flaherty to take care of Prudence; grabbed his coat and accompanied Montes to Marshal Kilburn's office. The suspected man endured hours of questioning but by the following afternoon, they were unable to prove he had anything to do with Najera. The marshal turned him loose, warning him to stay away from the Maynes ranch. Kilburn told Montes to tail the suspect discreetly. Frank went home and napped for a few hours; and told Prudence to go to her grandparents. He had to go to Pinos Altos to see Sadie.

A bone chilling wind spurred Frank up the mountain. He knew Sadie would be devastated by the news of Josefa Esquivel's death and dreaded telling her. Buck greeted him at the door when he arrived. Sadie rushed to hug Frank. When she saw his face her arms dropped to her sides.

"What's wrong? Did something happen?

Frank nodded. "I think you'd better sit down before I tell you."

Sadie sank into a chair by the fire. Frank held her hand and tears streamed down her face as she listened. When he was finished, Frank handed the box he'd brought to Sadie. She opened it slowly. It was impossible for her to believe the fun-loving woman who made this dress was gone. Her hands shook and she dabbed at her eyes with the corner of her handkerchief. Carefully, she lifted the dress out of the box. A small piece of paper fluttered to the floor. Frank retrieved the paper for her and watched her face as she read it.

In Josefa's delicate writing, the note read, *"I made this dress for Prudence. Not having her measurements, I just guessed at her size. Cherish your new daughter, she is a Gift from God."* Sadie handed her wedding dress to her father and removed the filmy paper under it to reveal a pale rose dress, designed exactly as her own but small enough for Prudence. She stroked the dress and wept. Frank knelt and put his arm around her.

Feeling uncomfortable, Buck laid his daughter's wedding gown on the table and went outside. Buck watched the sky darken and puffed on his pipe. He dreaded the day Sadie would leave and he'd be here alone. For over twenty years, this cabin had housed his family, and soon he'd be alone. Sadie was happy and he admired Frank but Buck was selfish and wished Sadie would stay with him. Maybe it was time he moved into town.

"You said that they were looking for Najera in Pinos Altos?" Sadie's voice was hoarse.

Frank nodded.

"While I was on my way to the store yesterday, I saw the old woodcutter, Clemente Baca, carrying a bulky sack into the woods. Clemente is a very small man and I could tell he was having trouble carrying it. He was hurrying but stopped every few minutes to look around to see if anyone was watching him. I thought it was strange but I knew nothing of Josefa's murder at the time," Sadie confided. "Under the circumstances, I'd like to postpone the wedding. I'm just too upset to think about our happiness. I know it will be hard on both of us, especially you, and I'm sorry."

"I understand, Sadie, I really do. We'll wait until you're ready. I have to get back to town. I'll try to come next week and we can discuss it." Frank hugged her and kissed her tearstained cheek.

"I'm coming with you. I'm sure the Jensens won't mind if I stay with them for a few days." Quickly, she threw some clothes into a bag.

Still outside, Buck's pipe had gone out as he stood staring at the sky.

"Pa, there are some things I need to do. I'm going to Silver City and will stay with the Jensen's for a few days." Standing on her tiptoes, Sadie kissed her father's beard roughened cheek, as he leaned down. "I love you."

"Be careful; you take good care of my girl."

Frank patted the older man's shoulder. He mounted his mare, pulled Sadie up behind him.

Chapter 32

Frank sought out the marshal early the next morning. Marshal Kilburn assured him he would investigate. The tired man returned home. While Prudence was at school, Frank decided to take a bath. He heated some water, poured it into the hipbath, and sat in the tub until the water was cold. Feeling relaxed, he prepared a nice supper for himself and Pru. The events of the past several days were a blur and he wanted to spend time with his daughter.

Eusebio Benavidez sat beside his niece, Rafaela, in his house across town. Her little face was pale against the white sheets. Najera had shot her in the leg while trying to escape the Esquivel house. She'd lost a lot of blood by the time the doctor arrived. Eusebio learned that Esquivel would recover from his wounds. Esquivel had abruptly informed Eusebio when he went to see him that he had no interest in caring for Rafaela and Felecitas.

Felecitas was so young she didn't understand what had happened to her mama. She was staying with Mrs. John Fleming but Eusebio planned to get her today.

When her uncle squeezed Rafaela's hand, she opened her eyes and smiled. It was obvious she was very tired. He bent to kiss her forehead. "I'll be back in a little while. You just rest now. I'm going for Felecitas."

Dressed in his best clothes, he went to the Fleming house on 6th Street. Mrs. Fleming met him at the door and escorted him to the backyard. He heard shouts and laughter coming from behind some trees. A large group of children were playing hide and seek and having great fun.

"Thank you so much for caring for my niece during this difficult time, Mrs. Fleming," Eusebio said warmly.

"It was my pleasure, sir. Felecitas is a special child," Mrs. Fleming smiled sadly.

Just then, Felecitas's flushed face appeared from behind a tree. She toddled over to her uncle with her arms wide open. He caught her in his arms, spun her around in the air and hugged her tightly. He choked back the lump in his throat; she looked so like Josefa.

"What will become of the girls now?" Mrs. Fleming asked gently.

"The Sisters of Mercy will take them. I'll stay in close touch with them, of course. A bachelor has no business trying to raise two little girls. My parents are too old to care for them, they have their hands full with Rumaldo, Rafaela's and Felecitas's brother," Eusebio told her.

"I'm glad you've decided. I know how hard it must be for you but I'm sure it's for the best," Mrs. Fleming said as she took them through the house to the front door. "Please keep in touch and let me know if I can help in anyway. I feel some responsibility toward Felecitas." She placed her hand on the child's head.

"Thank you, you've been most gracious," Eusebio bowed his head and carried his small niece toward the gate. Felecitas reached up and touched her uncle's cheek. She snuggled against him and smiled. He hugged her tightly and walked down the street. When they reached Bullard Street, Eusebio set her down on the ground and let her walk for a while. She reached up for him and he shook his head. He was so overcome with emotion he was afraid he would drop her.

Later Eusebio sat beside Rafaela, holding Felecitas. His pain was so acute, he was unable to speak for a long time. He couldn't remember ever having such difficulty finding the right words. When he finally regained his composure, Eusebio knelt beside her bed and explained to Rafaela he would be sending them to the Sisters of Mercy. He vowed silently he would find a way to provide the girls with the home they deserved.

Eusebio barely heard the tapping on the bedroom door. Rafaela laid her hand on her uncle's bowed head. Kneeling beside the bed so long, he was unable to feel his legs. Felecitas was sound asleep in the bed next to her sister, her thumb in her mouth.

"Come in, please," Eusebio croaked in a raspy voice. He stood respectfully.

Quetta, Li Soo, and Sadie entered. Felecitas' sleepy eyes lit up when Quetta laid a beautiful porcelain doll in her arms. Rafaela was also given one. Each doll was dressed exquisitely in formal dresses. Rafaela's doll was in blue and Felecitas's, in green. Rafaela's eyes filled with tears when she recognized her mother's work.

Quetta explained. "Your mama asked me to keep these for her until Christmas. She wanted to give you each a special gift and worked on the dresses while you girls slept. I know she would want you to have them now," Quetta paused. "She loved you both very much."

"It was very kind of you to bring them," Eusebio walked around the room, hoping to restore the circulation to his legs.

"Frank and I have decided to postpone our wedding out of respect for Josefa," Sadie announced as she sat on Rafaela's bed holding Felecitas in her arms.

"You didn't tell us," Quetta gasped. "When did you decide?"

Sadie's smile was unsteady. "Frank and I discussed it and decided it was the right thing to do."

"You can't postpone your wedding. Josefa wouldn't want that. She was so proud she had a small part in the planning. Don't do this!" Quetta was insistent.

"Señorita Tovar is right, you should go ahead with your plans. Life is short. Don't wait too long for happiness," Eusebio added, philosophically.

Rafaela smiled and nodded.

Sadie, Quetta, and Li Soo said their goodbyes and promised to visit the girls at the Sisters of Mercy. Each of the women wished they could take the children home with them.

Chapter 33

The sun shone brightly on the day of the wedding. St. Vincent's Church was sparsely decorated with fresh flowers and most of the pews were empty. Sadie wanted only people considered "family" to attend. She left the wedding reception in Florence's hands and didn't protest when told that there would be over fifty guests at the reception.

Buck helped Sadie and Prudence into the Jensen's carriage and climbed up beside the hired driver, uncomfortable in his new store bought suit. He hadn't been so dressed up in years and noticed Robert and R.D. wore their fancy suits like a second skin. Buck wondered what life in town would be like? Could he adjust to being on a daily schedule? Probably not, he decided.

Frank wrestled with his tie. Difficult to tie one with two hands, with only one, it was impossible. Li Soo caught a glimpse of Frank in the mirror as she passed down the hall to her room. Quickly, she went to assist him.

"I am not sure how to do it but I will try. You must hold still Mr. Frank otherwise I will never get it to look right," Li Soo scolded.

But after five minutes, Li Soo went to look for Robert who was just leaving for the church. Robert chuckled and went to assist Frank. Florence groaned impatiently.

"We can't leave without the groom. Just be patient, I'll be right back," Robert assured her, patting her hand. Florence nodded and smiled tightly. She was nervous and didn't know why. It was as though she was getting married. They hired several carriages to take everyone to the church because they didn't want to muss the gowns and Sadie wanted to arrive early.

Li Soo and Quetta were told to bring an escort. Mario arrived resplendent in a dark gray suit and hat. Li Soo was happy to see her escort, Mr. Coates's new assistant, Wong Lee, following closely behind Mario. Wong Lee, born in San Francisco, spoke English without a trace of an accent. He was working with the Chinese classes to help them perfect their English. Tall and nice looking, Wong Lee was sought after by several young women, but had eyes only for Li Soo. Wong Lee was dressed in a white suit. It was hard for Li Soo to adjust to the fact that Wong Lee wore his hair in the Western style and looked very natural in his suit.

Mario was very surprised to see a one-armed man enter the church with a beautiful young girl. The man looked vaguely familiar to Mario and it occurred to him that he had seen him driving a freight wagon a few years earlier. But it was the young girl who impressed him. She was dressed in a beautiful rose pink gown, her hair was in an upswept style that made her appear older than her actual age. As she walked up the aisle of the church, Mario noticed her unusual locket and how her hand kept reaching up to grasp it.

"Who is she?" Mario whispered to Quetta who was sitting beside him.

"That is Miss Prudence. It is her father who is getting married," she explained.

"I noticed that beautiful locket she wears. She keeps holding it in her hand," Mario told her.

"It is all she has of her mother's and she is unusually attached to it. Whenever she is nervous or unsure of herself, she holds on to it," Quetta smiled. "She is a wonderful person and I'm sure her mother was just like her."

A hush fell over the group when Sadie entered the church on her father's arm. She wore the stunning gown that Josefa had made so painstakingly. Frank Parnell stood at the altar, Robert at his side. The expression on Frank's face was one of pure wonder.

Mario gasped loudly and stood when he recognized the bride and her father. He patted Quetta's arm and whispered he needed some air. He put on his hat and pulled it down over his eyes. While everyone was watching the ceremony, he ducked out the door of the church.

Florence sat in the front of the church and dabbed her eyes. Prudence smiled through her own tears and patted her grandmother's hand. After the couple exchanged vows, Florence and Prudence left to be present to greet guests attending the reception.

When Sadie tossed the bouquet, Quetta caught it and smiled. She looked around to see if Mario had returned but did not see him. Disappointed, she held the flowers tightly and went to congratulate Frank and Sadie.

"We'd better get to that reception or Florence will panic," Robert warned the group.

Several carriages awaited them, all headed toward the Jensen house. Florence stood on the porch and greeted her guests. Quetta and Li Soo rushed to the kitchen and quickly donned aprons. They were stunned to see Florence had hired some girls to serve the guests. Florence came into the kitchen and took each of them by the arm and led them into the living room.

"Today our family is celebrating a wedding. You are part of our family and should enjoy yourselves," Florence explained to the surprised women.

Everyone who was anyone in the Silver City area were at the Jensen home that afternoon. The party grew from a guest list of fifty to close to one hundred people. The crowd spilled out into the yard and into the street. Elizabeth Warren came, accompanied by her eldest daughter, John and Mrs. Fleming, Marshal Kilburn, Dr. Woodville, Judge and Mrs. Newcomb, and many others attended. ·

It was nearly midnight when the last guests left. Robert and Florence were ready to collapse. Prudence planned to stay with her grandparents for the next few days to allow her father and his new wife some privacy. She kissed her father and Sadie and hugged her grandmother and grandfather.

"It was a very nice day but I'm tired. Are you going to go somewhere for a few days, Papa?" Prudence yawned.

"No, we plan to stay home," Frank smiled. "I love you. You get some rest and help Quetta and Li Soo clean up this mess."

Florence hugged Sadie and then Frank. "Don't worry, I have people coming tomorrow to do that. I want Pru to practice her piano for a few hours tomorrow. Next week, she begins giving lessons to Mrs. Newcomb and her son, Henry."

"I'm looking forward to it but I don't know if I'm good enough to teach yet," Prudence confided.

"You're good enough to teach. Nearly the whole town turned out to hear you play and you were wonderful," Frank told her.

Prudence smiled and yawned again. "I need to go to bed. I'll come home for the weekend, if that's all right?"

"Of course, I love you, Kitten. Sadie and I would like some time alone but we want you home soon."

"I understand, Papa, I really do. I'm not a child," Prudence hugged her father and Sadie again and went upstairs to bed.

Sadie thanked Florence and Robert for their kindness. Buck planned to stay the night at the Southern Hotel and go back to Pinos Altos in the morning.

Frank took Sadie's arm and helped her into their rented carriage. *It'll be nice to have a wife to come home to again*, Frank thought.

Chapter 34

The day began like many other hot summer days. Rain threatened several times in the morning, it sprinkled, the sun broke through and it clouded over. It was August and the "monsoons" were somewhat late this year. In the past several years, in an attempt to control run-off, dams were built and washed away, then bridges were built and they were washed away.

Prudence was now giving piano lessons to Laura Newcomb and her son, Henry. She went directly to Newcomb's apartment over the Silver City Enterprise after she completed her own practice. When the weather looked threatening, Laura Newcomb sent her carriage and driver to pick up Prudence and take her to their home.

That afternoon Henry Newcomb was struggling with an etude on the beautiful grand piano. Prudence lost her patience with him because he wasn't concentrating. Prudence had been helping Florence with a benefit all day and their lesson was later than usual. She had considered canceling but decided it was too important.

"Henry, please play that part again. Keep repeating that section until you play it correctly otherwise you'll never do it right," Prudence told him, holding tightly to her locket.

Henry glared at her. Prudence squeezed the locket and felt the delicate chain break in her fingers. Instantly, she felt remorse for her anger toward the little boy. Carefully, she removed the chain and locket and laid it on the piano.

Smiling at Henry, she sat beside him and demonstrated the correct way to play the passage. Henry realized Prudence was trying to help him and tried hard to concentrate. His fingers were short and uncooperative. Prudence wondered if a six-year old boy had the patience to learn to play the piano.

Judge Newcomb rushed into the room holding Prudence's coat. "It's raining very hard. If you're going to make it home tonight, you'd better leave now. We must hurry, Miss Parnell." Judge Newcomb took Prudence by the arm and pulled her toward the door.

"What's wrong, is it Grandfather?" Prudence grabbed her bonnet from the hook near the front door as she went by.

"No, no, nothing like that, but you must leave now!" Judge Newcomb's voice shook with emotion.

"I don't understand. Did I do something I shouldn't have?" Prudence pulled her arm from the Judge's grasp and tied her bonnet strings before going outside. The force of the pelting rain stung her face as she adjusted her bonnet.

Judge Newcomb laughed nervously, "Of course not, it's just the weather is getting really bad. The streets are treacherous and it is still raining. I'm afraid if you don't leave now, you won't be able to get home."

"My Papa is coming for me soon. I should wait for him," Prudence insisted as Judge Newcomb picked her up and set her inside his carriage.

"There is no time. Tuttle get going right away, be careful, and be sure this young lady gets home safely."

Prudence sensed the urgency in the Judge's voice and didn't argue. Settling herself on the seat, she adjusted her damp skirt and reached for her locket. Her locket! She had left it on the piano.

"Mr. Tuttle, Mr. Tuttle, please stop the carriage!" Prudence stood and leaned out the window. The roar of rushing water drowned her voice. She looked around for something to pound with to get the driver's attention. There was nothing.

Prudence removed her shoe and pounded on the roof of the carriage to get Mr. Tuttle's attention. She suddenly realized there was water on the floor of the carriage. She leaned out the window again and gasped. Water and mud was completely surrounded the carriage and Mr. Tuttle was struggling with the frightened horses.

"Mr. Tuttle, Mr. Tuttle can you hear me?"

The horses were screaming unable to maintain their footing. Mr. Tuttle held the reins tightly but the carriage started to rock. Roiling mud was nearly up to the window. Prudence screamed. "Mr. Tuttle, please help me!" Prudence cried but she knew the poor man couldn't help her. There was floating debris coming toward them. Mud was up to Prudence's knees and her skirt dragged against her legs. *Oh, Papa, where are you?* she thought desperately.

She saw Mr. Tuttle's head looking through the window. He was leaning down from the driver's seat.

"Take off your skirt, Miss Parnell. Do it now, else you'll drown," he insisted.

Prudence wasn't sure she heard him correctly. There was so much noise outside. People yelling, horses neighing, water and mud swirled as far as she could see. Numbly, Prudence's fingers struggled to take off her heavy skirt. Mr. Tuttle's hands reached toward her as he braced himself on the top of the carriage.

"Hurry, Miss there is no time. Please, please!" Tuttle yelled.

A loud thud caused the carriage to shiver violently. Prudence pulled her legs out of her skirt, put her hands in Mr. Tuttles's, and wriggled through the window. On the top of the carriage, Prudence was tossed from side to side. Tuttle attached a rope to the driver's seat and gave the free end to the girl.

Silver City Roils

"Hold on. It is going to get worse...Aaaagh..." Tuttle was hit in the side by a large branch. *The water was up to the top of the carriage.*

Prudence clutched the muddy rope tightly and prayed. Pictures of ships flashed through her mind. This must be how sailors felt. But this wasn't a boat and it felt like the wood she was lying on was loose.

"LOOK, Miss, we're going back toward the Judge's house. Can you swim?"

Prudence shook her head fiercely.

"You've got to try, it's our only chance. When I say go, hold on to my leg," Tuttle swung his leg toward the girl, "We have to jump."

"I don't think I can Mr. Tuttle. I'm scared. Please don't make me do it."

"I'll tie the rope to you and to me. Just let go when I tell you. We might drown, the water is too fast and I can't swim, neither."

Prudence's throat clogged with a huge lump, she couldn't breathe. Tuttle struggled to tie the rope to his arm and around Prudence's waist. The knots didn't hold. He had to do it again. The water churned toward the back of the Silver City Enterprise building. The foundation was eroding and the building started sliding toward them.

"Somebody, anybody, help us!" Tuttle shrieked.

The back of the building opened up and Mrs. Newcomb's grand piano appeared suspended in the air for a moment then crashed with a cacophony of sound down a steep bank into the hurtling torrent. Prudence pictured her locket sitting on the top of the piano. It was gone as her mother was gone. Tuttle grabbed Prudence's arm and yanked it hard. Her hands skidded over the muddy rope and stung unbearably. They were in the water.

Pieces of debris hit them from all sides as they struggled to keep their heads above the mud. A mouthful of muck caused Prudence to struggle harder, she thrashed her legs and arms, Tuttle wasn't holding on to her, he needed both of his arms to keep his head above the water. Prudence could see people standing near demolished buildings, they were yelling but she couldn't hear what they said and didn't care.

A chunk of wood hit Prudence in the head. She found the strength to grab it and hold on. It was a piece of plank, probably off a building. She held onto it with one hand and tugged on the rope around her waist, Tuttle was no longer on the other end.

Mud clogged her nose and mouth, sneezing and spitting, the brave girl clung to the piece of wood as it dragged her through what was left of Main Street. She closed her eyes and prayed again. Everything stopped.

Prudence opened her eyes. The plank snagged on a tree root protruding from the mudslide but it was slipping. She reached for the root but her hand was coated in slime and it slid off. Mud flooded her nostrils and she opened her mouth to scream.

Then a miracle occurred. Prudence was lifted up into a pair of bony arms and held tightly against a skeletal chest. Her muddy eyes made it impossible to see her rescuer. The stranger dragged her away from the deadly water and even wiped her face with a filthy rag as he struggled to run.

Chapter 35

Lan Soo and Mai Soo, his wife, sat on the roof of their house, huddled in blankets. As they surveyed their surroundings, Lan Soo told his wife it probably wasn't necessary to stay on the roof but the water was rising and he was a cautious man.

They watched the seething water sweep people in carriages and on foot along helplessly. Mai Soo gasped and pointed. "Look there my husband. Did you see that?"

Lan Soo squinted and looked in the direction Mai was pointing. A tall thin person, presumably a man, was pulling something out of the water. Even from a distance, the couple could see the man had a lot of difficulty holding on to what appeared to be a muddy bundle of rags.

"What do you think it is?"

"I do not know but it doesn't belong to him. See how he keeps looking around," Lan Soo noted.

"You are right. What is he doing now?" Mai leaned forward to get a better look.

"It must be heavy, he is half carrying and half dragging it up the hill. It must be valuable or something he wants badly." Lan Soo's curiosity was piqued. He imagined the bundle to be all kinds of things.

The sky was awash with pink, purple and gray light as the sun peeked through the clouds momentarily then slid behind Chihuahua Hill out of sight. It appeared the man had reached his destination, the old opium den on Yankie Street. He dropped the bundle and got down on his hands and knees. Furiously digging the mud away from the door, he was finally able to pry it open and drag his treasure inside.

"I must see what that man has taken," Lan Soo insisted.

"Be careful, my husband, he could be dangerous!" Mai Soo knew it was useless to argue with him and huddled down further into her blankets. It was beginning to rain again.

It was so dark. Crusty remnants of mud clung to her face and scalded her skin. Perhaps she was dead. Her breath caught in her throat; she clawed at her neck. A stream of vomit erupted as she gasped hungrily for air. But the air she breathed was dank and redolent with a sickening foul odor.

"Don't worry little miss, you are not dead." An inky voice whispered hoarsely.

"Ppplease, I'm frightened. Who are you?"

"A friend. Don't be frightened, you will not be harmed." The voice slithered toward her.

"I must find my Papa, he will be looking for me. Please, help me ff…find my Papa."

Prudence reached for her locket. She must find it.

"Where am I? Please tell me. Are you sure I'm still alive?"

A loud hissing wheeze, she interpreted as a laugh, made Prudence shiver and whimper.

"You are the granddaughter of the Jensen that owns the Miner's Mercantile?"

"Yes sir, that's right. Will you take me home, please?" Prudence pleaded.

Silence.

When the deluge engulfed Main Street, Frank was at home fixing a broken chair leg. Sitting behind the row house, he was so absorbed in his work, he didn't realize what was happening. It had rained off and on all day but not very hard until late afternoon. Taking advantage of the lull in the storm and the coolness outside, Frank pounded a nail into the chair leg.

Florence had enlisted Sadie and Prudence to help with a benefit. Mr. Coates, the Methodist minister, and English teacher to the Chinese immigrants, needed supplies. Li Soo was busy preparing that list. The other women and Prudence were mending clothing to be sold at a rummage sale. Prudence left for the Newcomb's house when the carriage arrived for her. When Frank heard the loud roar preceding the flood, he dropped his hammer and ran to the Jensen's.

Sadie was on the porch, struggling with her bonnet, when Frank bounded up the steps.

"Frank, Prudence is downtown!" she wailed.

"Dear God!" Frank leapt off the porch and disappeared into the storm.

Lan Soo tripped and fell over an overturned bucket and his foot was tangled in something. It was dark and his path was treacherous. He knew he was in the vicinity of the opium den because even with all the obstacles, he could sense the overpowering evil of the place.

In China, he had many encounters with opium eaters and felt the men and women who misused the drug were indescribably malevolent and they terrified him.

When Lan Soo finished untangling his leg from what felt like a greasy rope, he slogged through the muck until he reached a solid wall. He inched along leaning against it, feeling for a door. Something snuffled against his hand and he drew it back instinctively.

"Dutch, did you find something?" a voice came from the darkness surrounding him.

A match flared revealing a pale, haunted face, then blew out.

"Whose there?" the man demanded.

"It is Lan Soo. Is that you Mr. Parnell?" The dog, Dutch was shoving against Lan Soo's leg and whining.

"I think my dog found something. My daughter, Prudence is missing."

"I'm trying to find the door to the opium den. It is around here somewhere. I saw a man take something inside and I must find out what it is."

Dutch barked sharply then growled. Frank and Lan Soo realized the dog had located the door. He was digging and throwing mud everywhere. The men rushed to help him and managed at last to pry the door open. Dutch bounded into the room and disappeared into the darkness. Lan Soo tripped over something in the middle of the floor. Frank struck several matches one right after another on his boot until he located a kerosene lamp sitting on a shelf. He lit it, with Lan Soo's help, and they found Prudence huddled in the corner. Dutch was groaning and licking her face. She didn't respond. Frank ran to her and knelt down. She was breathing.

Lan Soo surveyed the room holding the lamp up. He saw a figure lying on a mat near the door, where he had tripped. He shook the skeletal shoulder of Chan Cho and Chan opened his eyes and looked at him without recognition. "What were you going to do with the girl?" Lan Soo demanded.

"Whhaaat girl? Ohhh? I was going to take her home when it quit raining. Leave me in peace, take her with you," Chan Cho muttered.

"Thank you for rescuing my daughter," Frank knelt beside the man and laid some money beside him.

Lan Soo snorted in disgust. "Do not give money to the likes of him. He is no good," Lan Soo paused. "I will help you take your child home. Then I must return to my wife."

"Bring your wife and come stay with us for awhile." Frank hoisted Prudence over his shoulder and held her with his arm. Lan Soo walked beside Frank to help him keep his balance and the two men trudged up the hill followed closely by a heroic dog.

Chapter 36

Prudence was very sick. Sadie managed to bathe her and get her into bed but she hadn't even opened her eyes. Florence burst into the room just as Sadie was covering her new daughter with clean quilts.

"What are you doing? You shouldn't have bathed her yet. She will catch pneumonia," the older woman shoved her aside. "Were you afraid she might get the sheets dirty?" Florence scolded.

"Mrs. Jensen, I have been taking care of people my whole life. I think I am qualified to make the decision to remove all kinds of unspeakable filth from a sick child. Now she can rest comfortably. Come into the kitchen and I will make us some tea," Sadie coaxed.

"I should stay with her until she wakes up. She needs to know I am here," Florence insisted.

"Let her rest for a few minutes. She will be all right, I promise," Sadie took Florence's arm. Frank sat by the fire snoring gently.

"How can he sleep at a time like this?" Florence said loudly.

"Mrs. Jensen, Frank had to carry Prudence home, up the hill through the mud. He is exhausted, please let him sleep."

"I came to tell you that Robert can bring the carriage over to collect Prudence's things and we can take her to our house. Li Soo's parents will be staying with us for a short time but we can still have a room prepared for our granddaughter."

"Prudence will stay here with us. I will take very good care of her," Sadie announced calmly. She went outside to get water from the rain barrel to boil for tea. A loud noise on the front porch caused Frank to wake up abruptly.

"Is someone in there?"

Frank went to the door and encountered Li Soo's escort to the wedding, Wong Lee.

"Hello, Mr. Parnell. I am looking for Li Soo, do you know where I might find her?"

"She is at my home with her parents. Weren't you at the wedding?" Florence eyed him suspiciously.

"Yes, madam. I was Li Soo's escort. I have been very worried about her and was finally able to get up here. Is she all right?"

"Of course, she is," Sadie said kindly. "Come inside, I was just about to make some tea, won't you join us?"

"Thank you, Mrs. Parnell but I must see Li Soo," politely Wong Lee left.

"Why did he come here I wonder?" Florence asked.

Frank shrugged. He took her arm and led her to the table. "Have some tea, I'll check on Pru."

Prudence was awake. She had vomited all over the floor by the bed and was crying.

"Papa, I'm so sick. Please help me."

"I know you're sick, Kitten. Don't worry, Sadie, your grandma, and I are all here to see that you get better. Lie down and try to sleep. I'll get this cleaned up."

Sadie hurried into the room armed with a mop and pail of sudsy water. She shooed Frank and Florence out of the room and cleaned up the mess. She put her arms around Prudence and rocked back and forth gently. "You will be fine, just fine."

The next day, Prudence was able to sit up and even sip water. She reached for her locket and remembered it was gone. As she cried inconsolably, Frank, Sadie and Florence assured her that they would get her another locket just like the one she lost.

"But it belonged to Mama. It can't be replaced," she sobbed. "Papa will you go look for it, please?"

Frank nodded. He knew it was useless but he would try everything in his power to find the locket that had meant so much to his wife and now his daughter. He was also preoccupied by something else. Three days earlier Marshal Kilburn had informed him that the search for Maximiano Najera had been called off. Many believed he had made it to Mexico. *How was he going to tell Sadie?*

Chapter 37

Two weeks after the ruinous rain, Li Soo decided to go to the Chinese Gardens. The topsoil, that had provided such good crops, had all been hauled in by wagon and depending on the extent of the damage, would need to be replaced. Quetta and Mario offered to escort her. Mario, jobless until parts of the printing press could be repaired or replaced, was impatient and restless. Li Soo packed a lunch and she and Quetta ventured downtown for the first time since the flood.

Diligent work had cleaned up much of the wreckage and they were able to walk to Li Soo's parent's home without too much difficulty. Their house had withstood most of the storm but the roof had been damaged and needed repair. Her parents had returned to their home last week. Li Soo's father appeared tired but her mother was radiant.

"My daughter, the English has helped me so much. I was able to talk to some people who came to see what they could do for us. They told me they would bring some wood for the roof and help us with repairs. The man and woman were so kind. They even brought us food and dry blankets," she told Li Soo, Quetta, and Mario.

"None of our precious possessions from the old country were harmed. I am so thankful," Mai Soo continued, asking tentatively, "Is everything all right at the store and at the Jensen home?"

"We have not been downtown but have been told that the mercantile had only minor damage. We have decided to go to the gardens to see if there is anything we can do to keep the topsoil from washing away if there is another flood. It is getting cloudy again. Did your roof get repaired?" Li Soo asked.

"The man brought his sons to help your father. I think they have nearly finished," Mai Soo touched her daughter's arm gently. "Do not worry too much about the gardens. We will be able to plant again in the spring."

Li Soo brushed tears from her eyes. Her mother's faith had always been stronger than hers. Much of the Chinese people's income was provided by the gardens. Li Soo's family had the laundry but they were more fortunate than most. Since her family had come, Li Soo looked forward to her times she could spend peacefully working in the life-giving sunshine.

Mario went outside to check on the progress of the roof repairs. He was very surprised to see that the men working on the roof were *gringos*. Shaking his head, he smiled; it was strange how people behaved during hard times. He offered to help and started handing supplies to a young man of about fifteen years of age, on the roof. The lad had been climbing up and down the ladder and Mario's assistance was greatly appreciated.

Nearly an hour later, the women emerged from the small house. Mario said goodbye to the workers and went to escort the women to the Chinese Gardens. It was worse than they could have imagined. All of the improvements, including fences to keep out animals and specially constructed beds, were gone. But there were about four wagons approaching when the three arrived. The wagons were having difficulty because the ground was eroded and still very muddy in places.

Today was a day of surprises. About twenty people climbed out of the wagons, *gringos*, Mexicans, Chinese, Negroes, all of them dressed to work. They went to work clearing the garbage that had been washed in from town. They loaded large pieces into the wagons and stacked much of the wood into piles to be burned later. Li Soo began to sob. Quetta put her arms around her friend. Mario pitched in to help and so did the women as soon as Li Soo had recovered her composure. Wong Lee walked toward Li Soo with a bright smile on his face.

"I am so happy to see you here today. I think about you often," he took her arm and led her toward one of the wagons.

Covered with grime, Mario smiled at Quetta, his clean teeth shining against the darkness of his skin and the drying mud. She smiled back and brushed her hair away from her face with the back of her blackened hand.

"You look beautiful," Mario exclaimed.

"So do you," Quetta laughed and smeared mud on Mario's cheek. She giggled and walked toward the wagon where women were handing broken machinery bits to men who were in the bed of the wagon, stacking it in piles.

A large piece of wood was partially buried but standing upright in the drying mud. Mario grabbed it and pulled with all of his weight. It didn't give an inch. He tried again, he felt it move slightly and was encouraged. The third time it moved a little more. Finally, Mario managed to dislodge it, after digging around it and using a lever. With an enormous sense of accomplishment, he hefted the very large piece of wreckage to one of the wagons. Just as he reached the wagon, he tripped and fell forward, launching the piece of wood like a catapult, into the large pile.

Mario didn't fall down but against the edge of the wagon. Disgustedly, he turned to see what he had tripped over. It appeared to be what was left of a glass vase. He stooped to pick it up because he didn't want someone else to trip. His eyes widened in surprise. Under the piece of glass was a silvery strand in the mud. Quickly, Mario looked for a stick and he carefully dug around the strand. His eyes widened in surprise at his discovery. Carefully, he retrieved the treasure, took out his bandanna, wrapped it inside and placed it in his shirt pocket. He recognized it immediately.

It was nearly dark and the workers decided to return the next day to complete the cleanup. The tired workers followed the loaded wagons toward Bullard Street. Many stopped to shake hands. Most of the men accompanied the wagons to a designated place to dump refuse where most of it could be burned later. Mario escorted Quetta and Li Soo to Li Soo's parent's home and went to assist with unloading wagons.

Mario went to stay with a friend that night. As he lay in bed, he considered his options. That locket was probably worth a lot of money. Maybe he could ask for a reward. If he could get enough money, he could ask Quetta to marry him. They could move to a big city and live in style. Well, perhaps the locket wasn't worth that much. He didn't like struggling with his conscience; there was a time, not so long ago, when he didn't have one.

The next morning, Mario got cleaned up and went to see Quetta. She was preparing breakfast for the Jensens when he arrived.

"You are a very good woman and I am a very good man. Maybe we should get married?" he grinned.

Quetta's mouth dropped open and she nearly dropped the pan she was holding. Speechless, she set down the pan and threw her arms around him. Mario nodded happily and walked out of the kitchen. Quetta let him go; she had to sit down.

Prudence was well enough to get out of bed. She sat in a chair by the fire with Mr. Whiskers curled up in her lap. Her whole demeanor expressed the sadness she was feeling.

There was a knock on the door and Sadie came from the kitchen to answer it. When she opened the door, she blinked hard. It couldn't be. It was the man, she and her family had taken care of in their cabin. She reached out to touch his arm to be sure he was real. He laughed when he saw her reaction.

"Señora, I know this must be a shock to you. But I have some important business to discuss with you and your family. May I come inside?"

Sadie gulped and remembered her manners. "I'm sorry, of course, come in. Please sit down. I will get my husband."

Frank was getting ready to go to work. He was surprised when Sadie told him they had a visitor. He was angry when he recognized the man who had teased him so outrageously about not knowing how to handle a burro. It had been quite awhile but the man's appearance was hard to forget.

"This man was injured. My brothers and I found him on the trail to Pinos Altos and took him back to our cabin. He didn't stay very long but I am so relieved to find him looking so well."

"Now, I must apologize for taking your silver hairbrush. I am so sorry but at the time, I felt I had no choice. I needed money to live until I recovered from my wounds. I hope you will forgive me, Señora."

"Of course, I forgave you right away when I realized you had taken it. I knew why."

"You are so kind. Mr. Parnell, I am familiar with your name, since I am a very good friend of Quetta Tovar. As a matter of fact, we are to be married."

"Congratulations, that is wonderful," Sadie was ecstatic. Frank added his congratulations.

Mario continued, "Now for the reason for my visit. I am here to return a most valuable piece of property. I confess, I considered keeping it but would not be able to sell it and enjoy the money it brought. I found your daughter's locket and I would like to give it to her personally."

Prudence's smile lit up the room. She rose to her feet unsteadily and hugged the tall, blond, dark-skinned man. He took a box from his pocket and placed it in her hand.

"*Vaya con Dios*, little one. *Vaya con Dios*."

THE END

About the Author

Diane Stuart Wright is married to David M. Wright and has two daughters, Paula and Amy, and a grandson, Clell. She has been a nurse since 1973 and lived in the Silver City area since 1984. Diane loves to read, write, hike, study history, and spend time with her family and animals.